Kemp: Warrio

Jonathan Lunn studied history at the University of Leicester, where he became involved in politics. He worked for six years as a spin doctor for the modern-day equivalent of the Whigs. He is the author of six Killigrew Naval Adventures, and two Medieval action thrillers featuring Kemp, an English Longbowman in The Hundred Years' War.

Also by Jonathan Lunn

The Kit Killigrew Naval Adventures

The Jungle War

Arrows of Albion

JONATHAN LUNN

WARRIORS
in the
SNOW

CANELO

First published in the United Kingdom in 2022 by

Canelo
Unit 9, 5th Floor
Cargo Works, 1–2 Hatfields
London, SE1 9PG
United Kingdom

A CIP catalogue record for this book is available from the British Library.

Print ISBN 978 1 80032 860 0
Ebook ISBN 978 1 80032 135 9

Look for more great books at www.canelo.co

Printed and bound in Great Britain by Clays Ltd, Elcograf S.p.A.

MIX
Paper from
responsible sources
FSC® C018072
FSC
www.fsc.org

To Dave

Martin Kemp and the Burnt Candlemas, 1356

One

Dark blood was still slick where it streaked the pallid skin of the five corpses sprawled in the mud. Their horses had been taken, naturally, and all five had been stripped: purses, arms and armour, even their clothes. Crows had gathered, though at the approach of two-and-twenty mounted archers they flapped up, cawing raucously, to settle on the bare boughs of the trees, waiting for the horsemen to ride on so they could resume their feast.

Kemp saw the wounds in the bodies where the arrows had entered their flesh. Those who had stripped the dead had retrieved the arrows. Kemp had reclaimed his own arrows from corpses many a time in the fields of France and Brittany, so he recognised such wounds. Not all the injuries had been fatal: three of the men had had their throats slit to put them out of their misery.

'The Scots shot from over yon.' Looking up from the confusion of hoofprints, footprints and splashes of blood on the ground, Ieuan ap Morgan gestured at the trees on one side.

Kemp felt a pang of guilt. These men had only been under his command for three weeks, not long enough for him to be able to put names to all their faces, but he recognised them. He was the one who had sent them to forage for victuals in the village on the far side of the woods; his orders had led them to their deaths.

'Fothergill and the rest of his lads urged their horses into a gallop and rode on.' Ieuan indicated the hoofprints gouged in the mud. 'Should we follow?'

'What good will that do?' sneered one of the archers halted behind Kemp and Ieuan. Like most of his companions, Kenrick Haine spoke in the dialect of the north country; and like them, he carried his bow stave slung across his back in a greasy woollen bow-bag and wore a leather bracer on his left wrist. A gammon-faced butcher from Ulverston in Furness, Haine's earlobes were ragged where they had been nailed to the boards of a pillory as a punishment for selling rotten meat. When a man's time in the pillory was over, the bailiffs removed the upper plank, but if a man's earlobes had been nailed to the lower plank, then it amused them to leave him to tear his own ears free, or else stay at the pillory and starve to death. 'If Fothergill and t'others were still alive, they'd ha' ridden back by now. If we follow them, belike whatever befell them will likewise befall us.'

'Hold your tongue, Haine.' Lambert Tegg had been working as a shepherd near Kirkby Kendal in Westmorland when he had heard the king's commissioners of array were raising troops for a campaign in Scotland, and had answered the call at once. It was the custom to organise large numbers of labourers into twenties, with the most responsible of them nominated 'twentyman' to have command over his companions. Tegg had been appointed twentyman over the troops of archers currently riding with Kemp, having fought at Neville's Cross nearly ten years ago.

'We don't know they're dead.' A tall, broad-shouldered man scarce past his six-and-twentieth winter, Martin Kemp wore a brigandine over his chain-mail habergeon, the studs in the leather betraying the presence of steel plates below, and a kettle helmet over the coif that hid his close-cropped blond hair. 'And until we do, we owe it to them to learn the truth of it. But we'll string our bows before we ride any further. I warrant whatever knaves ambushed Fothergill and his men are long gone by now, but let's be wary lest I'm wrong.'

Tegg and nine of his men dismounted, handing the bridles of their rouncies to the other ten to hold while they unslung their bow staves, stripped off the bags and braced the lower nocks of the staves against the inside of a foot, bending them until they could slip the bowstring over the upper nock. They tucked the empty bags under their belts and slung the bows across their backs by their strings before mounting again. Then they held the bridles of the other ten men's rouncies so they could do the same.

Like most yeomen in England, they were broad-shouldered and barrel-chested from practising weekly if not daily at the village butts, and many of them were ploughmen, an occupation that did not breed weaklings. But few of them were inured to the rigours of campaigning. When the Scots had laid siege to Berwick before Christmas, the king had hurried north to relieve the town. The men Kemp now found himself in command of had been recruited to the king's banner while His Majesty had celebrated Christmas at Newcastle upon Tyne, but they had come from all over the north country: Northumberlanders, Cumberlanders, Westmorlanders, Dunelmians, Yorkshiremen and Lancastrians. If their quality was any indication, they had been chosen based on which could most readily be spared from their everyday occupations by their lords and masters. But they were young, hale enough not to have been turned away by the commissioners of array, and – so far at least – obedient to those appointed to command them.

'Lead on,' Kemp told Ieuan, once they had all strung their bows.

The Welshman swung himself into the saddle of his rouncy and rode on at a walk, reining in from time to time to lean down and study the ground. A short, stocky man with a bushy, drooping moustache, he wore a Monmouth cap over his bowl-cropped hair, and a quilted green aketon that came down to his knees. He was past his fortieth winter, but if he was no longer quite as spry as he had been in his youth, his eyes remained as sharp as ever, and Kemp trusted his friend to read the tracks while he himself scanned the trees ahead.

A short way further on they came across the corpses of two more of Fothergill's men, along with Fothergill himself. Perhaps it had been luck, or perhaps a Scottish bowman had seen which of the English archers was giving orders, and picked him off deliberately.

'More Scots waited there.' Ieuan gestured to some trees nearby.

'Whoever laid this ambushment laid it well.' Kemp spoke the dialect of the East Midlands. 'He arrayed some archers back there, and knew when they loosed their first volley, our lads would gallop this way, so had more men hidden here.'

More bodies awaited them further down the trail. Like the first five, their horses taken, their bloody corpses stripped of every last stitch.

Seven had tried to surrender: their hands had been bound. They did not lie on the ground, but had been hanged from the boughs of an ancient, wide-spreading oak deep in the forest. The Scots had not hanged them by their necks — that would have been too quick — but by their bound hands, before slitting their bellies. Their entrails had slithered out to pile on the ground below in obscene, glistening coils.

'God's nails!' gasped Hob Gudgeon. A ploughman from a village somewhere in Northumberland, he was typical of the men recruited for the king's campaign, if a little more slow-witted than most. 'What manner of savages would do such a thing?'

'Men little different from you,' said Kemp. 'I warrant you'll do much the same to any Scots unfortunate enough to fall into your hands, if you get the chance.'

'Is that an order, Cap'n?' Haine asked with the leer of a man who would enjoy hanging a few Scots from a tree and slitting their bellies.

Kemp turned flint-blue eyes upon him, eyes that had seen too many such atrocities committed in France and Brittany, and not always by the foe. 'That's human nature, Haine.'

Something rustled in the undergrowth off to his left. Pretending not to have heard it, Kemp swung himself down from his rouncy, trying to look casual as he unslung his bow. He drew an arrow from the sheaf tucked under his belt and nocked it, whirling to aim at where the sound had come from. Seeing a face scarcely recognisable from the mud and blood covering it, he very nearly loosed, but the man thrust out a palm towards him, the terrified eyes pleading for mercy.

'It's Wilcock Dodd!' Swinging himself down from the saddle, Gudgeon handed the bridle of his horse to a companion before dashing across to where Dodd lay.

Kemp took another searching glance at the surrounding trees before relaxing his draw on his bow: if some Scots still tarried in these woods, a wounded man might have been left as bait to distract the Englishmen.

Dodd had not been stripped. An arrow stuck out of his ribs in a way that suggested his chances of surviving until nightfall were slim. It was a miracle he had survived this long. Crouching over him, Gudgeon pulled the bung from his costrel and held it to Dodd's lips. The wounded man drank greedily.

'Keep an eye on the trees,' Kemp murmured to the Welshman, who nodded, his sharp eyes darting about everywhere except where Gudgeon crouched over Dodd.

Kemp knelt on the other side of the injured man. 'Hold still, lad,' he said, trying to examine the wound through the hole punched in the blood-soaked quilting of his aketon. Even if the arrowhead was not barbed, Dodd might bleed to death if they pulled it out.

'It was Black Rab and his reivers,' gasped Dodd. 'They came at us out of the trees… they were everywhere!'

Dodd had fought alongside Kemp once before, and though the young captain had not recognised him at first, he had remembered the occasion when Dodd reminded him of it. About five years ago, they had both been members of a *posse comitatus* the Sheriff of Roxburghshire had led in pursuit of a gang of border reivers that attacked Melrose Abbey. Black Rab Nixon had slipped through their fingers that night, but Kemp and Dodd had got their first view of the reiver chief. If Dodd said Nixon and his reivers had ambushed Fothergill's troop, Kemp did not doubt it was true.

'Save your breath,' he told Dodd. There were barber-surgeons with King Edward's host: if they could get Dodd to wherever the king intended they should camp for the night, there might still be a chance for him. 'Hold still.' He grasped the shaft of the arrow sticking out of Dodd's ribs as close as he could to the wound, holding it steady. The shaft was no different from that of an English arrow, half an inch thick and made from good ash wood, no easy thing for Kemp to snap in two in his hands, but he managed it, albeit provoking a wince and a sob from Dodd. Kemp was careful to leave a couple of inches sticking out of the wound, enough for a barber-surgeon to extract.

'Help me get him on your horse,' he told Gudgeon.

They got Dodd on his feet and managed to support him as far as Gudgeon's rouncy, but he went limp before they could lift him into the saddle. Kemp and Gudgeon lowered him to the ground and the captain drew his ballock-knife from its sheath, buffing the blade on Dodd's sleeve before holding it an inch above his lips. When he looked at the steel, no breath had clouded it. Kemp drew his eyelids down.

'I make that twenty,' murmured Ieuan.

Kemp nodded: the mystery of what had befallen Fothergill and his men was a mystery no more. 'Mount up,' he told Gudgeon, swinging himself into the saddle of his own rouncy. 'We'll ride back to Musselburgh.'

'What about Wilcock and t'others?' demanded Haine. 'Shall we just leave them as they are?'

'The crow must have his meat as well as the worm,' said Kemp. 'Unless you'd to stay behind to bury them? Though I wonder how you'll do that without a spade.'

Riding at a brisk canter, it took them a quarter of an hour to reach to Musselburgh, a fair-sized town of houses with shingled roofs and corbelled façades. By the time they got there, the rest of the king's army had caught up with the foragers sent on ahead. Companies of men-at-arms trotted across the three-arched stone bridge over the river on their way to Edinburgh, the wintry sunlight gleaming on their polished bascinets, colourful pennants snapping in the breeze at the tips of lances, crotal bells jingling on the destriers' harnesses. Lightly armoured hobelars rode bareback on small, stocky hobbies.

Kemp found the other three troops of his company loitering idly by two wains drawn up on the high street. He could not help noticing the wains were as empty as they had been an hour ago. The three twentymen – Henry Earnshaw, Dickon Outhwaite and Tom Metcalfe – stood upright at his approach and touched fingers to their helmets in a gesture that was a cross between reaching up to tug a forelock and a knight raising his visor to address his liege lord.

'Did I not order you to ransack these houses for food?' Kemp spoke with more ire than he intended. He was angry about what had happened to Fothergill and his men – angry at himself for letting it happen – and he did not mean to take it out on his twentymen, but on the other hand he could not abide idling.

'We already did,' said Earnshaw. 'Someone was here before us. There's nowt to eat in this town but a couple of loaves of mouldy bread, a keg of flour crawling with weevils, and this hog.' The twentyman indicated a piglet tied to one of the wains. Clearly it had been the runt of the litter. A healthy pig would have been trotting all over the place, sticking its snout into everything, but this one just lay on its side, wheezing through its snout as if it was having difficulty breathing and watching the world mournfully through rheumy eyes.

'Did you try asking the townsfolk where they've hidden their food?' Kemp asked Earnshaw.

'They've fled,' said the twentyman. 'Taking their victuals with them. And anything else of value. All except one old cripple who says he's too old to fear death.'

Kemp would have found it hard to believe there could be so little to eat in a town of this size, had they not encountered the same situation in every town, village and hamlet they had passed through since marching into Scotland three days earlier. When they had prepared to set out from Roxburgh a week earlier, intent on avenging the Scots' attack on Berwick, Lord William Douglas' pursuivant had come to the castle to negotiate terms with King Edward. But after the pursuivant had ridden to and fro between the castle and Douglas' camp a few times, it had become obvious his lordship had no more intention of making peace with the King of England than Kemp had of casting aside his bow and becoming a cloistered monk. As they marched north into Lothian, the reason for the futile negotiations had become clear: Douglas had been buying time for the people to carry all their victuals and valuables north of the River Forth, leaving behind nothing that would feed or profit the English invaders.

'Did the old cripple say what he means to eat for his supper?' Kemp asked Earnshaw.

'I gave him some cheese and bread I'd been saving.'

Kemp smiled. 'I set you to ransack this town for victuals, and you take the last of your food and give it to the only local you can find?'

'He was an old man,' Earnshaw said defensively. 'What was I supposed to do?'

'So tonight we go hungry again!' grumbled Haine.

'The king's ships are sailing up the coast from Berwick with holds full of victuals,' Kemp told his men. 'They'll be here in a day or two. Till then, we must tighten our belts.'

'What of Fothergill and his men?' asked Earnshaw. 'Did you find them?'

'We found them.' There must have been enough weary resignation in Kemp's tone for the twentyman to understand not to enquire any further; not of Kemp, at any rate. If Earnshaw wanted the grisly details, no doubt Tegg would be willing to supply them, perhaps with an added commentary on how Kemp's lapse of judgement in sending only one troop through the woods had cost Fothergill and his men their lives.

The men dismounted to stretch their legs. Kemp could hear them muttering to one another and more than one of them scowled in his direction. 'Hell's teeth, but it's a mutinous pack of dogs the king has given me to command!' he muttered to Ieuan.

'Give them time,' said the Welshman. 'They just need to get used to you, that's all.'

'And if they don't?'

'Then pick out the brawniest and give him such beating, none of the others will dare oppose you for fear of getting the same treatment.'

There was no question which was the brawniest of Kemp's men: he glanced across to where Haine stood absent-mindedly tugging one of his ragged earlobes while talking to a comrade. 'You'd have me pick a fight with Kenrick Haine?'

'Beat him, and none of the others will dare defy you.'

'If I could beat Haine, I warrant the Devil himself would think twice before defying me!'

Seeing Kemp, a knight peeled away from one of the troops of men-at-arms riding towards the bridge.

Kemp recognised him as Nompar de Savignac, Bourc de Cazoulat, by the blazon of a white cockerel on his black shield. The Gascon was the half-brother of the Captal de Cazoulat, his father's natural son. Technically, he was Kemp's prisoner: the Midlander had a contract signed by Nompar promising to pay him the princely sum of twelve hundred *escudoes*. And if Kemp had learned one thing about the *bourc*, it was that he would honour that debt as soon as he had the resources. How he was going to get the resources was another matter entirely, but for men like Nompar and Kemp who lived by the sword and the bow, the Wheel of Fortune was always turning. Since being captured, Nompar had switched his allegiance from John of Valois to Edward of England.

The *bourc* raised the visor of his polished bascinet to reveal a saturnine face with a hooked nose, stubble on his jaw and melancholy brown eyes. 'The king bid me ask you to join him on Arthur's Seat.'

'Arthur's Seat?' echoed Kemp, confused.

'It's a big hill a mile east of Edinburgh,' said Ieuan, who had campaigned against the Scots when Kemp had been no more than a boy. 'I can show you the way.'

Kemp nodded to Nompar to indicate he understood. 'Then I'll see you in Edinburgh!' said the *bourc*, wheeling his horse to rejoin his troop of men-at-arms.

Kemp ordered his twentymen to take headcounts, and once they had all confirmed no one had wandered off, he ordered them to mount up. The archers swung themselves into the saddles of their stocky rouncies.

'Lead the way,' he told Ieuan, who nodded and rode on. Signalling the others to follow, Kemp rode on. 'Everyone keep your eyes open for trouble,' he growled over his shoulder.

They followed the tracks of the rest of the king's host, the road churned to mud by so many hoofs and wain-wheels. Beyond the bridge, they rode along the shore for a short distance, with the cobalt waters of the Firth of Forth on their right stretching across to where Kemp could just make out the coast of Fife in the distance. A couple of miles ahead, a high hill rose above the relatively flat landscape of Lothian. Drawing closer, Kemp saw that what in the distance looked to be a hill was in truth a jumble of craggy hills, gullies and escarpments. While the rest of the king's host rode on to where a church tower rose above the trees, Kemp signalled for his men to rein in beneath a crag with a small stone chapel perched atop it on the northern flank of the hills. Beyond the chapel, a path led up a gully between gorse-covered slopes. 'Yon's Arthur's Seat,' Ieuan told Kemp, pointing to where an outcrop of bay-hued rock with a rosy tinge to it rose above the upper end of the gully.

Kemp indicated the church tower. 'Is that Holyrood?' Ieuan nodded.

'Take the men to the abbey and await me there. I'll join you there after I've presented my compliments to the king. See to it the men wisp down their horses and water them.'

While the rest of the company rode on to Holyrood, Kemp wheeled his rouncy and headed up the gully leading into the hills. At the far end, the path turned, climbing the shoulder of the hill, and Kemp dismounted, tying a leading rein to his horse's bridle to draw her along the narrow path, which doubled back on itself where it led up to the rocky outcrop at the top. Half a dozen knights in full armour stood at the highest point while their squires waited a short way below the peak, holding the bridles of their horses. One came forward to take Kemp's rouncy. The west side of the hill fell away steeply, cliffs plunging down more than a hundred feet to the valley below. He hastily stepped back from the brink, and hovered a discreet distance from the knights, waiting to catch the eye of one.

From up here he had a fine view of the countryside to the west. Immediately below, a hill seemed to curve around the foot of Arthur's Seat, a grassy crescent rising to what might have been an escarpment: he could not see the other side, but it looked as though the ground fell away steeply. Half a mile further west, two rows of town houses flanked a broad street that ran along the crest of a low ridge, with tofts stretching back down the slopes on either side: the city of Edinburgh. The houses and their tofts were surrounded by an earthwork rampart topped by a palisade. Where the street met the palisade at the near side of the town there was a gate flanked by the wooden towers of the Netherbow Port. The far end of the town terminated in a great, sheer-sided rock thrusting up above the surrounding plains, surmounted by the battlements of a stone castle.

Kemp had seen London, Paris and Avignon; Edinburgh was tiny in comparison. From the foot of the castle rock to the Netherbow Port, he guessed it was no more than half a mile; even Musselburgh seemed larger. But before David Bruce had been captured at Neville's Cross, Edinburgh's castle had been one of his favourite residences; and judging from the fine quality of those town houses, there was money in the city.

One of the knights on the hilltop beckoned Kemp to approach. A tall, well-made man, his visor was raised to reveal crow's feet at the corners of a pair of piercing blue eyes and part of a golden-brown beard. Kemp dropped briefly to one knee: he knew the king did not like men to waste time in too much ceremony, but he also knew he was not impressed with those who neglected it altogether.

'Did you find many victuals in Musselburgh?' asked the king.

'No, my liege,' Kemp said bluntly. 'The Earl of Dunbar's men had stripped every granary, pantry and larder in the town, just as they have everywhere else.'

'Did you send a troop to Dalkeith as I suggested?'

'I did, sire. They never returned. The Scots ambushed them in the woods on the way and slaughtered them to a man.'

The king scowled. 'Less than three weeks since I gave you a company of archers, you have already lost one in five? Had you ordered them decimated, you would have lost half as many!'

The rebuke stung Kemp. 'The men left under my command will soon avenge them,' he asserted.

'Then perhaps I can give them the opportunity to do so.' The king pointed at the suburbs lining the road running from the Netherbow Port to Holyrood Abbey. 'See yon houses?'

'Aye, sire.'

'Despoil them and put them to the torch. Then withdraw to Haddington.'

Kemp glanced at the suburbs to the east of Edinburgh once more. He had marched in the same host the king had led to the battlefield at Crécy and he understood it was an accepted strategy of war to lay waste the foe's territory to force him to come to battle. But he was also conscious the folk who lived outside the palisade would likely be the poorer citizens of Edinburgh; men, women and children who had had nothing to do with the previous year's attack on Berwick.

He cleared his throat. 'If only a small force were to attack the suburbs, sire, and show themselves close to the Netherbow Port, the Scots might be tempted to make a foray. If we have additional men approach stealthily to hold themselves in readiness, we might take the gate; and thus the town.'

'We might,' the king agreed, a little tetchily. 'But the Scots would still hold the castle. And we cannot hold the town while they hold the castle.'

'But with the town in our hands, we might launch an assault on the castle.'

'We're not here to take the castle, Kemp.' The king made no attempt to hide his annoyance. He rarely lost his temper, but when he did it was a short path from tetchy to furious. 'Only do as I order. Do not make it more complicated that it need be.'

Kemp dropped to one knee again. 'As you command, sire.' When he rose, the king had already resumed his conversation with the other knights. The captain of archers could consider himself dismissed.

He rode back down the hill to Holyrood Abbey, where Ieuan and the others waited in the courtyard. Kemp ordered them to fetch torches from the abbey's stores. A flame was brought from the embers in the hearth in the abbot's lodge, so that by the time Kemp's company rode forth, several of the men held aloft blazing torches.

When they reached the houses outside the Netherbow Port, a couple of over-eager archers immediately held their torches to the eaves, trying to set them alight.

'Hold!' shouted Kemp. 'We burn these houses when I give the order, not before! First they must be plundered.

Metcalfe, take your men and guard the Netherbow Port. Have your men ready with arrows nocked lest the Scots foray out, and sound your horn if they do! Earnshaw, set up picquets guarding the approaches from the north, east and south. Tegg, your men will plunder the houses on the north side of the street for victuals, and owt else worth taking. Outhwaite, your men will do likewise on the south side. And don't let me catch anyone slipping a few coins in his purse! Whatever plunder we take goes in the common pot, and we'll share it fairly after the king has claimed his portion. Go to it!'

Earnshaw's and Metcalfe's men rode off to their positions while Tegg's and Outhwaite's eagerly set about plundering the houses. Their enthusiasm soon waned when they found themselves emerging carrying nothing more than fistfuls of farthings, or pewter crockery.

'It seems cattle were not the only valuables Dunbar had moved beyond our reach while Lord Douglas delayed us with blandishments,' Kemp remarked to Ieuan.

The Welshman nodded at the Netherbow Port. 'I warrant we'd find enough plunder on the other side of yon palisade to make us all rich men.'

'No doubt... along with enough Scots from the castle to make us all prisoners. We'll not return to England as rich men if we're burdened with crippling ransoms to pay off. We'll follow our orders: plunder these houses and put them to the torch.'

'I thought you sought redemption for the sins of your youth?'

'This is different. I've orders from the king.'

'Weren't the sins of your youth carried out at the king's orders?'

'We're at war, Ieuan. We cannot be squeamish. If I'm loyal to my king, I must do as he bids me.'

'Even if what he orders you to do is immoral?'

'A captain of archers mayn't pick and choose which orders to obey and which to refuse.' Kemp lowered his voice so only the Welshman could hear him. 'I may be a freeman now, Ieuan, but most folk know I was born a bondsman. All my life I've suffered noblemen looking down their noses at me as though I were summat less than a man. But not the king: he sees my worth. Why else would he trust me to captain one of his companies of archers?'

'I doubt he's all that different from any other great man. Be we bondsmen or freemen, our lords see our worth for as long as they reckon we'll be useful to them. And not a moment longer.'

'Then I owe it to my liege to prove myself worthy of his trust by showing him how useful I can be.'

A woman's scream came from one of the houses. Kemp and Ieuan exchanged glances. 'Still think we cannot be squeamish?' asked the Welshman.

Kemp winced. It was tempting to stand by and not get involved... such things were a part of war. No one would have blamed him for turning a deaf ear; indeed, many would think him daft for doing otherwise. And yet... he knew his conscience would trouble him in the small hours of the night if he did nothing, and he had enough sins weighing on his conscience without adding to them.

Another shriek came from the house. 'God damn it!' Kemp slid down from the saddle and quickly tied a leading rein to his rouncy's bridle, handing it to Ieuan. 'Wait here.'

He entered the house: the door had already been broken down. On the ground floor was a cooper's workshop, with barrel staves stacked here, iron hoops stacked there. A flight of stairs led up to the living quarters immediately above. A corpse he did not recognise sprawled on the steps. He picked his way over it and climbed the rest of the way to the first floor. Another bloody corpse sprawled in the dining hall. Hearing sounds of a struggle coming from one of the doors leading off, he stepped into a bedchamber and found a young woman struggling in the arms of Simkin Fisher, a fat, bearded cooper's apprentice from Cockermouth. The slashed remnants of her kirtle already littered the floor, and now Kenrick Haine sliced open the front of her undershift, exposing the bare flesh below.

Damn it to hell, thought Kemp, *why did it have to be Haine?*

Two

'Let her go,' said Kemp.

Fisher released the woman, but Haine immediately caught her and swung her around, holding her from behind. 'I'm entitled! Bitches are fair game. Divven't tell me you never had your way with a squealing bitch like this.'

Kemp blushed with shame and could only hope Haine and Fisher would think he was flushed with anger. He knew he was a hypocrite; but he also knew he would never atone for his own sins if he stood back and allowed others to commit the same crimes.

'Entitled, Kenrick? I'll remember you said that, the next time Loathsome Letty is on the prowl. If you're not getting any, maybe you should look to your own short-comings, instead of blaming it on lasses wi' more sense than to fall for your dubious charms. You're entitled to nowt, except maybe my boot up your arse.' Kemp took a step towards Haine.

The butcher pulled a knife from his belt and held it to the woman's throat. 'Stay back, Cap'n. Or I'll cut her, I swear.'

Kemp smiled, though he could think of few times when he felt less like smiling. 'Hiding behind a woman's skirts? Aye, I reckoned you for a gutless whoreson from the first.'

Haine threw the woman aside. She banged her head against the wall and slumped to the floor, maybe dead, maybe just stunned, though in that instant she was the least of Kemp's worries. He glanced at Fisher and saw the cooper's apprentice standing to one side. Aye, Kemp had nothing to fear there: if Haine knocked him to the floor, Fisher might grow bold enough to step up and kick him in the ribs, but until then he would loiter on the sidelines, waiting to see which way this fight turned out.

Haine was another matter. The butcher tossed his cleaver from one hand to the other and back again. He did not give a damn about anyone or anything, least of all Kemp. He might yet make a good soldier, given time, but looking at the wolfish grin on his face, Kemp reckoned time was the one thing he lacked.

The captain pointedly left his sword in its scabbard, beckoning Haine to come at him. 'Think you can best me? Come on, then! Show me what you can do.'

'Will you not draw your sword?'

'Against a whoreson like you?' Shaking his head, Kemp raised his fists. 'Come on, then, boy! Do your worst.'

'I divven't god-damned need this!' Much to Kemp's relief, Haine threw his cleaver down so that the blade buried itself in a floorboard. He flung himself at Kemp, swinging a wild, roundhouse punch at the Midlander's head. Kemp ducked it easily and threw a right cross at Haine's chin, clipping the point of his jaw.

Too late he saw Haine's left coming at him. It seemed to move impossibly slowly, but then time itself seemed to have slowed, nailing Kemp's boots to the floor. He tried to brush Haine's punch aside, but it was like trying to swing his arms through glue. The knuckles slammed into his cheek like a battering ram. Then time ran at a normal speed again, perhaps even faster, as the room whipped around him. A burst of blinding pain erupted inwards from Kemp's cheek, spreading through his whole head like a shockwave, and his legs turned to water and crumpled beneath him.

Haine drew back a foot to kick Kemp in the ribs. The Midlander rolled away from it, felt it slam into his brigandine. The steel plates must have hurt Haine's toe more than the kick hurt Kemp's spine; even through the brigandine, it knocked the breath from his lungs. He rolled back, swivelling on his buttocks and slamming the sole of one boot into Haine's crotch. The butcher doubled up with a gasp, bringing his face within range of Kemp's foot. The Midlander lashed out again, but judiciously: he wanted Haine bruised and bloody but fit for duty, so he restrained from pulping his nose — you could easily slay a man that way — or even breaking his jaw. Instead he merely slammed his heel into Haine's forehead, just hard enough to knock him on his rump.

Dazed, Haine writhed on his back for a few heartbeats, long enough for Kemp to ignore the shoots of pain that hampered his limbs as he struggled to his feet. White-faced, Fisher cowered in a corner, while the girl had evidently not been hurt as badly as all that, for she had taken advantage of the brawl to flee the room.

Haine suddenly made a grab for his cleaver, still sticking up out of the floorboards. Kemp was waiting for it. He brought a boot down on Haine's wrist, not hard enough to break it, but enough to make the butcher screw up his face in agony. Kemp stooped to pluck the cleaver from his fingers, then straightened, taking his boot from Haine's wrist and backing off.

'On your feet, Kenrick.'

Haine rose, nursing his wrist. Kemp could see the imprint of his heel livid on the butcher's forehead. His own cheek felt tight and swollen where Haine had punched him. He held the cleaver out towards him, handle first. 'Try that again,' he suggested. 'Only this time use the cleaver. Clearly you need it.'

Haine snatched it from him, but just stood there, glowering. After a moment, he tucked it back under his belt.

Kemp shook his head. 'I'd say today's lesson is that you can't beat me. But the trouble with oafs like you is that you never learn.' He turned to the stairs.

He did not hear the cleaver's blade whisper from under Haine's belt, but he heard his boots on the floorboards. They made it easy to keep track of him as he charged at his back. Kemp waited until the last moment, then dropped, swinging a leg at Haine's ankles as he did so. The butcher went head-first down the stairs. He pitched up at the bottom and for a moment Kemp thought perhaps he had broken his neck, but after lying still for a couple of heart-beats, Haine winced, tried to get up again, then slumped. Kemp descended the stairs, stepping unconcernedly over his opponent.

'As I said,' he sighed. 'You never learn.'

Hearing a footfall above, he glanced up to see Fisher standing at the top of the stairs.

'Pick him up and put him on his horse,' ordered Kemp. 'For that, you can both do double guard duty tonight.'

Emerging from the house, he crossed to where Ieuan stood. 'Are you hurt?' the Welshman asked him.

'Not as sore as he is.' Kemp gestured to where Fisher helped Haine over the threshold behind him. 'You obey orders in my company, Kenrick,' Kemp called, making

24

sure that the other men nearby heard him too, leaving them in no doubt who was the victor of the brawl. 'Orders are what bind a host together. Without orders, we're nowt but a rabble. I'll have no such misrule.' He turned back to Ieuan. 'Have all the houses been searched?'

'Aye, though we've not found enough spoil to fill a handcart.'

'Have Tegg and Outhwaite carry out headcounts. When every man's present and accounted for, put these houses to the torch.'

They started with the buildings closest to the Netherbow Port, knowing that once the flames took hold, the westerly wind would carry them down the road leading to the abbey, which was far enough from the end house for there to be no danger of the blaze leaping across the gap. The fire engulfed the timber-framed houses greedily. There was a destructive pleasure in watching houses that had taken months if not years to build be destroyed in a matter of minutes, especially for those of them who knew that unless they benefitted from an unusually profitable day's plundering, most of them would never have the fortune to own such fine dwellings. Though Kemp could not help but think that the truly rich whoresons owned houses within the town's palisade. *It's always the poor who suffer*, he thought bitterly. *The wealthy see to that. The wealthy, and their hirelings*, he reminded himself ruefully.

The inferno provided welcome warmth against the chill of winter, but the smoke did not rise high in the cold air and the wind blew it back in the faces of Kemp and his men.

'Send word to Earnshaw and Metcalfe that we're falling back,' he told Ieuan. 'We'll rally by the abbey.'

'Hold up, Cap'n,' said Tegg. 'One of my lads is missing.'

'Which one?'

'Dunstan Young.'

A lanky youth with greasy, unkempt hair that reached down to his shoulders emerged from a house nearby, his aketon unfastened at the front, reaching under the hem of his tunic to fasten his braies.

'Shift yourself, lad!' called Tegg. 'We haven't got all day.'

'I'm not even supposed to be here.' Young was a scholar studying to join the clergy at Oxford's Merton College, though he had been at home with his family in Kingston upon Hull when the king had called for men. 'I've already missed three weeks of lectures...'

'You'll miss three *years* of lectures, if the king so orders!' said Tegg.

'After what happened in Oxford this time last year, I'd ha' thought you'd appreciate the peace and quiet of the Scottish Borders,' Kemp said with a smile.

'What does the cap'n mean?' asked Gudgeon. 'In't the Scottish Borders supposed to be famous for strife?'

'He's in jest,' explained Tegg. 'There were riots in Oxford last Saint Scholastica's Day. Did you not hear? Three days of fighting, they say, and sixty clerks slain.'

'Three-and-sixty,' said Young. 'And thirty of the townsfolk. We gave as good as we got.'

'Three-and-sixty to thirty, and you call that giving as good as you got?' Tegg grinned. 'Is that the sort of arithmetic they teach you at Oxford?'

'What were they fighting about?' asked Gudgeon.

'The townsfolk decided they'd had enough of overeducated, overprivileged clerks looking down their noses at them.'

'Aye, well, don't let the king hear you speak so,' said Kemp. 'He fined the town five hundred marks for what befell, and had the mayor and bailiffs locked up in the Marshalsea for letting it happen.'

'The king knows England needs clerks as well as ploughmen if it's to thrive,' said Ieuan.

They mounted up – Hob Gudgeon helped Fisher put the dazed and battered Haine in his saddle – and trotted down the road to Holyrood. When Earnshaw's and Metcalfe's twenties joined them, Kemp cast a final glance towards the burning houses and saw the fire had spread beyond all hope of control. He had carried out his king's orders. Then he thought of the people who had lived in those houses, and atonement with God seemed further away than ever.

'Let's go,' he growled through clenched teeth.

It took them a couple of hours to reach the town of Haddington. It was Candlemas – the Feast of the Purification of the Blessed Virgin Mary – and those houses which had not been abandoned entirely by townsfolk fleeing from the English host all had candles burning behind the oiled parchment in their windows to mark the occasion.

While his men entered the Franciscan friary where they were billeted, Kemp rode to Lethington Castle, a fortified manor house half a mile beyond the town's southern palisade, where the king had ensconced himself with his retinue. His Majesty received Kemp's report with a dismissive nod, as if to say, *what do you expect from me for doing no more than your duty? A knighthood?*

Kemp bowed out of the king's presence. *For that, I put my immortal soul in peril?* he wondered bitterly.

Returning to the friary, he entered the pilgrims' lodge, doffing his brigandine and habergeon, and the quilted gambeson he wore beneath both for padding. Ieuan was there, washing his hands and face in a basin of water.

'What's for supper?' Kemp asked him.

'There is no supper. We ate the last of their victuals last night. The friars are going hungry, too, before you ask.'

'What of the other foragers? Did they find nowt?'

Ieuan shook his head grimly. 'Dunbar's men were thorough.'

'Then until the king's ships land the victuals they're supposed to be bringing from Berwick, we needs must tighten our belts.'

'The men won't like it.'

'The men will have to lump it. Do you see me dancing a jig at the prospect?'

'They say a good captain is like a father to his men.'

'What would you have me do? Tell them reassuring lies?' Kemp shook his head. 'I need men who can think for themselves, not wet-behind-the-ears thumb-suckers looking for someone to make promises he cannot keep.' Grimacing, he ran a hand over his hair. 'What about summat to drink?' A man could keep hunger pangs at bay by filling his stomach with liquid. 'Friars always have good ale to hand.'

Again Ieuan shook his head. 'Dunbar's men broached all their barrels of ale and emptied them to the drains. There's nothing to drink but water.'

'Water! Drinking water gives you the skitters.'

Kemp and Ieuan had scarcely regained their former strength after spending two and a half months on short commons during the Siege of Berwick, and now they must go hungry again? Kemp wondered if this was God's punishment, swift and sure, in retribution for burning those houses at Edinburgh. If so, he suspected that God had only just started, and wondered what other horrors the Lord intended to inflict on him for his sins.

Sir Alexander Bulchett and his squire reined in their horses outside the gate to the Greyfriars. Two archers were on guard there, a hulking ruffian with a battered face and the torn earlobes of a man who had been in the pillory, and a fat, bearded fellow. Evidently recognising the knight from the blazon on his jupon – a golden unicorn *couchant* on an azure field – they made no attempt to bar him from entering the friary precincts. Bulchett nonetheless felt an explanation for his presence was in order.

'I have orders from the king to speak to the abbot.' A stout man well past the first flush of youth, with porcine eyes almost lost in a pouchy, bloodless face, Bulchett frowned. Did friaries have abbots? He was not sure. Well, no matter. The two archers made no attempt to prevent him from entering. Act with enough boldness, he had learned, and few men would challenge you. He rode into the friary, signalling his squire to follow.

A friar emerged from a lodge to greet them. 'May I take your horses, lordings?' he asked in a Scottish accent.

'Take good care of them,' Bulchett ordered as he and his squire swung themselves down from their saddles. 'They cost me 120 marks apiece. Where is the library?' Haddington Greyfriars was famed throughout the world as *Lucerna Laudoniæ*, 'the Lamp of Lothian', as much for the knowledge stored in its well-stocked library as for the clearness of the light that shone forth from the quire of its handsome and graceful church.

The friar gestured to the large building on the opposite side of the courtyard. 'But it's kept locked frae sunset to sunrise.'

'Then fetch the key,' ordered Bulchett. 'And bring a lanthorn.'

'Nae lights are permitted in the library,' said the friar. 'The risk of fire is too great. That's why it's kept locked after dark.'

'Surely you don't think such pettifogging rules apply to *me*?' Bulchett said indignantly.

'Aye.' His squire, Rowland Crawley, basked in his master's self-importance. 'Surely you don't think such pettifogging rules apply to him?'

'Fetch the key and a lanthorn at once,' Bulchett snapped at the friar, 'or I'll have you flogged for your impertinence!'

'Aye, my lord.' The friar started to turn away, then paused, gazing up into the night sky, his eyes darting this way and that as if in search of something.

Bulchett looked up, but all he could see was ragged storm clouds racing across the face of a crescent moon. 'What are you looking at, fellow?'

'Did ye see that, my lord? A bat! It's unheard of to see one at this time of year: it must be an omen.' He chuckled. 'Remember the auld wives' tale about... how does it go? "Whosoever shall see a bat before the Feast of Saint Euphrasia shall lie cold in his grave ere Saint Fulbert's Eve".'

A shudder ran down Bulchett's spine and his stomach churned. He loathed bats, with their leathery wings, beady little eyes, piggish snouts and savage fangs. One only had to look at them to know they were creatures of Satan: no Christian animal would only come out at night, and spend its days hanging upside down. Such beasts were unnatural. Just the thought of them unmanned him.

'D'ye fear bats, my lord?' asked the friar.

'Me, frightened of bats? Don't be ridiculous! I fear nothing and no one, least of all bats!'

'To think the brave Sir Alexander would fear bats!' snorted Crawley. 'Ludicrous!'

'Now hurry away and fetch that key, before I have you pilloried for back-biting!'

Bulchett and Crawley tethered their horses to a rail outside the stables and crossed the courtyard to wait by the library. The knight kept an anxious eye overhead for fear the bat might return, one hand on the hilt of his sword lest he need to fend it off.

At last the friar returned carrying a lanthorn and led the way upstairs to the library. Producing the key, he made to unlock the door, but Bulchett snatched it from him with a podgy hand. 'Make yourself useful. See to it our horses are fed and groomed. Nay, give the lanthorn to my squire.'

'But how am I to make my way back downstairs without any kind of light?' protested the friar.

'You should have thought of that when you only brought one lanthorn!'

Bulchett waited until the friar had disappeared into the shadows of the stairway before fitting the key in the lock and trying to turn it. 'The infernal fool has given me the wrong key!'

'Perhaps it turns the other way, my lord,' said Crawley.

'What do you mean, the other way?'

'Widdershins as opposed to sunwise.'

'Don't be foolish!' snapped Bulchett. 'Keys always turn sunwise.'

'Surely that depends what side of the door one stands on, my lord.'

'Nonsense! It boots not which side of the door you stand. Sunwise is sunwise.'

'If I may, my lord?' The squire turned the key the other way, and the lock snapped open.

'I loosened it for you,' Bulchett said sulkily.

'Of course, my lord. A weakling such as I could not possibly have opened it, had it not first been loosened by a man as mighty as you.'

They entered the library. There were shelves on three sides – the fourth side having a row of south-facing windows – with bound books resting flat on them to keep the strain off their binding, and scrolls stored in pigeon-holes. There must have been over two hundred books in the place, which seemed like an astonishing number to Bulchett, but then he did not have much experience of libraries. Finding learning tedious in his boyhood, he had soon decided the ancients had little wisdom to teach anyone as brilliantly clever as himself. Between the shelves there were three rows of writing desks.

'What is it we seek?' asked Crawley.

'*The Confessions of Saint Augustine*.' Which was not true, but Bulchett had not got where he was in life by sharing information he had no need to share with minions like Crawley.

'There's a copy of that in the solar at Bulchett Manor,' said the squire.

'Yes, but there are pages missing from it. Key pages.' Bulchett pulled a tome down at random and carried it across to one of the desks, opening the cover to peer at the title page in the glow of the lanthorn: Frontinus' *De re militari*. Bulchett tossed it on the floor. It was important to be systematic: if he threw the books he had already looked at on the floor, that way he could keep careful track of which ones he had not yet examined. He took down another, glanced at the title page, saw it was not the book he sought, and threw that on the floor after Frontinus, heading back to the shelves for a third.

Crawley was also glancing at title pages, his younger eyes managing to read them in the distant glow of the lanthorn without carrying them across to the lectern, and when he closed them he returned them carefully where he had found them. 'It seems the librarian stores the books in some kind of order, my lord,' he said after they had both been searching for a while. 'These ones are all histories, those ones works of theology.'

Bulchett turned his attention to the histories. The third he looked at was the very tome he sought: the *Chronica Johannis Glasguensis*, the Chronicles of John of Glasgow. He rested it on a lectern and began leafing through its parchment pages in search of the information he needed. He had to squint to read it: the monk who had copied it had done so in infernally small letters. Needing more light, he removed one of the horn panels in his lanthorn, so the flame of the candle within shone directly on the parchment.

'Here is a copy of Saint Augustine's *Confessions*,' called Crawley.

'Put it to one side,' said Bulchett. 'I'll view it presently.'

Turning a couple more pages of the *Chronica Johannis Glasguensis*, he found the very reference he sought. His heart pounded with excitement as he followed the text with the tip of a podgy finger, his blubbery lips silently forming the words as he read. 'Ragman's Law!' he finally exclaimed excitedly. 'Have you seen any maps?'

'Maps, Sir Alexander?'

'I need a map of Scotland.'

'Over there, my lord.' Crawley pointed to some pigeonholes, each with a parchment map rolled up and slotted into it.

Bulchett worked methodically, pulling out each one in turn and unrolling it, holding it up to the light of the lanthorn to see what it was. It was not long before he came to the maps of Scotland, though most were too small to show him what he was looking for. Then he found a map showing the boundaries of Ettrick Forest, which had the Tweedsmuir Hills marked. It was too large to go in the leather scrip he wore at his hip, so he used his knife to cut away the parts he did not need and threw them aside, knocking the lanthorn off the lectern in the process. It fell to the floor, where the candle rolled out, the wick still burning as it rolled under the pages of one of the books Bulchett had discarded earlier.

'Come along!' he told his squire.

'Should we not put out that fire, my lord?'

'There's no time for that.'

'But… there are centuries' worth of learning in this library. Ever since that abbey burned down in the Alps, many of the books here have been the last known surviving copies: Socrates' verse versions of Aesop's *Fables*… Suetonius' *Lives of Famous Whores*… Aristarchus of Samos' book on astrology—'

'For Christ's pain, Rowland!' Bulchett emerged from the library, which was rapidly filling with smoke, and hurried down the stairs. He heard Crawley's footfalls on the steps behind him. 'They're only books. The world is full of the infernal things; I hardly think a few less will make any difference. In any case, wasn't Aristarchus of Samos the fellow who thought the earth orbited the sun? I think the world can do without the scribblings of such a wooden-headed fool as that!'

The two of them emerged once more into the chill of the February night. They found the friar wisping down their horses in the stables.

'Did ye find whit ye sought?' asked the friar.

Bulchett grabbed the homespun folds of the friar's habit in his fists and slammed him back against the partition between two stalls. The knight was flabby rather than muscular, but he had learned how to use his bulk to intimidate men. 'Ragman's Law!'

'The hill in Tweedsmuir?' stammered the friar.

'Aye. How do we find it?'

'Where St Mary's Loch bends to the south, a glen leads west. Two leagues hence there's a standing stone in the shape of a bishop's mitre. Ragman's Law is the hill immediately to the north.'

'Thank you—' Breaking off, Bulchett stared at something behind the friar. 'God's love! What's that?'

The friar turned. Bulchett drew his knife and stabbed him in the back. The friar turned back, gaping with shock and horror frozen on his face as he crumpled to the straw. Bulchett wiped the blood off the blade of his knife with a rag before sliding it back into its sheath.

Crawley stared at him. 'God's heart, Sir Alexander! You've slain him!'

Bulchett furrowed his brow. 'You're not suggesting I'm the sort of man who would go around murdering defenceless men of God, are you?'

'But I just saw you—'

Bulchett gave him a warning glare.

Crawley quailed. 'Now that you mention it, I thought I saw blood on the friar's habit when first we entered the stable. It must have been one of the archers quartered here who murdered him. It was a miracle he was able to tell us anything before he died.'

'Nonsense. He told us nothing. He was already dead. I must remember to explain that to the king's marshal, if he should happen to question me about it.'

'And I shall do likewise, if I am asked,' said Crawley, throwing a folded horse rug over the back of his master's palfrey and arranging his saddle on top.

Bulchett frowned. 'I hardly think it's appropriate for my squire to indulge in tittle-tattle with the king's marshal. If he asks you any questions, you shall say naught other than to direct him to me.'

Crawley saddled their horses. By the time they had led them out into the courtyard, flames were licking hungrily from the windows of the library and the roof was ablaze. Archers and friars ran to and fro, yelling to their comrades to awaken, while someone tolled the bells in the church to rouse the whole community.

'Should we not help put out the fire, my lord?' asked Crawley.

'It's not our responsibility,' sniffed Bulchett.

No one tried to stop the knight and his squire as they rode out through the gate into the night, heading back to their own billets. Behind them, the flames licking from the windows of the library began to spread to the other buildings.

Three

Kemp stood outside the great hall of a castle. He was looking through the door to where the king and his nobles caroused around a roaring hearth. Outside where Kemp was it was bitterly cold, but inside all looked warm and cosy and everything was joyful. He wanted to enter, but some unseen barrier blocked his way across the threshold. He tried to call out to the noblemen inside, but he had no voice. Indeed, everything was oddly silent in his dream, except for someone shouting 'Fire, fire!', and when Kemp looked again, a burning log had tumbled out of the hearth, rolling across the floor to set fire to a tapestry. The flames spread quickly, but the king and his nobles did not seem to notice. He tried to cry a warning to them, but still he had no voice.

This is a dream, thought Kemp and, even as the realisation came to him, he found himself lying awake in one of the cots in the pilgrim's lodge at Haddington Greyfriars. As the dream faded, he heard someone shout 'Fire, fire!' again. Muzzy-headed with sleep, he tried to work out where the dream ended and reality began. The bells of the church tolled: no musical carillon to summon the brethren to matins but an urgent, insistent clamour demanding attention. After tarrying a heartbeat longer to brace himself against the cold night air, he threw aside the blanket and swung his legs out of the bed. He draped his mantle over his shoulders, padded across the rush-strewn floor to the door and threw it open. On the far side of the courtyard, one of the buildings was ablaze, casting a hellish orange light over the scene.

'Fire!' shouted Kemp. He made his way from bay to bay, shaking those who lay in the cots by their shoulders, kicking the soles of the feet of the men who lay sleeping on the floor. 'Rouse yourselves, you idle dogs! There's work to be done!'

They dressed hastily. Outside, Kemp intercepted a friar running past. 'Pails?'

'There are some in the brew-house...'

'Fetch them. Tegg, take your men and go with him, fetch owt you can find that'll hold more than a gallon of water. Form a chain from the well to the blaze.'

With Kemp giving clear directions, the men moved swiftly and with purpose, but by the time they had formed their chain, the building opposite was completely engulfed by so searing an inferno, the scorching heat was too intense for any to get close enough to throw a pail of water at it. A stiff breeze had spread the flames to the church, which was already on fire at one end, but most of the blaze seemed to be burning in the roof, where they could not get at it. Even where they could, the flames burned so fiercely, the water no more quenched them than a sponge might mop up an ocean. Burning timbers groaned in the nave, and a part of the roof collapsed while some of Kemp's men were still inside, trying to fight the fire. A great blizzard of sparks darted up from the conflagration, and the thick billows of smoke rising with them were illuminated from below by the ruddy hue of the inferno.

By midnight, the whole church was ablaze: the flaming tower must have cast its light for miles.

'Now it truly is the Lamp of Lothian!' Ieuan said grimly.

Someone clapped a hand on Kemp's shoulder. He turned to see Tegg standing there, his face blackened with soot, a finger directed to where sparks had set alight the thatched roof of the stables. Only a small part of the roof was burning, but it would soon spread.

'Get the horses out!' shouted Kemp.

'Where should I tether them?'

'I know not. Somewhere they'll not burn to death before dawn. Use your wits, damn your nose!'

Townsfolk flocked to help with the fire as did men-at-arms and archers from the rest of the king's host. More pails were fetched, scooping up water from the riverbank. Working tirelessly through the night, they managed to stop the flames from spreading to the surrounding houses, but the friary was lost: church, chapter house, dorter, refectory, stables, brewery, pilgrims' lodge, library, everything.

As dawn rose, Kemp surveyed the charred, still-smouldering ruins. Men with red-rimmed eyes and soot-blackened faces sifted through the rubble. Charred corpses were dragged from the ruins of the church. At least one had a leather bracer on his left wrist, and an archer's calluses on his fingertips. *My men*, Kemp thought bitterly. To die in battle was one thing: only a fool did not accept it might come to that when he took up arms for his king. But to die in a fire? How had it started, anyway? Had it merely been an accident, or had the Scots started it in the hope of killing some Englishmen? If the latter, why had his sentries not spotted them?

He turned to Ieuan. 'The fire started in the building opposite the stables. Speak to the sentinels, and any of the friars who might know owt. I want to know how this fire began.'

Ieuan nodded. As he hurried off, Kemp was distracted by a low rumble from the north. Gazing over the rooftops of the houses on the high street, he saw a great, black thundercloud bearing down on the town.

—

Jagged lightning tore the night sky asunder with a crash like the wrath of God. The flash lit up the breakers where they foamed against the black rocks of the shore, vast clouds of spray erupting high into the rain-drenched air. Silhouetted against the white water, a cog was hunched over the rocks like a vast, wounded beast, her mast canted over at a crazy angle, the tattered remnants of the canvas sail flapping from the yardarm in the howling wind. Then darkness returned, cloaking land, sea and ship in a night blacker than a paynim's heart.

As the horsemen picked their way down the coast road, Red Rory Reid nudged his hobby forward until he drew level with Rab Nixon, who rode at the head of the troop of reivers. 'Did ye see that, Rab?'

'See whit?'

'There was a cog, wrecked on yon rocks.' A short, stocky man with an unkempt ginger beard adorning a vulpine, ruddy-cheeked face, Reid pointed to where he had seen the ship.

Nixon stared into the darkness as if waiting for another flash of lightning to reveal it again; but the storm, which had raged across the coast all afternoon, disobligingly turned coy.

'Once we've settled matters at the friary, ye can take Tam and Gib down to the beach to search for shipwrecked mariners.' Nixon was past the age of fifty now, his crinkly black hair turning silver at the temples, his heavily jowled face dominated by a boot-shaped nose. 'The friars can care for them. Unless the mariners turn out to be Inglishers, of course. If they're Inglishers, ye can slay them where ye find them. All but one. Ye'll bring him to me. Yé can slay that one after Ah'm done questioning him.'

'Aye, Rab.'

The road turned away from the coast, and a mile inland they came to the charred ruins of the town of Aberlady. Reid's knuckles whitened where they gripped the spear he carried in his right hand and he wondered what had become of the townsfolk. There were no corpses in the street, so perhaps they had got out before the murderous English whoresons had come. Those with kin in Edinburgh might have taken shelter behind the town's palisade, if they could persuade the guards at the Netherbow Port to let them in; others would have had a longer journey to the bridge over the River Forth at Stirling. But there were always some who did not heed the warnings, who would cleave to their homes and hope against hope that the English would not come. No doubt they sheltered from the storm in some woods nearby. There would be old folk amongst them, men and women too elderly to make the journey to Stirling, and young children besides. Reid wondered how many of them would perish from cold before the storm passed and the thin warmth of a winter sun returned.

An earthwork rampart topped with a wooden palisade surrounded Luffness Friary, a few furlongs to the east of the town. The torrential rain hissing into the puddles in the road masked the clop of the hobbies' hoofs as they approached. Nixon reined in a short distance from the timber-framed gatehouse, signalling his men to do likewise with an upraised hand. 'Open the gate, Rory,' he growled. 'Gi'e him a hand, Howk.'

Howk was the only man in the troop who did not ride a hobby, partly because he had never learned to ride bareback but mostly because no hobby could bear his weight on its back. He had been christened John and his father's name had been Hawick, his grandfather having hailed from that town; but someone had asked John his name once and, when the big man had volunteered his surname, the asker had misheard and made a joke about its aptness, 'howk' being a Scots word for a large and heavily built man. The name had stuck.

Howk ascended the rampart, stood with his back to the palisade and clasped his huge hands before him. Reid reached up to grasp Howk's shoulders and lifted a leg to put the sole of one shoe on the big man's upturned palms. Howk effortlessly boosted Reid up, and he perched awkwardly atop the timber palisade for a moment before dropping to the reverse slope of the rampart. He rolled down it, rising on one knee and surveying the shadows of the friary. The rampart behind him provided some shelter from the driving rain. A few lights flickered behind the waxed parchment in some of the windows. On a night like this, the brethren were all tucked up inside. But it was not the friars that Reid was worried about.

He crossed to the gatehouse, leaning close to a parchment window to listen. Someone – Nixon or Howk – tolled the bell to summon the porter. The gatehouse door opened and a Carmelite friar emerged, a ghostly figure in his white habit. Reid pressed himself up against the wall of the gatehouse and drew his maul from under his belt: a long-hafted war-hammer with a flat mallet on one side of the steel head and a heavy spike on the other. The friar was followed out by a man-at-arms, almost invisible but for the faint gleam of his bascinet and the links of his hauberk. He stood with his back to the gate and nodded to the friar, signalling for him to open the spyhole. He did not see Reid step up behind him. The reiver swung the head of his maul so the spike punctured the back of the man's bascinet. As the man sank to his knees, Reid jerked the maul out of the hole, and a trickle of blood ran down the steel, only to be swiftly washed away by the rain.

The friar cringed away with a gasp.

'Calm yourself, brother,' said Reid. 'Ah'm a friend.' He tucked the maul's haft back under his belt and was lifting the timber baulk barring the gate from its brackets when the friar hissed a warning.

'Look to your back!'

A second man-at-arms had emerged from the gatehouse. Reid slammed one end of the baulk into the man's face. As the man reeled with blood gushing from his nostrils, Reid adjusted his grip on the baulk, swinging it against the side of his head, breaking his neck with an audible snap. He handed the baulk to the astonished friar and heaved the gate open to admit the other reivers.

Nixon glanced down at the two dead men-at-arms sprawled at Reid's feet. 'Where are the rest?'

'Sir Andrew Welles is in the prior's lodge,' said the friar. 'His men are either in the pilgrims' lodge or the calefactory.'

Before Nixon could begin issuing orders, a dozen shadowy figures emerged from the slype between the church and the chapter house, chain mail chinking, swords whispering from scabbards. The reivers pulled battle-axes from under their belts and ran to meet them gleefully. The Englishmen might be better armoured, but the Scots outnumbered them three to one. Some worked in teams, two men grabbing a man-at-arms between them and holding him with his arms outstretched so a third could seek a chink in his armour at his leisure, before sliding the slender blade of a misericord through it to deliver the death stroke.

Reid had his own way of fighting, with his maul in his left hand and a sharp reaping hook in his right. When an armoured figure lumbered out of the rain at him, he parried the man's sword stroke with the steel haft of the maul, before slashing at his face with the reaping hook. The tip of the curved blade stabbed into the man's eye and he fell so swiftly, the hook was almost torn from Reid's hand.

Tugging it free from the corpse, he looked around for another man to fight and saw Howk standing in the midst of the melee, holding aloft a struggling man-at-arms with one meaty hand on his throat. The man-at-arms had a sword in his hand and he tried to swing it at Howk, but the big man caught his wrist in his other hand, staying the blow. The man-at-arms' feet kicked in the air. Howk's fingers must have been crushing the man's wrist, for the man shrieked and dropped the sword. With his other hand he clawed at Howk's forearm, trying to prise his thumb from the side of his throat, but he might as well have tried to bend an iron bar. Howk's right hand exerted the same crushing force on the man's throat that his left had already inflicted on the man's wrist, choking off his screams. When he went limp, Howk tossed his lifeless corpse at another man who ran towards Nixon with a spear in his hand. The man went down, and by the time he had crawled out from under the corpse flung at him, Reid stood over him and dashed his skull in with his maul.

The melee was over as swiftly as it had started. A couple of the reivers were dead and several had received wounds, one of them quite bad, but the Englishmen had been butchered. Emerging from his lodge, the prior crossed himself when he saw the bloody corpses strewn in the mud.

'Where's Sir Andrew Welles?' demanded Nixon.

The prior indicated one of the corpses. 'That was him.'

'Damn it! Ah wanted him alive for questioning. Are none of them living?'

'Only the mariner they brought in.'

'Whit mariner?'

'Some of Sir Andrew's men went down to the coast just before sundown. They returned an hour ago with a half-drowned mariner. I understand a ship was wrecked off the coast near here.'

'Take us to this mariner,' said Nixon. 'Ah think Ah'd like to have a word wi' him.'

The prior showed them to the cloister, where they found a white-haired friar washing his face at the lavabo. He had stripped off his habit, revealing a back criss-crossed with the scars of a whipping from long ago. Reid might have wondered if he had been one of the flagellants, but the scars looked much older than that.

'Ah'd know that back anywhere,' Nixon greeted the old man genially.

'And I'd know that voice,' replied the old man, fumbling for a towel to wipe soap from his eyes. He spoke good English, but with a hint of a French accent. 'Rab Nixon, you old rascal!'

'Ye have a guest in the infirmary?' asked Nixon.

Brother Constantine nodded and pulled his habit over his head.

'How did he get those scars on his back?' Howk asked Reid as they followed Nixon and Brother Constantine to the infirmary.

'Many years ago, before he joined the Carmelite Order, Brother Constantine was a serjeant in the Knights Templar,' murmured Reid.

'The Knights Templar? Were they no' heretics?'

'So the auld King of France would have had the world believe. He was a grasping devil who always needed money for the royal coffers. First he plundered the Lombards, then the Jews. But still he needed money. So he turned his avaricious eyes on the Templars. He had men falsely accuse them of witchcraft, and had many of them tortured until they confessed to heresies and blasphemies they never committed.'

Constantine overheard them. 'I was a serjeant at the Old Temple in Paris at the time. In truth, the men who tortured me were more interested in learning what had become of the treasure we kept in the strong room than in any heresies the knights of our order might have committed. But I was small fry to them and, thanks to the mercy of God, my tormentors let me go when I convinced them I could tell them nothing. The pope ordered the disbandment of our order, and I escaped from France with a few companions. We came to the one place we knew we would be beyond the pope's reach, for Robert the Bruce was under a papal interdict then, and he had always been a good friend to our order.'

Entering the infirmary, they found a bearded man with dark, curly hair fast asleep in one of the beds. 'This is the man you seek,' whispered Constantine. 'I pray you will let him rest. He has been through a terrible ordeal.'

'Dinnae fash yourself,' said Nixon. 'It's no' as if we're gaunae ask him to start doing handsprings.' Standing over the bed, he patted the mariner gently on the cheek until the man opened his eyes. Not recognising the reiver, but seeing he was clearly no friar, he looked fearful.

'Be you one of Sir Andrew Welles' men?' he asked in the dialect of the south country.

'That's reet,' said Nixon. 'Whit ship were ye in?'

'The *Jonette* cog.'

'Frae Berwick?' guessed Nixon. He had heard from the Earl of Dunbar – who had spies in Berwick – that a fleet of the English king's ships had sailed from the harbour a few days earlier.

The mariner nodded.

'And where were ye bound?'

Suspicion showed on the mariner's face. 'If ye bist one of Sir Andrew's men, ye should know whither we were bound.'

'Oh aye,' said Nixon. 'We ken. We jist need to make sure ye are who ye say ye are. Ye can prove it by telling us where the *Jonette* was bound.'

The mariner nodded slowly. 'We were bound for—' Breaking off in mid-sentence, he leaped out of the other side of the bed, dodged past Reid and would have been out of the infirmary door, had Howk not been blocking it. The giant caught the mariner by the throat and lifted him off the floor.

'Gently with him!' cried Nixon. 'We need him to talk.'

Howk lowered the mariner to the flagstones. Cringing, the man backed into a corner of the infirmary. 'You be meaning to slay me!' he groaned.

'Answer my questions truthfully, and Ah swear – on my mother's grave – Ah'll no' harm a hair on your heid. Now, where was the *Jonette* bound?'

'Aberlady. But we were driven onto the rocks by the storm.'

'She was part of the fleet bringing victuals to King Edward's host?'

'Arr.'

'And the other ships of the fleet?'

'I doesn't know. Either wrecked as we were, or sunk, or scattered far and wide. That be all I knows, I swear!'

'Ah believe ye,' said Nixon. 'Howk!'

The giant seized the mariner by the throat and dashed his skull against one of the ceiling beams before dropping his lifeless body to the flagstones.

Nixon chuckled. 'Ah never promised Howk widnae harm him, mind!'

Kneeling over the body, Brother Constantine buffed the blade of a knife on his sleeve before holding it over the mariner's lips, then looked up at Nixon with anger in his eyes. 'You are a cruel man, Rab Nixon. May the Lord have mercy on your soul.'

'If King Edward was depending on his fleet to bring him victuals and his ships have been wrecked or scattered to the four winds, whit will his men do for victuals now?' Reid asked Nixon.

'Whit indeed? Let's ride back to Yester Castle. These are tidings to warm Lord Douglas' heart. Summat tells me King Edward's host will no' be troubling us much longer.'

–

Kemp descended the stairs of the house he was occupying with Tegg's men to find Ieuan hunched over a kettle

48

suspended over the hearth. A savoury aroma filled the kitchen. Ieuan scooped some of the simmering stew out with a wooden spoon, tasted it gingerly, and smacked his lips.

'You found some meat, then?' Kemp asked him.

'It stopped raining for an hour or so after first light,' said Ieuan. The storm that had lashed Luffness Friary had lashed the rooftops of Haddington besides. 'I managed to shoot a couple of birds.'

'Pigeons?'

'It will *taste* like pigeon, with any luck, if I can get the balance of the herbs right.'

'If not pigeon, then what…?'

'Best you don't ask.'

Hoof beats clopped in the street outside. Kemp was already on his way to the door when someone hammered a mailed fist against it. Kemp opened it to reveal Wat Jepson and Jankin Quarmby – two of King Edward's serjeants – the rain falling from the gutters above running down their polished bascinets to stain jupons blazoned with the king's arms.

'The king wants to see you,' said Quarmby. Both he and Jepson hailed from the south country. They had difficulty understanding the language spoken by the northerners of the host, just as the northerners had difficulty understanding the two serjeants; or pretended to, at least. As a Midlander, Kemp was generally able to understand both, though the occasional linguistic peculiarity sometimes caught him out.

He nodded. He had been expecting such a summons since the previous morning; indeed, he was surprised it had not come sooner. But then he did not doubt the king had more pressing matters to attend to than a fire at a friary where some of his men were billeted.

'The king wants to see me,' he called to where Ieuan crouched by the hearth.

The Welshman indicated the kettle. 'I'll keep some warm for you then, shall I?'

'*Not* pigeon, you say?'

'But it will taste like pigeon. With any luck.'

'You and the lads go ahead and eat your fill; I'll see what I can scrounge at the castle.'

Flanked by Jepson and Quarmby, Kemp was marched across Nungate Bridge. From there it was half a league to Lethington Castle. There was hardly anyone in the great hall where Kemp found the king in conference with a handful of his nobles. Usually he would be surrounded by petitioners, flatterers and flunkeys all jostling for his attention. That this detritus of the court was noticeable by its absence was a sure sign the king was in one of his fouler moods, a circumstance that was confirmed almost the moment Jepson pulled aside an arras and jerked his head for Kemp to enter. Sir Alexander Bulchett was there, and a young chaplain in the king's retinue, a grave young man called William of Wykeham.

Kemp knew Bulchett by reputation only: he was known to be a hail-fellow-well-met sort of man, a man said to conceal a keen intellect behind a façade of being a genial buffoon. He and his squire stood in a corner, trying desperately not to catch the king's eye.

'All of them?' the king asked Sir Walter de Mauny, whose fine cote-hardie and mantle were bedraggled and salt-stained.

'All of them,' confirmed Mauny. Though a Hainaulter by birth, he had spent most of his life in England and spoke with the same Anglo-Norman accent as most English noblemen. 'And many loyal mariners besides.'

The king clenched his fists, pacing up and down in silence for a few heartbeats, then suddenly swung around, aiming a kick at the high table. The sole of the king's shoe hit it with such force, the board shot off the trestles and crashed to the floor below the dais. 'God's passion!' he roared with such fury that Kemp, Jepson and Quarmby all flinched. Then, as an afterthought, the king turned again and kicked over one trestle, then the other.

'One of the ships is caught on a reef off Craigielaw Point,' said Mauny. 'It may be possible to salvage some of the barrels of victuals and sacks of fodder from her hold—'

'Enough to feed our entire host?' snapped the king.

Mauny gestured helplessly.

The king resumed pacing, clenched fists pressed to his temples. Then he seemed to slump, and lowered his arms. 'Then what more is there to say?' he sighed more calmly, though it clearly took him an effort to keep his anger in check. 'We must march back to Roxburgh.'

Roxburgh was where they had started out from nine days ago. Kemp had privately doubted this campaign would have a happy conclusion, but he had not imagined the king would be forced to abandon it after little more than a week.

'My spies report the Earl of Dunbar has only marched the cattle to a place on the north side of the River Forth,' ventured Mauny. 'If we were to push on deeper into Scotland...'

The king shook his head. 'If we do, we'll play straight into Dunbar's hands. There are neither bridges nor fords east of Stirling, and that's four days' march west of here. And we may be sure we'll find the bridge well-guarded when we get there. No, Sir Walter, it is over... this time, at least. There will be other campaigns. But our path now is clear. We must march south, or risk seeing our host starve. Send word to the marshals: I want all the arrangements made in good time for us to set out at dawn tomorrow. We'll divide the host into three columns so the men will have a better chance of living off the land. Lord Neville will march back to Berwick by the same road we marched hither, across Coldingham Moor; Lord Percy will follow the ancient road south-west through Penicuik and Biggar to Annandale, and from thence to Carlisle; and I'll lead the third through Lauderdale and Liddesdale. And all three columns will leave nothing standing betwixt here and England: no castle, no manor house, no cottage. We'll teach these impertinent Scots they trifle with the English at their peril. Tell Neville and Percy.'

'Very good, my liege.' Mauny bowed out of the hall.

'I suppose the men will be pleased to learn we are heading south, at least,' said the king.

'Not a bit of it, sire!' blustered Bulchett. 'They cannot wait to get stuck into the Scots! They'll be bitterly disappointed by these tidings.'

'Bitterly disappointed,' echoed Crawley. Kemp shot a dirty look at him. If he had had to suffer a fawning lickspittle like the squire following him around, he would have given the obsequious turd a clip around the earhole and commanded him to hold his tongue until he had something useful to say.

The king pasted a smile on his face. 'What say you, Wykeham? You must hear the men talk when I am not within earshot. Is their morale high?'

'If it is, it will not remain so when they learn of the destruction of the fleet in yesterday's storm,' remarked the young chaplain. 'Some would see it as God's punishment for the destruction of the Greyfriars.'

'What stuff!' the king said scornfully. 'If God is angry for the destruction of the friary, I cannot see how he avenges it by drowning a parcel of mariners.'

'For the sins of the mariners I cannot speak, sire. But it was the men of your host who put the friary to the torch, was it not? And who shall suffer most now that the fleet is sunk, but those same men?'

The king beckoned Kemp to approach. 'You were quartered in the friary, were you not? Who gave the order to put it to the torch?'

'I do not know anyone gave an order, sire. Arson by the Scots, perchance, or – more likely – an accident.'

'A day has passed since the friary has burned down, and still you don't know whether it burned by accident or design?' Bulchett said scornfully. He turned to the king. 'If Kemp's men were quartered there, surely the responsibility to safeguard the place lay with him? What of the friar who was murdered?'

'What friar?' asked Kemp.

'Do not pretend you know naught of it! A friar, brutally stabbed by one of your men.'

'Brutally stabbed!' agreed Crawley.

'Stabbings in the stables, fires in the library,' snorted Bulchett. 'Is that your notion of keeping order in your company?'

The king nodded. 'Sir Alexander speaks true: whether or not you know what happened the night before last, you were responsible. It seems my judgement was at fault when I appointed you to command your company. If you cannot maintain discipline amongst your men, then you are not fit to command them. I must make an example of you. Quarmby, Jepson... put him in chains. I'll decide what's to be done with him when we get to Carlisle.'

Kemp felt as shocked as if he had been kicked in the stomach by a mule, with both hind legs. He accepted that he was responsible for the behaviour of his men, but it seemed the height of injustice to be stripped of his command and treated like a common criminal because someone had set the friary on fire.

The king turned to Bulchett. 'Sir Alexander, you will take command of Kemp's archers.'

Smirking, the knight bowed low. 'I shall be honoured, sire. You'll not regret reposing such trust in your most loyal servant!'

Four

Light flurries of snow fell on the Friday after Candlemas, but the fields, pastures and roads were too wet for it to settle. Scouting towards Sir Adam Hepburn's castle at Hailes, Nixon and his men were looking to cross the river at Linton, two leagues from Haddington, when they almost blundered into a picquet of archers guarding the eastern approach to the ford. Realising just in time that the archers must be English, Nixon and his men hastily wheeled their hobbies and retreated up the road towards Lord Douglas' castle at Tantallon. The archers loosed a couple of shafts after them, but were too disciplined to abandon their post by giving chase.

'We'll cross by the ford at Gourlay's Mill,' Nixon told Reid.

Gourlay's Mill was less than two miles downstream. As the reivers drew near, however, they saw a troop of mounted archers putting it to the torch. Swinging themselves back onto their rouncies, the archers galloped back across the ford and rode to where a larger body of troops could be seen about three furlongs away, marching down the road to Berwick. Even as Reid watched, billows of smoke rose from the turf roofs of a nearby farmstead as that too was put to the torch, but the smoke drifting across the countryside at least provided enough cover for the reivers to get closer to the column of troops. They crossed the ford, following the archers at a discreet distance, and dismounted, leading their own horses to where they could watch the road from a coppice less than a hundred yards away. They saw men-at-arms in bascinets and habergeons carrying their lances upright, and archers with their bows slung across their backs, sheaves of arrows tucked under their belts. The brightly painted wains of the baggage train seemed few, even for so small a host. Banners and pennants twitched fitfully in the breeze.

'That's never two thousand men,' said Nixon. 'No' even half that.'

'Less than seven hundred,' agreed Reid. 'The Inglishers must have broken up their host. Is yon Lord Neville's banner?'

'Aye. Ah dinnae see King Edward's arms, though.'

'He must be with the rest of his host... wherever that may be.' Reid shook his head. 'It disnae make any sense. Breaking his host up into smaller units will only make it easier for us to defeat them piecemeal. King Edward is nae sumph; why would he make such a simple error, unless he meant to entrap us?'

'There can only be one reason why he'd break up his host: because he has nae other choice. With his ships sunk in yesterday's storm, he's left with nae means of feeding his troops. They're withdrawing to the border, Rory, and they've broken up into smaller units to stand a better chance of being able to forage for food on the way!'

Once the English troops had marched out of sight and Nixon was confident there were no more units bringing up the rear, the reivers crossed the Berwick Road and headed south-west towards Yester Castle.

'If the Inglishers have broken their host up into smaller parts, is this no' a chance to defeat them piecemeal?' asked Reid. 'Maybe even kill King Edward himself?'

'Defeat them piecemeal, aye,' said Nixon. 'But the Earl of Dunbar will no' want Edward slain.'

'Why not?'

'Because if we slay Edward then we have his eldest son, Edward of Woodstock, to deal with.'

'Prince Edward's in Gascony—'

'And if he gets word his father's been slain campaigning in Scotland, he'll be hame on the next ship. And dinnae forget King David's still a prisoner at Windsor. The moment the prince sets foot ashore, he'll send word David's to be pit to death to avenge the death of King Edward. And then he'll raise an army and march up here to complete his vengeance. If ye think King Edward's given us a rough time, ye wait till his son comes looking for blood. He's no' nearly so merciful as his father, frae whit Ah hear.' Nixon fell silent, his double chins resting on the breast of his travel-stained jupon. 'But,' he continued after a few moments, raising his head again, 'if we should chance to *capture* King Edward... that would be another matter entirely.'

Yester Castle stood on a promontory high on the west side of the ravine of the Hopes Water. Once it had been a motte-and-bailey castle, but now the stone donjon-keep was crumbling on its mound and the main stronghold was the bailey, surrounded by forty-foot-high walls of russet freestone ashlar. The flagstaff on the highest point of the castle flew the banner of Sir Hugh Giffard, who owned the castle, and above it that of his liege lord, William Douglas.

Nixon and his men approached the twin drum towers flanking the main entrance by a wooden bridge spanning the ravine. Nixon identified himself to the sentinels, and the gates were opened to admit him and his men to the triangular bailey. Within, timber-framed buildings had been built against the insides of the curtain walls: the great hall on one side and stables on the other.

'Ah must speak with Lord Douglas,' Nixon told one of Giffard's men-at-arms, a smooth-faced fellow with a red rose blazoned on the jupon he wore over his shiny habergeon, and a polished bascinet neither scratched nor dented by battle.

'His lordship is with my master,' sniffed the man-at-arms. 'Whom should I say you are?'

'Rab Nixon. They'll want to hear whit I have to tell them. It's urgent.'

'I'll let them know,' sneered the man-at-arms.

Nixon was left waiting like a common servitor in the bailey while the man-at-arms entered the great hall. After a few minutes, a tall, raw-boned young man emerged, the corners of his thin-lipped mouth downturned in a scowl beneath a mop of black hair. Reid recognised him as Sir Archibald Douglas, the bastard son of Sir James Douglas and a kinsman to Lord William. Sir Archibald cast a thoughtful eye over the reivers in the bailey before his eyes fell on Nixon. 'I'm sorry you were kept waiting. Please come with me.'

Nixon turned to Reid. 'Stay with the men. Make sure they dinnae shit anywhere they shouldnae...' He glanced at Archibald, then leaned in to speak privily with Reid in a low voice. 'On second thoughts, tell them they can shit where they like. If Lord Douglas' men insist on treating us like dirt, then dirt is whit they'll get.'

Reid grinned. 'They'll no' invite us back again.'

'Aye, they will,' growled Nixon. 'They need us a damned sight more than we need them. Remember that, Rory.'

Reid watched Nixon follow Sir Archibald into the great hall, then fell to pacing up and down in the bailey. Sometimes folk asked him why he insisted on riding with a ruffian like Black Rab Nixon, when he might have taken service with any number of lords. 'Ye cannae trust a lord,' he invariably told them. 'Too many Scottish lords haud land on both sides of the border, and they change sides depending on which way the wind blaws. The knight who asked ye to die for King David yesterday will ask ye to do the same again for King Edward tomorrow. Say whit ye like about Black Rab, he's only got one foe, and that's the same folk who slew my parents, raped my sisters and burned us out of house and hame.'

The castle servants brought out food for the reivers while Nixon was closeted with Douglas and Giffard in the great hall. It was only bread – coarse maslin, and stale at that – but it was better than nothing, and they provided half a bushel of oats for the hobbies, along with loaves of horse bread, baked from beans and peas mixed with oatmeal. Though given the reivers were being employed to scout for Lord Douglas, seeing to it their mounts were fed seemed like the least they could do.

Nixon was smiling when he emerged from the great hall. 'Sir William Ramsay reports there's another seven hundred Inglishers marching south-west to Lauderdale,' he told his men. 'And King Edward's banner is amongst them.'

'God's nails!' exclaimed Reid. 'Lauderdale! It's too perfect a place for an ambush. It *must* be a trap.'

'It'll be a trap, reet enough,' agreed Nixon. 'But for King Edward, no' for us. Ramsay will send outriders to keep an eye on the men we saw marching for Berwick, and there's another seven hundred men marching east – Ah suppose they'll cut south through Annandale. If either of those hosts doubles back towards Lauderdale, we'll have warning of it. Rory, Ah want ye to ride to Selkirk, Hawick, Jedburgh and Kelso. Raise every man capable of bearing arms. Tell them we've got a chance to give the Inglishers such a bloody nose, they'll never dare show their faces north of the border again. It'll take King Edward's host four days to march through Lauderdale, so ye've got three to meet the rest of us at Thirlstane Castle.'

–

Heavy frost had primed the earth for the snow that fell the Sunday after Candlemas, lightly at first, but persistently, so that within a couple of hours an inch of snow-blanketed fields, meadows and pastures, and settled even upon the boughs of the bare trees that looked black in contrast to the whiteness all around. If the snow lay thick on the road ahead of King Edward's column, however, it formed no impediment to the baggage wains following at the rear: by the time their iron-rimmed wheels reached it, hundreds of horses had trampled it into dung-spattered slush, turning many stretches of the road into muddy sloughs.

Kemp rode with the baggage train, with Jepson and Quarmby close by to guard him. It was humiliating to ride in irons, with a couple of serjeants-at-arms riding herd on him; and besides, the cold and heavy cuffs of the manacles chafed his wrists, and made it difficult for him to wrap rags around his hands to protect them from the chill. He wondered what punishment the king was dreaming up for him for when they reached Carlisle.

The quilted gambeson he wore beneath his habergeon helped to keep him warm. Some of the noblemen riding with the king's host suddenly produced furs to wear over their armour, but lesser men-at-arms and archers had to settle for what rags they could plunder from any cottages they passed. Men trudged along with snowflakes settling on their helmets, dripping noses red from the cold, and each man's breath formed clouds in the air where it issued from his lips.

It was the second day of their march, and they had crossed the border back into England; at least, back into what King Edward called England. Kemp knew that many a Scot would insist that Berwickshire and Roxburghshire were parts of Scotland, and the border lay further to the south. For the past ten years, King Edward had had a fair claim to be in the right, if only by virtue of the English patrols roaming all over this district. But with King Edward himself retreating to Roxburgh with a part of his host, once again it was a fair description to call this territory 'the Debatable Land'.

They climbed steadily into the Lammermuir Hills during the morning, crossing a snow-swept moor before descending in the afternoon into a valley leading south with a steep slope rising on their left, a gentler one on their right. By the time dusk swept over the countryside and the order to camp for the night was given, Kemp reckoned they had marched little more than six leagues from Haddington, which was good going for a host on the march at this time of year.

Quarmby built a fire under the trees not far from where the wainmen of the baggage train camped for the night, and Jepson scrounged enough flour to make hasty pudding for the three of them. Picquets had been set, and within their cordon, roped-off areas delineated where the marshals had decreed the men should make camp, with the banners or pennants of their captains affixed to upright lances to show where each company was to settle. The king and some of the more senior nobles with him had tents to sleep in, but most of the men slept out in the open. Somewhere in the English camp, someone strummed a gittern to keep his companions' spirits up. The wainmen talked amongst themselves in low voices. Someone coughed in the darkness. A sentinel challenged a straggler arriving late at the camp. Kemp, Jepson and Quarmby huddled around a crackling fire.

'How long till we reach Melrose?' Kemp asked Jepson.

'Robert le Marshal reckons we'll be there the day after tomorrow,' said Jepson.

'What be it to you?' asked Quarmby.

'I'll be much happier when we're out of this valley,' said Kemp. 'I reckon we'll be safe when we reach Melrose.'

Jepson pushed himself to his feet. 'Mind watching him while I stretches my legs?' he asked Quarmby, indicating Kemp with a jerk of his head.

'Stretches your legs, my arse! You've got a flap-tail amongst the camp followers!'

'And when you gets a flap-tail amongst the camp followers, I'll take a turn watching him while you'm swyving her.' Jepson scrunched off through the soft snow that had gathered in drifts beneath the trees to where the camp followers – mostly laundresses-cum-whores – had erected their tents or crawled under their wains.

Jepson had only been gone a few minutes when a shadowy figure approached Kemp and Quarmby. The serjeant-at-arms reached for his sword. 'Rest easy,' said Kemp. 'It's only Ieuan.'

'Keep back, Welshman,' said Quarmby. 'No talking to the prisoner!'

'Kiss my arse!' Ieuan replied scornfully.

The king did not employ cowards as serjeants-at-arms, but he did not employ fools in that role either, and Quarmby had sense enough to weigh the consequences of challenging the Welshman's defiance against the likelihood of there being any consequences for not challenging it. He held his tongue and turned a blind eye.

Ieuan proffered Kemp an upturned kettle helmet containing stew. 'With food being in such short supply, I wasn't sure if they'd be feeding you proper, isn't it?'

Kemp took the helmet in his manacled hands. 'They're feeding me.' He proffered it back.

Ieuan shook his head. 'I've already had my fill of it.'

'What is it?'

'One of the sumpters in the baggage train died.'

Kemp could well believe it. For several days now, most if not all the horses in the column had had nothing to eat but what they could forage at the roadside. He marvelled that no more of them had died before now, and wondered how many more would perish before they reached the stores of hay and oats waiting for them at Melrose.

'... Seemed a shame to leave the meat for the Scots,' added Ieuan.

'Horsemeat?' said Kemp.

'Don't tell me you've never eaten horsemeat, boy!'

If experience had taught Kemp anything, it was to never turn down good meat when it was offered; especially when it might be several days before he got another chance to eat a proper meal. 'Thank you.' Producing his spoon, he dipped it in the stew. The shortness of the chain on his manacles meant he had to raise the helmet halfway to his face to put the spoonful between his lips, but it could be done. He chewed the meat ruminatively: he had tasted worse. 'The others have eaten their fill?'

'Oh aye, there was plenty to go around.'

'Sir Alexander is looking after the men, is he?'

Ieuan rubbed the back of his neck. 'Sir Alexander's not what I'd call a man who attends to the details. He leaves that sort of thing to his squire, Rowland, and Rowland leaves it to me.'

Kemp swallowed another mouthful. 'Are you drawing a captain's wages?'

'Don't be daft.'

'It's not right that you should do the work and Bulchett should get the credit.'

'Someone's got to do it. I fancy it'll never be Sir Alexander.'

'Till we reach Melrose, make sure the men stay close together. The Scots will be looking to pick off stragglers.'

Ieuan nodded. 'I'll keep an eye on them. Till you're re-instated as captain, that is.'

'*If* I'm re-instated.'

'You'll be re-instated,' Ieuan asserted confidently.

Kemp remembered what Bulchett had said when the king had ordered him put in chains. 'Was a friar murdered at the Greyfriars the night of the blaze?'

'Aye, since you mention it. Godwin Vertue says the friars pulled the corpse of one of their brothers out of the charred ruins of the stable. Only the funny thing was, he hadn't burned to death. He'd been—'

'Stabbed?' guessed Kemp.

'How did you guess?'

'Sir Alexander told me on Thursday.'

'But the friar said they only found the body yesterday morning,' protested Ieuan. 'How could Sir Alexander possibly have known a friar was stabbed in the stables on Thursday, unless...' The Welshman stared at Kemp. 'You don't think...?'

'If he did not slay the friar, he witnessed the murder,' said Kemp. 'Or learned of it from one who did.'

'But why should Sir Alexander be party to the murder of a friar?'

'I know not. If we knew why the friar was slain...'

'Maybe he saw something he shouldn't have seen.'

'Such as who started that fire?'

'Maybe. But if it was Sir Alexander, why should he want to do such a thing?'

'And if Sir Alexander came to the Greyfriars on Candlemas Night, how did he get past our sentinels unseen?'

Ieuan shrugged. 'Should I tell the king?'

Kemp shook his head. 'Best not to throw around accusations till we're sure of our facts. But keep an eye on Sir Alexander. Whether or not he slew the friar, he's involved in it somehow.'

'All right. I'll keep my ears open. And I'll have a word with Haine and Fisher. They were supposed to be guarding the gate that night. If Sir Alexander came to the Greyfriars, they should ha' seen him.'

'Be wary: if Haine and Fisher did see someone at the Greyfriars who had no business there that night, they never came forward to tell anyone about it. That tells me they're up to their necks in it, too.'

'Or Haine wants revenge on you for thrashing him that day, and him and Fisher are happy to keep their mouths shut when coming forward with the truth might prove you guiltless in the matter.'

'Whatever their motives, keeping silent makes them abettors to the murder. And Haine's the kind of man who'd gladly murder to silence an accuser.'

'Don't you worry about me, boy. I can handle Haine.' Having scooped the last spoonful of horsemeat stew into his mouth, Kemp swallowed and handed the helmet back to Ieuan. 'Leave Haine to me. I'll deal with him as soon we get to Carlisle, and I get this foolishness done with.' He rattled the chain on his manacles.

'As you will. I'd best be getting back. You know what that lot are like: turn your back for five minutes, and they're brawling about something. Nothing but trouble and strife, they are! The sooner you resume command, the better I shall like it.' The Welshman started to turn away.

'Ieuan!' Kemp called after him. 'Don't worry about me. I can look after myself. See to it the company gets safely to Carlisle.'

The Welshman nodded and headed back the way he had come.

Kemp crouched to clean his spoon in the snow.

'You don't really think Sir Alexander Bulchett would be involved in anything underhanded?' asked Quarmby, who could not have helped overhearing Kemp's conversation with Ieuan.

'Why do you find it so hard to believe?'

'He be a nobleman.'

'You think no nobleman ever committed a crime? Back home in Leicestershire, we had a family called the Folvilles...'

Quarmby shook his head. 'Sir Alexander be a good fellow. The kind of fellow you could be at ease with in an alestake.'

Kemp was amused. 'You think Sir Alexander would be at ease drinking in an alestake with the likes of us?'

'Why not?'

'He thinks he's better than us.'

'Er, he *is* better than us. He be a nobleman, remember?'

'And you think all noblemen must be better than commoners?'

'If they weren't, God wouldn't have made 'em noblemen.'

'Are we not all descended from Adam and Eve? Why did God make Heaven and Hell, if we're to have our reward for goodness in this life? Maybe nobility is a test that God makes for some men, as he tests us all, to see if we're worthy of eternal life?'

'If it be, then Sir Alexander has proved himself worthy.'

'How?'

Quarmby furrowed his brow. 'What mean you?'

'What has he ever done to prove himself worthy?'

'I told you: he be a good fellow. He makes I laugh.'

'Oh, well, in that case, he must be assured of his place in heaven!' said Kemp.

Glancing past the Midlander, the serjeant-at-arms clapped his hand to the hilt of his sword. Twisting, Kemp saw another figure tramping through the snow beneath the trees. The man stepped into the light of the crescent moon and Kemp recognised Nompar de Savignac. He noticed Quarmby did not even attempt to order the Bourc of Cazoulat to keep away from the prisoner.

'Martin,' Nompar said with a nod.

'Nompar,' returned Kemp.

The *bourc* hunkered down beside him in the snow and proffered a small parcel wrapped in waxed parchment.

'What is it?' asked Kemp.

'A couple of roasted blackbirds. I was not sure if they were feeding you, so...'

'Jepson and Quarmby let me share their hasty pudding. And Ieuan had the same thought as you: he just brought me a bowl of stew. In truth, I'm full. Though I'm glad for your kindness in thinking of me,' he added hastily when Nompar looked downcast. 'You eat them.'

Nompar shook his head. 'I too have eaten my fill. The horses ridden by two of the king's retainers have died, and his archers have been shooting birds besides...' He indicated the little parcel.

'Jankin and Wat have only had hasty pudding,' said Kemp. 'It would repay their kindness if I could give them summat in return...'

Nompar at once proffered the parcel to the serjeant. 'We couldn't...' demurred Quarmby.

'Please,' said the *bourc*.

'If you insist.' Quarmby took the parcel from him and unwrapped it to reveal the two plucked and roasted birds within. He wrapped one up again, saving it for his comrade no doubt, before tucking into the other ravenously.

'They are treating you well, then,' said Nompar.

'I've no complaints,' said Kemp. 'Except for being wrongly blamed for murder and arson.' He held up his manacles for the *bourc* to see.

'Have you any idea who might have murdered the friar?'

'I have my suspicions,' said Kemp. 'Until I have proof, though…' He noticed a fresh cut on Nompar's cheek. 'What happened to your face?'

'Hm? Oh!' Nompar raised a hand to his cheek, and grinned ruefully. 'I was out riding with a foraging party this afternoon when a band of Scottish hobelars sought to cut us off. We dealt with them right smartly.'

'Sounds as though I'm missing out on all the sport.'

'That's what you get for butchering friars and torching churches. I spoke to the king on your behalf today—'

'You did not have to do that.'

'And what manner of friend would I be, if I did not stand up for you when you were wrongly accused?'

'What makes you so sure I'm wrongly accused?'

'You are, are you not? You have your eccentricities, Martin—'

'*I* have my eccentricities!'

'—but you are not so foolish as to burn down the building where you have been quartered in wintertime. Besides, I saw your face when Sir Alexander Bulchett blamed you for what happened. There was nothing feigned in your indignation. You have many skills, but acting is not one of them, I think. Also, I would advise you to be wary of Sir Alexander, but I fear it is too late for that.'

'What did the king say?'

Like Kemp, Nompar was no actor. He could keep his face impassive, and did so now, but even that could be telling. 'He will come around. He knows he has treated you unfairly, I think. But it is difficult for kings and princes to admit when they are in the wrong. You must give him time.'

Kemp nodded. 'Do you know owt of Sir Alexander?'

'I tilted against him once, at Guînes a couple of years ago. That is to say, I tilted against a man wearing his coat of arms. He unhorsed me. He unhorsed every knight who jousted in that tournament. Though I never heard of Bulchett displaying any prowess in the joust before or since, and he has refused all my offers to break further lances between us. And after that tournament, there was a great scandal when Sir Thomas Dotterell – a man famous for his skill at the joust – claimed he had been the one wearing Sir Alexander's blazon that day; that Sir Alexander had offered him great riches to tilt in his place, and he had done so; but afterwards Sir Alexander had refused to honour his debt, saying none would believe Sir Thomas. And he was right: Sir Thomas was condemned for casting such aspersions on a noble knight like Sir Alexander, and went into exile, while Sir Alexander was exonerated of all blame in the affair. I heard Sir Thomas died trying to redeem himself fighting the Moors in Granada. But I've heard other tales of Sir Alexander's treachery... no more than hearsay, I'll own, but when so many stories should attach themselves to the same man, one cannot help but wonder if at least some of them have more than a whiff of veracity to them.' Nompar glanced up at the stars. 'The hour is late. I must be getting back now.'

Kemp nodded. 'Nompar?'

'Yes?'

'Thank you.'

The *bourc* shrugged. 'What are friends for?' He turned away and scrunched off through the snow.

'You trust him?' Quarmby asked Kemp as soon as Nompar was out of earshot.

'Why should I not?'

'He be a foreigner.'

'He's a Gascon; a subject of the same king as us.'

'Do 'ee speak English?'

'Well... aye. You just heard him speak it.'

'When he be at home, I means. Was he raised speaking English? No! He speaks an outlandish tongue, and that makes him a foreigner. Foreigners bain't to be trusted.'

'Aye, well, yon foreigner has twice saved my life, and I trust him far more than I trust Sir Alexander Bulchett.'

Kemp rubbed his hands together, trying to get some warmth into his fingers, and listened to the silence of the night. It was too quiet, in every sense. By now the Scots must have realised the king had divided his army into three parts and was headed for the border. He could not imagine they would let them go without some parting encounter to speed them on their way.

Five

'It be the treachery of it that gets I,' Jepson complained as he rode with Kemp and Quarmby in the baggage train a couple of days later. 'I gave her a parcel of presents.'

'What manner o' presents?' asked Quarmby.

'Dainties to eat, gifts of money—'

'What dainties? You never gives me any dainties.'

'You doesn't have a warm quim.'

'Where did you get the dainties?'

'From the king's cooks. What's that got to do with anything?'

'All I'm saying is, if you was getting dainties from the king's cooks, you might've brought me one. Especially after I saved that blackbird for you the night before last. If you wants to speak of loyalty—'

'Would you stop talking about your god-damned stomach for just a little while?'

'You stop talking about your god-damned pintle and I'll stop talking about my god-damned stomach.'

It was the fourth day of the march from Haddington and the host continued its tortuous progress down Lauderdale. A stream rushed parallel to the road, the stones of its bed black against the snow piled on the banks, though shelves of ice had formed where rocks jutting out of the water provided some shelter from the current, and rime-covered reeds glittered at the water's edge. Melted snow dripping from the trees in the small hours of the morning had formed icicles on all the boughs. It had snowed some more during the night, and Kemp noticed that despite having been trampled by hundreds of horses, the road they followed remained a blanket of white, unsullied by the mud even though impacted by the tread of hoofs. But where steaming horse droppings had landed, they had melted their way through to the mud underneath.

The snow fell in fat flakes, swirled by a driving wind that piled it into great, thick drifts beneath the trees. Combined with the fog, it reduced visibility to the extent that the troop of men-at-arms riding immediately ahead of the baggage train were little more than shadowy figures moving through the whiteness that surrounded them. The snow had a muffling effect: the iron-shod wheels of the wains no longer rumbled, the shouts of the marshals seemed a very long way off, and even the crotal bells on the horses' harnesses seemed to have their clappers frozen in place.

Huddled figures appeared, crouched over a shapeless mass by the side of the road. They resolved themselves into four men cutting up a dead palfrey. The blood looked black except where it had leeched through the snow, turning it crimson, the only splash of colour in a world turned black and white. The horse's piebald hide was peeled back, revealing glistening viscera caged within the protruding ribs. As Kemp, Jepson and Quarmby rode past, the impromptu butchers looked at them with hostility, as if suspecting them of planning to steal the meat. Jepson and Quarmby scarcely glanced at the men. The scene was nothing they had not witnessed a dozen times the previous day.

'And as for loyalty, what of that wife o' yourn back in Windsor?' Quarmby asked Jepson. 'Ere you blame your flap-tail for her lack of fidelity, you might think on your own lack of fidelity to your wife.'

'What of her? What she never knows can never hurt her.'

'It will if you picks up the hot piss from some dirty whore and pass it on to her.'

'Mary bain't a whore, she be a laundress.'

'Oh, a *laundress*, is she? So let me make sure I understand this aright: you gave her money, and she opened her legs for you. Sounds much like a whore to me. What say you, Martin?'

Casting a glance over his shoulder to watch the men resume carving up the horse as the falling snow swallowed them up in their wake, the Midlander nodded absently.

'It weren't like that!' protested Jepson. 'Mary and me had something special betwixt us.'

'Something special she didn't hesitate to turn her back on when something better came along,' said Quarmby.

Kemp turned his attention back to the road ahead. The swirling flurries of snow had entirely swallowed up the men-at-arms riding in front of them. Only two riders were visible, and they were no more than grey shadows in the whiteout, even as close as ten yards away. They had reined in side by side and one of them seemed to be passing something to the other. Except when the first man did not relinquish what the second man held, Kemp realised they were struggling for possession of something. It gleamed dully, reflecting the whiteness all around them with a flash, then swung across between the two men. Crimson droplets splashed the snow covering the road. One of the men tumbled from his saddle. The other seized the bridle of his horse, put his heels back and galloped off into the blizzard.

'Did you see that?' Kemp asked Jepson and Quarmby, though given the two serjeants were still arguing, the question was redundant.

'See what?' asked Quarmby.

'A man just slew him.' They had ridden to where they could now clearly see the bloody corpse sprawled in the snowdrift by the roadside.

'What man?' asked Jepson.

'Yon fellow who just rode off into the snow!'

'Were it a Scot?' asked Quarmby.

'It must ha' been.'

'I reckon we'd better try to catch up with the rest of those men-at-arms,' said Jepson.

'I reckon you be right,' said Quarmby, and the three of them spurred forward.

Kemp had thought the troop of men-at-arms was no more than a couple of dozen yards ahead of them, but it took them longer to catch up with them than he anticipated. They passed two more corpses on the way, blood already freezing on their grey faces, the crimson-splashed snow around them trampled with many hoofprints. At last two more riders loomed out of the swirling snowflakes, both wearing the black-and-yellow livery of Sir Richard Selby. So great was the muffling effect of the snow, Kemp had scarcely registered the sound of hoof beats before a third horseman cantered into view. He galloped dangerously close to one of Selby's men-at-arms. Something flashed between them, blood splashed, and a severed head rolled in the path of Kemp's rouncy, making the beast rear in fright.

An arrow appeared in the breast of the other man-at-arms. He stared down at it, then raised his head to stare at Kemp and his escort before slipping sideways out of the saddle. Another arrow whipped through the air, then another, and then a whole flight, so the air seemed as thick with shafts as it was with snowflakes.

'Wat?' cried Quarmby. 'I be shot!'

Kemp twisted in the saddle to look and saw another arrow jutting out of the studded leather of the serjeant's brigandine at his shoulder.

'Ride on!' said Kemp. 'We must catch up with the rest of the host.'

'Fall back to the baggage train,' said Jepson. 'For aught we knows, we be all that remains o' the host!' Grabbing the halter of Kemp's rouncy, he led his horse back, and Quarmby followed. Two more arrows soughed past their heads as they rode.

Kemp's horse stumbled, then reared. She was falling, and he took his feet from the stirrups and threw himself clear of the saddle, knowing that, if he did not, he might find his leg trapped and broken beneath her body. The snow provided a soft landing, and he rolled over, anticipating his rouncy would thrash about in her death throes, her flailing hoofs a menace to any who got too close. Rolling onto his stomach, his manacled hands beneath his chest, he glanced to his right and saw an arrow jutting from a bloody wound in his horse's rump. She whinnied, and he wanted to put her out of her misery, but another arrow landed in the snow only a couple of feet away.

He managed to push himself to his feet and dashed the last few yards to where the wainmen were arraying the wains of the baggage train into a square fort, a task made more difficult by the narrowness of the road, the lack of space on either side, and the fact the air was still full of arrows. The Scottish bowmen were aiming for the draught horses drawing the wains, and each time one went down, it had to be cut loose from the rest of the team before the work of positioning the wain could resume. Horses neighed and men shouted orders, or just yelled in incoherent terror.

Kemp dropped to squirm on his belly through the snow between the wheels of one of the wains, arising on the far side to take up position with Jepson and Quarmby, both of whom had dismounted. Quarmby still had the arrow jutting out of his shoulder, though someone – probably Jepson – had snapped off the shaft a couple of inches from the wound.

'Strike off these manacles!' pleaded Kemp. 'I cannot shoot with my wrists chained.' He knew his bow and arrows were in one of the wains, though he was not sure which.

Jepson shook his head. 'Couldn't do it even if I wanted to. 'Twould need the blacksmith's craft to knock out those pins.'

'Then at least give me my sword!' Kemp was used to fighting with his sword in one hand only, leaving his left arm free. Fencing with his wrists manacled would be a challenge, but under the circumstances he was prepared to give it a try: men with two-handed swords managed it, after all.

'Forget not you be a prisoner,' said Jepson.

'This is scarce the time for standing on such formalities!' protested Kemp.

A wainman screamed and fell as an arrow pierced his throat. Kemp glanced back in the direction from which they had marched. Somewhere behind them was supposed to be a company of mounted archers bringing up the rear, but there was no sign of it. For now the Scots seemed content to loose arrows at them from out of the swirling snow, but if they wanted to claim whatever plunder they imagined they would find in the baggage train, eventually they must charge the makeshift fort. When they did, Kemp and his companions would stand a better chance of surviving if they had even just a couple of twenties of archers to stand shoulder to shoulder with them.

They heard the Scots before they saw them. They came out the swirling snow like ravening wolves, howling battle cries. Some of the men with the baggage train had bows and loosed arrows into the brown of them, but the archers were too few to make any appreciable impact. The wainmen had still not finished arraying the wains into a fort: perhaps the diminishing number of gaps between the wains was what had prompted the Scots to attack so soon, rather than tarrying to pick off more of the English with their bows. The Scots surged through the remaining gaps, hacking with battle-axes and halberds. Steel cleft flesh, bones snapped and blood spattered the snow. Someone hurled a spear at Jepson with all his might: Kemp saw the serjeant stagger back with the shaft jutting from his chest, his face screwed up.

A Scot came at him, swinging his axe. Kemp managed to get his manacled hands up, catching the Scot by the wrists to stay the blow. The two of them grappled, circling with the axe above them, the Scot trying to hook an ankle behind one of the Midlander's shins to trip him. Kemp was wise to that trick and kept his feet back, but the soles of his boots slipped in the slush and he fell anyway. His stomach lurched with panic, but he kept a tight grip on the Scot's wrists, pulling him down after him. The two of them rolled over and over in the snow. Rolling on top, Kemp managed to dash the axe from the Scot's hands, but it landed just beyond his own reach, and each time he lunged for it, the Scot stabbed him in the side with his knife. Kemp's armour turned the blade, but the blows hurt nonetheless.

He got the chain between the cuffs of his manacles stretched taut across the Scot's throat and began to choke him. He was aware of mailed feet trampling all around them, the clash of steel against steel and ghastly shrieks as men felt their flesh slashed open. A terrific blow smacked into the back of his head, knocking off his helmet, and he became aware of blood running from under the hood of his gambeson, trickling into his eyes to blind him. A wave of nausea swept through him and he felt himself blacking out. Sheer desperation kept him conscious, for he knew the moment he let the blackness sweep over him, the Scot he grappled would finish him. All of which was academic, for the man who had struck him from behind could probably finish him with a stroke, though a moment later another body fell into the snow beside where Kemp and his opponent struggled, and since Kemp did not recognise the man, for all he knew it was the whoreson who had struck him.

The face of the Scot lying beneath him twisted into a hideous grimace as Kemp leaned with all the weight of his upper body upon the cuffs of his manacles, forcing the chain ever deeper into the man's neck. The Scot clawed at Kemp's hands, but his mailed fists could get no purchase. He kicked his heels into the ground until at last the death rattle sounded in his throat.

Feeling dizzy and shaken, Kemp pushed himself to his feet only for something to slam into his back, throwing him against the side of one of the wains. His legs could support him no longer, and the wain and the corpses lying around him seemed to whirl in the air with the flurries of snow, until everything faded to grey and then black and he knew nothing more.

Half a mile down the valley, Ieuan was unaware the baggage train had been attacked. He had more pressing concerns. Sir Alexander Bulchett's company – as Ieuan grudgingly accepted he must call it for now – had the honour of forming the vanguard of the column this morning, with the knight and his squire riding at their head. The snow on the road before them was virgin and the horses galumphed awkwardly where it had drifted as high as their girths. The snowflakes fell thicker than ever, and a bitter wind blew up the valley, driving them into the faces of Bulchett and his men.

Ieuan spurred his horse forward to ride alongside the knight. 'Perhaps we'd better call a halt until this weather eases, Sir Alexander. While this blizzard lasts, we know not what trouble we may be riding into.'

'Nonsense!' blustered Bulchett. 'This weather hides us well. The Scots will be tucked up at home in bed. All this talk of the bold Scots is so much blather anyway: they lack the spunk to stand up to Englishmen.'

'Tell that to the ghosts of Bannockburn!' Ieuan chuckled ruefully.

'We'll reach Melrose in a few more hours. The faster we push on, the sooner we get there.'

'You're so right, my lord,' said Crawley.

'Sir Alexander!' Metcalfe suddenly pointed into the driving snow.

'What is it?'

'I thought I saw someone.'

'You imagined it.' Bulchett raised a hand to his visor, which he wore down, presumably to keep the snow out of his face.

'I saw him, sir,' insisted Metcalfe. 'As plain as I see you now. Just past yon tree.'

'Belike 'twas some peasant.'

No sooner were the words past Bulchett's lips than an arrow whipped from the direction Metcalfe had pointed in. It missed the knight by inches, skewering one of the archers riding behind him. Even as the man who had been shot slid out of his saddle with a scream, two more arrows whirred out of the snow, from the left flank this time, burying their steel heads in men and horses, sowing chaos and confusion throughout the company.

'God's blood!' Bulchett hauled on his reins, wheeling his horse, and galloped back down the column.

'What in the devil's name?' gasped Ieuan.

'Belike he's gone back to warn the companies that follow behind we've ridden into an ambush,' said Crawley.

'Belike,' agreed Ieuan, though privately he doubted it. Most other knights he had known would have sent their squire back with the message, while they themselves remained with their men.

Another flight of arrows whipped out of the trees, taking their toll on the confused mass of men struggling to stay in the saddles of their plunging and rearing horses. Ieuan wondered why Metcalfe had not ordered his men to ride out of bowshot of their ambushers, then saw the twentyman sprawled in the snow beneath his horse's hoofs, eyes staring glassily up at the grey sky. Earnshaw was there, white-faced, fear in his eyes, looking this way and that in the confusion, without moving one way or another. There was no sign of Tegg or Outhwaite, but their twenties were further back, hidden in the swirling blizzard.

Another flight whistled out of the snow and more men and horses screamed, more bodies thudded to the ground. Why the devil in hell did no one take charge of the situation? Ieuan reckoned it was not his place to do so; but if no one did, it would quickly turn into a rout.

He rode across to where Earnshaw sat on his horse and grabbed him by the arm to make sure he had his attention. 'Get your men across the burn and rally on the opposite bank!' If the Scottish bowmen were as close as Ieuan guessed, Earnshaw and his men would not be out of range even on the far side of the stream; but visibility was so poor in the blizzard, perhaps they did not need to be.

'What of the wounded?' Earnshaw indicated a man sprawled in the snow nearby, clutching at an arrow sticking out of his side.

'Worry about those that can still ride! If we drive off the Scots, we can come back for the wounded.' It was a harsh decision – Ieuan was well aware they might not be able to drive off the Scots, and even if they did the wounded might be dead by then – but he knew this was not the time to second guess himself. He had to act on instinct, swiftly and decisively. Worrying about whether or not there had been better courses of action to take could wait until later.

Earnshaw nodded. 'Follow me, lads!' he shouted, waving them after him as he urged his mount into the thick snowdrifts between the road and the stream.

Ieuan turned his horse back up the valley. A knot of Earnshaw's men still sat on horseback on the road. They had not been able to see their twentyman gallop off, and had not heard his order in the tumult. They did not look as if they knew what to do, and when Ieuan told them to get across the river they did so at once, their gratitude at having someone else to do their thinking for them evident on their faces. Ieuan did the same with Outhwaite's twenty, though they were a lot fewer than a score now, and half of Tegg's twenty were missing too, including their twentyman.

Ieuan turned to one of Outhwaite's men, a young archer named Sam Atherton. 'Ride back up the valley and intercept Sir John Swinburne and his men. Tell him we've been caught in an ambushment – we'll rally on the far bank, ready our bows and counter-attack.'

Atherton nodded and wheeled his horse. Ieuan did not wait until he had been swallowed up by the swirling snow, but at once turned to the rest of Outhwaite's men. 'Follow me, you lot!'

They goaded their horses through the thick drifts on the bank of the stream, then splashed through its shallow waters. The stream bed was stony, and the horses crossed it with more confidence than they rode through the snow. As Ieuan drove his rouncy up the far bank, a momentary panic assailed him: what if more Scottish bowmen awaited them on the far bank? What if the ones who had loosed the first few flights were deliberately driving him into a worse position, and like a blind fool he was letting himself be harried into fitting in with their murderous plans? He shook his head, dismissing the moment of self-doubt. For the Scots to position men on both sides of the road would be to risk having their men shoot one another in the blizzard. Only a fool would make such an elementary mistake, and whatever else one might say about the Scots, they were no fools.

He saw shadowy figures mounted on horses on the west bank, and his hand reached instinctively for the short-bladed *bidog* he wore in a sheath in the small of his back, but it was only Earnshaw and his men.

'Dismount, and ready your bows,' Ieuan told them all. 'Outhwaite, pick some men out to guard the horses.'

'What about us?' asked one of Tegg's men.

'You're in Outhwaite's twenty for now,' said Ieuan. 'Take your orders from him.'

The archers stripped the bags off their bows and strung them. 'When I give the word, we'll recross the stream on foot in a line abreast, five yards between each man,' he told Earnshaw. 'Get your men arrayed.'

The twentyman nodded, and Ieuan made his way back along the line of men, retracing the path he had ploughed through the snow. He relayed the same orders to Outhwaite and his men, making sure they all understood to keep their companions on either side of them in view. Even then he was sorely tempted to baulk at giving the order to advance back across the stream, thinking of everything that could possibly go wrong, and wondering how he would live with himself if men died because he had given foolish orders. Not for the first time, he wondered how Kemp suffered these anxieties when he led men into battle, and wished he had thought to ask, instead of blithely putting his trust in the Midlander and merely doing as he was told.

Ieuan went to the men guarding the horses. 'Keep a sharp watch out, won't you, lads?' he told them. 'My hope is the Scots are all on the opposite bank of the stream, but if I was them I might be tempted to send men around the flank to cut out our mounts. Got your horn, Uphurst? Good – give it a good, loud blow if you see anyone you don't know.'

Returning to the centre of the line, he gave the order to advance. Holding their bows above their heads to keep the strings dry, the men descended the banks of the stream and waded across. The water did not come as high as their crotches, which was just as well, because it was freezing. Once they had struggled out on the opposite bank, Ieuan gave the order to nock arrows to their strings, running up and down behind the line making sure they kept moving, kept their alignment, no more than a few yards between each man... he shook his head in despair: the number of things he had to worry about was overwhelming.

They regained the road. The falling snow had already settled on the dead horses and corpses sprawled everywhere. Some of the men broke away from the line to attend to a wounded comrade. Ieuan ran across to chase them back into position. 'Let's make sure we've chased off the Scots before we tend to the wounded, eh?'

'Ieuan!' shouted an archer named Jancock Whitehouse, about halfway along the line.

The Welshman ran to where he stood. 'What is it?'

'I thought I saw someone.' Whitehouse pointed.

Ieuan squinted. He could see nothing but snow and had almost made up his mind Whitehouse had imagined it when he too saw a figure... no, three figures, grey shapes, men seated on horseback. 'Halt!' yelled Ieuan, running up and down behind the line once again to make sure everyone heard and the order was obeyed. 'Halt! Halt!'

Whitehouse drew his bow. 'Ease down,' Ieuan told him. 'They might be our men.' It was too easy to imagine that while Bulchett's archers had been rallying on the far side of the burn, Sir John Swinburne and his men might have missed Bulchett and Atherton and ridden into the gap. In the confusion of the blizzard, it was not beyond the realms of possibility that one of those shadowy figures might even have been King Edward himself. There were men back home in Striguil who would slap Ieuan on the back and buy him a tankard of ale if he became known as the man who killed the King of England; but plenty of others would damn him for a fool and a traitor. 'But keep your arrow nocked,' he added.

Whitehouse nodded, and Ieuan stepped between him and the next man, an arrow nocked to the string of his own bow as he edged forward.

'Who's there?' he called to the figures mounted on horseback. He could hear their voices faintly, talking amongst themselves, three out of four words whipped away by the wind, and what was left was too scanty for him to identify the accent. Seen as no more than shadows through the snow, the men loomed as large as fully armoured knights, but when one of them peeled away to approach Ieuan, he seemed to shrink. One of the weird effects of the snow was to distort the size of everything, and now Ieuan saw the man was only mounted on a small, stocky Irish hobby. The rider was a hobelar, wearing a travel-stained aketon and a rusty, dented bascinet on his head, and rode without saddle, stirrups or bridle, which lessened the weight on the horse but required skill and practice from the rider. There was a troop of hobelars in

King Edward's column, led by a Northumbrian knight named Thomas Featherstonehaugh: they wore his livery, scarlet trimmed with white. Beneath the snowflakes that clung to it, the aketon of the man riding out of the snow towards Ieuan was best described as bilious green trimmed with mildew.

Goading his hobby into a canter, he raised the spear he carried in his right hand as if to hurl it at the Welshman. Ieuan drew his bow and let fly. The arrow caught the rider full in the breastbone, piercing his chest and bowling him clean out of his saddle. Riderless, his horse veered away when it saw the row of archers ahead.

The other two hobelars followed the first out of the snow, levelling their spears at Ieuan. The Welshman turned and fled, ducking between Whitehouse and the next man. His feet skidding on the trampled snow, he twisted, drawing an arrow from under his belt. 'Shoot one, Jancock!'

Whitehouse did not hesitate, picking off the nearest of the hobelars. Ieuan nocked his arrow and, as soon as he saw which one Whitehouse was aiming at, drew and loosed it, shooting down the other.

A flight of arrows whipped out of the snow from the left flank. A couple of Bulchett's archers fell with arrows in them, one shrieking. The wind blew a hole through the snow flurries and Ieuan glimpsed a mob of bowmen coming towards them. 'On the left flank!' he yelled. 'Shoot!'

The snow had already closed in again, but the Scottish bowmen remained visible as a single, shadowy bunch, and that was a clear enough target for Bulchett's archers to aim at. When the second flight came out of the snow, there were fewer arrows than there had been before. The two sets of archers exchanged several more flights before a troop of men-at-arms galloped out of the snow, lances levelled, to plunge in amongst the Scottish bowmen. Some were spitted on lances, others trampled into the snow by the hoofs of the heavily built destriers, and the rest fled back into the snow.

Pushing up the visor of his bascinet, a man-at-arms wheeled his horse and cantered across to where Bulchett's archers stood. Ieuan recognised the blazon of Sir Walter de Mauny. 'Who commands here?' demanded the Hain-aulter.

Outhwaite pointed at Ieuan. 'He does.'

'These are Sir Alexander Bulchett's archers,' said Ieuan.

'Where is Sir Alexander?' asked Mauny.

'I know not. Did he not pass by you on his way to warn the king?'

'If he did, we missed him in the snow. If these men follow your orders, I suggest you continue giving them till Bulchett returns.'

'The king knows the vanguard has been ambushed?'

'He knows. Our foragers have found a path that leads over the hills to Melrose.' Mauny gestured vaguely back up towards the right-hand side of the valley.

'A path big enough for the wains of the baggage train?'

'The baggage train has been ambushed also. It's not as if the wains carried much of value. I need these archers to stay here and hold the Scots while the rest of the column follows the path over the hills.'

Ieuan thought of Kemp. He could not imagine his friend had been killed, but it might be he was in trouble. On the other hand, someone needed to take charge of Bulchett's archers, and Mauny seemed to think it should be Ieuan. The Welshman reluctantly accepted that Kemp would have to look after himself for a while.

'The king has sent for John Peplow's archers to aid you,' added Mauny, 'so shoot them not when they appear through the snow!'

Ieuan nodded, and Mauny shouted to his men to get their attention before signalling them to follow. The Welshman withdrew the archers a couple of hundred yards up the valley, so if any more Scots attacked them from the east, they were less likely to outflank them. He sent Whitehouse back across the burn to tell the men guarding the horses to lead them a couple of hundred yards upstream, so they would still be close to hand when the time came to pull back. Soon afterwards Peplow and his men arrived to take up position.

The Scots made a couple more probing attacks as the morning wore on, but they were easily chased off with a couple of flights of arrows. It must have been about noon – not that Ieuan could tell from the grey sky, though the flurries of snow had finally begun to ease off – when a marshal came to tell them it was time to follow the rest of the host over the hills to the west.

'You go first,' Peplow told Ieuan. 'We'll hold them to buy time for you to get away.'

'Give us as much time as it takes to recite ten paternosters, then follow,' said Ieuan. 'I'll array my lads where this path leads off. From there we'll cover you for a bit.'

Peplow nodded in gratitude, and Ieuan shouted for his lads to follow, keeping their bows strung. They marched back up the valley. Ieuan was worried he might miss the path, but in the event he need not have fretted: even with the snow still falling, there was no mistaking the trail of hundreds of hoofprints, with the occasional pile of dung serving as a marker. When Peplow and his men had filed past, Ieuan gave him time to get safely up the path, then cast a glance into the snow falling further up the valley, wondering if Kemp was still up there with the rest of the baggage train. For all he knew, Kemp had escaped and was already heading over the hills to Melrose with the rest of the host. Ieuan had visited the abbey there with Kemp a few years earlier, and he could easily imagine entering the calefactory to find his friend already ensconced by the fire with a cup of mulled wine in one hand.

'Mount up, lads,' he called to his men. They swung themselves into the saddles of their rouncies and started up the path into the hills.

Six

Cold.

Cold and pain.

Pain and cold. Kemp thought perhaps if he ignored them they would both go away, but after lying still for a while, he realised that was not likely to happen without him doing something about it. Doing something would require moving his limbs, which would take effort, something he felt in no mood to spare.

He opened his eyes: a small beginning, but he had to start somewhere and it seemed as good a place as any. Light flooded into his skull, dazzling him. He screwed his eyes closed again, wincing at the pain, then opened them once more, more tentatively this time. The dazzling glare took on a pale blue tint. With an effort, he focused his gaze. Everything was covered in snow; at least, everything he could see without moving his head. He was in no hurry to do so. The way his neck ached, he was not entirely convinced it would not fall off his shoulders if he did. He did not want to be parted from his head: he used it. Perhaps not as often as he should have done, he reflected ruefully, but occasionally.

And besides, he did not know who might be watching him, wondering whether or not he still drew breath; maybe a foe who would not hesitate to finish him off if he was careless enough to show any signs of life. If there was a foe, he was out of Kemp's line of sight. He listened. Not that he had been ignoring any signals from his ears up to that point, but there was so little noise there was not much to listen to: the faint susurration of a breeze in the bare trees; the harsh croak of a raven some distance off.

The cold and the pain were getting no easier to bear. Kemp raised his head, and at once regretted it. Shoots of pain lanced from his neck up into his skull, where they flickered and crashed like bolts of lightning. He closed his eyes and took a few deep breaths. But at least the movement had not prompted anyone to finish him off. He sat up – lumps of snow slithered off his mail coif – and gingerly turned his head to survey the scene.

His vision was blurred. He squinted, and raised a hand to rub his eyes, but the manacles chaining his wrist to the other arm brought it up short. *Sovereign*, he thought ruefully. He had forgotten the manacles. They would not make things any easier. Raising both hands, he used one to rub sleep from his eyes. Yawning, he squinted and blinked until the world outside his head came into sharper focus. The sides of the tree trunks downwind were black against the snow which stuck to the bark and weighed down their boughs. Even blanketed with snow, the shapes of the wains were unmistakable. There were other shapes beneath the snow, less regular in outline. Rime glittered on the shafts of the arrows sticking out of them.

Breath billowed from Kemp's mouth in the chill air, so at least he knew he was still alive. Up to that moment he had not been entirely sure. He could do nothing about the coldness of the air, but if he wanted to get warm, not lying in the snow would be a good start. Twisting to one side so he could put both hands against the snow together, he braced his arms and raised himself on his haunches.

Stiff joints protested as he pushed himself to his feet. At once the whole valley seemed to whirl around him and he staggered as if drunk, clutching at the side of a wain for support. Bowing his head, he took deep breaths, wondering if he was going to spew up. *Better out than in*, he told himself, but the moment passed.

His scalp itched. He pulled back his mail coif and tried to pull back the quilted hood of the gambeson beneath, but when he felt his hair tearing out from the roots, he quickly gave it up. Only then did he remember blood running down his face after receiving a blow to the head. A scalp wound, evidently, and now the hood of his gambeson was stuck to his hair with congealed blood. He would have to wash it off, when he came to a place where washing did not mean immersing his head in a stream as cold as ice. Although now that he thought about it, that was not such a bad idea. He scooped a fistful of powdery snow off the back of the wain and rubbed it in his face. It helped to sharpen his senses.

He felt better. Not perfect, but then he could not remember what perfect felt like, he only knew he fell a long way short of it. He was breathing, he was on his feet, and other than a possibly fractured skull he did not seem to have any broken bones. Those were the things that were well. It was important to think on the good, and not let thoughts of the bad overwhelm him.

But the bad had to be faced. He had got separated from the rest of the host; left for dead. With the Scots snapping at the host like seagulls tearing flesh from the corpse of a beached whale, maybe he was better off on his own. Perhaps by now even the king was dead, and all that was left of his host was a captain of archers with an aching head and manacles on his wrists. But none of that would count for anything if he blundered into any roving bands of border reivers.

His kettle helmet lay in the snow nearby. It was badly dented, but not so much he could no longer wear it. He put it on over his coif. The next thing to do was arm himself. When Quarmby had put his weapons in one of the wains, Kemp had made a note of the pattern painted on the side of the wain. He brushed some of the snow off the side of the wain he was leaning against, but the colours were all wrong. He moved from wain to wain, rubbing just enough snow off the side of each to reveal the pattern. Once he had found the one he sought, it was easy enough to reach down between the side of the wain and the barrels and wicker baskets stacked in the back to find his bow in its bag, his sheaf of arrows and his scabbarded sword, buried by the snow but otherwise unharmed.

He held the belt with the scabbarded sword attached in his manacled hands and thought: *now what?* After thinking it through, he ended up laying it out in the snow, then lying down on top of it, rolling to one side, grasping the tongue of the belt, and pulling it after him as he rolled towards the buckle. Even then it took him three tries, but at last he was able to thread the tongue through the buckle and draw it tight about his hips before rising.

Then there was his sheaf of arrows. Normally he would have tucked them under his belt at the back. He wondered if he should have arranged them on top of his belt when he had laid it out in the snow, but then decided his arrows were no good in their usual place when he could not reach behind him with one hand to draw one out; no good to him at all in fact when, as long as his hands were manacled, he could not even draw the bow. Nor could he sling his bow stave across his back. He was tempted to leave bow and arrows behind, at least until he could get the manacles off. But it might be many miles before he found a forge; if so, he did not want to have to walk all the way back here just to collect his weapons. And an archer without his bow and arrows was as much use as a horse without legs. In the end he had to settle for carrying both awkwardly under one arm.

His belly growled. He was tempted to search the wains for something to eat. Surely one of the wainmen would have had a cask of biscuits secreted somewhere? But the overcast sky offered no clue as to the hour of the day. He wanted to reach Melrose before dark, and he suspected he still had a few miles to go. Once there, he hoped, he would catch up with the king's host and, with any luck, get some meat to fill his aching belly. Perhaps the infirmarer at the abbey there could be persuaded to clean and bandage his head wound.

The snow that had fallen since he had lost consciousness had covered over whatever tracks the host had left in its wake, but that did not worry Kemp. He knew the stream to his right was the Leader Water, which flowed south until it met the River Tweed, which flowed from west to east until it reached the Almain Sea at Berwick. Melrose stood on the banks of the Tweed, no more than a league upstream from that river's confluence with the Leader Water. So all he had to do was follow the Leader downstream, and then follow the Tweed upstream to Melrose.

One thing he knew: he was not walking blithely down the road, as far as he could trace it through the snow. If the Scots had anyone out patrolling it, looking for stragglers, he would be walking straight into their arms. Instead he forded the Leader Water. He did not like getting his hose wet when it might be hours before he could dry them out again in front of a fire, but anything was preferable to staying on that road.

There were woods on the west bank. After tipping the icy water out of his boots, he trudged through the snow that had drifted beneath the trees. They gave him cover, while allowing him to stay close enough to the stream to keep an eye on anyone moving along the road. He knew he was leaving tracks wherever he went but, unless he could somehow grow a pair of wings, that could not be helped. He could only hope that anyone finding his tracks would see they belonged to only one man, and decide that one man alone was not worth troubling with, rather than viewing him as potential easy prey. Kemp was not accustomed to think of himself as 'easy prey', but on the other hand neither was he accustomed to defending himself with his hands manacled.

The chill breeze did nothing to dry his hose and only kept the wool cold and clammy against his legs. It was tempting to stop and light a fire so he could dry them, but he resisted the temptation. He would be wasting time – time he needed to reach a warm hearth in Melrose – and besides, the smell of woodsmoke might attract trouble.

He had covered no more than half a mile when a figure on horseback coming up the road on the other side of the burn caught his eye. He ran to the stout trunk of a tree, looking around it as the rider drew nearer. The horseman wore a polished bascinet, a black jupon over his habergeon, and the white cockerel of Cazoulat on his shield. He was about to step out from behind his tree and yell and wave to catch Nompar's attention, when two figures appeared in the road ahead of the *bourc*, one wielding an axe, the other a spear. Nompar reined in. Two more appeared out of nowhere behind him, cutting off his retreat. Kemp realised they must have been waiting in ambush. Had he stayed on the road, they would surely have caught him instead.

He stayed out of sight: if Nompar wheeled his destrier and managed to get past the two behind him, then he would ride off, and Kemp, charging across the Leader Water, would have to face the four Scots on his own.

The *bourc* raised his visor. Billows of mist formed before his face as he addressed the Scots, though he was too far away for Kemp to hear what was being said. Mist billowed from the lips of one of the Scots. Nompar lowered his visor and drew his sword. The Scot with the spear lunged forward, driving the head of his weapon into the breast of Nompar's destrier. The horse reared, and the *bourc* tumbled from the saddle. Kemp cursed: now he had no choice but to intervene. He dropped his bow and his arrows – they were no use to him while his hands were manacled – and broke out of the trees, drawing his sword awkwardly from its scabbard as he splashed across the burn.

The man who had spoken to Nompar came at him with an axe. The *bourc* blocked the blow with the blade of his sword, and pushed him back, sending him sprawling in the snow. The man with the spear was still trying to draw it out of the dead horse's breast. The other two men – both armed with axes – came at Nompar at once. Whirling to face them, he blocked one axe-stroke with his sword while he slammed the sole of a boot in the other man's stomach, sending him reeling. That bought him enough time to deal with the second axeman. He parried a second stroke and then, with the flat of his blade against the haft of the man's axe, forced it down, then to the right, then up, then to the left, until it had described a complete circle.

Then he did it again, and the next thing Kemp or the axeman knew, Nompar had tweaked the axe from the Scot's sweaty hands and sent it flying into a snowdrift.

Kemp was halfway across the stream. The icy water dragged at his thighs, impeding his progress.

The first axeman had picked himself up. He charged at Nompar, swinging his weapon at his head. The *bourc* ducked beneath the wild stroke, and swung his sword under the man's guard, slashing him across the stomach. The man's entrails spilled into the snow from the rent in his belly.

Kemp tried to climb up the east bank of the river, but it was steep here, and the snow made it slippery. Only a few yards away now, the third axeman ran at Nompar's back with his axe raised. 'Behind you!' yelled Kemp.

The *bourc* turned, sidestepped, and tripped the charging Scot with an extended foot. The Scot went flying headlong, his axe skittering from his hand.

The second man, meanwhile, had grabbed the axe from the hand of his slain comrade. He charged at Nompar, swinging. The *bourc* diverted the stroke, driving the tip of his sword into the man's throat on the follow-through.

Kemp managed to get a foothold in the snow to boost him out of the water. He put all his weight on it, but there was nothing beneath the overhanging snow and it crumbled beneath him, dropping him back into the stream.

The third axeman had retrieved his weapon. He swung at Nompar's head. The *bourc* caught the stroke against the blade of his sword, controlling it, swinging it to the side while he booted the Scot in the crotch. The man doubled up, and Nompar brought the pommel of his sword down against the back of his skull, cracking it. The man fell heavily into the snow and lay still.

Kemp threw his sword up on to the bank of the stream so he could use his manacled hands to grasp at a tuft of reeds growing up there, using it for purchase to try to haul himself up out of the water.

The spearman had finally withdrawn his weapon from the dead horse. Now it was just him and Nompar. The two of them circled on the road, the spearman jabbing the tip of his weapon at the *bourc*'s helmet. The tip glanced off the visor, and Nompar reached up, catching the shaft of the spear with his gauntleted left hand. He tugged it towards him. The spearman refused to relinquish his grip on his weapon. It was a fatal error, for it brought him staggering onto the tip of the *bourc*'s sword. Nompar gave the blade a twist to make sure of him, before dropping the spear and withdrawing his sword point to allow the Scot's corpse to flop into the snow.

Finally getting a knee up onto the bank, Kemp clambered out of the stream. Snatching up his sword, he ran the last few yards to join the *bourc* on the road, gasping from the exertion of crossing the stream, waterlogged boots squelching. The *bourc* raised his helmet to glance at Kemp, before looking pointedly at the four dead Scots. He was not even breathing hard.

'I came as swiftly as I could,' Kemp panted defensively.

'I'm obliged to you,' said Nompar. 'Your warning cry was timely. Had I not already heard the rasp of the man's breath draw nigh, you would have saved my life.'

'It was my pleasure,' Kemp said ruefully. He sat down and once again removed his boots to tip out the water.

The *bourc* crossed to where his destrier lay, blood spreading through the snow it lay in. There was fear in its eyes, and a sadness too, as though it knew it was dying, but perhaps that was just Kemp attributing his own emotions to it. Crouching beside it, Nompar patted it reassuringly on the withers. He murmured soothingly to it in his own tongue and then, with a sudden, spasmodic motion, thrust the tip of his sword into its heart.

'I'm sorry,' said Kemp. He knew only too well how attached a man might become to a good mount.

Nompar wiped the blood from the blade of his sword before slotting it back into its scabbard. 'The king loaned him to me. My own horse was slain when Sir Richard Thirwall captured me last year.'

'Will the king make you pay for him?' It took generations of breeding and years of training to make a good destrier, and if you found one for sale at a horse market for less than ninety pounds, you could be confident there was something amiss with it.

Nompar shook his head. 'If he had been my horse and he had died in the king's service, I would be entitled to compensation.'

'Where were you bound when they attacked you?'

'Looking for you, as a matter of fact.'

'What have I done to deserve such an honour?'

Nompar glanced at him in surprise. 'You are my friend, are you not? You would have done the same for me.'

Kemp shrugged. He was not sure he would have done. Then he remembered the times Nompar had saved his life in the past. Not to mention how he himself had rushed from cover when the *bourc* was ambushed. Yes: if Nompar had been left for dead, and Kemp had been with the rest of the host, and at liberty, he would have ridden back alone to search for him, if not out of friendship then certainly out of a sense of obligation.

'What became of the rest of the column?' he asked Nompar.

'The vanguard was ambushed.'

Kemp remembered his men – he grimaced; Bulchett's men – had been riding in the vanguard that morning. 'Ieuan?'

'Alive and well,' Nompar assured him. 'He took command when Sir Alexander disappeared.'

Kemp was not surprised to hear Bulchett had made himself scarce the moment danger reared its head. He had known the knight's type before: all mouth and no ballocks.

Then something else Nompar had said sank in. 'Ieuan took command?' he asked in astonishment.

'Someone had to.'

'Aye, but... Ieuan? You know how he feels about taking responsibility for owt.'

'Yes. But we both know he is not fool enough to be unable to see what needs to be done in the hour of danger, nor coward enough to shun the responsibility when no better man presents himself. He will get your men safely to Carlisle, I think.'

Nodding, Kemp pulled his boots back on. 'I think so too.'

'You and I, however, I have less confidence about.' Stooping, Nompar retrieved two axes from the ground, then threw one at Kemp's feet. 'Stretch the chain of your irons across the axe head.'

Kemp got down on his knees and did as the *bourc* bid him. Nompar knelt opposite, raising the other axe a few inches. He brought it down against the chain, but scarcely notched the links. 'I need to take more of a swing at it.'

Kemp nervously eyed the axe head raised over the *bourc*'s shoulder. 'You know what you're doing?'

'Certainly.' Nompar swung the axe down. Kemp panicked at the last moment, whipping his wrists away before the edge of the axe in the *bourc*'s hands clanged against the axe head below the chain.

'You distrust me?' asked Nompar.

'It's not that. But you've only to miss by a couple of inches...'

'You can see where my axe notched the axe below. Had you not moved your hands, the chain would be broken now.' The *bourc* jerked his head at the axe flat on the ground. 'Again.'

Kemp swallowed, and stretched the chain across it. Again Nompar swung the axe down, and again the Midlander pulled his hands out of the way at the last moment.

'You did it again,' said the *bourc*.

'If you miss, I must forsake archery and turn beggar!'

'Look at the fresh notch: a fraction of an inch from the first. Have more faith, *mon amec*.'

Kemp took a deep breath and stretched the chain across the axe head.

Nompar raised the axe again. 'This time I will count to three,' he said. 'Ready?'

Kemp nodded. 'Third time's the charm.'

'One... two...' Nompar suddenly looked off to one side. 'What is that?'

Kemp looked in the direction Nompar glanced in. 'What's what? I don't see—' His eyes were still scanning the snow when he felt the axe smash down against the links of his manacles.

'Son of a whore!' gasped Kemp. The stroke had split one of the links of the chain clean in two, leaving him with two heavy iron cuffs chafing each wrist, a couple of links dangling from each, but at least he could move his arms independently now.

'You're welcome,' said Nompar.

The two of them pushed themselves to their feet. The *bourc* retrieved his saddlebags from his destrier, slung them over one shoulder, and scanned the hills on the west side of the valley. 'Melrose lies to the south-west,' he told Kemp, pointing. 'If we cut across yon hills, we may save time. We will certainly avoid any reivers seeking stragglers in this valley.'

Kemp nodded and slithered back down the bank of the stream to cross to the other side. 'Where are you going?' asked Nompar.

The Midlander pointed to the trees on the far bank. 'I left my bow and arrows over yon. Besides, if we mean to climb yon hills, we must cross the burn sooner or later.'

Nompar shrugged and followed him through the shallow water to the far bank, where they both clambered up through the snow piled there, before taking off their boots to tip out the water, for the third time in Kemp's case. Retrieving his bow stave in its bag, he slung it across his back, and tucked his arrows under his belt. He pointed to where the ground sloped up further through the trees. 'These woods will hide us from the Scots until we cross the ridge at the top.'

The two of them trudged through the snow beneath the trees. In places the thick drifts concealed thorny, entangling brambles that obliged them to retreat and cast about in search of another path. When they drew near to where the slope began to curve towards the spine of the ridge, concealing the bottom of the valley in dead ground, they found themselves at the treeline. Kemp paused to cast a final glance into the valley below. Seeing figures moving up the road to where they had left the bodies of the four Scots Nompar had slain, he pointed them out to the *bourc*.

'Scots?' asked Nompar.

'They're not English. They'll find the bodies of the men you slew, and from there they'll follow our tracks in the snow.'

The *bourc* indicated the bow stave slung across Kemp's back. 'Can we ambush them with that thing?'

'We can try, but that'll mean waiting for them to catch up with us. I reckon it took us a quarter of an hour to climb up here. It'll be dusk soon, and I'd hoped to reach Melrose ere nightfall. If the king tarries there with the rest of the host, I warrant yon Scots will rue it if they follow us.'

'Let us keep moving, then.'

'Let's try to put some distance between us and them,' suggested Kemp. There were fewer snowdrifts up here and they jogged along for the best part of a mile. The track descended into a valley with a small hamlet at the bottom. The ringing of a hammer against an anvil led them to a blacksmith's forge.

Nompar clapped Kemp on the back. 'A chance for you to divest yourself of your new bracelets, *non pas*?'

Kemp glanced back up the road to the ridge behind them. If the men they had seen in Lauderdale really had followed them, they would have more than enough time to catch up to them while Kemp was having the cuffs of his manacles removed by a smith. But for all he knew the Scots they had seen were not following them; might not even have noticed their tracks. And the iron cuffs were heavy and chafed him cruelly, and it seemed foolish to wait until they had reached Melrose to have them removed, when there was a blacksmith right here.

'You'd best do all the talking,' he told Nompar.

'You do not think my Gascon accent will draw suspicion?'

'Four months ago you fought alongside the Scots nobility. If anyone seems suspicious, just tell them the truth: you came to Scotland with Sir Eugène de Garencières and were left behind when he and his men returned to France.'

'No need to mention switching my allegiance to King Edward in the meantime, you mean?'

Kemp nodded, and looked around, making sure there were no troops of Scots men-at-arms in the vicinity. If the villagers were suspicious of Kemp and Nompar – which they probably would be regardless of any yarn the *bourc* spun them – they would send word to the nearest Scottish nobleman. The question was, how far could Kemp and Nompar get before that nobleman arrived?

Approaching the forge, they peered inside. A youth – probably the smith's apprentice – worked the bellows on the forge while the smith himself gripped a piece of red-hot metal between a pair of tongs with his left hand, holding it steady on the anvil while he pounded it with a mallet. The anvil rested atop a wooden log, to which it was firmly nailed. Although only three feet of the log showed above ground, Kemp knew it would be perhaps seven foot long, the rest of it going four feet into the ground to provide a steady platform for the anvil.

Looking at the slender piece of glowing iron, Kemp guessed the smith was making a nail. Despite the cold air outside, it was hot enough in the forge for the brawny smith to be stripped to the waist under his leather apron. The apprentice had his back to the opening at the front of the forge, but the smith must have seen Kemp and

Nompar watching him. He did not acknowledge them until he was sufficiently satisfied with the nail to drop it into the water-filled bosh at his feet. Laying down his tongs, he leaned across with his left hand to touch the apprentice on the shoulder. When the apprentice glanced at him, the smith nodded to where Kemp and Nompar stood. To the apprentice, that seemed to be the signal to stop working the bellows.

The smith did not put down his mallet. 'Whit can Ah do for ye gentlemen?'

'I ordered my man be manacled for his insolence,' said Nompar. Kemp held up his hands so they could see the iron bands around his wrists. 'Now he has redeemed himself in battle against the English, I wish the cuffs to be removed.'

The smith beckoned for Kemp to approach. The Midlander expected the warmth of the forge to be welcome after the cold outside, driving the chill from his bones, but it was too far into the other extreme, the heat from the furnace searing his face and squeezing sweat from his pores.

He held out his wrists so the smith could inspect the cuffs.

'These cuffs look like English work to me,' said the smith.

'I would know nothing of that,' said Nompar. 'Perhaps the smith I hired to put them on learned his trade in England.'

'Would that be Iain Gough of Hawick?'

Nompar was too sharp to fall for that one. 'I do not recall his name. He kept a forge just outside Edinburgh.'

The smith did not reply. Releasing Kemp's hands, he turned to his workbench. His hand hovered over the haft of a sledgehammer for a moment, until he glanced up and caught Kemp staring at him. The Midlander shook his head warningly. With a guilty flinch, the smith moved his hand away from the sledgehammer and instead picked up a mallet and a chisel.

He beckoned Kemp to approach. Gripping one of his cuffs, the smith positioned it at a corner in the anvil, with the cuff to one side of it, but the top of the holding pin threaded through the interlocking knuckles resting on the edge. He placed the chisel's cutting edge under the flattened top of the pin, then struck the butt of the chisel's handle lightly but firmly with the mallet. Taking the chisel away before repositioning it between each stroke, in about a dozen blows he had sheared off the head of the pin. He was then able to pull the pin out of the knuckles so Kemp could open the cuff. The skin below was chafed and discoloured with heavy bruising. The smith repeated the procedure with the other cuff.

The apprentice must have slipped out while Kemp and Nompar were watching his master work, for he returned now carrying a loaded crossbow, which he levelled at the *bourc*. The blacksmith quickly took the crossbow from him, aiming it at Kemp and Nompar in turn. 'Move into yon corner, the pair o' ye. Keep your hands where Ah can see 'em, and dinnae make any sudden moves. Wullie, run to the castle and tell Sir John we've captured a brace of King Edward's men.'

Seven

Kemp stood in the corner of the forge with Nompar and stared at the crossbow in the blacksmith's brawny hands. He heard hoof beats outside as the smith's apprentice mounted a hobby and rode off in the direction of 'the castle'. Kemp guessed that was Thirlstane, the nearest castle as far as he knew, about two leagues to the northeast. It would take the apprentice nearly half an hour to ride there, and who could say how long for 'Sir John' and his men-at-arms to don their armour and saddle their horses before riding back to the forge? But suppose Sir John and his men were already in armour, their horses saddled? Suppose the apprentice ran into them on his way across Lauderdale?

'Shoot one of us, and the other will slay you before you can reload,' he told the smith.

'Aye, but Ah reckon neither of ye will be willing to be the one to hazard getting a crossbow bolt in your guts.'

'And yet if we stand here and do nothing, then we will both die when Sir John and his men get here and put us to death for the crime of not being Scottish,' said Nompar.

'Dinnae expect me to shed any tears for ye. Nobody asked ye to invade Scotland.'

'Actually, King Edward asked us to invade Scotland,' said Nompar.

'Ordered us, in fact,' said Kemp.

'Aye, well, he didnae have the right to. And ye should have had more sense than to obey him—'

Nompar suddenly lowered his head and charged. The smith did not hesitate, squeezing the tricker to release the crossbow's ratchet. The bolt shot from its groove to clang resoundingly against Nompar's bascinet, and the *bourc* fell in the narrow space between the anvil and the workbench.

Kemp tried to get at the smith by moving the other way around the anvil. The smith did not waste time trying to reload, instead throwing the crossbow at Kemp's head before reaching for his sledgehammer, so the Midlander had to waste precious moments batting the crossbow aside, moments which might have been better spent drawing the broadsword still scabbarded at his hip.

The smith came at him, swinging the sledge. Kemp threw himself sideways to avoid it, and the heavy iron head splintered one of the workbenches. As the smith swung it back over his head for a second blow, Kemp snatched up the first thing that came to hand – a horseshoe – and flung it at the smith's head. The hammer fell from his hands, thudding heavily to the ground behind him. Blinking, he staggered, tripped over the hammer and sprawled on his back. Kemp moved in again, jamming the heel of a boot into where he judged the smith's crotch was behind the leather apron. He must have hit the mark, for dazed though the smith was, he sat up sharply, clutching at himself with a yowl. Kemp moved in again, smashing a kneecap into his face. This time the smith fell back, dead or stunned, Kemp did not know which and did not much care.

He turned to where Nompar lay. The *bourc* rose unsteadily to his feet.

'Are you hurt?'

'It was nothing.' Nompar rapped gauntleted knuckles against his steel bascinet, where the bolt had glanced off it. 'Good Gascon steel.'

Kemp was relieved to hear it. 'Thick Gascon skull beneath it. You damned fool! Did you seek death?'

'Come – let's be gone, ere the prentice boy returns with Sir John and whatever armed men he can muster.'

Kemp paused long enough to bind the smith's wrists and ankles with the straps of his apron – the knots would secure him until his apprentice returned, at least – and then he and Nompar emerged into the gathering dusk. It felt even colder outside than before, or perhaps it just seemed that way after the heat of the forge. What little daylight was left was reflected by the snow in the surrounding fields, casting a dour blue light across the valley: enough to make out a dark shadow over the hills to the south-west, extensive woods on the spine of the ridge like a saddle cloth on a palfrey's back. Kemp pointed to the woods, and Nompar nodded, understanding at once. In less than an hour it would be too dark for anyone to follow their footsteps in the snow, but unless it snowed overnight, their trail would be plain enough to follow come sunrise. They would stand a better chance of dodging any pursuers in the trees above than they would out in the open.

The two of them jogged across the snow. It was a good three-quarters of a mile to the trees, uphill all the way, and by the time they reached them, Kemp's lungs were raw from panting in the wintry air. They paused to gaze back down into the valley below, looking to see if anyone followed, but the fields were empty. The throbbing ache in Kemp's skull, which had not left him since he had regained consciousness a few hours earlier, suddenly flared up, and he had to doff his helmet to press a palm against his right temple, waiting for the pain to subside.

'What ails you?' asked Nompar.

'An aching head. I was struck on the skull earlier today. It's nowt, it'll pass.' Even as he spoke, the throb seemed to recede, and he replaced his helmet and turned to where a thick hedge grew on the low embankment surrounding the woods, presumably to stop the livestock grazing the surrounding pastures from getting in amongst the trees and feeding on the shoots from the stumps of coppiced trees. Kemp and Nompar followed the ditch at the foot of the embankment until they came to a gate.

'You think there'll be another gate on the far side?' asked the *bourc*.

'If there isn't, we'll have to turn back this way,' said Kemp. 'But it's growing dark, and I doubt we'll find any other cover before twilight's end.'

He noticed that while snow lay thick upon everything else, it had fallen off the rails of the gate, as if knocked off when someone slammed it behind him. Fresh footprints in the snow led into the woods: at least half a dozen pairs.

Nompar saw them too. 'There's someone in these woods,' he murmured. 'And honest men come to harvest timber and withies would have gone home to their beds by now.'

Nodding, Kemp shrugged off his bow and strung it.

'We could skirt these woods and seek shelter elsewhere,' said Nompar.

Taking an arrow from the sheaf under his belt, Kemp used it to indicate the footprints. 'They might be friends. We cannot be the only ones who became separated from the column this morning.'

'Then why are you readying your bow?'

'They might *not* be friends.' Passing through the gate, Kemp held it open for Nompar to follow him before closing it behind him, then nocked his arrow, ready to draw and loose in an instant should the need arise.

The Scots managed their woodlands in much the same way the English did, with the woods subdivided into parts covering only a few acres. Where Kemp came from, these sections were called 'burrows', though he had heard men from other parts of England call them by various other names. There were no physical boundaries between these burrows, but it was easy to see where one ended and the next began: the trees in each burrow were at different stages of the coppicing process. In one they had been freshly cut down, in the next the shoots growing from the stumps could only boast one year's growth, elsewhere they had been growing for years, and in another burrow the shoots had grown thick enough to provide poles and would likely be sawn down before the winter was out. Here and there an oak or a hornbeam had been left to grow to its full height to provide timber. Cart trails ran through the woods to make it easier to carry the poles out after they had been cut down.

Kemp and Nompar followed one of these trails, moving slowly, partly out of caution lest they ran into a foe, but mostly because it was so dark beneath the trees they could scarcely see where they were going, and ran the risk of tripping over a root or walking slap into a tree trunk at every other step. They had scarcely gone two furlongs when Kemp spotted the glimmer of a fire through the trees. He reached out an arm to stop Nompar, walking alongside him. When the *bourc* glanced at him, he indicated the fire. Even as the two of them stared, the light was blotted out, but only for a heartbeat, as if someone had walked in front of it.

'Let's take a closer look,' Kemp murmured to Nompar. 'Keep your eyes and ears open: unless they're fools, they'll have sentinels set.'

They crept closer to the fire, expecting a cry to challenge them from the darkness at any moment. The closest thing to a challenge was a whinny from the shadows up ahead: whoever had lit the campfire had horses nearby. Soon Kemp and Nompar were close enough to make out eight men huddled around the fire, warming their hands. Sir Alexander Bulchett was there with his squire Rowland Crawley as well as Lambert Tegg and five archers from his twenty: Haine, Fisher, Young, Gudgeon and Godwin Vertue, their faces strained in the orange glow of the fire.

Kemp stepped out of the shadows into the firelight. 'Whoever you set to keep watch, they're doing a sovereign job!'

Tegg and Haine at least clapped hands to the weapons they had tucked under their belts before realising it was only Kemp. The rest of them just sat there and gave him bovine stares.

'That's what you think,' said Bulchett. 'I have a dozen men concealed in the shadows. One signal from me, and you fall, pierced with a dozen arrows.'

Kemp smiled. 'Drivel.'

'Impertinent rogue!' protested Crawley. 'How dare you address my lord with such impudence? You, who are not worthy to kiss the ground upon which he walks!'

'There is no need for sentinels,' said Bulchett. 'None shall find us here.'

'We did,' said Kemp.

'Your wrists should be in irons for putting the Grey-friars at Haddington to the torch. How is it your hands are now free?'

'My manacles must have slipped off.'

'You and you!' Bulchett gestured at Haine and Fisher. 'Seize him and bind his wrists.'

The two archers started to rise, then froze when Kemp clapped a hand to the hilt of his sword.

Nompar stepped past Kemp into the circle of firelight. 'What foolishness is this? We are lost in the country of our foes. If we are attacked, we will need every man's hands free to fight.'

'You may be lost,' said Bulchett. 'I happen to know exactly where we are.'

'You do?'

The English knight nodded. 'Melrose lies yonder.' He gestured vaguely into the darkness. 'We'll come there tomorrow.'

'Sir Alexander will get us safely back to the rest of the host,' said Crawley. 'We may depend upon it.'

'Where are your horses?' asked Bulchett.

'We lost them,' said Kemp.

'Lost your horses!' scoffed the knight. 'You're a disgrace, Kemp. A shameful excuse for an archer, never mind a captain. Whatever the king thought he was doing, putting you in command of the company, I cannot imagine.'

'At least we only lost our horses, and not the whole company barring six men,' retorted Kemp.

'You impudent dog! I'll have you flogged for such insolence! I tell you, Kemp: tomorrow we'll ride out of here. If you and your French friend cannot keep up, that's your ill-fortune.'

'I'm Gascon, not French,' Nompar corrected him.

Bulchett ignored him. 'I'll not have my men slowed down by having to share horses with you.'

'Fret not,' said Kemp. 'Nompar and I can look after ourselves. Mind if we share the warmth of your fire?' He sat down without waiting for a response from Bulchett, too grateful for an opportunity to warm himself to worry about whether or not the light would draw the attention of any Scots in the woods. Nompar followed his lead.

Kemp turned to Tegg. 'Where's the rest of your twenty?'

'Ackroyd got shot through the neck by an arrow. Ramsbottom were trampled beneath the hoofs of a riveling's hoss.' 'Riveling' was a derogatory term for a Scot, after the rawhide shoes the Scots wore. 'I didn't see what befell t'others: we were separated in the blizzard.'

Kemp noticed the twentyman's right arm was swathed in bandages and supported by a makeshift sling. 'What happened to you?'

'It's nowt.'

'He got stabbed,' said Young.

'Just a cut,' said Tegg. 'It in't deep. I reckon I'll live, if it divven't rankle.'

'God-damned Scottish whoresons!' growled Haine. 'Lord Christ! I wish we could send every last one of them to burn in Hell for eternity!'

'That's blasphemy,' sneered Vertue, an usher from Durham Cathedral whom the bishop had decided his staff could spare for a few months. 'The Lord will punish you for taking his name in vain. The ground will open up beneath your feet, and you'll be dragged down to the fires of the Hell-pit!'

'Kiss my arse!' Haine said cheerfully. Like most men in the company, he swore freely – amongst the French, the English were known as '*les Goddams*' for their fondness for blasphemy – and Vertue's holier-than-thou condemnation washed off him like water off a duck's back.

'Does anyone have aught to eat?' asked Nompar.

Bulchett shook his head. 'I warrant there'll be food enough when we reach Melrose on the morrow.'

'We'd better take turns keeping watch,' said Kemp. 'Haine, you can keep watch till the moon sets.'

'And you can kiss my arse, too,' said the butcher. 'You're a prisoner, divven't forget. I divven't have to take orders from you.'

'Haine speaks true,' said Crawley. 'It is not your place to give orders! Or had you forgotten you no longer command here? That privilege belongs to Sir Alexander.' The squire bowed fawningly to his master.

Bulchett, who had been staring moodily into the fire, glanced up at the mention of his name. 'Eh? What's that?'

'It is your privilege to decide which men will take turns on guard tonight,' said Crawley.

'Yes. Yes, of course. Er… you take the first watch, you take the second and you take the third.' Bulchett pointed at Haine, Young and Vertue in turn.

Young cleared his throat. 'How am I to know when it is time to rouse Vertue, Sir Alexander?'

'Well, you know. When it's about two-thirds of the way through the night.'

'Do they teach owt of astronomy at Oxford?' Kemp asked the scholar.

'Aye, it's one of the subjects of the quadrivium.'

'Then you'll know where to find Sirius in the night sky.'

'The brightest star in the constellation *Canis Major*, or "the big dog" as it is vulgarly termed.'

'When Sirius sets in the south-east in the small hours of the morning, then it'll be time for you to rouse Vertue.'

Grumbling, Haine went in search of a place where he could keep watch. The rest of them wrapped themselves in their mantles and lay down to sleep by the fire. 'I shall dream of loin of beef tonight,' sighed Young.

'I'll dream of veal pies,' sighed Gudgeon.

'What do you know of veal pie?' sneered Fisher.

'I ate one from a hot pie shop in Westminster once.'

'That's a lie!' said Fisher. 'You've never been south of the Humber.'

'I have too! When I were a wee'un. Me father were a pedlar. Usually when he went out on the road he'd leave me with us mam, but when I got older he'd take me with him, trying to teach me the trade.'

'So how is it you became a ploughman?'

'Didn't want to spend my whole life traipsing about on the highways and byways of England, did I? A man's got to put down roots... a rolling stone gathers nay moss. Anyroad, one time we were in Westminster and me father took me to this hot pie shop to get us summat to eat. We had a veal pie, the meat were cooked in gravy but they added other things, spices and must and verjuice. It were a right fancy hot pie shop, 'cos when the king's parliament were in session, the knights of the shires and the bishops from all over would send their servants there to fetch them pies. God's belly, it were a reet canny collop!'

'Divven't blaspheme!' said Vertue. 'How many times must I tell you? If you take the Lord's name in vain, the ground will open up beneath your feet and you'll be dragged down to hell!'

Grinning, Fisher nudged Young, indicating Gudgeon. 'It weren't the hot pie shop owned by the Countess of Huntingdon, were it?'

'The Countess of Huntingdon never owns a pie shop!' protested Gudgeon.

'She does too. In't that right, Dunstan?'

'Aye, I seem to recall hearing summat about that,' agreed Young.

'She owns the land on which the pie shop stands,' explained Fisher. 'And the pieman pays her rent. Only instead of paying her in coin, he pays her in blood.'

'Get away wi' you!' gasped Gudgeon.

'It's true! The countess and all her noble friends are devil-worshippers and they drink the blood of Christian babies in their satanic ceremonies. I heard all about it from a friend of me aunt's cousin who knows one of the countess's scullions.'

Gudgeon grew saucer-eyed at this revelation, oblivious to Tegg, Vertue and Young all trying to stifle their sniggers at his credulity behind his back.

'Why dun't somebody do summat about it?' asked Gudgeon.

'What can they do?' asked Fisher. 'The countess is too powerful. Even the local sheriff is in her husband's purse.'

'Someone should tell the king!'

'Aye, when we get to Melrose, you should tell him.'

'Hob!' said Kemp. 'Remember when we spoke last week, how I told you that when people – and Simkin Fisher in particular – tell you stories, before you believe them, you should stop and ask yourself how plausible those stories are?'

'Aye, so?'

'So even if it were true that the Countess of Huntingdon was a devil-worshipper who drank the blood of Christian babies, do you truly think word of it would reach your ears before it reached the ears of the king; or think you His Majesty, learning of such vile practices, would do nowt to end them?'

Gudgeon's eyes became even wider. 'You mean... the king's in on it too?'

Kemp stared at him in disbelief. 'No, I... oh, for Christ's sake! You're a silly fool, Hob.'

'Blasphemer!'

'Hold your tongue, Godwin! And as for you, Simkin: you may reckon pulling the wool over Hob's eyes proves you sharp-witted; but it only proves your wits sharper than his. That's nowt to boast of.'

Kemp tipped his helmet forward over his eyes and hugged his mantle more tightly about him to keep out the cold. He was too cold and wet to sleep, and spent most of the night tossing and turning by the campfire, worrying about whether or not they would find their way to Melrose before they were caught and butchered by Scots. And yet he must have drifted off at some point, for the next thing he knew he was waking from a dream where he was trying to protect the Countess of Huntingdon from a mob of halfwits like Gudgeon, whipped into a frenzy of bloodlust by Simkin Fisher's teasing.

It was still dark, so he rolled over and tried to get back to sleep, but it was even colder now. Seeing the vaguest hint of light in the sky to the east, at last he gave up trying to sleep and pushed himself to his feet, heading to where Vertue should have been keeping watch. He had been meaning to have a private word with the usher anyway. Vertue's habit of picking up on every blasphemy that issued from the lips of his comrades was growing wearisome, and Kemp suspected that when the day came the usher had to give an account of himself to Saint Peter, whatever advantage he thought he had gained by discouraging blasphemy would be more than countered by his being a sanctimonious whoreson.

Searching for Vertue, however, he instead found Young, fast asleep in the place where Haine had been on guard. Evidently he had fallen asleep on watch, leaving Vertue to sleep through to first light.

Kemp grabbed a fistful of Young's cote-hardie and dragged him to his feet, slapping him awake. 'You stupid whoreson! You stupid, stupid whoreson!'

'Wha—? What did I do?'

'You fell asleep on watch! The Scots might ha' marched in here and cut all our throats while you lay there snoring.'

The others began stirring around the campfire. 'What's going on?' asked Bulchett.

'It's Young, Sir Alexander,' said Kemp. 'He fell asleep on watch.'

'Oh, well. No harm done.'

'No harm done?' Kemp echoed incredulously. 'Will you not punish him, Sir Alexander?'

'I'm sure there's no need for that. Least said, soonest mended.'

'Falling asleep on watch is the worst error any fighting man can commit,' said Kemp. 'If I'd fallen asleep on watch when we marched to Crécy, Sir Thomas Holland would ha' had me flogged for it!'

'Seems a bit harsh to me,' said Bulchett. 'And I think we're all mightily sick of Crécy veterans like yourself puffing out their chests, pretending they know it all.'

'You'll not even dock his wages?'

'Need I remind you yet again? I command here, not you. Very well, perhaps the Scots might have stumbled across us in the dark and slit all our throats. But they did not, so I fail to see what the need for any fuss is.'

'When a man lets his team down as badly as Young has, it's customary to make an example of him so his companions understand how needful it is not to make the same mistake.'

'Given what a mess you made of leading this company when you were given the chance, it ill-behoves me to take any lessons from you!' Bulchett said scornfully, before turning to Crawley. 'Fetch my palfrey.'

'Aye,' said Tegg. 'Kenrick, Simkin, you twain can round up all us hosses.' In the absence of any fodder, the archers would have hobbled their mounts overnight to prevent them from straying too far, letting them crop at what grass they could find growing beneath the snow.

'Nay morrow-meat to break us fast?' grumbled Young.

'Nay use in asking,' said Tegg. He clutched at his wounded arm as if it pained him.

'Never mind, lads,' said Bulchett. 'We'll eat our dinner at Melrose Abbey ere noon.'

'If the rest of the king's host ha'n't already eaten the brethren out of house and home by the time we get there,' muttered Young.

'When Fisher and Haine return with the horses, Tegg, you can give yours to Sir Nompar,' said Bulchett.

'Mine? How am I to get to Melrose?'

'You'll walk with Kemp, make sure he's not tempted to flee into the depths of Scotland rather than face the king's wrath. 'Tis but a couple of leagues.'

'Thank you!' Kemp said scornfully. 'I do not fear the king's justice.'

'I would not dream of obliging a wounded man to walk,' said Nompar. 'It is no fault of Tegg's that I have no mount.'

'And you'll see to it Kemp is delivered to the king's justice at Melrose?' Bulchett asked anxiously.

'A promise easily given,' said the *bourc*. 'Senher Kemp does not shy from accepting responsibility for his actions.'

While Crawley, Haine and Fisher were rounding up the horses, the rest of the party went their separate ways to ease nature. Kemp was wiping his backside with some moss when the squire returned with the two archers. 'They've been taken!' he told Bulchett, white-faced.

'Who's been taken?'

'The horses! We found the tracks... someone came in the night and led them back towards that village to the east.'

Eight

'No harm done, eh?' Kemp told Bulchett scornfully. 'And while Young lay snoring, some Scots rascals crept up here by night and helped themselves to your horses!'

'The dirty whoresons!' said Haine. 'I say we go down there, take us hosses back, and put their whole shitten village to the torch to learn 'em a lesson.'

'And while we put their hovels to the torch, belike the lord of Thirlstane Castle already rides hither with his men-at-arms to capture us and put us to death,' said Kemp. 'I warrant the folk in the village have already sent him word of two knights, a squire and seven archers snoring their heads off in these woods.'

'But that palfrey cost me a hundred and twenty pounds!' protested Bulchett.

'Try docking *that* from Young's wages!' said Kemp.

'Things done cannot be undone,' said Nompar. 'Now we must hasten to Melrose. If we have no horses, we must go on foot.'

They gathered up what little gear they had left, buckled on sword belts, slung bow staves across their backs and tucked sheaves of arrows under their belts.

'Did they take the rope also?' Bulchett asked Crawley.

'No, my lord. I hung it from a branch when I unsaddled my palfrey. 'Tis still there.'

'Go and fetch it, then.'

Crawley plunged into the bushes and re-emerged a moment later, shrugging a coil of good hempen rope over his head and one arm so it hung crosswise over his torso.

'What's that for?' asked Kemp.

'I always take a coil of rope with me wherever I go,' said Bulchett. 'You never know when it will come in handy.' He led the way to the hedge-topped embankment at the western edge of the woods. The hedge was made from plashed hawthorn reinforced with briars and brambles.

'We'll never get through that.' Kemp had worked on hedges as boon-work on the manor where he had grown up, and he knew how impenetrable a plashed hawthorn hedge was. 'We'd best head back to the gate and make our way around the outside of the woods.'

'Nonsense!' said Bulchett. 'You're a worrywart with too much black bile in your humour, that's your trouble. We'll get through this hedge in no time.' He strode into the brambles, immediately startling a family of thrushes out of its depths, then spent the next few minutes thrashing about with his sword, trying to hack his way through and instead only becoming more thickly entwined in the brambles. At last Kemp and Nompar, growing impatient, had to drag him out.

'Unhand me!' protested Bulchett. 'Damn your noses, I had almost made it through!'

'You were no closer to the far side than you were the moment you stepped into it,' said Kemp. 'And in the time you wasted, we might be on the other side already had we gone the long way around.'

'Perhaps we should split into two parties?' suggested Nompar. 'Those of us who are in haste to reach Melrose can leave by the gate, and those of us who wish to spend all day locked in brutal hand-to-hand combat with some briars may do as they please?'

Kemp suppressed a smile. 'No,' he said firmly. 'If we split up, that'll only make it easier for the Scots to defeat us piecemeal. Until we rejoin the rest of the host, we stick together. But I still say we leave by the gate.'

It was broad day by the time they got back to the gate, with a grey, wintry sky louring over a landscape blanketed with snow. Kemp and his companions jogged around the outside of the wood. The stocky Bulchett was soon panting and wheezing like an elderly sow run ragged by a boisterous dog. 'We could have been there by now had we persevered at the hedge!'

'Keep an eye on me,' Kemp murmured to Nompar. 'If it seems I'm about to lose my temper and flatten the whoreson, hold me back!'

A road from the valley below led past the north-western corner of the wood to a saddle between two hilltops. On the other side, a gully ran down to where a stream no more than three dozen yards wide ran black between snow-covered banks. Pausing at the brink, Bulchett produced a piece of parchment from his scrip, consulting it. Guessing it was a map, Kemp tried to get close enough to look at it over the knight's shoulder but, as if sensing his presence, Bulchett hurriedly folded the parchment once more and slipped it back into his scrip. He slithered down the bank and began to wade across the stream, knee-deep.

'Whither away, Sir Alexander?' cried Kemp. 'This stream must join with the River Tweed. Surely if we follow it downstream it'll lead us to Melrose soon enough?'

'Not before we run slap into Galashiels Castle!' Bulchett pointed to where a road on the far bank led into a gap between two large hills. 'If we follow yon road, we'll steer safely clear of Galashiels and reach the Tweed upstream.'

Tegg and the others were already scrambling down the bank into the stream and wading across after Bulchett. 'That valley leads to the south-west,' murmured Nompar. 'I fancy we are already well to the west of Melrose.'

'Aye, but once we reach the Tweed we can follow it back downstream,' said Kemp. He nodded at Bulchett's back. 'He seems to know whither he's bound.'

'He seems to *think* he knows whither he's bound,' said Nompar. 'A subtle distinction, but an important one, I think.'

'Let's stick with him for now,' said Kemp. 'If it turns out he doesn't know where he's bound, we can always turn back later.'

'Later may be too late. Are we to let him lead us to perdition?'

'Better we stick together.' Without waiting to see if the *bourc* followed, Kemp slithered down the bank of the stream. The water was icy enough to stab fresh icicles of pain into feet he had thought numbed with cold, but there was nothing for it but to wade across and scramble out on the opposite bank. He helped Nompar up after him, and once again the two of them pulled off their boots to drain them before pulling them back on and following Bulchett and the others into the gap between the two hills.

'Do you know the story about the old man who had three sons who were constantly quarrelling?' Kemp asked Nompar.

'Is this the one where he takes three sticks, bundles them together and invites them try to break them together, then individually?' The *bourc* nodded. 'It is one of Aesop's Fables.'

'Then you understand there's strength in unity,' said Kemp.

'There is,' agreed Nompar. 'Whether that strength is used to do good or ill, on the other hand...'

A couple of hours' march brought them into another valley. The river running through the bottom was deep and serene, with shelves of ice creeping out across the placid surface from the reeds growing in the shallows close to the banks.

'We could swim across,' said Crawley.

'Don't be a wooden-headed fool,' said Kemp. 'Aye, we might swim across. And freeze to death in this cold, with no way to dry our clothes on the far bank.'

Bulchett took out his piece of parchment again. 'If we head upstream, we'll come to a bridge in a couple of leagues.'

'Two leagues!' protested Kemp. 'And all the while we'll be marching further west of Melrose. Surely this must be the River Tweed? If we follow it downstream, will it not take us to Melrose?'

'Aye, but there are no crossings this side of Monksford. We'll head upstream to the bridge, then double back to Melrose once we're on the south bank.'

'And kindly waste not our time questioning my lord's judgement,' added Crawley. 'You cannot doubt a man of his wisdom knows whither he's bound?'

Bulchett had already started marching along the road leading upstream along the riverbank. Crawley went after him, and once again the others followed.

'We're going with them?' asked Nompar.

'You have a better suggestion?' Kemp snapped angrily, then made an effort to reign in his ire: it was not Nompar who had put him in this difficult position. 'The king has put Bulchett in command whether I like it or no. I'll not regain his trust if I defy his commands.'

'Your loyalty to him is admirable,' said Nompar. '"*Toujours de la perdrix!*"'

'"Always partridge"? What do you mean by that?'

'There is a story of a king of France – I forget which one – who kept many mistresses. One day, his confessor took him to task for his infidelity to his wife. The king asked him what his favourite food was. "Partridge," said his confessor. "Very well," said the king. "Then you shall have all the partridge to eat you could wish for, and more." And so he ordered it that the confessor should dine on partridge, for dinner and supper, and when the confessor woke up hungry and called for some morrow-meat, he was served cold partridge then as well. After a month, the king asked him how he liked his new diet. "*Toujours de la perdrix!*" sighed the confessor.'

'An amusing tale,' said Kemp. 'There is a point to it?'

'Your loyalty to your king and your companions-in-arms is admirable,' said Nompar. 'But one can have too much of a good thing.'

–

Nixon and Reid crouched behind the snow-covered embankment of an ancient fort that stood on a ridge north of the Tweed. Occasionally breaking off from rubbing their hands together to cup them and blow into them for warmth, they gazed down to where the river meandered through the valley below. A church tower rose over the snow-covered rooftops of the buildings of Melrose Abbey. There was a lot of activity down there, troops of hobelars and mounted archers patrolling the riverbank and the fields around the town.

'We could ambush them again,' said Reid. 'If they head south-west towards Carlisle, we can ambush them as they cross Wauchope Forest—'

'And if they head south-east towards Jeddart, or east for Roxburgh?' Nixon shook his head. 'We had our chance. Douglas let the English king slip through his fingers.'

'The weather was against us,' said Reid. 'Impossible to see who was fighting who in that blizzard. In any case, we left nae shortage of English deid for the crows to feast on.'

'Aye, and nae shortage of Scottish deid, for that matter,' said Nixon. 'Though in truth, Ah warrant we got the better of it.'

Running bent double, he dashed through the snow lying in the ancient fort, and Reid went after him. The two of them climbed over the rampart on the opposite side, then descended through the snow on the northern slope of the ridge to where Howk and the rest of Nixon's men waited in a quarry with their horses. With the men Reid had raised from Tweeddale, less those slain in the battle or too sore wounded to ride, there were three dozen of them now, a few armoured with rusty habergeons or worn brigandines, most wearing nothing more than a jupon or an aketon, and armed with axes or spears.

'Tam, Gib, ye twa can take a turn watching the abbey,' said Nixon. 'Come back and let us know if there's any sign of Edward's army marching out. We can yet pick off a few stragglers. Otherwise, I'll send someone to relieve ye both at midday.'

While Nixon was speaking, Reid saw two men in armour riding from the direction of Lauderdale. 'Haud, Rab!' he said, pointing them out.

Gib and Tam stayed by their horses as they watched the two riders approach, waiting to see if they were friend or foe. As the horsemen drew nigh, Reid saw one of them carried a shield blazoned with the red heart of Douglas on a white background beneath a blue band with three white stars on it. His companion's shield was blazoned with a red rose.

'Stand easy, lads,' said Nixon. 'They're Lord Douglas' vassals.'

The two men rode straight into the quarry and raised their visors. The man bearing the red heart of Douglas on his shield raised his visor to reveal Sir Archibald Douglas' face. 'Nixon,' he greeted the reiver chief coldly, before gesturing at his companion, who raised his own visor to reveal the smooth face of the man who had looked down his nose at the reivers at Yester Castle a few days earlier. 'You remember Peter Sneith.' Archibald might have been born a bastard in a bothy, but his kinsman Lord Douglas had seen to it he had been educated in France, and like all Scots noblemen he spoke English with the same Norman accent as their English counterparts.

'Whit can Ah do for ye, Sir Archibald?' asked Nixon.

'We've received word of a party of English stragglers in the woods on Ladhope Hill.'

Reid glanced to the north-west. He could see the woods Sneith spoke of about a league off, backed by an even higher ridge beyond.

'How many stragglers?' Nixon asked Archibald.

'Ten.'

'Ah'll send a dozen men to round them up.'

'Lord Douglas would have you take all your men to be sure.'

'Eight-and-thirty of us, against ten?' snorted Nixon. 'Dinnae be ridiculous! A dozen of my men can deal with them, while the rest of us shadow King Edward's army, picking off stragglers.'

'Sir William Ramsay and his men will shadow the English host,' said Sneith. 'Lord Douglas commands you to pursue the stragglers on Ladhope Hill.'

'Is that so?' Howk strode across to where Sneith sat on his horse. He reached up – he did not have to reach very high – and grabbed Sneith by the throat. The man-at-arms at once pulled the battle-axe from under his belt, but Howk caught him by the wrist with the other hand and stayed the blow. A moment later, Sneith had tumbled from his saddle and rolled in snow. His face suffused with fury, Sneith crawled to where his axe had fallen and gripped the haft, but Howk stepped on the axehead, pinning it to the ground. 'We dinnae take orders frae Lord Douglas,' he sneered, and was about to smash a knee into Sneith's face when Nixon called out.

'Howk! Let him up.'

The big man stepped back, regarding Sneith with contempt.

The man-at-arms rose to his feet, his axe in his hand. 'I should have this dog whipped for his insolence!'

'Howk is my man,' Nixon said mildly. 'Ah'll decide whether or no' he deserves a whipping. He spoke nae more than the truth.'

'Put your axe away, Peter,' said Archibald. 'Is it any wonder the English defeat us so often, when so many of us are more passionate about picking quarrels with our own countrymen than our true foes? Our only hope of defeating the English is to unite against them. A realm divided against itself cannot endure.'

'Ye speak true enough,' said Nixon. 'But we all ken that when your kinsman Lord Douglas speaks of Scots uniting, he only means they should unite behind him and do as he says. Me and my lads are no' vassals of his. Sometimes we have a common foe. Sometimes we work together. But that disnae mean we take orders frae him.'

Sneith pointed an angry finger at Howk. 'The churl had the temerity to lay hands upon me!'

'If you've a quarrel with that big ruffian, Peter, I suggest you settle it yourself,' said Archibald. 'Or hold your tongue.'

Sneith glared at the big man a moment longer, then tucked the haft of his axe back under his belt.

'You should keep your ruffian on a shorter leash,' Archibald told Nixon.

'As should ye,' the reiver chief replied pointedly. 'These stragglers on Ladhope Hill... are any of them noblemen?'

'A couple of knights and a squire.'

'And if there are ransoms to be squeezed from them? Who earns those?'

'If any of them are prisoners of importance, you're to take them alive and hand them over to Lord Douglas. Though he gives you his word, you'll get a fair share if there are ransoms to be paid.'

Reid hawked and spat. 'The word of a nobleman, eh?'

'Whisht now, Rory,' said Nixon, before turning back to Archibald. 'Noblemen, eh? Ye should have said as much in the first place. That's another matter entirely. Very well, Sir Archibald. Ye may ride back to Thirlstane Castle and inform Lord Douglas we'll do his bidding – this time.'

Archibald shook his head. 'Lord Douglas bids Sneith and I ride with you, to see his wishes are carried out.'

'His lordship reposing his trust in us as usual, Ah see,' Nixon said drily. 'Very well, Sir Archibald: ye and your man-at-arms may ride wi' us — if ye can keep up. But if ye get in our way, well... jist dinnae get in our way, that's my advice to ye!'

Nine

Bulchett and his companions followed the valley as it wended its way westwards. The slopes of the hills rising on either side showed no sign of furrows beneath the snow that covered them, suggesting they were pastures rather than fields. In places, woods stretched from the water's edge up to the ridges above, the trees bare of leaves and black against the snow. Beyond the trees, they came to where a flock of sheep picked at what little grazing grew through the snow covering their pastures.

'Mutton for dinner, lads!' cried Haine, and at once broke away from the others to charge towards the sheep. Fisher went with him.

'Those are the first sheep I have seen since we entered Scotland a fourteen-night ago,' said Nompar.

Scouring the hills rising above them with his eyes, Kemp nodded. 'Given how thoroughly the vassals of the Earl of Dunbar and Lord Douglas drove their livestock out of our path, that must mean we've travelled further west than ever they thought we might come.'

Seeing Haine and Fisher approach, the sheep at once bolted, moving in a herd. The two archers veered after them, but they moved with less co-ordination than the sheep. Then one sheep stumbled. Haine moved towards it. Seeing him approach, the sheep panicked. Separated now from the rest of the flock, it headed into a shallow gully in the pasture. Haine went after it, trying to cut it off, but he slipped and fell in the snow. Fisher's laughter echoed off the surrounding hills. By the time Haine had regained his feet, the lone sheep had given him the slip and rejoined the rest of the flock.

'They'll never catch a sheep that way,' scoffed Tegg.

'Strange,' said Nompar. 'You'd expect to see a shepherd watching over a flock of a sheep.'

'Shepherds are there to protect the sheep from wolves, not gangs of armed men,' said Kemp. 'Any shepherd will have made himself scarce when he saw us coming. Belike he watches us now from yon woods.' He indicated more trees growing on the far side of the pasture.

'I little think we have aught to fear from a shepherd,' said Bulchett.

'And if he runs to the nearest castle to complain to his lord that a parcel of brigands has butchered one of his sheep?'

Bulchett jabbed a stubby finger at Vertue and Gudgeon. 'You and you, run up to yon woods and see if you can find the shepherd. See to it he does not bear tidings of our presence here to whatever lord rules over this valley.'

The two archers did as they were bid without hesitation, though they did not exactly run: the snow was too deep and the hillside too steep for that. Haine, meanwhile, realising he was never going to catch a sheep with his bare hands, had unslung his bow, stripped off its bag and strung it. He loosed at one of the sheep from a few dozen yards. The shaft buried itself in the fleece, and the sheep fell, rolling on its back in the snow, legs thrashing at the air. The rest of the flock fled further up the slope, while Haine and Fisher converged on the injured sheep, hooting with glee. The rest of them trudged up the hill to where Haine set to work butchering the sheep expertly.

'My ancestors fought with King Richard in the Holy Land,' said Nompar. 'I wonder what they would say if they could see their descendent reduced to a stealer of sheep?'

'If they were experienced campaigners, they'd understand,' said Kemp.

'It's the owner of the sheep has my pity,' said Tegg.

'They stole our horses, we stole one sheep,' said Crawley. 'I'd say thus far they have the better side of the bargain.'

'We do not know the folk who own these sheep are the same ones that stole your horses,' said Nompar.

By the time they got to where Haine was carving up the sheep, a great pool of blood stained the snow where he had slit its throat, and now he was peeling off the fleece. A flock of crows began to settle in the boughs of the trees overlooking the pasture as Haine slit the sheep's belly and drew out its entrails. Revealing its ribs, he severed its spine with a delicate jab of the tip of his cleaver, then chopped off the back legs. He cut the breasts off the ribs, then the loins, hacking at the bones with Fisher's hatchet. 'I'd usually use a saw for this bit,' he explained. His hands were red with gore. 'A hatchet dun't cut as nicely, but it'll do.'

While Haine was working, Vertue and Gudgeon returned from the trees above. 'Did you find the shepherd?' Kemp asked them.

Vertue shook his head. 'We found tracks leading east, but I reckon he'd put too much distance between him and us to make it worth us chasing him.'

'You mean you were afeared you'd catch him,' said Fisher.

It took Haine less time to butcher the sheep than it took to walk a mile. When he was finished, he divided up the cuts of meat and shared them out with his companions.

Gudgeon at once began tearing mouthfuls of meat off one of the cuts with his teeth. 'Don't eat it raw, you wooden-headed fool!' said Kemp. 'That's how you get the bloody flux.'

'I canna help it,' said Gudgeon. 'I'm that hungry!'

'Put it in your pokes for now,' said Kemp. 'We'll push on and find somewhere under cover where we can risk lighting a fire.'

'I give the orders around here,' growled Bulchett.

'As you will,' said Nompar. 'Shall we push on and find somewhere under cover where we can risk lighting a fire, or would rather we wait here until whoever the shepherd has gone to fetch arrives?'

Bulchett thrust forward a petulant lower jaw and gave the *bourc* a long, hard stare. Indifferent, Nompar inspected his fingernails. 'Follow me,' Bulchett said at last, turning away.

A league further on, they came to where a valley leading north out of Tweeddale was choked with trees. A short march through the woods brought them to a grove where Kemp reckoned they could light a fire without a risk of any travellers getting a whiff of wood smoke. Making skewers of twigs, they roasted some of the mutton and ate the meat hungrily. After eating nothing but horse-meat or worse for the past few days, and little enough of either of those, it tasted heavenly. Kemp kept a close eye on the men, fearing some of them might be tempted to gorge themselves until they were sick.

Peeling back the mail coif of his habergeon, he squatted in the shallows of a stream and buried his head in the water, seeking to soak the hood of his gambeson so he could peel it back without ripping half his scalp off in the process. The clear water was so icy it was like dipping his head into a furnace, and the cold forced him to take his head out long before he ran out of breath.

He looked up to find Nompar standing over him on the bank of the stream. 'Struggling to keep awake?'

'I took a blow to the head yesterday and my hood's stuck to my scalp with blood. Could you…?'

'*De segur.* Sit down.'

Kemp squatted at Nompar's feet and the *bourc* gently peeled back the quilted hood a fraction of an inch at a time, until Kemp felt it pull at the roots of his close-cropped hair. He winced and hissed through his teeth.

'Ah, yes, I see. There is much dried blood here, but I think it looks worse than it is. Yes, there is a gash, but not too deep. Let me clean it up for you.' Producing a clean rag, Nompar dipped it in the stream, wrung it out and began to dab at Kemp's head. 'It has started bleeding again. Let me put this rag over it and bind it in place with this coverchief… there.'

Tegg kicked the remains of the campfire into the stream and threw snow over the ashes while the others packed up their gear. 'Come along, you two!' Bulchett jeered Kemp and Nompar. 'When you've quite finished picking lice off one another!'

'He has a head wound that needed tending,' said Nompar. 'Bah! He is a fool!' he added to Kemp in French. 'Why should we care what he thinks?'

'Will it rankle?' asked Kemp.

'I wish I had some wine or vinegar to splash on it,' said Nompar. 'Wear your hood down, until it has dried out. Your head will freeze otherwise.'

Kemp's kettle helmet helped to keep some of the warmth in his head, but it was sized to fit over his hood and mail coif, and without them he had to wear it on the back of his head to stop the brim from falling over his eyes. Without the close-fitting hood of the gambeson, Kemp's ears stung from the cold, but he could not deny the wisdom of Nompar's advice about giving it a chance to dry out.

The bridge Bulchett had spoken of proved elusive, but after another mile they found a ford shallow enough for them to wade across without getting wet above the knee. On the south bank, the road branched left and right. Kemp immediately turned to the left to follow the branch leading back to Melrose.

'Not so hasty, Kemp,' said Bulchett.

'Are we not headed for Melrose?'

'We'll not get there ere sundown. If it's our intent to rejoin the king's host, we'll not find it there tomorrow. Belike he spent last night there and marched on for Carlisle this morning. By the time we reach Melrose, the king's host will be two days ahead of us.'

Whose fault is that? Kemp was tempted to ask.

Bulchett consulted his scrap of parchment. He pointed down the opposite branch of the junction, leading to the west. 'If we continue this way, on the other hand, there's an old drove road through Ettrick Forest that will lead us to Liddesdale. If we push hard, I warrant we'll reach Hermitage Castle ahead of the king's host.'

'If we're headed for Hermitage we must pass through Selkirk, which lies two leagues south-west of Melrose.'

139

Once again Kemp pointed to the east. 'From there we can march to Hawick and from thence to Hermitage.'

Bulchett shook his head. 'That's going the long way around. This is a shortcut.'

'Either way, I warrant we're at least three days' march from Hermitage. How are we to feed ourselves in that time? The sheep we just butchered will not keep us so long.'

'Nonsense!' said Bulchett. 'We have plenty of meat. Come on! Follow me, I know the way.'

Half a league west of the ford, they passed a village on the opposite bank of the Tweed: a few dozen stone bothies with turf roofs clustered around a church. Bulchett and his men kept to the woods on the hillside above the road until the village was out of sight behind them, and even the Tweed had veered away to the north. Bulchett led the way up a tributary valley. Half a mile further on, the road split, the left-hand branch continuing up the valley, while the right-hand fork looked like a drove road, leading up into the hills to the south-east.

To Kemp's surprise, Bulchett turned right.

'Sir Alexander!' he cried, and when the knight stopped and turned back, Kemp indicated the left-hand fork. 'I thought we were bound for Hermitage?'

'We are!'

'Surely Hermitage lies to the south-east of here? Why are we headed south-west?'

'We're not. That's north, this is south-east.' Bulchett pointed.

'That's east!'

'Nonsense! How would you know, when the sun is nowhere to be seen?'

'I need not see the sun to know east from west, Sir Alexander. The rust-coloured lichen on the trunks of yon beech trees shows which way north lies.'

'Aye. It grows on the west side, where it gets the sun in the evening.'

'What? No! It grows on the north side, where the sun does not dry out the bark.'

'What stuff! It grows on the west side. Even a child knows that.' Satisfied he had won the argument, Bulchett continued up the valley without waiting to see if the others followed.

Kemp shook his head in disbelief. His father had told him about the lichen when he was a boy. All his life he had navigated on sunless days by keeping an eye on the lichen, and it had never steered him wrong yet. Or had the blow to his head addled his wits? 'It grows on the north side,' he told Crawley. 'Does it not?' he added weakly, conscious that the very fact he had to ask admitted that suddenly there was doubt in his mind.

'I think Sir Alexander knows which side of a tree trunk lichen grows on,' the squire declared loftily, before following his master.

Kemp turned imploringly to the others. 'Tell them!' he pleaded, gesturing after Bulchett and Crawley. 'That lichen grows on the north side!'

Tegg scratched his injured arm through his bandages. 'If Sir Alexander says it grows on the west side, I reckon he would know.'

Kemp looked at Gudgeon. 'Hob! You're a coun-tryman.' *Hell's teeth*, he thought, *I cannot believe I'm turning to a witless oaf like Gudgeon for support.* 'Tell them: that rusty-looking lichen grows to the north.'

'Sir Alexander wouldn't make a mistake about summat like that.'

'But you know he's wrong! You *know* he's wrong.'

'You're the one who's in the wrong,' sneered Haine. 'And you're too proud to admit it. You think you know everything, but you're not as wise as you think you are. It only goes to show: Master Knows-a-Lot knows a lot of rot.'

Kemp turned to Young. The scholar shrugged. 'Divven't draw me into your quarrel, Master Kemp. It has nowt to do wi' me. I just obey orders.'

Vertue and Fisher followed the others, leaving Kemp rubbing his throbbing forehead in bewilderment, wondering if he was going mad.

'If it is any consolation,' said Nompar, 'I too thought such lichens grew on the north side of trees. At least, they do in Gascony. I confess, I have neglected to pay attention to such things since I came to Scotland.'

'I can understand Sir Alexander getting it wrong.' Kemp shook his head. 'But not all of them. They cannot *all* be wrong.'

'A wise man knows all men are fallible, so a wise man doubts himself. Only a fool speaks with utter certainty. When he does, wiser heads are loath to contradict him, thinking that to speak with such certainty, he must know something they do not.'

'Maybe he *does* know summat we don't. Maybe we'll crest the brow of the ridge after next and see Liddesdale stretching out before us.'

'My father once told me when two men say contradictory things, you should never trust the man who's telling you what you want to hear just because it's what you want to hear.' Nompar pointed up the fork Bulchett and the others had not taken. 'If you say that is the road that leads to Hermitage, I put more faith in your judgement than in Sir Alexander's. Perhaps we would do better to forge out on our own.'

Kemp was sorely tempted. He had had a bellyful of Bulchett's folly and pomposity. But he knew the king would not give command to the sort of man who would abandon his companions-in-arms when the going got tough. No matter how much taking orders from Bulchett might rankle, he had to curb his irritation and buckle under. 'We cannot abandon our companions,' he told Nompar.

'Even when they prefer to follow a fool?'

'If they prefer to follow a fool then they're in trouble, and when they're in trouble, that's when they're most in need of our help.'

'When a man jumps off a cliff, you cannot save him by jumping after him.'

'We've not come to a cliff-edge yet. Come on.' Kemp hastened after Bulchett and the others, and Nompar followed.

Climbing the spur of a hill, they left the pastures of Tweeddale behind, entering a wilderness where the drove road snaked across moors where the snow rested thickly atop the wiry heather growing on either side.

Kemp glanced up at the gravid sky. 'I'd say there's more snow to come, Sir Alexander!'

'Nonsense!' said Bulchett. 'It's too cold to snow!' He marched on.

Kemp and Nompar exchanged glances. 'I fear this will end in tears,' murmured the *bourc*.

'I will settle it my own way before it comes to that.' Kemp patted the hilt of his sword.

'You'd cross swords with Sir Alexander?'

Kemp chuckled. 'You think I've owt to fear from such a fool as that?'

'Beware you do not underestimate him,' said Nompar. 'Some say you shouldn't be fooled by his silly manner, that he's a wise man only pretending to be a fool.'

Kemp snorted. 'I warrant *he* is fool enough to believe that!' He glanced after Bulchett. 'Some men are such great fools, to underestimate them is an impossibility!'

--

There was such a confusion of footprints in the woods on Ladhope Hill, even Reid could not make head nor tail of them, and he was acknowledged to be one of the finest huntsmen in the Merse. But he knew that in such a situation, the best thing to do was to search the periphery for clear indications of tracks leading away, so it did not take him long to find the footprints in the snow leading down towards the Gala Water.

'They're on foot?' Sir Archibald Douglas observed in astonishment. 'Why would they give up their horses?'

'Ye'd have to ask the villagers at Langshaw about that.' Reid climbed back on his hobby. 'Ah noticed them herding a destrier, a palfrey and half a dozen rouncies into a barn when we arrived.'

'It disnae say much for the wits of these Inglishers if they didnae have sense enough to guard their horses overnight,' sniffed Nixon. 'Still, it'll no' take us long to catch up wi' them if they're on foot.'

Where the tracks disappeared into the Gala Water, they easily picked them up on the far side. Reid hesitated, eyeing where the footprints led into the valley leading to the south-west.

'Why do you tarry?' asked Archibald. 'You can see plain enough which way they went.'

'Aye,' said Reid. 'But if they're trying to rejoin their army, why did they no' follow the Gala Water downstream through Galashiels? They could have crossed the Tweed at Abbotsford, and frae there it's a short walk to Melrose.'

'Maybe they have nae sense of direction,' said Nixon. 'They dinnae hail frae these parts, remember.'

Reid shrugged and they rode on, following the fresh prints to the bank of the River Tweed. He was even more puzzled when the tracks turned upstream rather than down. 'Even if they didnae ken this is the Tweed, they must have known all rivers hereabouts feed into the Tweed. Where's the sense in heading upstream?'

'It's too deep to ford here,' said Archibald. 'If I was looking for a place to cross and I did not know the area, I would head upstream rather than downstream.'

A league upstream, they found a shepherd staring glumly at some sheep-bones, entrails and pieces of fleece scattered about in a patch of bloody snow.

'Did they pay you for it?' asked Archibald.

'Of course not!' spat the shepherd. 'God-damned English whoresons!'

'You spoke with them, then?'

'Nae. Ah hid in yon trees.' The shepherd gestured with his crook. 'A pack of English ruffians comes towards ye, whit would ye have done? If ye'd been me, Ah mean. But Ah heard them talking.'

'Ten of them? Two knights, a squire and seven archers?'

'Aye, that sounds about reet. Are ye chasing them?'

'We are.'

'If ye catch them, make the thieving whoresons suffer.'

'We will.' Archibald took a couple of coins from his purse and leaned down from his destrier to press them into the shepherd's palm.

The shepherd scowled. 'Ah dinnae ask for charity.'

'That's not charity,' said Archibald. 'I'll soon replace them with coins from the purses of the men who did this.' He indicated the remains of the dead sheep, and rode on, following the tracks where they continued upstream. The others rode after him.

'Ah thought your cousin had had all livestock that couldnae be hidden herded north of the Forth?' Nixon remarked to Archibald when the knight rode alongside him.

'Only in the path of King Edward's host. That was a big enough task, without adding to it herds so far west. No one ever imagined the English would come this way.'

'The men we're chasing came this way. Whit d'ye think King Edward will do, if these men rejoin his host and tell him there are enough sheep and cattle in the Moorfoot Hills to feed a thousand men?'

Archibald set his jaw. 'Then the men we're chasing must not be allowed to rejoin King Edward's host.'

They rode on, past Innerleithan. At the head of the troop of reivers, Reid halted his hobby when he saw the tracks of their quarry led up the old drove road across Blake Muir. Glancing to the west, he saw dark storm clouds gathering over the Tweedsmuir Hills.

'Howie Ure's?' he asked Nixon.

The reiver chief nodded. 'Howie Ure's,' he agreed, and all thirty-eight of the reivers wheeled their mounts and rode back the way they had come.

Archibald and Sneith tarried. 'You'd give up?' the knight called after the reivers. 'You can see clearly enough which way they went. Do not tell me three dozen of you fear ten men?'

'It's no' the Inglishers we're afraid of.' Reid pointed to the clouds. 'Yon blizzard will be here in less time than it takes a man to walk a mile. God help anyone caught on Blake Muir when it does. Innerleithan's less than a league back that way. We can shelter at Howie Ure's inn for the night.'

'All the more reason to press on! If we tarry till the morrow, the snow will have buried the tracks of the men we're after.'

'Yon tracks are less than an hour old. The men we're chasing will no' make it to the far end of the drove road before yon blizzard forces them to seek shelter. Which means all we need do is follow the road on the morrow and we'll pick up their tracks long before they reach the Yarrow Water. Assuming the blizzard disnae finish them off for us, that is.'

Ten

All was white. The sky was white, the ground was white, and the air was thick with millions of fat white snowflakes driven over the desolate moors by the mournful threnody of the wind. Only the other members of Bulchett's party offered a break from the eye-aching whiteness all around – those close enough for Kemp to make out through the flurries – and they were little more than dark grey shadows. The snow stuck to their clothing and seemed to grow thicker on the ground with each step. Already it was knee-deep even where it had not drifted; if it kept falling so thickly, it would not be long until it was waist deep, then chest deep, and how would they move through it then?

And it was growing dark. Kemp fancied that if they were caught out on the moors by nightfall they would be frozen to death before dawn. He welcomed a little privation, in the hope it would teach Tegg and the others the folly of following a man like Sir Alexander Bulchett, but he had not imagined anything like this. In his own way, he had been just as foolish as they, and now they would all pay for it with their lives.

He saw one of the shadows up ahead grab one of the other shadows to address him. Only the occasional handful of words was whipped his way by the wind.

'—must get out of this blizzard!' said Nompar.

'—see any shelter—' said Bulchett.

Kemp grabbed them both. 'We must hold on to one another! If we become separated, we may never find one another again!' He started grabbing the other shadows as they stumbled within reach, forming them into a chain with each man holding the belt of the man before him. As he did so, he took a headcount. 'Someone's missing!'

White faces stared back at him, red noses glowing between eyebrows and beards thick with snow, eyes dull with misery and fear.

'Where's Tegg?' Kemp cupped his hands around his mouth. 'Tegg! Lambert Tegg!'

The others took up the cry, bellowing into the snow. 'Are you sure it's wise?' Bulchett asked Kemp. 'Giving away our presence to anyone within earshot?'

'Who but Tegg is like to hear us? No one in his right mind would be out on the moors on such a day as this!'

'Lambert Tegg!' Gudgeon stumbled away from the huddle of men as he sought to project his voice further through the blizzard. Kemp realised the ploughman was about to get lost, too. 'God damn it!'

'Blasphemy!' said Vertue. 'The Lord will punish you for taking his name in vain.'

'I know, I know,' sighed Kemp. 'The ground will open up beneath my feet and I'll be dragged down to the fires of the Hell-pit. Trust me, Godwin: at my final judgement, blasphemy will be the least of the sins I must answer for.' Now Gudgeon had disappeared into the driving snow. 'Stay here, everyone. Keep together!'

Kemp plunged through the blizzard after Gudgeon. The twin furrows the ploughman had ploughed through the snow on the ground were easy to follow. If Kemp moved fast enough, they would help him find his way back to the others before the drifting snow covered them.

Gudgeon had moved further and faster than Kemp had anticipated, however. He had thought only to dart a few yards away from the others to drag the ploughman back, but it seemed to take an inordinately long time to catch up with him. The thick snow dragging at his legs did not help, and he had to keep blinking as the icy wind drove fat flakes into his eyes.

'Gudgeon!' he shouted. 'Hob Gudgeon!'

At last he saw a figure ahead of him through the snow. He grabbed him by the arm. Gudgeon turned to face him.

'We must stay together!' Kemp yelled at him. Gudgeon just looked at him with eyes dull with incomprehension. When Kemp began to retrace his footsteps in the snow, dragging Gudgeon after him, the ploughman made no effort to resist.

Already the falling snow had begun to cover their traces behind them. As thick as it fell, the track they had left was too deep to be missed even beneath a covering of fresh snow, though perhaps if Kemp had taken a few minutes longer to find the ploughman, things might have turned out differently. As it was, they were able to stumble back to where the others waited. And when they got there, they found Tegg had found his way back to them, too.

'There's a croft o'er yon!' Tegg pointed into the swirling snow with his uninjured arm.

'Lead the way!' said Bulchett.

Tegg set off, following his own footsteps, and Bulchett held on to his belt, while Crawley held on to the scabbard of Bulchett's sword, Nompar held on to Crawley's belt, and so on. Kemp brought up the rear, clutching Gudgeon's belt. Tegg must have been retracing his own steps through the snow: he could not possibly have found his way through the blizzard otherwise; it was a miracle he had found the croft in the first place.

After they had trudged down a slope the best part of a furlong, heads bowed against the driving snow, the shadow of a grey hump loomed out of the blizzard. On closer inspection, Kemp saw stones piled beneath the drifted snow on the leeward side and, when he moved closer still, he saw a door amongst the stones, and a tiny, shuttered window.

Bulchett struggled with the latch for a moment, then got the door open and led the way in. The others followed. Kemp stepped over the threshold into a wall of warmth, so welcome after the stinging cold of the blizzard, he scarcely minded that the reek of smoke from the peat fire stung his aching eyes. Despite the few rush-lights burning about the place, making it stink of tallow, the smoke from the fire reduced visibility inside the croft almost as much as the blizzard did outside. Kemp felt his cheeks tingle as sensation returned to his numbed face. While the others brushed the snow off their shoulders and stamped numb feet against the earth floor, shrugging off their gear and unbuttoning their cote-hardies, he looked around to see who had started the fire.

A young couple in their twenties huddled in the far corner, their faces pallid in the firelight as they stared at the ten strangers who had invaded their home. The man was well-made and handsome, with crisp black hair, his jaw clean-shaven to reveal a strong and dimpled chin. The woman was fresh-faced and flaxen-haired, buxom and pretty. Kemp would have preferred a wart-faced hag: he glanced at the others, saw leers on the faces of Bulchett, Haine, Fisher, Vertue and Gudgeon, and foresaw trouble ahead. In Kemp's world women had their place, and that place was a stew-house, where the women had little left to lose and had been sufficiently toughened to know how to handle men like Kemp. This lass lacked that hardened look.

But it was obvious the couple presented no immediate threat to the ten men who had barged uninvited into their croft, so Kemp closed the door behind him to keep out the cold, snow-laced air.

'Have no fear, good people,' said Bulchett. 'We mean you no harm. My men and I only seek shelter for the night.'

'You're English!' The young man looked pale in the glow of the fire, and the woman clung to him fearfully.

'We are,' said Kemp. 'But give us no trouble and we'll give you none in return.'

'You live here alone?' asked Tegg. 'Just the two of you?'

The man did not answer, no doubt reluctant to admit to their vulnerability. Kemp cast his gaze around the interior of the croft: a byre at one end with a cow, a couple of pigs and some chickens in it, a little pottage simmering in a kettle suspended over the peat fire in the central hearth. A rough piece of sacking hung over an alcove opposite the byre. Kemp tweaked it aside to reveal a bed place that would be very cosy for two. He let the sacking fall back. There was no sign of any children or any other relatives.

'How far to your nearest neighbours?' asked Tegg.

'Niall Fraser lives in the next glen.' The man fidgeted as he spoke, his eyes glancing up to the timbers supporting the roof. Kemp could see white all around his irises, and was sure the man was lying. 'And Sir James Hay's men-at-arms often patrol all the glens about Neidpath Castle.'

'Making sure all his sheep are safe, like a good shepherd.' Kemp did not believe a word of it.

'The next glen might as well be a thousand miles away, on a night such as this,' said Crawley.

'I am Nompar de Savignac, Bourc of Cazoulat,' the Gascon told the crofters, as formally as if he had met them in the great hall at Westminster Palace rather than in the course of invading their home. 'And these gentlemen are Sir Alexander Bulchett, his squire Rowland Crawley, and Martin Kemp, Lambert Tegg, Kenrick Haine, Simkin Fisher, Dunstan Young, Godwin Vertue and Robert Gudgeon.' He gestured to each in turn.

Kemp was impressed Nompar had taken the trouble to remember all their names. He wondered that the *bourc* had bothered to introduce them to the crofters at all. If something bad happened at the croft this night – and Kemp would have laid odds-on that it would – and either of the crofters lived to tell the tale, then the names of Savignac and Bulchett would ever after be impugned. Then it occurred to him perhaps that was exactly why Nompar had performed the introductions: now Bulchett had an incentive to see to it that the men under his command behaved themselves. He smiled; the *bourc* could be a cunning devil, in his way.

'Ah'm Michie Liddell,' said the man. 'This is my wife, Tibbie.'

Haine leered. 'A handsome wife!'

Kemp clipped him around the back of the head. Haine scowled at him. 'Do that again,' he told Kemp, 'and I'll kill you.'

Kemp did it again. 'Keep a civil tongue in your head.'

'You're frae France, Sir Nompar?' Tibbie asked shyly.

'From Gascony,' the *bourc* corrected her. 'I am a vassal of King Edward.'

Fisher eyed the stew simmering in the kettle. 'D'you have any food?'

'We've scarce enough to feed ourselves,' said Liddell.

'Kill a pig,' said Haine. 'Then there'll be plenty to go around.'

'We cannae afford to kill a pig this year!'

'No need to kill a pig,' said Kemp. 'The meat will turn rotten before we can finish our mutton. Everyone give some of your lamb to Mistress Liddell. She can put it in the stew, and perhaps bake some oatcakes to eat with it.'

Tibbie glanced at her husband. He nodded. She took some oats from a lidded bucket and began to grind them in a mortar with a pestle. Kemp, meanwhile, took some mutton from his poke, putting it on a dish he found. He handed it to Young. 'Pass it around. Make sure everyone adds at least as much mutton as I have.'

'Owt to drink in this hovel?' asked Haine.

Liddell poured some ale from a jug into a wooden mazer. Bulchett took a swig and passed it to Nompar. The men began to make themselves comfortable amongst their discarded gear on the floor. The tension that had dominated the room from the moment Bulchett and his men had entered began to ease. Even Liddell and his wife began to look as though they could imagine living until dawn. Kemp took a sip of ale and wondered if that was true.

'This ale's not bad,' said Fisher. 'You brew this yourself, Tibbie?'

'It's my mother's recipe.'

'Ye know why they have ale tasters in London, divven't ye, Hob?' said Fisher. 'They slip wolf's-bane in every ale tub that's brewed in the city. That way if there are any werewolves amongst the folk of London, their power to turn into a wolf is quashed.'

'Is that true?' asked Gudgeon, wide-eyed.

'It's drivel, Hob,' said Kemp. 'Pay him no heed.'

'It's God's own truth, I tell you,' said Fisher. 'And it works: that's why there are so few werewolf attacks in London. The only trouble is, the babies of women who swallowed wolf's-bane while they were with child grow up to be barren. If it wasn't for all the country folk that move to London in search of work, in two generations the city would be bereft of all living citizens.'

'You're a barrel full of turds, Fisher,' growled Kemp.

'Divven't believe me if you divven't want to. But I'll touch no ale brewed in London.'

'Put a bit more mutton in than that, Godwin,' said Young.

Vertue was trying to pass the dish to Tegg. 'I put in as much meat as anyone.'

'You added that piece.' Young pointed. 'Half as much as anyone else.'

'That piece and that piece.' Vertue pointed to another collop of mutton. 'You weren't watching close enough.'

'I were watching like a hawk. That's one of the pieces Hob added.'

While Young and Vertue argued, Kemp saw Liddell whisper in his wife's ear. She blanched, but nodded. 'What are you two whispering about?' he asked.

'Nothing!' protested the young crofter. 'Ah swear, as God's my witness.'

'Don't take the Lord's name in vain. It upsets Godwin there. I saw you whisper in Tibbie's ear. What did you tell her?'

'Ah was only warning her that we must be on our best behaviour while you're our guests.' Once again Liddell fidgeted as he spoke and his eyes darted nervously about the room. Kemp did not believe a word of it, though Tibbie nodded eagerly as if to confirm what her husband said.

'Come and sit on this side of the hearth, Michie,' said Kemp. 'If you've got owt to say to your missus, say it so we can all hear. It's ill-mannered to whisper before guests.' He glanced at Bulchett. 'Is it far to Hermitage Castle from here?'

Liddell furrowed his brow. 'Hermitage Castle? Hermitage is in Liddesdale, eight leagues south-east of here.'

Kemp frowned. If they had been marching towards Hermitage as Bulchett claimed, they should have been a good deal closer than that. 'Are you sure?'

'I ken where Hermitage lies. Which way did ye come?'

'Over the moors from Tweeddale.'

'Frae Tweeddale! You're heided in the wrong direction if ye came here frae there on your way to Hermitage. Ye'd have done better to follow the river downstream to Selkirk, then heid south by way o' Hawick.'

'Pay him no heed,' said Bulchett. 'You cannot trust what he says. He's our foe. There's nothing he'd like better than to send us the wrong way.'

'Maybe so, but I know Hawick lies south of Selkirk,' said Kemp, 'and I know it's but four leagues from Hawick to Hermitage because I've ridden that way myself. Christ's blood! Hold your tongue, Vertue. I warrant we're not even in Teviotdale yet!'

'Teviotdale!' Liddell laughed heartily. 'You're a long way frae Teviotdale, Inglisher. There's all of Ettrick Forest lies betwixt here and there.'

'God damn it!' Kemp glared at Bulchett. 'I knew that lichen grew on the north side of trees. You don't know west from north, Sir Alexander. You've been leading us the wrong way since noon! Since we left Lauderdale, I warrant.'

Gaping like a wronged man who had never known such injustice could exist in the world, Bulchett turned to Tegg and the others for support. 'Some peasant who'd like nothing better than to see us all caught by Lord Douglas' men tells you I've led you all astray, and you'd sooner believe him than me?'

'Pay no heed to Kemp, my lord,' said Crawley. 'He's a fool who knows naught of which he speaks.'

'Damned Midlanders,' growled Haine. 'They in't got the brains God gave 'em, nor sense enough to know when they divven't know what they speak of.'

'What say you, Sir Nompar?' asked Kemp. 'Shall we continue to follow Sir Alexander on the morrow, or should we set out on our own and head south with any of these men who have sense enough to follow us?'

'You're not going anywhere,' Bulchett growled before the *bourc* could reply. 'You're a prisoner, don't forget. You'll come with the rest of us, or I'll see you hanged from the next tree we pass with a bough strong enough to bear your weight.'

Tibbie saw Tegg scratch at the bandages on his wounded arm. 'You're hurt,' she said.

'It's nowt,' said the twentyman.

'Let me see. Ah might be able to make a poultice that will help to heal it.'

Tegg peeled off the bandages. The wound had stopped bleeding, but the skin around it was inflamed. 'That's bad,' said Tibbie.

'One of your countrymen did that to him,' said Haine. 'I'd not put any poultice any damned Scottish bitch prepared on a wound if I were you, Lambert. Belike it'll be poisoned.'

'Why do ye hate the Scots so much?' asked Tibbie.

'Because you're all scum. You invade our country, rape our women, put our homes to the torch and steal our cattle.'

'Remind me what we've been doing for the past two weeks?' Nompar murmured to Kemp.

Haine overheard him. 'They started it!' he insisted angrily. 'Why can the rivelings not stay in their own country, and accept that we're just better than they are?'

'The Scots are God's bairns too,' said Vertue.

'No, they're not,' said Haine. 'They're sons of Belial! What about the Moors, Godwin? Did God make them too? Of course not! They're nowt but... imitations of men; demons put on this earth by the Devil himself to torment good, honest, God-fearing Christian Englishmen.'

'Pay him no heed,' Tegg told the Liddells. 'He's a worthless whoreson and in his heart he knows it. Thinking being English makes him better than foreigners as a matter of course is the only way he's got to feel good about himself.'

'Like Godwin jumping down everyone's throat whenever they blaspheme,' said Young. 'They're as bad as each other, just wanting to feel superior to someone.'

'If I correct you when you blaspheme, I do it for the good of your soul. There's nowt in it for me.'

'What?' asked Young. 'Not even a sense of smug self-righteousness?'

Vertue sniffed and did not deign to reply.

Tibbie turned to Haine. 'If ye need to feel superior to others, did ye ever think about… trying to be a better man?'

'I divven't have to try,' the butcher asserted sullenly. 'I *am* better. Better than you and your husband, anyroad.'

Tibbie turned her attention back to Tegg's arm. 'Is there owt you can do for it?' he asked.

'Maybe. Ah'll need to prepare that poultice. Silver-weed, pennywort, nettles, mistletoe, meadowsweet, mallows, lamb's-tongue, horsemint, groundsel, chick-weed, and twa stems of red and rotting dwarf elder. It must be boiled wi' wheat meal, then allowed to cool and mixed with egg yolks, butter and swine's grease.' She turned to her husband. 'Could ye pass me my herbs, dearest?'

'Of course.' Liddell stood up, reaching for a basket hung from a nail hammered into one of the roofbeams along with several pans.

The pitchfork must have been resting across the beams above them: Kemp did not see it until Liddell had it in his hands and was lunging its tines at his chest. The Midlander barely had time to throw himself aside. Rising to his feet, he caught hold of the pitchfork's haft before Liddell could thrust again. Chest to chest, the two of them grappled for possession of it. Liddell was as strong as he looked, and with a sudden jerk sent Kemp staggering back. The Midlander felt something against the back of his calves – probably Gudgeon – and fell over, sprawling. But he kept his grip on the pitchfork's haft, and pulled Liddell down after him.

As the two of them rolled over and over on the floor, Kemp was vaguely aware of the shouts of alarm from the others as they moved around, trying to get out of the way. The door must have opened, for Kemp was conscious of a gust of icy wind laced with snow slashing through the warm fug inside the croft. Liddell rolled on top, leaning on the pitchfork with all his weight, trying to crush the haft into Kemp's throat. The Midlander managed to lock his elbows, holding him at bay long enough for Nompar to step up behind Liddell and kick him in the crotch. The crofter's face turned puce in the firelight, and Kemp managed to throw him off sideways.

Liddell fell across the fire in the hearth. Shrieking, he rolled off it again, but not before his tunic caught fire. He beat at it, screaming, until Fisher snatched up the jug of ale and splashed it on him, dousing the flames. Kemp buried the tines of the pitchfork in the floor and grabbed a fistful of Liddell's chaperon, holding him up while he slammed a fist into his dimpled jaw. The crofter reeled. Kemp caught him before he crumpled to the floor, thrusting him towards Young and Vertue.

'Tie him up!' The door was still open. 'Who went out?' he asked. But he already knew who had gone out: only one thing could have induced Liddell to risk throwing away his life in a fight with ten men, and that was trying to buy his wife time to escape.

'The woman,' said Bulchett. 'The fellow with the torn ears went after her.'

Haine. Kemp was not sure which thought disquieted him most: Tibbie Liddell somehow fighting her way through the blizzard to raise the hue-and-cry for Bulchett and his men at Neidpath Castle, or the thought of Haine getting her to himself.

'Keep everyone in here,' he told Nompar, who nodded. Kemp swept his mantle about his shoulders and dashed out, pulling the door to behind him.

The snow still fell as thick as before, but now night was falling and it was colder and darker. There remained enough light for Kemp to make out the fresh footprints, Tibbie's leading the way, Haine's bigger prints criss-crossing them, trampling over them in places. Kemp reckoned they would have to catch Tibbie quickly if they were to find their way back to the croft before the snow hid their tracks.

The ground sloped down: someone had cut steps in the hillside here, perhaps even paved them with flagstones. At the bottom, Kemp sensed the tracks he was following veered off the path. He saw a hunched figure with snow on his shoulders up ahead and reached for his sword, but it was only a bush, its foliage weighed down with snow. The tracks led past it. The wind blew the snow into his eyes now, blinding him. He raised an arm to his brow, trying to shade his eyes against the flakes that pelted him. He could barely see where he was putting his feet, much less follow the tracks. Then the ground fell away beneath him and, before he knew it, he was falling into darkness.

Eleven

Kemp's guts clenched with a sickening lurch. For one moment his heart was in his throat as he feared he had charged headlong over a high cliff. Scarcely had he time to realise he was falling before he plunged into a thick snowdrift. Shaken, frozen and struggling for breath, he tried to stand. The banked snow hemmed him in on all sides and every time he tried to put a hand down to push himself to his feet, the snow only crumpled beneath it.

At last he managed to get up and wade out of the drift. There were no other tracks in the snow nearby, and if Tibbie and Haine had come this way, not enough time had passed for the snow to cover their footprints. He tried to climb back up to the top of the bank he had fallen down, but it was too steep and his boots could gain no purchase in the snow. He started to trudge along the foot of the slope, hoping he would come to a place where it was shallow enough for him to climb up.

A woman screamed nearby; not from the top of the slope, but somewhere off to Kemp's right. He hurried towards the cry, or at least to where he had thought it had come from. The wind whipping snow over the crest of the slope distorted sounds, making it difficult to tell where they originated. He peered through the curtain of snowflakes falling through the darkness, listening for other sounds that might lead him to Haine and Tibbie. But the snow was not moving as swiftly nor as thickly here, and though it was more shadowy, without the icy wind burning his cheeks it felt less cold. A black burn trickled through the snow to his left, the shadow of another slope rising beyond it, and Kemp realised he had fallen into a small glen.

The burn meandered around a spur of ground jutting into the glen. Kemp was thinking that the spur offered a path a man might use to climb back out when he saw two sets of footprints leading down it, and knew he was on the right track. On the far side of the spur, Haine had Tibbie backed up against the trunk of a tree, trying to force a kiss upon her while she turned her head this way and that to avoid it, revulsion on her face.

Kemp grabbed a fistful of the cape of Haine's chaperon at the back, yanking him away from her. Frustrated lust transforming rapidly to hate, the butcher drew his cleaver from under his belt and slashed at his attacker. Kemp jumped back, the cleaver's razor-sharp edge missing his throat by inches. Kemp thought about drawing his broadsword, but he wanted to get Bulchett and all the men with him safely to Carlisle; even a whoreson like Haine.

The butcher slashed again. Kemp tried to catch him by the wrist, but Haine only slashed him across the palm, drawing blood.

While Kemp and Haine circled, Tibbie dashed away, disappearing into the darkness and the swirling flurries. Kemp realised he had to end this fight quickly if he was going to capture her before she reached Neidpath Castle.

Haine lunged again. Kemp ducked beneath the stroke. He slipped, making it look like an accident, and rolled on the ground. Rising on one knee, he reached out with his right hand as if to steady himself. Instead he scooped up a fistful of snow and threw it into Haine's face. The butcher reeled, wiping his face with his sleeve. He was only blinded for a couple of heartbeats, but that was all the time Kemp needed. He launched himself to his feet, catching hold of Haine's wrist and twisting his arm up between his shoulder blades until he cried out and dropped the cleaver. Kemp pushed him away, slamming the sole of one boot against the butcher's rump and sending him sprawling in the snow. He stooped to snatch up the cleaver, brandishing it at Haine when the butcher rose to his feet and turned to face him.

Kemp gestured with the cleaver to where Tibbie's footprints led away through the snow. 'After her, damn your nose!'

Haine looked at Kemp with suspicion, wondering why the Midlander had not already killed him.

'I don't care what anyone says,' said Kemp. 'You're still one of my men, and I don't slay my own men. As long as you behave yourself, that is: the next time you try to force yourself on a woman, you're a dead man. Now stop wasting time!'

Haine nodded and began following the footprints. Kemp went after him.

'What about my cleaver?'

'You don't need a cleaver to catch a slip of a girl. You can have it back when you've earned my trust. And believe me, you've got a way to go.'

The two of them ran through the falling snow. The ravine broadened out again and the tracks swung away from the burn, then curved back towards it, disappearing into the water. Kemp saw no footprints on the opposite bank.

'Silly bitch thinks she can throw us off the scent by splashing through the beck,' said Haine. 'She's too foolish to see all we have to do is follow the beck till we catch her, or find her footprints leading out again.'

'Which way did she go?' asked Kemp.

Haine indicated where her footprints led into the water at an angle. 'Downstream, of course!'

'You're the silly bitch, Kenrick. If she's clever enough to realise her footprints will lead us to her, she's clever enough to throw us off the scent by doubling back on herself.' Kemp followed the bank of the burn upstream and after a couple of hundred yards he saw where she had disturbed the snow by climbing out on the opposite bank.

Kemp and Haine picked their way through one of the shallower parts of the burn – it was not a night for going about with wet hose – and followed her footprints up a path angling up the opposite side of the glen. The wind and the snow grew thicker once more as they breasted the crest of the slope and emerged from the trees.

They were moving across open ground now. Kemp could not see more than a couple of dozen yards and wondered that Tibbie could find her way in such a blizzard, for he saw no landmarks that might guide her, but her steps seemed to run straight for all that. After a couple of furlongs, he caught a glimpse of her green kirtle, grey in the twilight. She had not had time to grab a mantle on her way out of the croft and if they did not catch her, Kemp feared she would freeze to death before she got halfway to Neidpath Castle.

She was moving fast, but the kirtle's hem impeded her. Kemp redoubled his efforts and soon overhauled her. He reached out to clap a hand on her shoulder. With a sob, she twisted out of his grip and dodged in another direction, doubling back, only to see Haine moving to cut her off. Again she changed direction, trying to duck past Kemp, but her shoes slipped in snow and she fell. He expected her to get up again, but she just lay there, sobbing.

Kemp and Haine stood over her, hands on their knees, both panting. 'Come on,' Kemp told her. 'Let's get in out of this blizzard before we catch our deaths. If you and your husband will but behave yourselves, I promise no harm will come to you. In the morning we'll let you both go and be on our way.' He helped her to her feet, shrugging off his mantle and draping it over her shoulders.

They traced their own footsteps back to the croft, Kemp keeping a firm grip on Tibbie's upper arm to discourage her from making any more attempts to escape. By the time they had climbed up the spur on the other side of the ravine, however, the snow had covered their tracks to the extent where it was impossible to follow them. Haine criss-crossed the ground, trying to pick up the trail again, but at last had to give it up. 'Do you know which way your croft lies?' Kemp asked Tibbie.

She looked at him disdainfully and said nothing.

'You'd freeze to death for the pleasure of making life difficult for us?' he asked her.

'One Scottish life for two English ones. That seems like a fair exchange to me.'

Kemp thought he saw a light through the snow. Staring in that direction, he caught sight of it again. It was difficult to make out what it was through the blizzard, but there was definitely something there. He headed towards it, dragging Tibbie behind him, and Haine followed them both. In a couple of dozen yards, the light had resolved itself into a lanthorn held aloft, and soon they saw Nompar holding it. Seeing them approach, he lowered the lanthorn and smiled.

'I was worried you might get lost.'

'We might've, if you hadn't shown us the light.' Kemp tried to move past him into the croft, but the *bourc* moved to block his way. 'Stand aside, Nompar! It's as cold as marble-stone out here.'

'Best not to let Domaisèla Liddell in without preparing her to be stunned in her wits.'

'Did someone dent one of her dishes?' sneered Haine.

Tibbie picked up on Nompar's grim tone before Kemp did. She jerked her arm from the Midlander's grip and dodged past the *bourc* to tug the door open. She stepped inside, and a moment later Kemp heard a shriek of despair. He raced in to see what the fuss was about, and saw her standing just beyond the threshold, her eyes fixed on where her husband lay on the floor, his eyes staring sightlessly, a bloody gash in the small of his back where someone had stabbed him.

As Nompar and Haine followed Kemp over the threshold, the latter pulling the door to behind him, Kemp stared at the others as they sat around, indifferent to the corpse at their feet. As the full horror of it dawned on her, Tibbie gave a keening wail and sank to her knees, tears flooding from her eyes.

'What the hell did you kill him for?' demanded Kemp.

'He broke free and grew frenzied,' said Nompar. 'He attacked Fisher.'

'There was no need to slay him!' protested Kemp.

Fisher glared at him. 'What were I supposed to do? He would ha' killed me!' He looked pale and shaken: Kemp was willing to believe the cooper's apprentice had acted in self-defence out of genuine fear for his life.

Tibbie rose to her feet and attacked Kemp, pounding his chest with her fists. 'Ye told me Michie and I would come to nae harm! Ye promised...'

Kemp let her pound away a little while longer, then caught her by the wrists and gently but firmly pushed her away from him. Putting an arm about her shoulders, Nompar led her away. Young filled a beaker with ale and handed it to her. She accepted it without raising it to her lips, staring only at her husband's corpse.

'You might at least have covered the body over,' said Kemp. 'Or better yet put it outside.'

'Dinnae touch him!' Abruptly restored to life, Tibbie flung the beaker at Kemp's head, and he only ducked it narrowly. She knelt on the floor by her husband's corpse, raising his head and shoulders so she could clasp him in a final embrace. 'Stay away frae him, ye dirty English whoresons!' Tears streaming down her cheeks, she bowed her head over the body. Her shoulders heaved with sobs. Nompar tried to lead her away so they could carry the corpse out, but Kemp only touched the *bourc* on the shoulder and, when Nompar glanced at him, he shook his head. They had taken her husband from her; the very least they could do was allow her to grieve.

Bulchett dipped a ladle into the mutton stew simmering in the kettle over the hearth. 'Supper's ready!'

'How can you think of your stomach at a time like this, Sir Alexander?' asked Vertue.

The knight shrugged. 'Got to keep body and soul together. A healthy mind in a healthy body and all that.' He ladled some of the stew into a dish and began spooning it between his blubbery lips.

Bulchett was right, in a way, if not particularly sensitive about it: there was no sense letting good food go to waste, especially when in a day or two they might be starving again. Each man helped himself to a receptacle to hold his portion – there were only two bowls, but when a man was not too fussy about what to eat out of, there were plenty of alternatives – and retired to a corner of the croft to eat in silence. When the last man had taken his share, there was a portion left over. Perhaps feeling guilty, Fisher poured it into a skillet and proffered it to Tibbie. She ignored him, so he put it on the floor beside her so she could help herself later if she changed her mind. Something told Kemp she would not.

When they had finished eating, they sat around the hearth, playing at dice and telling jokes and stories for an hour to try to raise their spirits. Tibbie did not move from where she cradled her husband's body in her arms.

'I suppose we had best turn in for the night,' Bulchett said at last.

Tegg rubbed his bandaged arm. 'Should we set guards?'

Crawley opened the door a couple of inches and peered out, but only for a heartbeat: even through the narrow gap, a flurry of snowflakes was borne in on an icy draught. He slammed it again. 'I doubt we need fear anyone coming hither while this blizzard keeps up, and the weather doesn't look like breaking soon.'

'Someone must keep an eye on the prisoners,' said Bulchett.

'What prisoners?' asked Tegg.

'Kemp and the woman.'

The Midlander smiled. 'You frightened I might run off in the night and go to throw my lot in with Lord Douglas's men?'

'I'd not put it past you. And who knows what mischief the woman may get up to if she's left unattended? Slit all our throats in revenge for her husband, I shouldn't wonder. These Scots are a wild, savage folk.'

'We should tie her up,' said Crawley. 'Then there'd be no need for anyone to keep watch over her and we'd all get a good night's sleep.'

'Tie them both up,' agreed Fisher, jerking his head towards Kemp.

'Give her to me.' Haine leered. 'I'll keep her too busy to get up to any mischief.'

'Hey! If he gets a turn at her, I want a turn too,' said Fisher.

'Anyone touches that woman does so over my dead body,' said Nompar.

'What difference does it make?' asked Haine. 'We'll slay her in the morning anyroad. Happen we'll have some sport with her first.'

Kemp glanced at where Tibbie still cradled her husband's head on the floor, wondering what she made of all this talk of raping and killing her. If she was even taking any of it in, she gave no sign of it.

'Who said aught of killing her?' asked Nompar.

'Yon fellow speaks true.' Bulchett indicated Haine. 'It's not as if we can turn her loose to run to Neidpath Castle and rouse Sir James Hay's men.'

'At least let's sleep on it,' said Nompar. 'Let us not murder her tonight and then wake up in the morning to find some turn in our fortunes renders her death needless. Gudgeon and Young were on watch last night. I suggest Haine, Vertue and Fisher take turns keeping watch tonight.'

'And who'll watch the watchmen?' asked Kemp. 'If Mistress Liddell needs guarding, Haine and Fisher are the ones she needs guarding from.'

'You need have no fears on that accompt,' said Nompar. 'I'm a light sleeper. And if aught befalls Mistress Liddell tonight, I vow, by the bones of Saint Miramunda, Master Liddell will not be the only man we leave behind who'll be in need of a grave.'

That settled, they doused the rushlights and Bulchett crawled under the blankets in the bed place while the rest of them made themselves as comfortable as they could on the floor. Tibbie's sobs, which had been inaudible while the men's talk had filled the croft, now seemed loud when the only other sound was the wind howling about the eaves.

Kemp had killed so many men in King Edward's service he had lost count, but Michie Liddell's death preyed on his conscience more than most, even though he could not see that he was directly responsible for the man's death. Nevertheless, he turned over the evening's events in his mind, wondering if things might have turned out differently if he had followed some other course of action. A few months ago he had decided the best way to atone for the sins of his youth was to protect those who could not protect themselves. The Liddells were exactly the sort of people he had in mind; thus far, his efforts at redeeming himself could hardly be called an unqualified success.

–

Reid was woken at first cockcrow. His instinct was to turn over and go back to sleep, but he managed to overcome it. Rising from where he slept on the rush-strewn floor of the hall – Howie Ure's inn at Innerleithen did not stretch to private rooms – he stumbled through the darkness to the table, prompting sleepy grumbles from the other reivers as he inadvertently kicked them. Finding a rush-light, he lit it with his tinderbox, then used its glow to find where Nixon slept. He shook him by the shoulder.

'First cockcrow, Rab. Ye said we'd rise at first cockcrow and be on our way before dawn.'

'Go to Freuchie and fry mice!' muttered Nixon.

'Come on, Rab! The early bird catches the worm. The sooner we catch these Englishmen, the sooner we can return to Roxburghshire.'

'Awreet, awreet! Ye heard the man, lads. Rouse yourselves!'

With much yawning, stretching, hawking and spitting, breaking of wind and scratching of groins, the reivers roused themselves. The noise roused Ure himself from his bower, a wizened old man with white hair and unkempt eyebrows.

'That'll be sixteen shillings and sixpence,' said the innkeeper.

'Pay the man, Sir Archibald,' said Nixon, stumbling out into the snow.

Reid left the knight reaching for his purse with a bewildered and indignant expression on his face, following Nixon out into the cold. It was still dark out, with scarcely any trace of the sunrise approaching from the east and no stars in the sky, though the snow which lay thickly everywhere reflected what little dingy-blue light there was. The reivers took turns at the pit that served as a latrine for the inn. Clouds of condensation billowed from their lips as they complained of the King of England choosing to campaign at such a bitter season.

As Reid fetched his hobby from the stables, he noticed Sneith hanging a crossbow from a peg on the cantle of his saddle.

'Did ye borrow yon toy from your lassie?'

The man-at-arms glowered. 'That's no toy. I can slay a man at a hundred yards with that.'

'Ye should learn to use a man's weapon,' said Nixon. 'In the time it takes ye to reload yon jim-crack, there's no' one of my men cannae shoot half a dozen arrows the same distance.'

They led their horses out into the snow and mounted up. 'Will we not take some morrow-meat?' asked Sneith.

'Morrow-meat!' snorted Nixon. 'Morrow-meat is for maids. The sooner we set off, the sooner we'll catch these English skybalds. Now let's make haste, and hope we pick up their trail this side of Yarrowdale!' Urging his horse into a trot, he signalled the others to follow him.

Twelve

Despite his troubled conscience, Kemp must have drifted off at some point, for the next thing he knew he was dreaming he was in a house that was on fire. The flames were all around him and the only way out was through an opening in the roof. He tried to climb up to it, but then someone caught hold of his foot and held him back. He glanced down and saw Sir Alexander Bulchett, who explained that the house was not on fire and he was only imagining the flames searing his cheeks. Then the whole house collapsed, the floor fell away and Kemp plunged through it into a great, dark pool of cold water. The shock of the splash was so great that he woke up to find the only fire was the embers in the hearth in the middle of the floor. Fisher was closing the door.

Kemp sat up. 'What hour is it?'

'Gone terce, I reckon.'

'Terce' was midway between dawn and noon. 'Gone terce! For Christ's sake! Why did you not wake us?'

'Calm yourself, Kemp!' sneered Fisher. 'It's not yet first light. God's truth! I can scarce believe you were taken in so easily.'

'Bravely done,' Kemp acknowledged ironically. 'You told a credible lie, and like a fool I believed it. I bow to my superior in wit and cunning.'

He roused the others. Tegg looked grey and sickly and muttered deliriously even after the Midlander had patted him lightly on the cheek a few times. 'Ephraim is as an heifer that is taught, and loveth to tread out the corn; but I passed over upon her fair neck: I will make Ephraim to ride; Judah shall plough, and Jacob shall break his clods.'

'What's he saying?' asked Gudgeon.

'Summat from the Bible,' said Vertue. 'The Book of Hosea, I think.'

Kemp laid the back of a hand to Tegg's brow. 'He's feverish.'

Tegg clutched at Kemp's arm. 'Ye have ploughed wickedness, ye have reaped iniquity; ye have eaten the fruit of lies: because thou didst trust in thy way, in the multitude of thy mighty men. Therefore shall a tumult arise among thy people, and all thy fortresses shall be spoiled, as Shalman spoiled Betharbel in the day of battle: the mother was dashed in pieces upon her children.'

'He's delirious,' said Haine.

'Is he well enough to walk?' asked Bulchett.

'He'll have to be,' said Kemp. 'We can't leave him here for the Scots. If they should find him lying here next to the body of their neighbour, they'll tear him to pieces!'

While Vertue got the fire going in the hearth, Gudgeon carried the kettle outside, scouring out the traces of supper with fistfuls of snow. They made some oatmeal pottage. Kemp saw that the skillet of mutton stew Fisher had given to Tibbie remained untouched, but he was reassured to see her accept a dish of pottage when Young handed it to her. It seemed to signify that while she might still be grieving for her husband, she was not despairing to the point where she no longer cared for her own life.

'What's the use in feeding her?' asked Haine. 'If we're going to slay her—'

'No one is slaying her,' said Kemp. 'She's coming with us.'

'The devil she is!' protested Bulchett. 'She'll only hold us up.'

'Want her for yourself, do you?' Haine sneered at Kemp. 'Can't say I blame you for that. She's a tasty morsel. But I divven't see why you should have her all to yourself.'

'Hold your tongue, you lickerous caitiff!' snapped Kemp. 'Just because you cannot govern your lusts, don't judge the rest of us by your own foul standards.' Even if he could atone for all his other sins, he fancied his hypocrisy alone would be enough to condemn him to the fires of Hell for eternity. He turned to Bulchett. 'She'll not hold us up; I'll see to that. And tomorrow morning, when we've put another day's march between us and Neidpath Castle, we'll turn her loose.'

'It is a good plan,' Nompar said before Bulchett could object further. 'If she does go to warn Sir James Hay, he and his men will be two days behind us. If we push hard, in three days we can be across the border and safely back in England.'

'Very well.' Bulchett jabbed a finger at Kemp. 'But I'm holding you responsible. If anyone dies because she holds us up or betrays us to her countrymen...'

They spooned down their pottage, performed their ablutions and gathered up their gear. Kemp went through the chest containing the Liddells' clothing and bedding. There was a good woollen mantle for Tibbie, and a pair of gloves and a hood trimmed with rabbit fur that would keep her warm. 'Wear these,' he told her. 'You have a good pair of boots?'

176

She produced a suitable pair from an alcove.

'Good,' said Kemp. 'Put them on. Do as you're told, and no harm will come to you. I give you my word.'

'Last night ye gave me your word nae harm would come to Michie.' She looked pointedly at her husband's corpse.

'I failed you once,' he admitted. 'I'll not do it a second time.'

Bulchett opened the door to find the snow had piled high against it during the night. He fought his way through, and the others followed him out to find that while the sky remained grey and threatening and a cold wind still gusted, at least it had stopped snowing, and they could see down the glen for a couple of miles to where it opened out into a valley with the peaks of snow-covered hills rising high on the far side. There were no other houses in sight, neither crofts nor villages, no church spires rising in the distance, and Kemp wondered that the Liddells had chosen to live in such a desolate place. He glanced back up the valley behind them, trying to work out where he and his companions had descended the previous afternoon. There were woods up there, but he was pretty sure they had not passed through them in the blizzard.

Those of them who thought the past few days had been exceptionally cold got an unpleasant shock. The frozen air tingled with unpleasant severity on their faces. 'Sweet Jesu, it's cold!' gasped Crawley, clouds of condensation billowing from his mouth at each syllable.

'Th-th-that's b-b-blasphemy!' Vertue stammered through chattering teeth.

Everyone paused to rearrange mantles, collars and mufflers, trying to make sure as little of their skin was exposed to the cold as possible.

After pausing to consult his scrap of parchment, Bulchett led the way. Heading down the valley, he immediately began to ascend the slopes on the right.

'Should we not make for the valley below?' Kemp called to him, pointing.

Bulchett indicated a pass between two hills. 'Shortcut!' he called back.

'Shortcut to where?' wondered Kemp. 'Perdition?'

He kept a close eye on Tibbie as they trudged on through the snow; or rather, stayed close to her and kept an eye on Haine. Gudgeon loyally stayed by Tegg, occasionally taking him by the elbow to steer him in the right direction when the delirious twentyman's feet seemed inclined to lead him astray. The going was heavy enough to make them pant, and each indrawn breath of the icy air felt like brimstone in their lungs, but at least the exertion helped to warm them up.

When they crested the brow of a saddle between two hills, they saw a frozen lake dusted with snow covered most of the valley bottom. It was impossible to see how long the lake was – a couple of miles away the valley forked, and the lake curved out of sight into the southern branch – but it was nearly half a mile in breadth.

'Is it safe to cross?' wondered Crawley.

'Certainly,' said Tibbie.

'I'd not take her word for it!' said Haine.

'We've no need to cross,' said Bulchett. 'We'll skirt the northern shore.'

'When do we start heading south?' demanded Kemp.

'Soon enough. Upon my word, Kemp! You're a most untrusting fellow. How I pity you, going through life with such a bleak outlook, blind to all the joys and wonders that the world has to offer!'

'I'll pause to appreciate the joys and wonders that the world has to offer just as soon as we're all safely back in England.'

Bulchett began to pick his way down the icy slope with Crawley at his elbow, ready to reach out and steady his master any time it looked as though he might lose his footing.

Haine fell into step alongside the *bourc*. 'Is it true you were a vassal of John of Valois till last year, Sir Nompar?'

The *bourc* inclined his head.

'How do we know we can trust you?'

'I have sworn homage to your King Edward. Your king is my king.' He gave Haine a sidelong glance, and saw the sceptical look on the butcher's face. 'Ask Master Kemp, if you do not believe me.'

'Not sure I'd take that rascal's word for owt. If you can betray your allegiance to John of Valois so easily, how do we know you'll not switch back again?'

'As God is my witness, the decision was by no means taken lightly.'

'Why change your allegiance, then?'

'I heard Kemp made him a prisoner,' said Fisher. 'Switching to King Edward's allegiance was a good way to dodge his obligations.'

Nompar smiled. 'Any debts between Kemp and I are no man's business but our own; yet I will assure you that no change of allegiance on my part could negate any debt I owe to any man.'

'Why did you change your allegiance?' asked Gudgeon.

'I used to think loyalty was like a system of rivers: each peasant like a little stream, paying homage to his lord; each lord a river paying homage to a greater lord, and the greatest of lords paying homage to his king, who is the greatest of all rivers, emptying into the sea.'

'And now?' asked Crawley.

'Now I understand better, I think: loyalty is like the tides in the sea, first flowing one way, then the other, as necessity demands.' Nompar turned to Haine. 'You call my change of allegiance a betrayal of Valois; perhaps it is. But my forefathers were loyal to Valois' forefathers for generations. When an enemy of my family used his blandishments to falsely persuade Valois that my father was a heretic, Valois too easily believed him, without troubling to hear my father's side of the story. My father was tortured to death by the Holy Inquisition when a word from Valois would have spared him; my brother and I have been declared fugitives from justice, and the estates my brother should have inherited have been handed to the very enemy who spread such calumnies against us. When loyalty only flows in one direction – when a man's liege offers him nothing in return for his homage but injustice and betrayal – then for a vassal to persist in his loyalty to that liege is worse than folly: it is an act of wanton self-destruction.'

They followed the northern shore of the lake for half a league, to where it curved to the south. Another road branched off, leading west, up the other fork of the valley, where craggy mountains loomed on all sides. Bulchett paused to check his parchment again, and suddenly veered up the road to the west, into the mountains.

'Sir Alexander?' called Kemp.

Bulchett turned back. 'Aye?'

'Where are you bound?'

The knight pointed into the mountains. 'To England!'

'That's west. England lies to the south.'

'We must go west to go south.'

'That's drivel! Enough of your lies, Sir Alexander! Where are you leading us, and why?'

Bulchett sighed. 'Very well, then. If you must know the truth… we seek the Brazen Head of Pope Sylvester.'

Kemp felt as though he had strayed out on to the surface of the frozen lake, and the ice was cracking beneath him. 'What in hell is the Brazen Head of Pope Sylvester?'

'Pope Sylvester II was a powerful necromancer,' said Bulchett. 'The legends tell how he had a great head forged in brass, and trapped a demoness named Meridiana within it. Once trapped inside the head, this demoness was bound by sorcery to answer any question put to her by whoever possessed the head. Any question, Kemp! Can you imagine how much power it would grant to a man, if he could be given the answer to any question that might vex him?'

Kemp gestured to the west. 'And you believe this head lies somewhere in yon mountains?'

'I'm certain of it! You've heard of Michael Scot, who was court astrologer to the Emperor Frederick II?'

'No.'

'Oh. Well, according to Matthew of Rochdale's *Vita Silvestri Papae*, after the emperor's death, Scot visited Rome, where he discovered the Brazen Head in a secret chamber in the papal palace. He brought it back to Scotland, after which it disappears from the pages of history. But, according to the *Chronica Johannis Glasguensis*, Scot was a disciple of Ranulf de Soulis, a necromancer who had a secret temple in a cave on Ragman's Law, a mountain not a day's march from here. Piecing those two facts together, I realised: would not Scot have inherited the lair of Soulis after the necromancer died? And if he continued to use it, where else would he hide the Brazen Head?'

'Do you tell me we're on a quest for a demoness entrapped in a brass head which can answer any question posed to it?'

Beaming, Bulchett nodded.

'I know what question I'd like to ask it.'

'Oh yes?'

'"Has Sir Alexander Bulchett lost his god-damned wits?"' Kemp gestured at Nompar, Tegg and the others. 'You put these men's lives at risk – deliberately led them astray, when they were in peril enough as it was – just so you could go chasing after a legend?'

''Tis no legend,' said Bulchett. 'It's there in Matthew of Rochdale's *Life of Pope Sylvester*.'

'Any damned fool with a quill and some ink can write some nonsense on parchment. That doesn't make it true. The world is full of copies of Aesop's Fables, but I never heard a fox nor a cockerel speak. Surely you know there's no such thing as magic, outside of fairy tales?'

Bulchett shook his head. 'You're wrong, Kemp. There *is* magic in the world. When I was a boy, one Yuletide a sorcerer from the Indies came to my father's castle, and entertained us by performing many wonders. Most marvellous of all, he took a cord and threw one end of it into the sky, where it hung unsupported. Then he shinned up it, and fought a battle with demons. The demons cut him up into many pieces, which they threw back to the ground. Yet through his mastery of necromancy, the sorcerer was able to draw the pieces together and heal himself. This I saw with my own eyes!'

Kemp gaped at him. Such credulity he could believe in a witless village oaf, but surely a courtly knight like Bulchett was not to be taken in so easily. 'That's a conjuring trick! I've seen similar tricks performed at castles and inns from Berwick to Avignon. I'll swear the men that did them are no more wizards than I! They're conjurors who use flashes of serpentine powder and mirrors of glass to distract your gaze from their trickery.'

Bulchett chuckled and shook his head, as if Kemp were the naïve one for believing that such wonders could be performed by conjuring rather than sorcery. 'There you go again with your melancholy temperament, seeing naught but dullness, blind to the marvels that surround us.'

'Even if there is a temple in a cave in Ragman's Law, you'll not find a brazen head with a demoness trapped inside because there are no such things as demons! You're chasing a chimera.'

'But what if I'm right?' asked Bulchett.

'You're wrong.'

'But hypothetically speaking… if I could lay my hands upon the Brazen Head… think of the power it would grant me, to have any question answered!'

Kemp shook his head. 'Some folk say you're a fool, Sir Alexander; others that you're a clever man, only feigning foolishness. I say you're as foolish as you feign, and fool enough to think otherwise.'

'Knowledge is power. There's always a way: you've just got to believe in it hard enough. I will be omniscient, and from omniscience it is but one short step to omnipotence! I will have the power to make myself emperor.'

'Good luck with that. I'm heading for England.' Kemp turned to the others. 'Coming, lads?'

'I go where Sir Alexander goes,' said Crawley. 'When he is emperor, he has promised to make me King of England.'

Kemp laughed. 'You plan to be King of England, do you? I'd call that treason, were it not such arrant nonsense. Come on, lads.'

Nompar moved to stand with Kemp. The other archers hesitated. Tegg was moving to follow Kemp when Gudgeon called after him. 'Hold up, Lambert. What if Sir Alexander's telling the truth, like?'

'Telling the truth?' Kemp said scornfully. 'Sir Alexander is incapable of telling the truth. He knows not the meaning of the word. He could not tell the truth if his life depended on it!'

'It's a two- or three-day march from here to England,' said Gudgeon. 'But if Sir Alexander becomes all-powerful, he can use sorcery to whisk us to Carlisle in less time than it takes to say a paternoster!'

'Hob's right!' Fisher said excitedly. 'We could be in Carlisle ahead of the king's host.'

'Hob's a credulous fool,' said Kemp. 'You of all folk should know that, Simkin. Will you allow him to sway you?'

'I'll go you one better than that,' said Bulchett. 'I've promised Rowland here the throne of England, but there are other kingdoms in Christendom, other thrones. How would you like to be King of France, Sir Nompar?'

The *bourc* smiled. 'No, thank you. Have you not heard the tale of the Sword of Damocles?'

'I'll be King of France!' said Haine.

'You speak nay French,' said Young.

'First thing I'll do, I'll make a law that all Frenchmen must speak English.'

'Can I be King of Castile?' asked Vertue.

'If you like,' said Bulchett.

A spot of scintillating light sparkled in Kemp's vision. He blinked his eyes and shook his head, trying to clear it, but it would not go away. He tried to ignore it. 'Giddy fools!' he spluttered at the others. 'D'you not hear yourselves? You've all turned lunatic!'

'Let those who want to be kings follow me,' said Bulchett. 'Those of you too blind to recognise the possibilities that the Brazen Head will grant us, well… you may trudge the long, weary miles to the English border if you will. When I am emperor, I may be merciful to you, though you need expect no special favours from me.'

'Thank you!' sneered Kemp. The spot of scintillating lights had turned into a shard that started at the periphery of his vision and stabbed into the centre of it, like a dagger. Again he blinked, hoping it would go away. 'Rest assured, we'll ask for none.'

'Bring the woman, Haine,' ordered Bulchett.

Leering, the butcher moved to grab Tibbie by the arm. Kemp interposed himself. 'The woman's with me.'

'You're in no position to give orders,' said Bulchett. 'Do not forget you're a prisoner yourself.'

'I gave her my word no harm will come to her…'

'Then you exceeded your authority. Come along, men.' Bulchett began marching up the road into the mountains. Crawley, Fisher, Gudgeon, Vertue and Tegg all followed.

Grinning victoriously at Kemp, Haine grabbed Tibbie by the arm and dragged her after him. She went unwillingly, gazing pleadingly over her shoulder at Kemp and Nompar. 'Ye'll no' leave me a prisoner of these madmen?'

After a moment's hesitation, Young set off after the others. 'Do not tell me someone as learned as yourself believes this folly?' Nompar asked him.

Young glanced guiltily after the others, then hurried back to where Kemp and Nompar stood at the junction. 'Of course not. But what can I do? Sir Alexander is my captain now.'

'Sir Alexander is a fool and a madman. There's naught but death awaits you in those mountains if you follow him.'

Young only shrugged, turning to scurry after the others.

'We cannot abandon them,' Kemp said to Nompar.

'It seems to me *they* are abandoning *us*. If we go with them, then whatever doom Sir Alexander leads them to will just as surely befall we two.'

'They're my men, Sir Nompar. I care not what anyone says. I've a responsibility to them and I'll not abandon them to Bulchett's madness. And then there's Tibbie. What do you think will become of her if we leave them now?'

Even as he spoke, the scintillating lights in Kemp's eyes spread until they blotted out his vision entirely. He squeezed his eyes shut again. The background behind the sparkling dimmed, but the scintillating remained. When he opened his eyes again, he could see nothing else. A feeling of panic constricted his throat.

'Why do you stare?' he heard Nompar ask.

'I have a slight problem.' Kemp waved a hand before his face, but saw nothing through the mass of sparkling lights twinkling in his eyes like sunlight splintered through a thousand tiny shards of ice. 'I'm blinded!'

Thirteen

Reid pulled back a corner of the fleece to reveal the face of a dead man, his pallid, grey-green face frozen in a grim rictus of agony. 'God damn them!' he said. 'God damn them to hell!'

'You knew him?' asked Sir Archibald.

Reid let the fleece fall back into place. 'Aye. Michie Liddell. He was a good man.'

'You think the Englishmen we're chasing did this?'

'Who else would do such a thing?' said Nixon. 'They must have spent the night here.'

'Whit did he ever do to them?' Reid wondered out loud as the three of them emerged from the croft. The rest of the men waited outside on their hobbies.

'When did the English ever need a reason for their plunderings and butchery?' Nixon swung himself back astride his own mount.

Reid wiped his lips on his sleeve. 'Michie had a wife.'

'They took her with them?' asked Archibald.

Reid studied the footprints leading away from the croft. If there were any footprints amongst them small enough to belong to a woman, they had been trampled over by the men at the rear of the file. He climbed on to his hobby's back. 'There's nae sign of her in the croft, and I dinnae see any other tracks leading away frae here.'

'They've taken a woman with them?' exclaimed Sneith. 'What for?'

Nixon eyed him with amusement. 'Whit d'ye do wi' a woman when ye get her alone?'

'It's nae good asking this bloodless gelding whit to do wi' a woman, Rab,' said Reid. 'Ah reckon he prefers the company o' men, if ye ken whit Ah mean.'

'By my faith!' exploded Sneith. 'You'll pay for that insult, you viperous caitiff!' He rode his horse at Reid and tried to punch him. Reid caught him by the wrist, staying the blow, and the two of them struggled until their horses shied apart. Sneith was pulled out of the saddle and Reid, relinquishing his own grip too late, was pulled down after him. The two of them rolled over and over in the snow until Nixon ordered Howk to dismount and pull them apart.

'You must learn to govern your temper, Sneith,' growled Archibald. 'We Scots will never defeat the English if we spend all our strength fighting one another!'

'Forgive me, Sir Archibald! But he deliberately provoked me—'

'Aye, and you let yourself be provoked. Now hold your tongue.' The knight turned to Reid. 'How far ahead of us are they, would you say?'

'Nae more than an hour. And they're on foot.'

'Then Ah suggest we get after them!' Putting his heels back, Nixon led his men down the road leading towards Yarrowdale.

—

'If Kemp cannot see, we must leave him,' said Bulchett. 'We cannot let a blind man slow us down.'

'If we leave him, the Scots will catch him and kill him,' said Nompar.

'That's his problem,' said Bulchett.

Kemp was on his hands and knees in the snow. Unable to see, he did not even trust himself to stand. He saw nothing but the scintillating lights sparking in his eyes. He felt sick. Under his gambeson, his skin was clammy with a cold sweat. What use was a blind archer to anyone? When he had chosen to make his living by the bow and the sword, he had always accepted he would die a bloody death, but this was something else entirely. If Bulchett and the others left him behind for the Scots, he would have no chance of defending himself. Blinded, scrabbling around in the snow, he would die like a dog, a pathetic and inglorious death.

'Let us wait a moment,' said Nompar. 'Perhaps the fit of blindness will pass.'

'We have no time to wait,' said Bulchett. 'Leave him. If his sight returns before any Scots find him, let him make haste to catch up with us. Otherwise...' Bulchett let the sentence hang in the air.

'I will not leave him,' said Nompar.

'Then stay and die with him,' snorted Bulchett. 'The rest of us will tarry no longer.'

God bless you, Nompar, thought Kemp. *And God damn you, Sir Alexander!*

'Come along, men!' said Bulchett, and Kemp heard boots scrunching in the snow and the swish and chink of armoured men moving off.

Someone gently laid a hand on Kemp's shoulder. 'I do not like leaving Domaisèla Liddell in the hands of a ruffian like Haine,' he heard Nompar say.

'Then go with them,' said Kemp. 'Protect her. I'll be all right.'

The *bourc* laughed without much humour. 'Alone and blind in a strange land, where every man's hand will be against you? I think not. Is your vision dimmed, my friend, or can you see nothing but blackness?'

'I see lights sparkling, twinkling in my eyes, blotting out everything else.'

'It sounds like a megrim. My father's wife was plagued by them. I think that blow to your head did you more harm than you realise.'

'What would you have me do?' Kemp demanded bitterly. 'Seek out a physician?'

'When we reach a town in England, it would do no harm to consult one.'

'No harm but to the weight of my purse! Your father's wife can see between her megrims?'

'Oh yes. And they rarely last above a short while, though her head aches fiercely afterwards!'

Was it Kemp's imagination, or were the sparkling lights thinning out? He waved a hand in front of his eyes and thought he saw a shadow...

'What is it?' asked Nompar. 'Is your sight returning?'

Kemp was reluctant to answer for fear getting his hopes up might be tempting fate. But he could definitely see his hand now, and Nompar's feet in the snow. He stayed on his hands and knees for a moment, drawing deep breaths to calm his racing heart. A few sparkles lingered, but in less time than it took to say a paternoster those too had vanished. And now a sharp headache pounded in his skull, so bad he felt sick to the pit of his stomach.

'I can see again.'

'God be praised! Can you stand?'

Taking his time, Kemp pushed himself to his feet. He felt a wave of giddiness pass through him and for a moment he feared the sparkling lights would return, but then his head seemed to clear, even if the ache remained as sharp as before. He felt slightly foolish for thinking the blindness would be permanent. Megrims were supposed to be something that plagued old women, not hale young archers. And yet the fear still lurked at the back of his head: what if the sparkling lights returned? What if a second attack came, and this time it did not pass?

'Can you walk?' asked Nompar.

Kemp put one foot in front of the other. The jogging of his head did little to dispel the ache in his skull, but at least he was moving. There was no sense in worrying about a second such attack before it had happened. The Scots were a more immediate threat. Though he reflected it might not be a bad idea to follow Nompar's advice and consult a physician about his fit of blindness at the next opportunity.

'Come on,' he told the *bourc*.

The two of them hurried through the snow, following the footprints left by Bulchett and the others until they caught up with them a mile further on, striding up the valley leading into the mountains.

'You can see again?' asked Bulchett.

'Aye,' growled Kemp.

'I divven't think he ever lost his sight,' sneered Haine. 'I reckon he just made the whole thing up, to make us feel sorry for him.'

'Keep testing my patience, Haine,' said Kemp. 'I've a whoreson of an aching head, and I warrant giving you cause to feel sorry for yourself might be just the distraction I need to take my mind off it.'

They trudged on. Sheep grazed on stalks of reeds and sedge grass jutting above the snow covering the meadows on either side of the stream running through the wide valley. Where the ground sloped up to the hills on either side, moors presented a blanket of white, unbroken but for the black rock of an occasional crag, or clusters of trees growing here and there.

'Can you truly imprison a demon in a head of brass?' Gudgeon asked Vertue.

'A demon may possess a man's body. But you can't drive a demon from a man's body without providing an alternative vessel for the demon to occupy. Remember how Christ met with a man possessed by demons at Gadara?'

Gudgeon nodded. 'When Christ asked the name of the demon possessing the man, they replied "My name is Legion, for we are many".'

'That's right,' said Vertue. 'And when Christ exorcised them, they asked to be transferred to a herd of swine foraging nearby. Possessed by demons, the herd rushed over a cliff into the Sea of Galilee and was drowned.'

'A herd of swine going mad and hastening to its own destruction,' Nompar murmured to Kemp. 'What does that put me in mind of?'

'You believe in demons?' Young asked Fisher.

'Of course! Even the law recognises the existence of demons.'

'How so?'

'When I were a lad, me Uncle Absalom hanged himself from a beam in a neighbour's barn. Because he'd committed suicide, the sheriff said all his chattels were forfeit to the Crown, along wi' the instruments he'd chosen to destroy himself: in this case, the rope and the beam in the barn, both of which belonged to his neighbour.'

'You mean, if I steal your knife and use it to stab myself, then not only my property but also your knife is forfeit?' asked Gudgeon.

'Aye, that's right,' said Fisher. 'It's called the "deodand". Only the thing was, after the beam was taken out and delivered to the sheriff, a couple of days later the whole barn collapsed.'

'Go on!' protested Young. 'That's another of your stories, is it not?'

'Swear to God,' Fisher said piously.

'How does that prove the law recognises the existence of demons?'

'Because after the sheriff confiscated Uncle Absalom's chattels, me Aunt Wensliana consulted a man of law, and was able to provide evidence that her husband had not been in possession of his own mind when he hanged himself, but had been possessed by a demon. Therefore he weren't responsible for his own deeds and couldn't be accused of suicide. The case was tried at the assizes and the justice decreed the sheriff had to return Uncle Absalom's chattels to my aunt.'

Gudgeon shook his head in wonderment. 'I'd never hang meself. Not even if I were possessed by a demon.'

'You wouldn't know,' said Fisher.

'What d'you mean?'

'If you were possessed by a demon, you wouldn't know it. The demon would have so much power over you, even your thoughts, you'd think you were in control of your own deeds, but really it'd be the demon telling you what to do. That's how it works. I mean, suppose a man were possessed by a demon and knew it? 'Twould be the easiest thing in the world for him to go to a priest to have it exorcised. Stands to reason. Why, you might be possessed by a demon even now, and none of us would be any the wiser, least of all you.'

'Get away wi' you!' said Gudgeon. 'That's drivel, in't it?'

Fisher shook his head solemnly. 'As God is my witness.'

Gudgeon grabbed Young. 'Look into me eye, Dunstan. Can you see a demon in me head?'

Young pushed him away. 'Divven't be a silly fool, Hob. There's nay such things as demons.'

'Dunstan says there's nay such things as demons,' Gudgeon told Fisher.

'The Bible says there are,' said Vertue. 'Do you say the Bible in't true? Is that what manner of blasphemy they teach at Oxford nowadays?'

'Nay, but...' Young gestured helplessly. 'Have you ever seen a demon?'

'I have not,' admitted Vertue. 'But I've never seen a cameleopard neither. Doesn't mean there's nay such thing.'

'Dunstan's a liar,' Fisher told Gudgeon. 'If he doesn't believe in demons, why's he coming with us to find the Brazen Head?'

'Calm yourself, Hob,' said Kemp. 'Simkin's teasing you again. I see no signs that you've been possessed by a demon.'

'But how would you know?' demanded Gudgeon, panic-stricken. He clutched his head as if he felt as though it would burst asunder if he did not hold it together. 'How could anyone know?'

Nompar cleared his throat. 'I heard that when a man is possessed by a demon, his eyes glow red.'

Kemp felt a flood of gratitude for the *bourc*'s quick-wittedness. 'Aye. That's how Fisher's Aunt Wensliana was able to convince the justice that her husband had been possessed by a demon when he hanged himself. Is it not?' he added, grabbing a fistful of Fisher's chaperon and twisting the material so it was drawn taut about the apprentice's flabby neck, half-strangling him.

'Aye, that's true,' gasped Fisher. Kemp released him.

'Are me eyes glowing red?' asked Gudgeon.

'Nay,' said Kemp. 'Now calm yourself! No demon possesses you.'

They trudged on through the snow. A cold wind blew down the valley from the mountains ahead, bearing a few fat snowflakes and a threat of plenty more where those came from.

Kemp realised the only way to save Tegg and his men from Bulchett's folly was to try to reason with them, and make them understand that what Bulchett promised them was nonsense, madness. The problem was that so many of them were weak-minded and easily led. But perhaps he could turn that to his advantage. If they were easily led, then the more of them he could persuade of the folly of this quest, the easier it would be to convince the remainder.

Deciding that of the other six archers, Dunstan Young was the cleverest, most level-headed and amenable to reason, Kemp fell into step alongside him. 'You know this is folly, don't you?'

'Aye.'

'Will you help me persuade the others? If Bulchett is fool enough to march to his death in these mountains then I reckon the world will be better off without him. But we can still save Tegg and the others.'

Young shook his head. 'Leave me out of it.'

'What do you mean?'

'If there's a quarrel betwixt you and Sir Alexander, I want nay part of it.'

'Seems to me you're up to your neck in it whether you like it or not. You may say you don't want to take either side, but if you follow Bulchett then you're taking his side.'

'The law says I must obey his orders. It divven't mean I trust him.'

'But if you follow him and do nowt to thwart him, that makes you as much party to his folly as if you chose to abet him. Nowt makes it easier for the wicked to triumph than for righteous men to stand idly by.'

'And you reckon you're righteous, do you?'

'Anything but! Yet compared to Bulchett—'

'As far as I can see, you're both as bad as each other.'

'At least I don't lie to you. At least I don't take you for a fool. If you can see no difference between Bulchett and me, I know not what to say to you.'

'Say nowt. It's got nowt to do wi' me anyhow.'

'It'll have everything to do with you, if Bulchett leads you to your death!'

Young shook his head stubbornly. 'It's between you and Bulchett; it's got nowt to do wi' me.'

Kemp redoubled his pace until he fell into step alongside Haine. The butcher might be a brutish ruffian, but he was no fool. 'You don't believe this nonsense about the Brazen Head, do you?'

'Of course not.'

'Then why do you follow him?' Kemp gestured at Bulchett's back.

'To thwart you.'

Kemp was nonplussed. '*What?*'

'Folk like you make me spew. You reckon you're better than the rest of us. You reckon you know it all, but you divven't. Why do I follow him? Acos he knows how to thwart smug whoresons like you. I'm enjoying this, Kemp. If you could see the look on your face now, as you come to realise you divven't know everything... it's worth it, just for that.'

'And if Bulchett leads you to your death? Will it have been worth it then?'

'Me? I've got nowt left to lose. After I was pilloried for selling rotten pork, me landlord kicked me out of my shop. I lost everything. There were nowt wrong wi' that pork anyroad, nowt a little gravy couldn't hide. Just some fancy whoresons with over-delicate tastebuds and weak stomachs, that's all. I can die in these mountains or beg in the gutter. But just suppose... what if Sir Alexander's right? What if there really is a Brazen Head? I could be King of France. Not bad, for a lad from Ulverston.'

Kemp snorted. 'Even if there is a Brazen Head – which I don't believe for a moment – you're a bigger fool than I took you for, if you think a man like Sir Alexander will be willing to share any of the power it grants him with a man like you.'

'Aye, well... even if he dun't, at least I can have some sport on the way.' Haine grabbed Tibbie's arm and dragged her after him, leering at Kemp as he did so.

Kemp let him walk on. Fisher, Gudgeon and Young walked past him, until Nompar, bringing up the rear, joined him.

'I cannot fathom it,' he told the *bourc*. 'Some of them believe it... some of them want to believe it... can they not see it's no more than a pack of fairy tales?'

'A man like Bulchett gives them hope,' said Nompar. 'That is something men of their rank rarely get to enjoy.'

'False hope,' said Kemp. 'Any shitten swindler from the gutters of London might give them as much, and at less cost to them.'

'But unlike a swindler, Bulchett believes his own lies. That is what makes him so dangerous. We must make a plan. Tonight I will volunteer to take a turn on watch. While the others sleep, we will take Domaisèla Liddell and give the rest of them the slip. See if you can find a way to let her know without Haine or any of the others overhearing, so she can be ready.'

'How far do you think we'll get, when our footsteps in the snow will be so easy to track?'

Nompar gazed up at the ominous clouds. 'I think there will be more snow before the day is out. Perhaps we should go then, rather than waiting for nightfall.'

Before Kemp could reply, something soughed overhead and landed with a soft chunk. Glancing towards the sound, he saw the shaft of an arrow sticking out of the snow. Even as he turned his head, two more arrows landed nearby in quick succession, then five. One missed Nompar by only a couple of feet. Kemp glanced back the way they had come, and saw a crowd of two score riders coming from the direction of the lake: lightly armoured hobelars and mounted bowmen for the most part, but Kemp saw a couple of men-at-arms wearing habergeons and polished bascinets, and mounted on destriers. One bore the coat of arms of Sir Archibald Douglas on his shield. He did not recognise the blazon of the other, a red rose on a white field.

Another rider bore more than a passing resemblance to Black Rab Nixon. Though Kemp had not clapped eyes on the reiver chief for about five years, the combination of this man's build, the way he sat in the saddle, and the few details of his face Kemp could make out at that range all put him in mind of Nixon. Another man he did not recognise, a giant of a man, rode alongside him. Some of the bowmen had dismounted and hurried ahead of the others to shoot. They were less than a furlong away.

'Come on!' Kemp broke into a run. He and Nompar soon overhauled Young, Gudgeon and Fisher as they trudged on at the tail of the file. 'I'd get a move on if I were you!' Kemp yelled at them as he ran past. He grabbed Tibbie's arm and pulled her away from Haine as he passed. Taken by surprise, Haine released her before he realised what was going on, his confusion only exacerbated by a second volley of arrows that landed all around them.

Dragging Tibbie alongside him, Kemp soon passed Vertue, Tegg, Crawley and Bulchett. 'Reivers!' he shouted, pointing back to where their pursuers now chased them across the snow.

'God's love!' Bulchett broke into a run. He followed Kemp, Tibbie and Nompar. The others all followed Bulchett.

'Don't bunch up, for Christ's sake!' shouted Kemp. 'Spread out! You're all archers, you should know a dozen little targets are more difficult to hit than one big one!'

He knew they could not outrun horsemen; they had to stand and fight, no matter how impossible the odds might seem. He had faced worse odds at Crécy. But first they needed to put some distance between them and their pursuers: not much, just enough to buy them sufficient time to conceal themselves in some covert and ready their bows.

Up ahead, a pair of rocky crags about a furlong up the slope to their right marked the mouth of a ravine that would provide plenty of cover; but they would not even reach that if he did not find some way to discourage the reivers from drawing too near. Closer to, there was dead ground just ahead: nothing dramatic, the ground undulated gently enough, but it might be sufficiently deep for a man standing in the bottom to be hidden from anyone approaching until they came within fifty yards. If the bowmen amongst the reivers could not see their quarry, they could not shoot at them with any accuracy.

Tibbie pulled back against Kemp's grip on her upper arm, trying to break free. She knew their attackers were her countrymen and clearly reckoned she would be safer with them. He was tempted to let her go: it would be one less thing for him to worry about. On the other hand, the reivers might shoot her before they recognised her as a countrywoman. And part of him could not help thinking that if they did recognise her as a countrywoman, it might be useful to have her as a hostage.

'Stay with us,' he snarled in her ear. 'Unless you think Black Rab Nixon's reivers will be any more reluctant to rape you than Kenrick will.' He dragged her to the bottom of the dead ground, shrugging off his bow stave with his other hand. Turning, he saw the others skidding down the slope behind him. As he had anticipated, the reivers were still out of sight. 'Stand your ground!' he shouted at Tegg and his men, bracing the lower end of his stave against the inside of a foot and bending it until he could loop the string over the upper nock. 'Ready your bows!'

'Lambert can't use his bow with his arm in that sling,' said Young.

The twentyman looked almost as pale as the surrounding snow, and a sheen of sweat bathed his face while everyone else shivered. 'And he cried mightily with a strong voice,' he moaned, 'saying, Great Babylon is fallen, and is become the habitation of devils, and the hold of all foul spirits. For all nations have drunk of the wine of the wrath of her fornication.'

Kemp grabbed Nompar. 'When I give the word, I want you to take Bulchett, Crawley, Tegg and Tibbie, and head for yon ravine.' He pointed, and the *bourc* nodded.

The reivers crested the brow above the dead ground. For convenience, the bowmen carried their bows strung but slung across their backs.

'Nock!' Kemp drew an arrow from his sheaf. He glanced at the others to see how they were getting on: Gudgeon seemed to be having trouble stringing his bow for some reason, but Fisher, Haine, Vertue and Young all reached for arrows. When most of them had an arrow nocked – there was no time to wait for Gudgeon to sort himself out – Kemp yelled 'Draw… and loose!'

He pulled back on his string, felt the bow creak in his left hand, and let fly. The string thrummed against the leather bracer on his left wrist, sending his arrow soughing to where the reivers, realising they had cantered into an ambush, tried to wheel their mounts. Fisher, Haine, Vertue and Young all loosed at the same time. Of the five arrows, one stuck in the shoulder of a hobelar, another pierced the rump of a hobby, making the beast rear and throw its rider. Even if the other three missed, they must have come close enough to throw a scare into the other reivers. For a few heartbeats the huddle of horsemen was a tumult of plunging horses and men shouting incoherently.

Finally Gudgeon had his bow strung, and when Kemp ordered his companions to loose a second flight, there were six arrows in it rather than five. It was enough to decide the reivers: putting their heels back, they wheeled and galloped the way they had come until they were out of sight, though Kemp was too much of a pessimist to think that would be the last any of them would see of them.

'Martin!' shouted Nompar. Kemp glanced towards him, and the *bourc* pointed to where Bulchett had broken away from the others and was dashing up to the ravine on his own, Crawley following close on his heels.

Kemp followed the bottom of the dead ground to where Nompar stood, holding Tibbie by the arm. Here the dip was less deep, and he could see over the brow to where the reivers rallied about three hundred yards off, out of bowshot. Now three men lay in the intervening ground with the shafts of arrows sticking out of their bodies, four riderless hobbies trotted about friskily off to one side, and one man limped through the snow to where his companions rallied.

Kemp clapped Nompar on the shoulder. 'Go! Take the girl!'

Dragging Tibbie on one side of him and the delirious Tegg on the other, the *bourc* began to run up the slope, following Bulchett and Crawley to the ravine above.

Haine and the others did not hold their position, but ran up to where Kemp stood in the shallow upper end of the dead ground. It was poor discipline, but Kemp said nothing, for it saved him the trouble of waving them across. 'Nock arrows but don't draw yet,' he told them. 'Young, keep an eye on those reivers. When they come within a furlong, sing out.'

The scholar nodded.

'Right then,' said Kemp. 'Let's go!'

They began to sprint across the open ground to the ravine above. At once the reivers divided into two groups, both containing hobelars and bowmen. One circled around through the meadowland at the bottom of the valley, the other made directly for the mouth of the ravine: they would be too late to cut off Bulchett and Crawley, but they could still get there before the archers.

The riders making for the ravine were less than a furlong away now. 'Kemp!' shouted Young.

'I see them! All of you be ready to halt and loose a flight towards the reivers to our right when I give the word.' He ran a few more yards up the slope, keeping one eye on the hobelars cantering across to cut off Nompar, Tibbie and Tegg from the mouth of the ravine. 'Stop here!' he shouted to the others. They skidded to a halt. 'Aim for the hobelars. Draw and... loose!'

Another flight whirred away from the Englishmen, five of the arrows keeping in tight formation as they arced high towards the reivers, one veering off wildly: someone had gleft his shot. The other five fell amongst the riders. Again one man fell with an arrow sticking out of him, another was thrown from a wounded horse, and the remainder scattered in all directions.

Further across to the right, the bowmen amongst the reivers reined in and dismounted, lining up to loose a flight towards their English counterparts. 'Another flight!' Kemp drew another arrow from the sheaf under his belt and nocked it. 'Towards the archers this time. Draw and... loose!'

This time all six arrows flew true. The reiver bowmen loosed a flight in reply a heartbeat later, so both volleys passed one another in flight. Kemp did not wait to see where the English volley struck, but at once continued up the slope after Nompar, Tibbie and Tegg, shouting for the others to follow. As long as they were moving, they would present a more difficult target for their counterparts amongst the reivers.

Nompar, Tibbie and Tegg had reached the mouth of the ravine. Kemp and the rest of the men had almost joined them when a second flight of arrows from the reivers rained down all around them. Someone shrieked in agony, and Kemp turned to see Young fall, the feathered shaft of an arrow sticking out of one shoulder.

'Another flight!' Kemp and the rest of the archers nocked fresh arrows and loosed again. While the flight was still in the air, Kemp slung his bow across his back by its string and dashed across to where Young tried to crawl to the mouth of the ravine, leaving a trail of blood in the snow. Gudgeon ran across to help him, and the two of them dragged Young into cover.

'Keep an eye on the reivers!' Kemp told Fisher. 'Warn me if they approach.'

He crouched over Young. The shaft had gone deep. Young opened his mouth to try to speak, and then a fit of coughing wracked his body. A gobbet of blood gouted from his lips to stain the snow. He made another effort to speak, but no sound would come. Then he screwed up his face in agony, arched his back with a final spasm, and lay still, eyes staring glassily.

Fourteen

Kemp clenched his fists in frustration. Young had been a bright lad and would have been welcome in the ranks of any company the Midlander commanded, if he could have persuaded him to join.

He turned to where Bulchett stood a short distance up the ravine. 'Take a good look, Sir Alexander,' he snarled, pointing at Young's corpse. 'Yon's your handiwork.'

'We're at war, Kemp. Men die in war. You ought to know that. He died in King Edward's service. That's an honourable death.'

'That's drivel! He died because you insisted on leading him into these mountains chasing a myth, when he should have been fleeing for the border.' Kemp turned to Nompar. 'Those are Black Rab Nixon's reivers.'

'But they're led by Archibald Douglas.'

Kemp shook his head. 'Lord William Douglas might use Nixon as a cat's-paw from time to time, but I doubt they'd suffer Sir Archibald to lead them. Did you recognise the blazon of the other man-at-arms?'

'*Argent*, a rose *gules* stalked *vert*?' Nompar shook his head. 'One of Lord Douglas' vassals, no doubt.'

'Did you see the giant?' asked Gudgeon. 'They say Black Rab rides with a giant named Howk. They say he stands ten feet tall and can lift a full-grown ox over his head!'

'He was a big fellow,' admitted Nompar, 'but not ten feet tall. Barely a head taller than his companions.'

'Maybe not,' said Kemp, 'but I'd not care to be pitted against him in a wrestling match!'

'Ah dinnae understand,' said Tibbie. 'Why did they no' press hame their attack?'

'What's the matter?' demanded Kemp. 'One death not enough for you?'

'There were twa score of them. Against half a dozen of ye.'

'Hobelars are good for riding down a few fleeing foot soldiers, but when they see archers lined up ready to loose a volley, they'll take no comfort in the odds, only think on what if one of those arrows hits *them*.'

Her brow furrowed, Tibbie turned to Nompar.

The *bourc* nodded. 'It is the truth. In plays perhaps both the good and the bad fight with equal fervour; but on the battlefield, men are more inclined to think on whether or not they will live to see their womenfolk, and hang back in the hope the battle can be decided without them having to risk their necks.'

'That's sensible,' said Kemp. 'In any case, they don't need to slay us all at once. They'll harry us, wear us down, pick off a couple here, a couple there. Next time they charge we'll only be able to shoot five arrows in each volley. The time after that it'll be four, or three. Then two, or one. We're a long way from home and they know it. They've got all the time in the world.'

He glanced up the ravine. It was only a couple of dozen yards wide, with rocky cliffs on both sides, the ground at the foot of those cliffs sloping down to the stream running through the bottom. He crossed to where Fisher stood below one of the crags at the mouth of the ravine, gazing down to where the reivers rallied.

'You don't reckon they'll give up, then?' asked Fisher.

Kemp shook his head. 'Not so easily.' Unless the reivers were fools, they would not try following the English archers into the ravine. If Kemp had been in their shoes, he would have tried to box them in, keeping some archers watching the mouth, sending others to find the far end, while yet more could hunt them from the top of the cliffs on either side. If they only hunted from the cliffs on one side, then Kemp and his companions might take shelter from them at the foot of the cliffs immediately below. But if Nixon was cunning – and he was – he would send archers to search both sides of the ravine, and then there would be nowhere for those below to hide. All of which meant Kemp and his companions had to find a way out of the ravine before Nixon put such a plan into effect; preferably a way out that would enable them to give the reivers the slip.

'Let's keep moving.' Kemp turned and headed up the ravine, following the sloping ground between the stream and the cliffs to their left.

Bulchett hurried after him. 'Should we not leave some of the archers to cover our escape?'

'That's what the reivers will expect us to do, in't it?'

'Aye.'

'So they'll not send anyone charging into the mouth of this ravine. Instead they'll try to outflank us: there, there, and somewhere up ahead.' Kemp pointed to the brinks of the cliffs above, and then pointed up the ravine.

Around the next corner, there was a break in the wall of rock to their left. The ground remained too steep to climb, except for what might have been a goat trail angling up the slope.

'Wait here.' Kemp stepped over the stream and ascended the precipitous trail, his bow in his left hand with an arrow nocked ready, keeping one eye on the top of the cliffs opposite. At the top, he looked about. There was no sign of the reivers, not yet at least. To his left, the moorland sloped back down to the valley the reivers had chased them out of; to his right, it sloped up to the brow of a hill. Behind him, the ravine continued up the slope. He beckoned the others to climb up after him, and once they were all out of the ravine, they began to trudge up the snowy slope to the brow of the hill above.

Before they had covered a hundred yards, Kemp heard hoof beats and turned to see the reivers riding across the moorland beyond the far side of the gorge. Spying their quarry, they reined in and the bowmen dismounted. Bulchett and his companions broke into a run, Nompar dragging Tibbie, and Kemp leading Tegg. Vertue paused and turned back, nocking an arrow.

'Keep running,' Kemp told him. 'Save your arrows.'

The first flight of arrows fell all around them. There were a couple of near misses, but no one was struck. The arrows from a second flight all landed in the snow behind them: well over a furlong beyond the ravine, they were clearly out of range. And the ravine was too wide for even a mighty destrier to leap over, much less the little hobbies most of the reivers were mounted on.

Haine made an obscene gesture. 'Go kiss the Devil's arse in Hell, you riveling whoresons!'

'Before you provoke them overmuch,' said Kemp, 'bear in mind they might not be able to cross the ravine, but it'll not take them long to find some other way around.'

Bulchett's party crested the brow of the hill and descended the slope on the other side into the next glen. To their right, the glen forked, one branch continuing straight ahead, another curving around to the right.

'Which way?' Nompar asked breathlessly. 'North or east?'

'West.' Kemp pointed up the steep slope opposite. Even from the bottom of the glen, it was obvious that the higher one climbed, the steeper the slope became; towards the top, it was sheer in some places, though there were others where Kemp reckoned even a man with one arm in a sling would be able to clamber up.

'Up there?' asked Fisher. His obese frame ill-suited him for mountain-climbing.

'The reivers cannot follow us up there on horseback,' said Kemp. 'They must forsake their mounts, or forsake the chase altogether.'

He led the way up the snowy slope. It was easy at first and in no time at all they were about a third of the way up. Kemp paused to turn and see how the others were doing, and was surprised by how high they had climbed already. The slope seemed much higher than it had from below. It had become steeper than it seemed from below too: even here, if one of them slipped, they would probably slide through the snow all the way to the bottom, perhaps bouncing off the jagged rocks that jutted up here and there along the way.

He turned his attention back to the climb above, wondering if it was fair after all to expect Tegg and Tibbie to climb up. But when he gazed across at the hill on the opposite side of the glen, he saw horsemen coming over the ridge. Even if he and his companions abandoned the ascent and tried to climb back down now, the reivers would be the first to reach the bottom of the glen, cutting off their retreat. There was no turning back now.

Kemp resumed climbing. Before long he found he had to use his hands as well as his feet to ascend. He glanced down to see how Tegg was managing and saw Nompar helping him up. It really was a long way down now... best not to look, he told himself.

He turned his attention to the slope above. Only a few more yards. The crags at the top of the slope loomed over him, icicles hanging off them in places, but over to his right a ravine led up between two crags that looked eminently climbable. He began to traverse the slope to reach it. Before he had covered a few yards, however, one of his feet slipped. His stomach lurched sickeningly as he felt himself fall, grabbing instinctively at some wiry heather jutting out of the snow. He managed to roll on his back and dug his heels in, stopping himself before he fell too far, but it had been a close-run thing and his heart pounded in his chest. To fall from this high – even sliding rather than falling free – would be fatal. He clung there for a moment, clouds of breath forming before his lips as he panted cold air into his lungs, waiting for his racing heart to settle down to its normal rate. *This is madness*, he thought to himself. *You were a fool to think you could climb up here, much less get the others up after you.*

'Martin?' Nompar called anxiously.

'All's well!' he called back, pushing his doubts to the back of his mind. Turning on wobbly legs to face the slope again, he pulled himself up by the wiry sprigs of heather and managed to regain the place from which he had fallen. He clambered up to the gully without further mishap, only to find a dead end at the very top. There was a sheer wall of rock about ten feet high, without any handholds or footholds that he could see, topped with a thick blanket of snow that curled over the edge. Above that he saw nothing but grey sky: maybe it was the top of the slope, or perhaps there was a ledge with another rockface further back, even more impossible to climb.

Breathing hard, Bulchett followed him into the gully. 'You god-damned fool! We cannot climb that!'

In the glen below, the reivers had reached the foot of the slope. Some of the bowmen dismounted from their hobbies, but instead of climbing up after their quarry, they began to ready their bows. He pointed them out to Bulchett. 'We cannot climb down, either.'

'We're trapped, damn you!'

Kemp turned his attention back to the rockface. If Ieuan had been there, the stocky Welshman would already have put his back to the rock so Kemp could climb up on his shoulders. He turned to look at the others climbing up behind Bulchett. Seeing the rope still coiled about Crawley's torso, he got an idea. 'I don't suppose you have a grapnel to go with that rope?' he asked Bulchett.

'What in the world would I want with a grapnel?'

'At this moment, one would come in right handy!' said Kemp. 'Nompar!'

'Yes?'

'If we can get just one man up above that ledge, he can tie the rope to something and pull the others up after him.'

'But how do we get one man up there?'

'I reckon I can climb up on your shoulders, if you make a step-up for me by clasping your hands before you, thus.' Kemp cupped his hands in front of his stomach, fingers interlaced, by way of demonstration.

In the glen below, the reiver bowmen began loosing arrows up at them. The first few shafts soughed into the snow below where Fisher brought up the rear. The slope was not so tall that Kemp and his companions were out of range: evidently the bowmen had forgotten that when one shot uphill or downhill, it was necessary to aim even higher than usual to compensate for the angle. It would not be long before they realised their error and adjusted their aim accordingly.

The sloping ground below the overhang provided a poor surface for an archer to brace his feet on, but Fisher, Gudgeon, Haine and Vertue nevertheless unslung their bows and began shooting back at the men below, throwing them off their aim and forcing them to duck behind whatever cover they could find amongst the boulders tumbled at the bottom of the glen.

Nompar moved past Bulchett and Kemp to stand with his back to the rockface, cupping his hands before him. Kemp climbed up onto his shoulders, his cheek almost pressed to the frozen rock, fingers searching for the top of the ledge above. He thrust his hands between the rock and the overhanging curve of snow, which felt coarse and brittle against his knuckles. His fingertips located the angle of a ledge there. He dragged the snow away in chunks, brushing the lip of rock clear. Spluttering noises from below indicated some of the snow had been blown back in Nompar's face.

'Sorry!'

Kemp hooked his fingers over the exposed ledge. Shoulders strengthened by years of drawing his bow now drew him up, the soles of his boots scrabbling against the rockface below. He managed to pull himself up until his waist was level with the ledge, arms straight down, braced, struggling now only to get his centre of balance over the precipice. He tried to swing a leg up: if he could just hook one heel over the ledge, he would be able to boost himself up the rest of the way. An arrow clattered against the rockface a couple of yards to his left: the bowmen below had compensated for the angle of the slope, but they were still effectively shooting at extreme range, and at such a distance even Kemp would have struggled to be sure of his target.

He swung his right leg up, hooked his ankle over the precipice, leaned forward, and managed to roll himself on to the ledge. There was not much room to move about: after a couple of feet, the ground sloped up steeply again, but not sheer.

'Throw me the rope!' he called down to Crawley.

The squire unlooped the coil over his head and tossed it up to Kemp, who caught it. There was a rock on the ridge above. Kemp tied one end of the rope to it. There was more than enough to toss back down to where the others waited.

Bulchett was the next to climb up onto Nompar's shoulders. His eagerness to put some distance between himself and their pursuers overcame any fear of the scramble. He pulled himself up the rope and Kemp helped him over the precipice. Puffing and blowing like a beached whale with the chincough, Bulchett sprawled on the ledge for a moment, blocking the way of anyone who wanted to climb up after him.

'Move aside, Sir Alexander,' said Kemp. 'The others cannot climb up while you lie there.'

'Just let me lie a moment longer to catch my breath,' said Bulchett. 'I've no more strength left—'

An arrow cleared the precipice from below, missing the knight by less than a foot. Presumably discovering he had a little more strength left after all, Bulchett leaped to his feet and scrambled up the last few yards to the crest of the ridge.

'How's Lambert to climb up with but one hand?' Vertue asked as Crawley climbed up after his master.

'You and Hob will help him,' said Kemp. 'Once he's standing on Sir Nompar's shoulders, you'll put your hands under Tegg's left foot, Gudgeon will put his hands under his right, and the two of you push him up together while I clasp his hand and draw him up from above.'

Gudgeon and Vertue left off shooting at the reivers below to lead Tegg to where Nompar stood with his back to the rockface. Once again the *bourc* clasped his hands together before him.

Vertue indicated Nompar's clasped hands. 'You need to put a foot there and climb up, like Kemp, Sir Alexander and Master Rowland did. Do you understand?'

'Thou hast built thy high place at every head of the way, and hast made thy beauty to be abhorred, and hast opened thy feet to every one that passed by, and multiplied thy whoredoms,' said Tegg.

'Er... aye, if you say so.' Vertue clapped a hand to the twentyman's forehead, then glanced up at Kemp with anxiety etched on his features. 'He burns like one possessed by the Devil!'

Kemp spread his arms. 'What would you have me do? Send for a leach?'

An arrow narrowly missed Vertue, no doubt reminding him this was no time to tarry. 'Come on, Lambert. You can do it!'

Tegg put his foot on Nompar's upturned palms. The twentyman started to boost himself up, then began to topple back, but Gudgeon and Vertue were there to catch him, their hands on his back to steady him, pressing him forward until he could step onto the *bourc*'s shoulders. He reached up his good arm to grab the rope, but his left foot slipped off Nompar's shoulder and he began to fall. Kemp caught his outstretched hand and saved him, but it was a strain just to do that, pulling against all of the twentyman's weight. Vertue got his hands under Tegg's left boot, steadying him. Gudgeon tapped the twentyman's right boot. 'Raise your foot a little, Lambert, so I can get me fingers under.'

Tegg did as he was bidden.

'Got him?' Vertue grunted at Gudgeon.

'Aye. By God and Saint Joyce, he weighs a ton!'

Much to Kemp's surprise, Vertue did not berate Gudgeon for blaspheming. Instead he said, 'On three: one… two… *three!*'

With Gudgeon and Vertue pushing up from below and Kemp pulling from above, they managed to get Tegg almost up to the ledge, but when he tried to get his knee on the lip, it meant taking his foot off Vertue's upraised hands, so Kemp and Gudgeon bore his full weight between them. Kemp found himself straining so hard to pull the twentyman up, he feared he would tear his thews. Then Crawley was there, grabbing hold of Tegg's brigandine, helping to drag him to safety. The twentyman managed to get a knee on the ledge, and then Kemp's strength gave out and as he fell back it was all he could manage to pull Tegg after him, the twentyman sprawling across Kemp and Crawley together.

Crawley led Tegg away to where Bulchett waited, while Vertue climbed up. Gudgeon was about to follow, but Kemp shook his head.

'Send the woman up next.' Tegg had been the one he had had most doubts about getting up; if they could get Tibbie over also, he reckoned they were home and dry.

Gudgeon and Haine helped her climb on to Nompar's shoulders. Kemp proffered a hand to help her up, but she pointedly ignored it, pulling herself up the rope unaided with considerable agility.

With only Fisher shooting back at the reivers, the arrows from below started to come thick and fast, if no more accurately than before. Haine scrambled up next, while Vertue shot from the precipice above.

Fisher began to pull himself up the rope while Nompar and Gudgeon pushed him from below, grunting with effort. When he reached the top, Kemp grabbed one of his hands to help him over the precipice, and Haine grabbed the other.

An arrow whipped between them. Haine fell back with a cry, blood on his face, letting go of Fisher's hand. Suddenly Kemp was left bearing all his weight single-handed. He was pulled down, his chest hard against the ledge, Fisher's weight threatening to drag him off. The fat apprentice scrabbled at the rockface with his feet, while Nompar and Gudgeon hurried to support him again. But Fisher's pudgy fingers could not grip Kemp's hand.

He fell. It was only a short drop to the sloping ground where Nompar and Gudgeon stood. Fisher landed on his heels and for a moment Kemp thought all would be well, but then Fisher toppled over backwards. Nompar tried to grab one of his flailing arms, but was too late. Tumbling head over heels, Fisher made a couple of backwards rolls in the snow, then seemed to twist sideways as he continued to tumble down the slope.

'Simkin!' Gudgeon screamed in dismay, as if Fisher had been his best friend rather than someone who had delighted in endlessly tormenting him.

Fisher smashed against a rock and was thrown spinning out into space, plunging forty feet or so. Seeing the fat man hurtling towards them, the reivers scattered, and Fisher came to rest at the bottom of the valley, head and limbs twisted at awkward angles.

'Happen he's only hurt?' Gudgeon asked Nompar.

'After such a fall?' The *bourc* shook his head.

The bowmen amongst the reivers quickly rallied and resumed shooting up at Nompar and Gudgeon. 'Make haste, climb up!' urged the *bourc*, cupping his hands before him once again. Gudgeon clambered up on to his shoulders and hauled himself up the rope. The *bourc* came last, pulling himself up unaided until Kemp could help him over the lip at the top.

'Don't forget the rope, Rowland,' said Bulchett. 'We may need it again.'

Crawley unfastened the rope, coiling it in his hands as he followed the rest of them over the crest behind the ledge, where they were out of sight of the bowmen shooting at them from below.

–

'A yellow horse on a blue field.' Reid gazed up the slope to the escarpment where their quarry had disappeared. 'Whose coat of arms is that?'

'That was a unicorn, not a horse,' said Sneith. 'Did you not see its horn? That was the blazon of Sir Alexander Bulchett.'

'That fool!' snorted Archibald. 'If we slay him, it will be no great loss to King Edward's cause.'

'Aye, but his father's wealthy,' said Nixon. 'Ah warrant he'll pay a pretty penny if we ransom his eldest son.'

'You'd best hope Sir Alexander is the apple of his father's eye, then,' said Archibald. 'Were he my son, I'd pay you handsomely to take him off my hands!'

'Whit about the other?' asked Reid. 'A white cock on a black field.'

'Nompar de Savignac, the Bourc of Cazoulat,' said Archibald. 'I've met him: he is one of the knights who came to Scotland with Sir Eugène de Garencières. Indeed, I counted him an honourable gentleman, until he switched his allegiance to King Edward.'

'A traitor, then,' snorted Nixon. 'If there's one thing Ah cannae abide, it's treachery. Ah say we should teach him a lesson by demanding a particularly punitive ransom for him.'

'Aye, well, let's not count our cockerels before they're captured.' Archibald jerked his head at the escarpment at the top of the slope. 'How are we to get our horses up there?'

'We'll lose half a day if we go round the south side of Micklevencur's Head,' said Reid.

'They're only moments ahead of us,' said Nixon. 'We dinnae need our horses to catch them. Ah say we send a few of my men back to Innerleithan wi' the horses, and press ahead on foot. The Tweedsmuir Hills is bad country for horses anyway: too many perilous paths, and there'll be poor grazing beneath the snow at this time of year.'

'Press on without our horses?' snorted Sneith. 'And give up our advantage over them?'

'Ah widnae say our horses are our only advantage,' said Reid. 'Even if we send six men back with them, we'll still outnumber them three to one. And they must be running low on arrows.' He stooped to pluck up one of the shafts the Englishmen had loosed and peered at the fletchings with a critical eye.

Archibald shook his head. 'There's something about this business that makes no sense to me, something we're missing. When the rest of King Edward's host is heading south for the border, why are Bulchett and the *bourc* heading west into the Tweedsmuir Hills?'

'To learn the answer to that question, Sir Archibald, we must catch them and ask them,' said Nixon.

'Very well, then.' Archibald swung himself down from the saddle of his destrier. 'Let's waste no more time in talking, but get after them. Pick your men to take are horses back to Howie Ure's inn, Nixon, but warn them: my destrier's worth over a hundred pounds, and if I don't find him safe and in good health when we return to Innerleithan, there'll be the Devil to pay...'

–

Above the escarpment, Kemp and his companions sprinted across a broad plateau where a bitter and relentless wind chased spicules of ice around the sparse stalks of yellow grass jutting up from the thin covering of snow. Kemp wrapped his muffler about his head to keep the wind off his cheeks and drew his mantle tightly about him.

On the far side of the plateau, the ground sloped down again into another glen. They could see for miles, not that there was anything to see but league after league of snow-covered wilderness. If Kemp had kept his bearings, he reckoned they could not be more than six leagues from the town of Moffat at the upper end of Annandale – an easy day's journey in flat terrain on a summer's day – but for all he could see of it from here, it might as well have been on the dark side of the moon. He shivered at the insidious chill of the wind that seemed to find every chink in the clothes he had wrapped about himself and wished he was indoors in front of a warm fire. At that moment, the fires of the Holy Inquisition would have seemed inviting.

Leading the way, Bulchett paused to consult his scrap of parchment. 'We must find the Mitre Stone! That's the marker. The hill due north of the Mitre Stone is Ragman's Law.'

He led the way down the slope, at a more sedate pace now. Kemp glanced back across the plateau towards the escarpment, half expecting to see the reivers coming after them, but there was no sign of anyone. He did not know if that meant they were having a harder time getting over the escarpment than he and his companions had, or had set off in search of a way around that would save them from having to abandon their horses. It seemed too much to hope they would give up altogether.

The glen was a little more sheltered than the plateau had been, but the wind still howled about them and they had to wade through drifts of snow nearly waist deep in places. They slowed to a walk to catch their breath. Turning to face Kemp, Haine jabbed an index finger menacingly in his chest. 'You let Simkin fall!'

'I let him fall? You let go first!'

'What man would not, when an arrow came within a hair's breadth of cleaving his brain-pan in twain?' Haine raised a hand to where the arrow had scored a line through the hair above his left ear. Fresh blood still trickled down his cheek. Producing a rag, he wiped away the blood before pressing it to the wound.

Kemp noticed Haine had only three arrows left under his belt. He glanced surreptitiously at the arrows carried by Gudgeon and Vertue and saw they had two and five respectively. With so few arrows between them, they would not last long if they got into another shooting match with any Scots they might encounter on the way to England. Glancing at the sheaf under Tegg's belt, he saw he still had a dozen left. 'Lambert, will you share your arrows with Kenrick, Godwin and Hob? They'll not avail you with your arm in a sling.'

'One for you and two for me,' said Tegg. 'And three for Agnes by the sea! Four for a beggar and five for a knave, and six for the old king cold in his grave!'

Taking that as assent, Haine helped himself to Tegg's arrows. He handed four to Vertue and another four to Gudgeon, adding the rest to his own sheaf.

They reached the bottom of the glen. Here the ground was firm and level – if anything, it was weirdly flat – with only a couple of inches of snow on it, and devoid of trees or hedges. But the going was easy and they made good time.

Then something squeaked. It was an odd sound, reminiscent of something Kemp had heard before, though he could not place it. 'D'you hear that?' he asked Nompar.

'That creaking noise?' The *bourc* nodded. 'It seems to be coming from our feet.'

'What manner of earth is this?' wondered Vertue. 'It's too level for pasture.' He stamped a heel against the ground to try the soil under the snow.

Kemp felt the vibration – the ground seemed to pitch gently, as if he were standing on the deck of a ship barely perceptibly rocking at her anchor. The creaking noise sounded again, all around them now.

'Don't do that, Godwin!' said Kemp.

'I just want to know what manner of earth we walk on.' Vertue slammed his heel down again. The surface beneath his feet responded with a loud crack, then a whole succession of loud cracks. Vertue turned as white as the snow. 'Oh, Jesus Christ!' he cried out in dismay.

The ice shattered beneath his feet and he vanished, a little spout of water briefly fountaining up to show where he had fallen through. The water spread across the ice to wash away the thin covering of snow and reveal the cracks spreading outwards from the hole where Vertue had disappeared.

'No one move!' yelled Kemp. 'We've strayed onto a frozen lake!'

Fifteen

Gudgeon ran to where Vertue had disappeared. Kemp grabbed him as he ran past, realising that if the ploughman got too close to the hole, the ice would crack beneath him and they would lose two men instead of one. But Gudgeon was moving too fast. Thrown off balance, he slipped and went over, and Kemp was pulled over too. Both landed heavily and painfully on the ice, which cracked under the impact.

Sprawling on his side, Kemp stared in horror at the cracks spreading around him. He did not dare move, but Gudgeon was rising to his feet, heading towards the hole again.

'Hob, don't move!' cried Kemp.

'We've got to help Godwin!'

'If you get too close to that hole, you'll just widen it and then we'll lose you too. Even if we pull you out, you'll freeze to death before we can dry you out.'

'Everyone be still!' said Nompar. 'Get down on your hands and knees to spread your weight. Better yet, lie flat on your bellies. Then move slowly away from everyone else. If we all bunch together, we'll put too much weight on the ice in one place and it will break. If we spread out, we spread the weight. Then crawl to the nearest solid ground.'

Everyone who had not already dropped to their hands and knees now did so; everyone but Tegg, that was. 'Mother says "no", mother says "no", mother says "no",' he muttered anxiously to himself, over and over again. He wandered in tight circles on the ice, sometimes sunwise, then abruptly changing direction and going widdershins. He veered to where Haine lay.

'Get away from me, Lambert!' the butcher yelled fearfully.

Tegg flinched away from him, backing towards the hole where Vertue had disappeared.

'Lambert, halt!' Kemp shouted commandingly. 'Stop where you are!'

Tegg stopped. The ice creaked beneath his boots, but the twentyman's eyes were on Kemp.

'Look to your feet, Tegg. Look where you stand. Do you know where you are?'

Tegg looked down, then looked up at Kemp with bewilderment on his face. Kemp had the impression that the twentyman did not know where he was, but where he imagined himself to be was a mystery.

'I need you to get down,' said Kemp. 'Get down on your hands and knees and crawl.' It would have been better for Tegg to crawl on his belly like the rest of them, but with his arm in a sling that was out of the question.

Tegg dropped to his knees, a little too heavily for Kemp's liking; and too heavily for the ice's liking for that matter, if the way it crackled in protest was any indication.

Kemp pointed to a hummock in the snow on the shore of the lake. 'D'you see yon knob?'

Tegg shook his head.

'Just crawl in that direction.' Kemp pointed. 'You'll reach it soon enough.'

Tegg began crawling, leaning on his good arm, shuffling his knees towards the hand on the ice, then swinging the arm forward again.

Having done all he could for the twentyman, Kemp turned his attention to his own predicament. He shifted his position, rolling onto his stomach. His instinct was to stay perfectly still until he was satisfied the ice was steady, but in his heart he knew it would never be steady, not while nine of them crawled about on it. And if he did not keep moving, he feared he would get frozen to the ice. He began to inch his way back the way he had come. Gudgeon was on his right, crawling on a divergent course.

There was another crack, and a crackling noise. 'Sweet Jesu!' The ice had broken beneath one of Crawley's knees, and water welled up through it, spreading around him.

'Down on your belly, Rowland!' urged Nompar. 'Spread your weight!'

'I'll get wet!' whimpered Crawley.

'We'll light a fire and get you dried off as soon as we reach the shore. But if you go through the ice and go under, we cannot save you.'

Sobbing, Crawley lowered himself to the ice. Nompar, who was closest to the squire, took his knife from its sheath and slid it across the ice to where he lay. 'My knife in one hand, your own in the other: use their tips in the ice to pull yourself along.'

The squire did as Nompar instructed and had soon pulled himself out of the puddle of water which had welled up through the crack beneath him, and was already forming a new layer of ice. It was freezing where it had soaked Crawley's hose, too: his clothing crackled with each movement. But after he had gone a few yards without the ice cracking beneath him anymore, he returned his own knife to its sheath, slid Nompar's back across the ice to the *bourc*, and resumed crawling on his hands and knees.

'Where did you learn that trick?' Kemp asked Nompar.

'Crusading with the Teutonic Knights. If you think Scotland is cold, you should travel to Lettow, *mon amec!*'

Kemp's knees and elbows soon ached from crawling, and the cold from the ice seeped through his skin and into his bones. A distance he had covered in a few moments walking seemed to take an eternity on his stomach. He wondered how thick the ice was. Three, four inches? How thin could ice become before it snapped under a man's weight? But he knew that when a lake or a pond froze over, it froze from the edges inwards, so he had an idea the ice was thinnest at the centre, thickest at the edges. He reckoned Vertue had been in the middle of the lake when he had fallen through. And stamping his heel against it had probably not helped, either. But it meant that the closer to the shore of the lake Kemp got, the thicker the ice was beneath him.

He brushed the snow away to reveal the ice below his head. It looked dark and murky. He thought of Vertue being trapped under there, and wondered how it was he had never found his way back to the hole. Perhaps he could not swim, or perhaps the shock of the icy water had seized his thews with cramp. Even if Vertue could open his eyes under water, a man could probably not see more than a few feet through a lake, not well enough to pick out a hole from the surrounding ice. If he lost sight of the hole, his chances of finding his way back to it would be slim. In any case, by now far too much time had passed since his disappearance: no man could hold his breath so long.

Young, then Fisher, and now Vertue... all because Bulchett dreamed of finding some mythical artifact he thought would make him Emperor of the World. The knight was mad, and his madness was going to get them all killed. And yet, could Kemp lay all the blame at Bulchett's feet? For all that Young had had more sense than to believe the knight's nonsense, he had still passed up the opportunity to abandon this quest, following him as willingly as Vertue and Fisher... just as Kemp now followed him; Kemp, who now had nothing between him and a dark and watery death but two or three inches of brittle ice...

He looked up, blinking at the ice spicules the wind blew across the surface of the lake into his face, stinging his cheeks. Finally the lake shore was starting to look closer. He glanced over his shoulder. The distance to the hole was now greater than the distance to the shore. Gingerly, with infinitesimal slowness, Kemp rose on his hands and knees. The ice creaked a little, but did not crack. He crawled a short way in that manner, and once he had halved the distance to the shore a second time, he rose carefully to his feet, ready to drop to his belly again if the ice showed the least sign of cracking. It held. He walked the last few yards to the shore, and when he made it without falling through the ice, one by one the others did the same. Most of them arrived at different points on the shore of the lake, and had to walk around its perimeter to meet up again. Haine had gone after Tibbie to make sure she did not get any ideas about running off if she reached the shore ahead of the others. Now he took her by the arm and led her back towards where the others waited.

Nompar was the first to reach Kemp. 'You know he will get us all killed, *non pas*?' he asked in a low voice.

Kemp glanced to where Bulchett walked towards them. 'Not if I have owt to do with it.'

'If we persist in this folly, before you know it we'll have reached the point where the matter will be taken out of your hands.'

Kemp put a hand on the back of his neck, or at least the muffler wrapped around the neck of his habergeon. 'Remember what you said about loyalty flowing two ways? Tegg, Gudgeon and Haine are still my men. I cannot forsake them. And I promised Tibbie no harm would come to her.'

'Then you must work swiftly to persuade them to forsake Sir Alexander.'

'Tonight,' murmured Kemp. Bulchett had almost reached them. 'Tonight we'll break with Sir Alexander, and if we can persuade any of the others to come with us, we will.'

'Tonight may be too late,' muttered Nompar.

'Too late for what?' asked Bulchett, joining them.

'Too late to say a prayer for Vertue, if his soul is in Purgatory,' said Kemp.

'Nonsense,' said Bulchett. 'It's never too late to say a prayer for a soul in Purgatory.'

Crawley joined them, followed by Gudgeon leading Tegg, and Haine dragging Tibbie. 'Let's go.' Bulchett turned to lead the way around the top of the lake.

Gudgeon gazed mournfully towards the hole. 'What about Godwin?'

Nompar shook his head. 'I am sorry, *mon amec*. He is gone.'

'In that case… can I be King of Castile?'

Laughing – Vertue's death forgotten already, if it had ever mattered at all to Bulchett, which Kemp very much doubted – the knight clapped Gudgeon on the back. 'You may be king of the whole Iberian Peninsula, if you like.'

They clambered up to a saddle between two hills in the ridge to the west of the lake. As they neared the top, Kemp paused, breathing hard, to gaze back across the valley behind them. He could see distant figures, black against the snow, descending the slope to the tarn where Vertue had drowned. At that distance, Kemp could make out no details other than that they were on foot, and there were about two dozen of them. 'Sir Alexander!' he called.

The others turned back. 'What is it?' Bulchett called, a little tetchily.

Kemp silently pointed to the distant figures.

Bulchett flinched at the sight. 'That could be anyone,' he said, as if wishing would make it so.

'Aye,' said Kemp. 'From this distance it might be a troupe of dancing girls from far Cathay. But I'll wager it's Nixon and his men.'

'What must we do to throw them off the scent?'

Kemp glanced across to where Haine kept a tight grip on Tibbie's arm. 'We could let the woman go. For aught we know, she may be the only reason they're still chasing us.'

'She knows too much, Kemp. She can tell them whither we're bound.' Bulchett shook his head. 'We'll keep her with us: we may need a hostage. Think of some other way. Can we not catch them in an ambushment?'

'Four archers – one too sick to use his bow – and a knight, an arse-licking squire and a false, witless ape, against six-and-twenty reivers?' Kemp shook his head. 'By all means stay here and make a fight of it; I'm going on.'

Bulchett turned to Nompar. 'You count it no insult, to be called a false, witless ape?'

The *bourc* smiled faintly. 'I do not think I was the one he spoke of.'

On the other side of the saddle, they descended through some woods. They had to wade through snow-drifts that had banked high between the trees, and in many places the snow concealed thickets of brambles and briars that tugged at their ankles, tore their leggings and eventually barred their way entirely, forcing them to retreat and seek out some other path to the bottom of the valley. The tapping of a woodpecker in search of grubs in a tree trunk sounded sporadically, and here and there small birds had left the imprints of their feet where they had hopped about on the snow. The tracks of a pair of young deer foraging in the woods crossed the path of Bulchett and his men at one point. The mournful howl of a wolf sounded not too far away, almost at once taken up by the rest of the pack, which was a dozen strong if their eerie chorus was any indication. There were no wolves left in England, though Kemp had heard them howling in Brittany.

Tegg stumbled and fell in the snow. Kemp helped him to his feet, but it was clear from the pained expression on the twentyman's face he was nearing the end of his tether. And Crawley's teeth chattered with cold: he had not had a chance to dry out his wet clothes after he had almost fallen through the ice.

'We need to rest,' said Kemp. 'There's wood enough here to build a fire so Rowland can dry himself out.'

'No time for that,' said Bulchett. 'Ragman's Law is just beyond the next ridge, I'm sure of it. We'll be there in a couple of hours. Besides, if we tarry, do we not run the risk of being caught by Nixon and his men?'

'They're a couple of hours behind us,' said Kemp. 'I reckon we can pause for as long as it takes to walk a couple of miles. Besides, Tegg's weary. He cannot walk another step.'

Bulchett glanced at the twentyman, clearly contemplating whether or not he would be better off leaving him behind.

'P-p-please, Sir Alexander,' Crawley stammered through his clattering jaws.

Bulchett gave a long-suffering sigh. 'Very well, then. You lot wait here. I'll scout ahead.'

'Be careful, Sir Alexander,' said Crawley. 'I don't know what we'll do without you to lead us.'

Bulchett strode off.

'Such a courageous man!' said the squire. 'Letting us huddle here while he selflessly risks his life by going on ahead to find the way.'

'That's drivel,' said Haine. 'I reckon he's gone for a shit.'

'If we're waiting for him to empty himself of excrement, we could be waiting for some time,' Nompar said with a smile.

'How dare you say that?' demanded Crawley. 'Sir Alexander is a great and worthy man! We're privileged to serve him.'

'Do you hear yourself?' asked Nompar.

The squire turned to him with a frown. 'What mean you?'

'You're so lavish in your praise of Sir Alexander,' said the *bourc*. 'I mean no offence, but... there's some would call you a lickspittle.'

Crawley furrowed his brow. 'I only give praise where 'tis due. Sir Alexander is a prince amongst men: brave, handsome, intelligent, loyal to those who follow him, his prowess at the tourney matched only by his prowess in the chase—'

'That's just the sort of talk I speak of. Ordinary folk don't speak of other men so, not even the ones we truly admire. We'd fear lest others think us a… well, lickspittle. In any case, I wonder that you can look on a man like Sir Alexander and see naught but good in him. The man is patently an ass.'

'Then I pity you, for you are blind to his greatness.'

'Sir Alexander's a hen-hearted trifler,' said Kemp. 'He were at the Greyfriars when it burned down on Candlemas, was he not? Did he have summat to do with the fire?'

'How dare you impugn such an honourable servant of his king?'

'That's not a denial. He *was* at the Greyfriars that night, wasn't he? By accident or design, he started it, and when the king took me to task for it, none condemned me more loudly than he who was then made captain in my place. Damn that whoreson! He's already got Dunstan, Simkin and Godwin killed. We'll all be slain, if we persist in this insane quest.'

Gudgeon shook his head. 'Sir Alexander says he'll make us all kings.'

'He's lying, Hob. There are no such things as demons. There is no Brazen Head. There never was. It's a myth.'

'You're working for her, aren't you?' said Crawley.

'Who?'

'Meridiana! Everyone knows demons are real. They only try to trick us into thinking they're not real so they may work their evil unhindered. Why else would you seek to undermine Sir Alexander's noble quest to find the

Brazen Head, except to spare your demonic mistress the humiliation of being bound to serve him?'

Kemp stared at him. 'Do you truly believe the drivel you spout, or do you just say whatever you think Bulchett wants you to say?'

Crawley burst into tears.

With a sigh, Kemp turned to Gudgeon. 'Make a fire.'

'How am I to find any firewood under all this snow?'

'Break down a sapling if you must.'

'What if the owner of these woods—?'

'The owner of these woods is likely a vassal of David Bruce's,' said Kemp, 'in which case, he doesn't need the excuse of us having damaged one of his trees to justify doing us harm.'

'A shame we divven't have Simkin's hatchet,' said Haine.

Nompar drew his sword from its scabbard. 'Use this.'

Gudgeon took the sword from the *bourc*, admiring the craftsmanship of the jewelled hilt. 'A canny weapon! Was this your father's sword? Would using it to cut firewood not be tantamount to using a destrier to draw a dung cart?'

'My brother carries my father's sword. That I bought from a swordsmith in Toledo.'

Gudgeon hewed down a sapling and hacked it into logs. They built a fire beneath a tree and Kemp got it started with flint and tinder.

'Yon's green wood,' said Haine. 'It'll smoke and betray where we are to the rivelings.'

'The smoke won't rise high in such cold weather,' said Kemp. 'Besides, the reivers already know where we are. Our footprints will lead them to us long before the smoke betrays us.'

Crawley spread his mantle on the snow and sat down on it to remove his hose, hanging them on a bough above the fire to dry out. The others crowded around, warming themselves.

Gazing at the sky, Kemp saw leaden clouds massing on the horizon. He did not much care for the idea of being caught out in the open when that storm reached them. He turned to Tegg. 'How d'you feel?'

'Better,' said the twentyman. It was the first coherent thing he had said all day, and indeed there was more intelligence in his eyes than there had been for some time.

Kemp pushed himself to his feet. 'Think you can march a few miles?'

'I'll try. Where are we bound?'

'The English border. What about you, Rowland? Are your hose dry?'

Crawley reached up to finger the toes. 'Nearly. But surely you do not suggest we march on without waiting for Sir Alexander to return?'

'I'm not even sure he means to return. Stay here and wait for him if you have that much faith in him, but the rest of us are moving off. What about you, Hob? Will you come with us?'

'Sir Alexander says I can be King of Castile,' Gudgeon said sulkily.

'How? Because he's going to find a Brazen Head with a demoness trapped inside, and use her power to make himself emperor? Think for a moment: when have you ever heard of such a thing happening, except in a fairy tale?'

'You would say that! It's as Master Rowland says: you only want to undermine Sir Alexander!'

'A wise man once told me that when two men tell you contradictory things, you should never trust the one who's telling you what you want to hear, just because it is what you want to hear. Thus swindlers persuade their pigeons to fall for their lies. Belief, disbelief... that's a choice. When you find yourself floundering in a slough of woe because you swallowed such folly, you'll have no right to say, "But Sir Alexander told me..." Choose to believe nonsense, and you bear the blame for the outcome. Not Bulchett, not fate, not an uncaring God... *you*, Hob. So I'll ask you one last time: who will you believe? The man who promises you a kingdom, or the man who tells you the cold, harsh reality?'

'Ye divven't know how hard I've had it!' sobbed Gudgeon. 'Me parents died of the plague... all me life I've had to work us fingers to the bone to put bread on me family's table... every day that God sends, all I do is work, work, work, while folk born wi' silver spoons in their mouths have servants to wait on them hand and foot. When did they ever work a day in their lives? They divven't know what the likes of us have to put up with. Divven't I deserve a reward after so many years of labour? In't I entitled?'

'It's not a question of "deserve". Life simply isn't fair and, if you think otherwise, you're in for a great, big, god-damned disappointment. In your heart, you know that's the truth. Maybe in Heaven we get our reward, though I have my doubts.'

Gudgeon shook his head. 'I put me trust in Sir Alexander.'

Kemp sighed, and turned to Haine. 'Maybe you don't like me, Kenrick. I don't much care for you. But you're still one of my men, whatever anyone says, and that means I've a duty to you.'

'I'm not one of your men. I never was. You're just a commoner like me. Not like Sir Alexander. He's a proper nobleman. A cousin of the king, they say. I put my faith in him before I put it in the hands of a self-serving whoreson like you. And the more that sorrows you, the better I like it.'

'What about Tegg?' asked Nompar.

'Tegg's coming with us,' said Kemp. 'Canonbie Priory lies betwixt here and Carlisle. The monks there will care for him.'

'Whit about me?' asked Tibbie.

'You also,' said Kemp. 'We'll take you to a place of safety on our way to the English border.'

'Not so hasty!' said Haine. 'You heard what Sir Alexander said. She's his captive, not yours—'

Kemp placed a hand on the hilt of his sword. 'If you're that insistent you're not my man, then I'll gladly discuss the matter with you at swords' point.'

'Discuss what matter?' asked Bulchett, reappearing around a bank of snow-laden brambles.

'Kemp wants to betray you,' Crawley said at once. 'He says he's going, and he's taking Nompar, Tegg and the woman with him. And I simply will not repeat some of the foul and baseless words he used to describe you!'

Kemp clenched his fists. He had expected Crawley to betray him to Bulchett, of course, but he was a little shocked that he did it so swiftly and blatantly.

'Perhaps you and I need to talk,' the knight said to Kemp.

The Midlander shook his head. 'We've wasted enough time in talk.'

'At least have the courtesy to hear me out. There are matters you are unaware of, matters I think will be of great interest to you. But I can only discuss them with you privily.'

'Owt you've got to say to me, you can say in front of these others.'

'A noble sentiment.' Lowering his voice, Bulchett moved closer to Kemp, so he could speak to the Midlander without any of the others overhearing. 'But I think you should hear what I have to say before you decide anything. If you think it's appropriate to share with the others, on your own head be it...' He gestured for the Midlander to precede him.

Kemp sighed and began walking through the trees, virgin snow scrunching beneath his boots. His headache had never really gone away, but now it seemed to be pounding worse than ever. When he was about fifty yards from where the others huddled about the fire, he stopped and turned back to Bulchett. 'Very well. What is this great secret you wish to share with me?'

'A little further, I pray you.'

'They cannot hear us from so far off!'

'Indulge me.' Bulchett pointed to another thick bank of brambles. 'Let's stand on the other side of yon briars.'

Kemp cast another glance at the approaching storm clouds. The sooner he heard Bulchett out, the sooner he and Nompar and anyone else who chose to accompany them could begin their search for shelter. 'As you will.' He strode around the far side of the brambles and turned to face Bulchett. 'No more delay!'

'I'm less than satisfied with your behaviour, Kemp. You've done naught but seek to undermine me ever since you stumbled into our camp the night before last. As a prisoner charged with setting alight the Franciscan friary at Haddington, you should spend more time thinking about how you will account for your failures to the king than seeking to throw the blame upon me.'

'Even though you were the one who started the fire?'

'Ah. Oh. Ah! No! It won't do, Kemp, trying to blame me for your incompetence. I'll not have it!'

'Three of my men are dead now. That's just the three that have been killed since you started trying to lead them to Ragman's Law instead of heading for Carlisle. I'm not counting the ones who died in the fire you started, or the men who died in the ambush in Lauderdale because you didn't have sense enough to post outriders. Do you really think you'll find a secret temple in these mountains containing a demoness trapped in a Brazen Head? Or is that just another lie, to cover up whatever your true purpose is?' Kemp pressed a hand to his aching head. It made it difficult for him to concentrate on anything else, and he felt drained by the effort of venting his spleen upon the knight. 'Why am I even wasting my time bothering to ask you? You're so accustomed to lying, I warrant you could not tell me the truth even if you wanted to.'

'You impertinent dog!' spluttered Bulchett. 'I don't have to put up with your insolence—' He broke off suddenly, gazing at something in the snow beyond Kemp. As the Midlander turned to see what it was, Bulchett flipped the brim of his helmet at the back, hard enough to knock it from his head despite the chin strap.

Wondering what the hell Bulchett was playing at, Kemp stooped to retrieve it. Before he could rise again, something hard and heavy collided with the back of his skull. Blackness flickered behind his eyes and his legs would no longer support him. The next thing he knew, he was down on his hands and knees in the snow. He caught sight of something out of the corner of his eye, a blur moving towards him at great speed. When it reached him, it smacked into his temple.

The blizzard and the snow on the ground whirled around him. He was vaguely aware of Bulchett standing over him, too blurred for Kemp to make out the expression on his face. The blur darkened, until all Kemp could see was blackness, and then he could not even see that much.

Sixteen

'What d'you reckon Sir Alexander's saying to Kemp?' Haine wondered out loud.

'Does it matter?' asked Nompar. 'It will be a lie, whether Bulchett believes it or not.'

Crawley looked outraged. 'How can you say that? Sir Alexander is the most honest man that ever drew breath.'

Nompar only threw back his head and laughed. That annoyed Haine. One of the things he liked about Bulchett was the way smug whoresons like Kemp and the *bourc* got so worked up about his deceit. When Nompar laughed about it, no matter how cynically, it robbed him of his sport.

'Whatever he's saying, he's surely taking his time about it,' said Haine.

'Expressing himself clearly and concisely is not one of Sir Alexander's strengths,' said Nompar.

'Here he comes now,' said Gudgeon.

Haine turned to look in the direction Bulchett and Kemp had wandered. He could see the knight returning, but not the Midlander.

'Where's Kemp?' wondered Gudgeon.

They had to wait for Bulchett to reach the campfire so Nompar could repeat the ploughman's question.

'He's run away,' said the knight.

Nompar furrowed his brow. 'Run away?'

'He said he'd take no more orders from me. Then he punched me in the face and ran off. When we get back to England, I shall send his description to every sheriff in the land, with orders to arrest him on sight for desertion.'

'Where in the face did he punch you?'

'On the jaw.'

'I see no bruise.'

'I don't bruise easily.'

The *bourc* shook his head. 'I cannot believe he just ran off like that.'

Bulchett bridled. 'Do you call me a liar?'

Nompar opened his mouth, closed it again, thought for a moment, then spoke. 'If Kemp ran off, I think you have misinterpreted his motives. Let me go after him. I'll persuade him to return.' He started to walk towards the brambles Kemp and Bulchett had disappeared behind earlier, but the other knight caught him by the arm and held him back.

'He's long gone, Sir Nompar. You'll not catch him.'

'Nevertheless, I would try. Martin is my friend.'

'You will not go after him, Sir Nompar. That is an order.'

'I do not take orders from you.' The *bourc* broke free of Bulchett's grip and continued towards the brambles.

'Haine!' said Bulchett. 'Nock an arrow to your bow. Be ready to shoot the *bourc* at my command.'

The butcher took a bodkin-tipped arrow from under his belt and nocked it to his string with mixed feelings. He had slain plenty of men in the past and would feel no compunction in adding Nompar to the list. The *bourc* was a foreigner and Haine did not like foreigners. At such close range, the bodkin-tip would punch through his armour. Haine would shoot him where it would not kill him outright, but he would spend a long time bleeding to death.

On the other hand, Nompar was Kemp's friend, and as much as Haine wanted to believe Bulchett when he said the Midlander had run away, he shared Nompar's scepticism. Kemp was in these woods somewhere, perhaps secretly watching them from some hiding place nearby. If Haine slew the *bourc*, then Kemp might seek to avenge his friend. A shudder of disquiet ran down his spine.

Bulchett had spoken loudly enough for Nompar to hear. Now the *bourc* stood frozen a short distance away. Haine nocked his arrow, ready to draw and loose at Bulchett's word of command.

Nompar turned back with a quizzical expression.

Bulchett nodded. 'I mean it. I command here. If you'll not obey my orders, I'll have you slain.'

Nompar gestured towards the brambles. 'But Kemp—'

'Kemp is gone. What more is there to say? We must push on for Ragman's Law.' Bulchett resumed walking, heading down the slope towards the bottom of the glen. Crawley and Tegg followed him.

'Grab the woman, Hob,' said Haine. 'Make sure she dun't run off.'

Gudgeon took Tibbie by the arm. 'Come along, lass.'

That left only Nompar and Haine. The butcher still had his arrow nocked, waiting to see what the *bourc* would do. He jerked his head after the others, motioning Nompar to follow them. After a moment's hesitation, the *bourc* complied. Haine followed him down through the trees, his draw on his bow relaxed now but his arrow still nocked, ready to draw and loose in an instant: Nompar had acceded a little too easily for his liking and Haine itched for him to try something.

Tibbie stumbled in the snow. Haine's instinct was to help her up again, but he could not do that while he had an arrow nocked to his bow. She managed to rise without any help from him. God's nails, but she was a handsome woman! He would have some sport with that one…

Some warning instinct made him glance towards Nompar, only to find the *bourc* glaring at him. Nompar's penetrating gaze seemed to read Haine's mind. He looked away hurriedly, not back to Tibbie, but to the snow before him where it had already been trampled by Bulchett, Crawley and Tegg.

It began snowing again, thick curtains of fat, tumbling snowflakes that made the previous day's blizzard look like a light snowfall. A biting, blinding wind drove the flakes into their eyes and piled them on helmets and shoulders, plastering mantles, brigandines and cote-hardies. It piled on the ground, too, forming deep drifts Bulchett and his companions struggled to wade through.

'Bunch up, bunch up!' shouted the knight. 'If we lose touch in this lot, we'll never find one another again.'

Stumbling along, Tegg missed his footing and sprawled in the snow. Gudgeon helped him to his feet. *Why bother?* wondered Haine. It was obvious the twentyman was dying.

Haine hugged his mantle about him more tightly. It seemed like a lifetime ago when they had huddled around the hearth of the Liddells' croft, though that had only been the previous night. Now he felt so cold, he could scarcely remember what it was like to be warm, much less imagine being that way ever again. He yearned for it nevertheless, and cursed the day he had ever set foot in this wretched, wintry land. He felt so miserable, he even found himself wondering if perhaps Kemp had not been right after all:

Bulchett was going to lead them all to their deaths in this bleak and frozen wilderness.

It was pure chance they stumbled into the sheiling. Like the Liddells' croft, it was so thickly heaped with snow it looked like a part of the landscape. Visibility in the blizzard was so poor, they might have stumbled past twenty yards to either side without even realising it was there. Instead, fate led them straight to it. Men like Bulchett always enjoyed such good fortune, Haine reflected. They led charmed lives, and no amount of sinful behaviour would change that, not in this life at least. The fact they were generally born into the nobility was the first indication, for what better luck could a man have in life than to be born to wealthy parents? And surely whatever good fortune befell such men also benefited those with the foresight to hitch their own fortunes to them?

'Clear away the snow heaped in front of the door,' ordered Bulchett.

'What if there's someone inside?' asked Gudgeon.

'There won't be,' said Tegg. 'This is a sheiling: neat-herds bring their cattle up to these parts for the summer grazing, and back down into the valleys after harvest. We'll find none here at this season.'

They got the door open and ducked their heads under the low lintel. Within, they shrugged off bow staves and packs and made themselves comfortable. Haine crouched to make a fire in the hearth at the end opposite the empty byre.

Raising the visor of his bascinet to view his companions, Bulchett frowned. 'Where's the *bourc*?'

Haine looked around in surprise. The Gascon was no longer with them.

'He must have lost his way in the blizzard,' said Crawley. 'Poor devil! He'll not last long out in the open in this weather.'

'Good riddance!' said Bulchett. 'Foreigners are not to be trusted. Not even ones who owe fealty to King Edward.'

Tegg sank to his knees on the floor of the croft, then pitched forward. Tibbie ran to him, turning him over. 'Is he dead?' asked Crawley.

'Nae, he's but fainted.' Tibbie gently took Tegg's arm from its sling and unwrapped the bandage.

Haine recoiled from the sickly-sweet stench that emanated from the suppurating wound. 'It's rankled,' he said. 'The arm must be amputated.'

'You might kill him,' said Gudgeon.

'He'll die for sure if we divven't.'

'Are you volunteering to cut his arm off?' demanded Bulchett.

'Me?' Haine felt a shudder run down his spine. Butchering a cow or a pig was one thing, but butchering a living human being who was not an enemy? What if he made a mess of it? The others would blame him... 'Nay!'

'It needs a surgeon,' said Tibbie. 'Ye cannae just lop his arm off and hope for the best. Ye must leave enough skin to fold over the stump, and stop up the arteries, or he'll bleed to death.'

'Where are we to find a surgeon hereabouts?' demanded Crawley.

'Make him comfortable for now,' ordered Bulchett. 'We'll leave him here when this storm breaks. 'Tis but a few miles to Ragman's Law. In a few hours we'll have the Brazen Head. That will tell us what we must do to save him.'

Bulchett took Crawley up to the far end of the sheiling to talk to him privily. Gudgeon touched Haine on the arm and jerked his head towards the byre, indicating he wanted a word. Haine was reluctant to leave Tibbie – he knew she was just looking for a chance to make a break for it, and he did not think the blizzard outside would discourage her – but she was busy making Tegg comfortable, and Haine supposed he could just as easily keep an eye on her from the fence between the byre and the rest of the sheiling.

'What do you want?' he asked Gudgeon.

'I want you to kill me.'

Haine thought he must have misheard. 'What?'

His eyes wide with panic, Gudgeon grabbed two fist-fuls of the hem of Haine's chaperon. 'I'm possessed by a demon, Kenrick! I divven't know what's real and what's not anymore!'

Haine pried Gudgeon's hands from his chaperon. 'You're not possessed by a demon, Hob. There are no such things.'

'Then why are we bound for Ragman's Law?'

'Why are we——?' Haine laughed. 'Divven't be a wooden-headed fool. In any case, if you're that sure you're possessed by a demon, why not kill yourself? Why drag me into it?'

'Suicide's a mortal sin.'

'So's murder!'

'Aye, but you've slain men afore now.'

'Happen I have, but never because I thought one was possessed by a demon. Besides, if you were possessed, then if you did kill yourself, it wouldn't count as suicide. Folk would say you weren't in your right mind.'

'Only if someone told them. If I kill myself, will you tell them how the demon made me do it?'

Haine laughed again. 'I'll tell 'em you weren't in your right mind, aye.' He slapped Gudgeon hard. 'Stop being a silly fool. There are no such things as demons and you're not possessed by one. Simkin was only teasing when he said them things.'

That seemed to calm Gudgeon, but only for a moment. Then the colour drained from his face. He stared at Haine. 'You're one of them, too!'

'What?'

'What you just said. That's exactly what a demon would tell me to convince me I wasn't possessed by a demon. You've been possessed too!'

'Divven't talk daft!'

'Or happen it's the demon in my head, making me *think* you're telling me there are no such things as demons,' Gudgeon mused out loud. 'Happen you're not there at all; happen the demon's only making me imagine I'm talking to ye.'

Haine stared at him. He had heard stories of men being possessed by demons, though he had never seen it for himself. Usually a chapman passing through Ulverston would stop at one of the town's taverns to tell how a fellow he had met on the other side of the Pennines had told him a story about his sister-in-law's cousin had been possessed... folk were all a bit peculiar on t'other side of the Pennines... Haine had always assumed that somewhere along the line there would be someone like Simkin Fisher, telling tall tales purely for the pleasure of seeing who would be credulous enough to be taken in by them. But maybe it happened like this: some poor halfwit like Gudgeon got it into his head he was possessed, and lost his mind. Not that he had ever had much of a mind to lose in the first place... It was easy to see how credulous folk finding someone like Gudgeon spouting this kind of nonsense would believe he was truly possessed.

'If you reckon I'm just a figment of your imagination, then there's no use in me talking to you,' Haine told Gudgeon at last.

Tibbie cleared her throat. 'Ah need to ease nature.'

'I'll watch her.' Grabbing her by an arm, Haine dragged her outside, ducking his head under the low lintel and pulling the door to behind her. The snow still fell thickly and after the relative warmth of the sheiling, the air outside seemed colder than ever.

'Am Ah to pish wi' ye watching me?'

'Piss or not, I'm not taking us eyes off you for a moment.' Haine dragged her around the back of the sheiling. The building provided a little shelter from the driving snow. Haine pushed her away from him. 'Get on with it.'

Hitching up the skirts of her kirtle and the shift below, she squatted at the foot of the wall. A glimpse of her bare buttocks made Haine stiffen inside his braies.

'Will you piss or not?' he demanded at length.

'Ah cannae do it wi' ye watching.'

'You're just trying to put it off, aren't you?'

She furrowed her brow. 'I dinnae understand.'

'Yes, you do.' Reaching under the hem of his tunic, he pushed down his braies and showed her his stiff pintle. The kiss of the cold air upon it, and the expression of horror on her face, only excited him more. 'Happen we'd best get it over with.'

Rising to her feet, she tried to make a break for it, but he caught her, seizing her in his arms. He forced her down on her back in the snow. The more she struggled, the more it excited him. One time a woman had tried to give herself willingly to him, but he had found himself impotent on that occasion, and the woman had laughed at him. The thought of that humiliation still filled him with rage. The same rage filled him now. *God damn all bitches*, he thought to himself. *You're not laughing now, are you?*

It was near impossible to wrench up the hem of her kirtle and hold her down at the same time. He lay on top of her, pinning her down with his weight.

'Help!' she screamed. 'Help! Help!'

He punched her on the jaw. 'Shut up, bitch! There's no one going to save you. Lie still. Who knows? You might even enjoy it!'

She thumped him in the ribs. He caught her by the wrist, and pinned her arm in the snow. Was that his knife in her hand? The bitch had taken his knife! And there was blood on the blade. Had she stabbed herself? He looked down and saw blood on her kirtle.

While he was staring at the blood, she managed to lift a knee into his crotch. Pain erupted through his loins. He rolled off her, letting go of her wrist, and she slashed at his face with the knife. He leaped back from her, and she got to her feet and ran off into the blizzard.

'Run, bitch!' he called after her, laughing. 'You cannot hide from me! Your footprints in the snow will betray you!'

Had she cut his cheek? He had not felt it, but he kept the blade of his knife keen, and perhaps his cheek was numbed by the cold. He raised a hand only to find it was covered in blood before he even touched his face.

Crimson blossomed in the snow to his left. Where in hell had that come from? He turned to see, but there was no one and nothing there. More blood splashed into the snow, again to his left even though he had turned. And again – this time he saw a gout of it jet through the air before it spread through the snow. It was coming from him. He looked down at himself and saw a rent in his tunic where she had thumped him. Except she had done more than thump him, he realised: she must have already taken his knife by then.

The blood continued to spurt from his side. He clapped a hand over the wound, trying to stanch it. He felt sick and dizzy. How grievously was he wounded? By Saint Neot, that was a lot of blood!

Anger filled him. The damned bitch! She had murdered him. Well, he would teach her... he started to follow her footprints in the snow, but before he had taken more than a few steps a leaden hand on his shoulder forced him down. The snowflakes whirling around him whirled even more swiftly. The thick snow clasped his body in its icy embrace. He tried to get up again, but his limbs would no longer obey him. He was dying... anger gave way to despair. This was not fair! He was not even past his thirtieth winter... he did not deserve this!

Whimpering, snivelling, blind to his own sins to the last, Kenrick Haine felt darkness flood over him even as the last drops of his lifeblood gouted out into the cold, indifferent snow.

–

Pain.

Pain and cold.

Cold and pain. Regaining consciousness to find himself lying in the snow, Kemp had the weird feeling he had been here before. Then he remembered he *had*, only a couple of days earlier, after the Scots had ambushed King Edward's host in Lauderdale. But this was not then. Things had happened since then. He remembered meeting Nompar, and Bulchett and his men... Young getting shot... Fisher falling to his death... Vertue vanishing through the ice... Bulchett's insane plan to try to find the Brazen Head of legend.

Kemp's head ached. Someone had hit him. Bulchett... there had been something in his hand, the pommel of his knife. Kemp felt like a fool for letting it happen. Nompar had warned him against underestimating Bulchett, but he had been so convinced of the knight's cowardice he had not anticipated any kind of threat from him. He could count himself lucky Bulchett had not finished him off. Perhaps he thought he had killed him.

No use lying here in the snow wondering about it: he would catch his death. He had to get up, get after Bulchett and the others. The knight would rue the day... And then there was Haine... he hoped Nompar was keeping an eye on him, making sure he did not try anything with Tibbie Liddell.

He tried to get up, but to do that he needed to put a hand on the snow to push himself up, and to do *that* he needed to take his hands out of the small of his back. But he could not do that because of something cutting into his wrists. Bulchett had not thought he was dead, because no one in his right mind killed a man and then tied him up. But clearly Bulchett was not in his right mind.

He tried moving his legs. They were bound at the ankles. Snow fell off him as he rolled on his back, and he managed to sit up. It was still falling thickly, so he realised he could not have lain bereft of his senses for long. He tried to work the cord binding his wrists under his buttocks, but his hands were bound too closely for that.

He glanced down at where he kept his knife in a sheath on his belt, but it was gone. So was his sword. Kemp could see his bow in its bag a few yards away, partially covered with snow, and the fletchings of some of his arrows sticking out of the snow where they too had been discarded. There was no sign of his sword or his knife.

Why had Bulchett not killed him? Was he coming back for him? Kemp could not think why. Perhaps he was hoping he would freeze to death in the snow: if he could not find a way to break free before nightfall, that might prove to be a very real possibility. Still, it seemed strange to him that Bulchett had not simply slit his throat when he had the chance. But people could be squeamish when it came to spilling blood. When he had been a boy, a man had died of old age and his widow had inherited his dog, a mongrel she had never much cared for. She had been too poor to feed it and it had been such a notoriously ill-natured beast she had been unable to give it to anyone else in the village. In the end she had led it into the middle of Knighton Woods, tied it to a tree and left it there. She had been too squeamish to kill it, but had apparently lost no sleep over leaving it to starve to death. Maybe that was how Bulchett saw Kemp: a mangy, ill-tempered cur that was more trouble than he was worth. The thought made him smile.

A wolf howled in the woods, not far off. Once again, the rest of the pack took up the refrain. Kemp felt a shudder run down his spine. Of course, even in those places where there were still wolves, they rarely attacked men. But then they did not often find men lying in the snow, tethered like a goat...

Bulchett knew there were wolves in these woods: he had heard them howling, just as Kemp had. The whoreson had only left him alive to be torn apart by wolves! Was probably chuckling at the thought somewhere, regretting that he had been unable to stay and watch. When Kemp caught up with him...

But first he had to stay alive, and that meant breaking free of his bonds. By drawing his knees up, digging his heels into the snow and pushing himself backwards, he was able to squirm on his buttocks. With a little extra squirming he could change direction, too. He circled about laboriously, then wriggled back to where Bulchett had left his arrows. He found a tendril of brambles, hidden beneath the snow, with the underside of his thighs. The sharp thorns tore his hose and lacerated his skin painfully. A few more inches: something snapped under his weight. An arrow... his groping hands found the shaft. They worked their way along it to... the fletchings. The wrong half. He set it carefully aside and scrabbled in the snow with frozen fingers. At length he found the other half, worked his way along it to find the arrowhead. But it was a bodkin-tip. What he wanted was a broadhead, with two sharp edges which, with a little patience, he hoped he would be able to saw through his bonds.

Paws pitter-pattered in the snow. Glancing up, he saw a wolf trot into the clearing less than thirty yards away. The wolf halted, staring straight at him.

'Go the Devil's way!' Kemp snarled at it.

The wolf did not move. Maybe it was just because Kemp was sitting down, but it looked big. It had a lean, hungry look to it, but those jaws were strong enough to crunch bones.

A dozen more wolves trotted into the clearing, crowding behind the first. Kemp's blood turned to ice in his veins and his stomach shrivelled and knotted. Against one wolf, with his hands free, he would have taken his chances. Against thirteen, and him with his hands and feet bound…? He imagined Bulchett watching, guffawing at his predicament. If Kemp got out of this one, the knight was in serious trouble. But who was he fooling? There was no getting out of this. The best he could hope for now was not to die like a coward, but to go out fighting to the last. He could kick and head-butt, even bound though he was. Little use against wolves: it would not be long before he felt their fangs tear his flesh, their jaws crunch his bones.

They hung back. To them this must have seemed too good to be true: Kemp would have been equally suspicious if he had been walking through the woods and found a roast capon just sitting on a trencher as if someone had left it there for him. Perhaps the wolves were not hungry enough to tackle a man? They did not understand – yet – that his hands were bound and he could not fight back. But they looked hungry. He doubted he would last long once they overcame their suspicion.

Seventeen

The biggest wolf in the pack stalked towards Kemp, fangs bared in a snarl. Most of the rest crowded behind it, but another big wolf crept around to his left, a third skulking around to his right.

His bound hands scrabbled in the snow behind him for another arrow. 'Hie you hence! Get off out of it, you mangy whoresons!'

His groping hands found another arrow. He ran his fingers down the shaft. A broadhead! But now he had to angle the cutting edge of the head against the cord binding his wrists.

The wolves had circled him now. The biggest tried to clamp its jaws on one of his feet. Kemp managed to slam the soles of both boots into its snout and it twisted away with a yelp of frustration, but then another wolf caught his arm in its jaws. The chain-mail sleeve of his habergeon and the padded gambeson beneath provided some protection, but the sheer force those jaws exerted was agonising.

And then he dropped the arrow he was holding. With a groan of despair, he scrabbled for it in the snow behind him, but it seemed to have vanished.

The other wolves crowded around him, baying, frenzied with bloodlust. Kemp managed to slam his heels into another snout, but then a pair of jaws clamped on an unarmoured leg and he cried out as teeth ripped at his flesh. *This is it*, he thought. *This is where I die...*

A wolf's head exploded into a cloud of white powder. Someone had thrown a snowball at it. Startled, the wolf shied away from Kemp. Another snowball impacted against the hide of a second wolf, and then the others scattered, realising they now had to deal with an enemy who did not have his limbs bound. They rallied a short distance away, glancing from Kemp to another figure coming around the thicket of brambles.

The newcomer stooped to scoop up another fistful of snow, compacted it into a ball in his hands, and shied it with unerring accuracy at the biggest wolf.

'*Vai te'n cagar!*' shouted Nompar. He did not reach to make another snowball, but drew his sword from its scabbard. It was a moot point whether or not the wolves understood what the razor-edged steel could do, but they clearly understood that tackling an unbound man was a different kettle of fish from a helpless one. The biggest wolf turned and loped away through the trees, and the others streamed after it.

Nompar slotted his sword back into its scabbard and ran across to where Kemp sat. The Midlander's heart still pounded in his chest, but he was ready to weep with relief at seeing the *bourc*. If they ever made it back to England, he was going to have to find some way to pay his friend back for the many times he had saved his life.

Nompar crouched behind Kemp to untie the cord binding his wrists. 'Are you hurt?'

'A little gnawed on, but I'll live. What are you doing back there?'

'My fingers are too frozen to pick apart this knot.'

'Just cut it.'

'Cut it? This is good quality cord! Waste not, want not—'

'Cut it, for the love of Mary, before my arse freezes to the ground!'

Nompar sighed and produced a knife. He cut through the cord binding Kemp's wrists, then the Midlander took the knife from him and cut the cord about his ankles – one of his own bowstrings, by the look of it – before handing the knife back. He unfastened one of his hose from his braies and rolled it down to examine the bite in his leg. The tooth-marks oozed blood. Kemp tied a rag around the wound to stanch it, before rolling his hose back up and tying it to his braies again.

'Bulchett?' he asked Nompar.

'Leading the others down the valley. He told us you had run off, but I knew he was lying...'

'How could you tell?' Kemp scrabbled in the snow for the rest of his arrows. 'Were his lips moving?'

Nompar grinned. 'I gave him the slip in the snowstorm and came back to seek you.'

'You left Mistress Liddell alone with Haine?'

'I do not think Haine will try anything while the others are there watching him.'

'No doubt. The trouble with whoresons like Haine is they've way of arranging things so they're *not* being watched.'

Kemp gathered up the last of his arrows and tucked them under his belt at the back, then slung his bow in its bag from his shoulder. He was about to leave when he noticed the hilt of his sword, partially buried under the snow. He drew it out, dusted it off with his hand, then wiped the blade dry before slotting it back into its scabbard. He searched the snow for his knife also but could not find it, and time was pressing.

They followed Nompar's own tracks back to where he had given the others the slip. Beyond that, the falling snow had all but covered their footprints, but the tracks left by five men and a woman were too marked to be entirely covered up in the short time since Bulchett had knocked Kemp unconscious, and there was just enough of a trace for Kemp and Nompar to follow. They began to run, trying to catch up with their quarry before the snow could obliterate the tracks entirely.

–

Lambert Tegg woke up with a start and was amazed to find himself lying in a four-poster bed behung with drapes of diaphanous gauze. He threw off the sendal sheets and pulled back the drapes, looking about him in wonderment.

When he had been a boy – back in the days of the old king – Helsington Manor House had become empty and fallen into disrepair. The servants who had looked after the place would live there no more when there was no one to pay them; did not even want to be associated with it when it was said their former lord had been executed for treason. No one else moved in. Some said it had become the property of the king, but if that was so, His Majesty had more pressing matters to attend to than to employ a steward to look after the place.

Growing up in a village nearby, Tegg and his friends had often played in the abandoned buildings. Their parents had warned them against going anywhere near the place, making up all sorts of stories about how it was haunted, but that had only acted as an encouragement to youthful minds full of mischief. Tegg was usually obedient to his parents, but when the leader of the local youths had dared him to enter, he had easily been led astray.

He had enjoyed exploring the painted chambers, wondering what life must have been like for those who had lived there. Now he fancied he was back there and the murals daubed on the plastered walls were no longer faded, but were as bright and colourful as they must have been the day they had been painted. There was a writing desk by the window, and a muniments chest. The only discordant notes were a fat sow snoring in one corner, a piglet suckling her teats, and a curiously wrought cande-labra hanging from a ceiling beam. Something about the candelabra filled Tegg with disquiet, and suddenly he felt an overpowering urge to get out of the bedchamber.

His arm itched. He reached for it, and found it trussed up with a sling. He tore the sling off and discarded it, stretching his stiff and aching right arm.

He pulled aside an arras, expecting to emerge into the hall, but to his surprise the doorway led directly out into a summer meadow bathed in sunshine. The air was full of fluffy seeds like those blown from willow trees in early summer, like hundreds of floating fairies, and Tegg laughed with delight, raising his arms. He felt oddly light and carefree, as if a great weight which had been pressing down on him for as long as he could remember had been lifted from his shoulders.

Laughing with childlike innocence, he began to run across the meadow. It was muddy in places and sometimes he slipped, and sometimes he struggled to drag his feet from the clinging mire, but that was all part of the joy of living he felt coursing through every vein. And when he had exhausted himself and could run no further, he lay on the grass, letting the sun's warmth caress his face while the fluffy willow seeds settled on him, slowly covering him from head to toe.

—

A vague sense of disquiet troubled Bulchett the moment he awoke. He had not intended to sleep at all, and waking up he wondered how much time he had wasted.

Crawley lay beside him, his head pillowed on Bulchett's shoulder. Grimacing, the knight pushed his head away. The squire snorted in his sleep, then began to stir. Bulchett glanced around the interior of the sheiling to see what the others were doing and got a shock when he saw only one of them: the simpleton, hanging from the ceiling. His eyes bulged from their sockets and a black tongue protruded between crooked teeth. Urine still dripped from one leg, making elliptical patterns in the dust beneath the straw scattered on the floor as the corpse swung back and forth. The simpleton had clearly helped himself to Crawley's rope, clambered up the rails of the fence separating the byre from the rest of the sheiling, and tied the rope to one of the roof beams before jumping off. The crude knot fastening the noose about his neck had been clumsily tied, but it had done the job.

The door of the sheiling was wide open, and a few flakes of snow gusted in. Bulchett realised it was the cold draft that had aroused him from his doze. He remembered the archer with the torn ears closing it behind him when he had taken the woman out to ease nature, and wondered who had opened it again, as if in doing so they had allowed the wounded twentyman to wander off like an animal straying from its pen. For that matter, had the woman not yet finished easing nature? Bulchett had no idea how long he had slumbered, but he was sure it had been more than a few minutes. At least sunset was still some way off, judging from the amount of light that flooded into the sheiling through the open door. Perhaps there was still time for him to find his way to Ragman's Law before dusk.

He grabbed one of Crawley's shoulders and shook him violently. The squire opened his eyes and smiled dreamily.

Bulchett indicated the swinging corpse. 'The simpleton's hanged himself.'

Crawley looked in the direction his master pointed, and gave a yelp of alarm, before crossing himself. 'Where are Tegg and Haine?'

'You tell me,' said Bulchett. 'You were supposed to be keeping an eye on them while I slept.'

'You never said aught about keeping an eye on them.'

'I shouldn't have had to. It should have been self-evident that was what I expected.'

'Of course, Sir Alexander. I'm an incompetent fool, not worthy to serve a knight as noble as yourself. Can you ever find it in your heart to forgive me?'

Bulchett snorted and rose to his feet. Kicking at the straw strewn on the floor, Crawley found a black rag and picked it up, holding it up for Bulchett to see.

'What's that?' asked the knight.

'The sling Tegg was wearing. He must've torn it off.'

'Perhaps he's feeling better, then. Get the rope.'

Crawley glanced up at Gudgeon's swinging corpse. 'Must I?'

'We'll need it to climb down into the cave on Ragman's Law.' Leaving Crawley to do the dirty work as usual, Bulchett crossed to the door and stepped out. Snowflakes still drifted down from a grey sky, but they were few and far between. The blizzard was ended and now he could see the valley clearly. Thick snow, even thicker than before, blanketed everything. The only sound was the wind soughing over the moors.

He looked around. The archer with the ragged ears lay nearby, partially covered by snow which was stained crimson around his torso. The archer's complexion was a waxy hue of pale, greyish blue, his features frozen in an expression of astonishment and dismay. There was no sign of the woman: evidently she had fled with whoever had stabbed him. Their footprints had been covered over by the snow, unlike the relatively fresh set of tracks leading away from the door of the sheiling.

Bulchett followed the tracks for a few hundred yards to find the twentyman lying in the snow. His skin had the same hue as ragged-ears, his eyes the same glazed look. There were icicles in his beard, but he was smiling. Bulchett wondered what on earth he had to smile about. The smile seemed to taunt him, and he kicked the twentyman's corpse irritably in the ribs.

'What a handless mob of halfwits!' he said to no one in particular. 'Whatever did I do to find myself lumbered with such a parcel of wooden-headed fools? It amazes me how such dunderheads have not even the wit to see just how foolish they are. Whom the gods would destroy, they first make dim-witted.'

Crawley emerged from the sheiling, looking green about the gills as he coiled the rope in his hands. Looping it over his head, he joined Bulchett where he stood over the twentyman's corpse, and crossed himself.

'We are better off without him,' said Bulchett. 'Better off without any of them. They only held us back. We had better get on.' He took his map from his scrip and consulted it. Turning it this way and that, he got his bearings as best he could – though in truth all these hills looked the same to him – and started walking in what he reckoned was the most promising direction, while the ever-loyal Crawley trotted at his heels.

–

Hearing footsteps crunch in the snow up ahead, Kemp and Nompar squatted behind another thicket of brambles, then craned their heads to see over the snow-laden tendrils. Tibbie Liddell appeared through the trees, clouds of breath puffing from her lips as she ran.

Kemp stood up. 'Tibbie!' He waved to her, but she only blanched at the sight of him and veered off in another direction. He made to go after her, but Nompar caught him by the arm and held him back.

'Let her go, *mon amec*.'

'We cannot just leave her—'

'She does not want our help. We have not helped her so far. She will get better help from the people who live near here, if there are any. If there are, I warrant she will know where to find them. All will be well with her.'

'If she runs into Nixon and his men, she'll lead them straight back here.'

'Then we should get moving, and be far away by the time Nixon arrives. Besides, are you not curious to know how she escaped from Bulchett and the others? I cannot imagine they willingly let her go.'

The two of them hurried on, following Tibbie's footsteps back in the direction from which she had come. After a mile or so, they came to a sheiling at the bottom of the valley. Haine's corpse lay in blood-stained snow outside. Kemp unslung his bow and strung it, nocking an arrow before approaching the open door. 'If there's anyone inside, show yourself!' he shouted. 'If I must enter to find anyone within, I'll shoot them before I check to see if they're friend or foe, so whichever you are, you'd do well to come out.'

Nothing stirred in the sheiling. Outside, the only sound other than the soughing of the wind and the ragged breathing of Kemp and Nompar was the croak of a raven flying overhead, a black silhouette against a pale grey sky.

Kemp advanced to the door, stood to one side of it, looked around the jamb, then hurriedly pulled his head away again lest someone shoot at it. When no arrows or quarrels emerged, he stepped over the threshold, drawing his bow as he did so, and moved to one side as soon as he was within so he would not be silhouetted in the doorway. After the bright snow outside, the gloomy interior looked almost black until his eyes had adjusted.

Gudgeon's corpse lay sprawled on the floor. There was no sign of Bulchett, Crawley or Tegg. Easing the draw on his bow, Kemp returned the arrow under his belt and slung the bow stave across his back by the string. Crouching over Hob, he rolled him over and winced when he saw the bulging eyes and the black, protruding tongue. A rope had left a clear imprint on his throat, though there was no sign of it now.

'Martin?' Nompar called from outside.

'No one in here,' Kemp called back. 'None but Hob, and he's dead.'

The *bourc* followed him in. 'It looks as though he's been strangled.'

'He was hanged from yon roof beam.' The Midlander pointed to the ceiling, then indicated the circles of urine on the floor. 'Ever been to a hanging? They always piss themselves, and as the body swings the piss drips down their legs and makes circles on the ground.'

'The question is, did he hang himself or did someone do it to him?'

'Someone took him down and untied the rope after... no sign of chafing on his wrists to show his hands were tied... none of the cuts or bruises you'd expect if he defended himself. I'd say he did it to himself. Poor devil... all Fisher's talk of demons and hangings must have turned his mind. Not that he had much of a mind to begin with.'

The two of them emerged from the sheiling. 'Some footprints here,' said Nompar, pointing.

'Let's follow them, then.'

After a few hundred yards, they found Tegg's frozen corpse lying in the snow.

'I see no signs of violence,' said Kemp. 'It looks as though he just lay down to die.'

'And Sir Alexander and his squire made no attempt to help him?'

Kemp indicated the two pairs of tracks leading away from Tegg's corpse. 'Did you not see that one of the sets of tracks that drew us here was partially covered over compared to the other two? I think Tegg wandered off in his delirium, and Bulchett and Crawley followed later. When they found him dead, they went on.'

Kemp suddenly felt sickened and wearied. First Young, Fisher and Vertue, now Haine, Gudgeon and Tegg. All of them dead. They had been flawed and foolish, perhaps – that was just human nature – but, except for Haine, none had deserved to die. That Kemp had as good as foreseen their deaths was no consolation: if anything, the knowledge he had foreseen this yet failed to prevent it only made the guilt gnawing at his heart worse.

He reminded himself he was not the one that had led them to their deaths by chasing after some mythical artefact, believing it would grant him some demonic power. Bulchett was to blame for this, but Christendom was full of men like him, who inflicted their chaos on the world and were never called upon to atone for their sins, never took responsibility, nor ever received any kind of punishment for their indifference to the suffering they caused. And if the world was full of men like Bulchett, was it because the world did nothing to discourage such men from behaving as they did? If anything, fate seemed to conspire to reward them for their misdeeds.

'We go after them?' asked Nompar.

Kemp wanted to. He wanted to catch up with Bulchett and avenge the six dead archers. If an uncaring world would not punish the knight, perhaps Kemp's sword could make up the deficit. But how far into these mountains was he willing to chase Bulchett and Crawley? Was it worth risking his own life and that of Nompar by chasing after a pair of fools? It would not restore the dead to life.

'No,' he told the *bourc*. 'The Devil carry them to hell! Let's head for the border.'

'A wise decision, I think. Which way is south?'

Kemp looked about. There was no sunlight visible through the clouds to cast any shadow, and the trunks of the nearest trees were too thickly coated with snow to reveal any lichen on their bark. He could see the wind blowing plumes of snow from the crest of a hill on the opposite side of the glen. He knew the prevailing winds were westerly in Scotland just as in England. If the wind blowing the hill opposite matched the prevailing one, then the hill lay to the west. Of course, there was no guarantee it *did* match the prevailing one, but if it did, then it matched Kemp's gut instinct that if he and Nompar headed down the glen, they would be heading south.

The Midlander laughed.

'What is so amusing?' asked Nompar.

'I was just thinking, fate plays queer tricks.'

'I do not understand.'

'I think this way is south.' Kemp pointed in the direction that Bulchett's and Crawley's footprints led.

'That way, hmm?' Nompar glanced at the footprints, then gazed long and hard at Kemp's face as if trying to read his mind. At last he shrugged. 'Then I suppose we must go whither fate leads us.'

The two of them began following Bulchett's and Crawley's footprints down the glen.

—

'Any suggestions?' Nixon asked Archibald.

'At least let us press on a little further. We may pick up their trail somewhere below.'

'Aye, or we might jist wander in the Tweedsmuir Hills until we die of cold and hunger!'

The reivers had trudged through the snow on the slope above the tarn, making for the saddle above. They knew the men they were chasing had come this way because when they had first entered this valley, the track left in the snow by the Englishmen had been so clear, they had been able to make it out clear across the valley. But since then the blizzard had swept across the hills, forcing the reivers to huddle in a gully for shelter. When the weather had broken, they had emerged to find the tracks of the Englishmen entirely buried beneath the fresh covering of snow.

'This is your fault,' Reid spat at Sneith. 'If ye hadnae wasted so much time crossing Stanerie Rig, we might have got here before that blizzard o'ertook us.'

'My fault!' Sneith protested indignantly. 'You were the one who made us all wait while you eased your bowels.'

'A man must do as nature compels.'

'You should have done it before we set out.'

Reid slammed the palm of a hand against Sneith's breastbone. 'Ye dinnae get to tell me when I should or shouldnae ease my bowels.'

Sneith shoved him back so hard, Reid lost his footing and sprawled in the snow. Leaping to his feet, he pulled his reaping hook from under his belt. The man-at-arms drew his axe.

'Put up your weapons, both of you!' snapped Archibald. 'Honestly, you're like a couple of children!'

'He started it!' whined Sneith.

'You're each as bad as the other. How oft must I tell you? We'll never defeat the English while we're too busy squabbling amongst ourselves.'

Reid pointed a trembling finger at Sneith. 'Ah'd fain be a slave than ally myself to this heichlie, slekit willy-wisp!'

'Then be a slave!' Archibald spat back just as angrily. 'Not every man thinks as you nor lives as you. If there's no room for compromise in your heart, best learn to love the taste of gall and wormwood!'

'Whisht!' said Nixon. 'Someone's coming!'

A young woman trudged up the slope towards them, her arms gripping her shawl tightly over her kirtle against the cold. Reid caught her attention with a wave. 'Tibbie!'

She glanced at them, but did not stop, continuing back the way she had come.

'We saw whit happened at the croft,' Reid called. 'Did the Inglishers take ye captive?'

She hesitated, then sighed audibly and turned back to speak with the reivers. 'They did.'

'Did they harm ye?'

'They tried. One of them sought to rape me. Ah stuck him with his own bodkin.'

'How many of them are there?'

'Ah make it six now. One of them's wounded.'

'The man ye stabbed?'

She shook her head. 'He was wounded before. His wound's rankled and he's out o' his heid with the fever. The man Ah stuck is deid: when Ah stick a man, he stays stuck.'

'Do you know whither they're headed?' asked Archibald. 'I would have expected them to head south for the border, but ever since we picked up their trail they've headed west.'

'They're bound for Ragman's Law. Summat about a Brazen Heid?'

'The Brazen Heid of Pope Sylvester?' Reid had heard the legend, but he had never believed it, not even when he was a child. He had little time for stories of ghoulies and ghosties and long-leggedy beasties and things that went 'bump!' in the night. 'But that was back in the days when the popes lived in Rome. What would the Brazen Heid be doing in Scotland?'

'Ah dinnae ken. Their leader told a story about how some sorcerer brought the heid to Scotland and hid it in some cave.'

'Aye,' said Reid. 'There's a cave on Ragman's Law: Ah've seen it, though Ah never dared sclim down. It disnae look as though there's any way to sclim out again. Some say Soulis had his lair down there where he sacrificed virgins to the De'il; others say it's a portal to Hell.'

'That's all revil-ravel,' snorted Nixon. 'My father climbed down into that cave once. He said it's jist a big hole in the ground. But Ah suppose an English knight might be daft enough to reckon there's truth in such trumpery. There are gowks, glaikit gowks, and then there are Inglishers!'

'How far is it to Ragman's Law?' asked Archibald.

'It cannae be more than five miles as the crow flies, just past yon ridge.' Nixon pointed to the south-west, across the glen.

'Then we can still catch them.'

'Oh aye, we can that.'

Archibald turned to Tibbie. 'Can we send a couple of men with you to see you safely home?'

'Ah can find my own way hame,' she replied, striding on. 'Just see to it yon English whoresons get whit's coming to them!'

Eighteen

'What I cannot understand is how a level-headed man can believe in such nonsense as the Brazen Head,' Kemp panted to Nompar as the two of them jogged along the bank of the stream running through the bottom of the glen, following the footsteps of Bulchett and Crawley. 'A dim-witted oaf like Hob Gudgeon, God rest his soul, that's one thing. But Sir Alexander?'

'People believe what they want to believe,' said the *bourc*. 'Regardless of how fantastic it is. "This year's harvest will be bountiful, in spite of the heavy rains over the summer." "Of course the most beautiful girl in the village will fall in love with me, despite my beetle-brow, crooked teeth, squint, boils and hunchback." "If I can just lay my hands on this magical artefact, then I will have power over all Christendom and everyone will have to bow down before me as I so richly deserve." In any case, I must challenge your characterisation of Bulchett as "a level-headed man".'

Kemp laughed.

The temperature had plunged since it had stopped snowing, and although the day had brightened a little, the bitter air burned Kemp's windpipes and lungs each time he drew it in, and formed clouds of condensation in the air around his head when he exhaled. Less interested in catching up with Bulchett and Crawley than they were in putting some distance between themselves and Nixon's men, Kemp and Nompar ran as fast as they dared, mindful the snow made the going treacherous underfoot.

They reached the great valley running east to west: Kemp had lost his bearings but, if he had not known better, he would have said they were higher up the same valley where Nixon and his men had first attacked them earlier that day. After a league or so, they rounded a spur from a hill to the north, and saw two figures no more than half a mile head ahead of them, stumbling through the snow to where an irregularly shaped standing stone had been erected on the banks of the burn another half a mile further on.

'It is them,' said Nompar.

Kemp nodded, and the two of them redoubled their pace. Bulchett and Crawley had almost reached the standing stone when they heard the thump of their pursuers' feet against the snow, and turned, waiting for them to catch up.

'Remember what I said about holding me back if it seems I'm about to lose my temper with Sir Alexander?' Kemp panted to Nompar.

'You want me to hold you back?'

'Do so at your peril! I withdraw my request.'

They approached Bulchett and Crawley. 'Sir Nompar!' the knight exclaimed as if he was delighted to see the *bourc*. 'You still live! God be praised!' He pointed an accusing finger at Kemp. 'Whatever he told you, 'tis a lie.'

Kemp charged straight at Bulchett. The knight hastily lowered his visor and reached for his sword. Before he could draw it, Kemp pushed his visor up again and smashed a fist into his face. In the cold air, the punch hurt Kemp's knuckles even more than it would have done on a summer's day, but it was still worth it to see the look of astonishment on Bulchett's bloody face as he stumbled and fell on his back. He flailed his arms, struggling to rise.

Crawley moved as if to assist his master. Whether he meant to attack Kemp or merely to help Bulchett to his feet, Kemp could not say, but either way, Nompar caught the squire by the arm and held him back.

'Did Kemp bind his own hands and feet and leave himself a feast for the wolves?' asked Nompar.

'We were attacked by the reivers!' protested Bulchett. 'They struck me down. I was robbed of my senses, but when I awoke there was no sign of Kemp. I know not what calumny he has cooked up with them, but be sure that caitiff means to betray us all.'

'False traitor!' Kemp drove a booted foot into Bulchett's crotch with all his might. The knight curled into a foetal position, clutching at himself. Kemp drew his broadsword and brandished it over him.

'Slay me, and you'll never find the Brazen Head!' sobbed the knight.

'How many times must you be told?' Kemp asked him. 'There is no Brazen Head!'

Rising to his feet, Bulchett pointed to the standing stone which, seen close to, was only three feet tall. Blood trickled from one of his nostrils. 'See that? Yon's the Mitre Stone.'

Kemp wondered if Bulchett was trying to distract him. Taking a step back just to be on the safe side, he glanced at the stone. It did bear a passing resemblance to a bishop's mitre, as seen from the side. 'What of it?'

Bulchett indicated the tall hill rising to the north. 'Yon's Ragman's Law. There's no need for us to argue about whether or not there's a Brazen Head: before sundown, we can find the entrance to Soulis' lair and you'll see it with your own eyes.'

'We're not climbing all the way up there to learn what we already know: there is no Brazen Head, and you're a beguiled fool for thinking otherwise. Now draw your sword, you whoreson!'

'You fool!' sneered Bulchett. 'Surely you don't think a knight such as I would lower himself to cross swords with a churl like you—' Even as he spoke, Bulchett suddenly drew his sword and lunged at the Midlander, stabbing at his face.

Kemp had known too many knights who believed it was beneath their dignity to fight with churls to doubt it, even on Bulchett's lying lips. But when his eyes saw the knight's right hand grasp the hilt of his sword, instinct took over. He dodged the thrust, buying himself enough time to draw his own sword.

Nompar likewise unsheathed his blade. 'A dastardly blow! But say the word, Martin, and I'll fillet this caitiff like a herring.'

'Put up your sword, Nompar. This whoreson's mine!'

Kemp and Bulchett circled. The knight lunged, roaring incoherently. Kemp had been braced for a probing attack, and perhaps Bulchett had been counting on that, for he just came straight at the Midlander, all brute force and no subtlety, swinging his sword like a club at Kemp's head. The Midlander brought his own blade up to parry, but the strength of the blow was enough to throw him off balance. He reeled, lost his footing in the snow and sprawled on his back. Bulchett lost no time in following up his advantage, but he fought like one who knew nothing of swordsmanship, hacking at Kemp's head when a thrust would have served him better. Kemp rolled out of the way of the stroke, and while Bulchett swung his sword up – already puffing and panting – Kemp had an opportunity to rise to his feet.

Bulchett came at him again, roaring once more. Kemp was ready for it this time, and parried easily. On the third such attack, he slashed at Bulchett's bascinet. The visor broke open, and the tip of Kemp's sword scored a line of blood from the knight's cheek. Bulchett backed off, raising a hand to his face. There was insufficient blood in his pasty grey complexion for him to ever blanche, but his eyes widened in alarm when he saw a few traces of gore on his gauntlet.

'Blood!' he whimpered.

By now Kemp had the measure of Bulchett's swordsmanship. He slotted his blade back into its scabbard.

'Are you sure you know what you're doing?' asked Nompar. 'I've seen many a fair swordsman feign clumsiness to beguile an opponent.'

'We'll soon find out,' said Kemp.

Seeing the Midlander standing empty-handed before him, Bulchett charged again, thrusting at his throat. Kemp stood there until the last moment, then stepped aside, grasping Bulchett by the wrist as he passed and at the same time extending a leg to trip the knight up. As Bulchett crashed into the snow, his arm was twisted up behind him. Kemp easily prised the sword from his hand. The knight rolled onto his back only to find the tip of his own blade held unwaveringly an inch from his nose.

He at once began blubbering. 'Don't slay me! I'll give you anything you want. The Brazen Head… you can have it! Only spare my life.'

The knight was such a pathetic image of a gibbering, snivelling knave, Kemp could only think how little satisfaction he would get from slaying him. He remembered he was searching for redemption for the sins of his youth; if he slew an unarmed man who grovelled at his feet, he would only be adding to an already long list of sins he needed to atone for. To let such a fool make him feel such anger only made him as big a fool as Bulchett himself.

He flung the knight's sword into a snowdrift and turned to Crawley. 'If yon wooden-headed, hen-hearted braggart wants to march up there in search of a myth, then let him. But I warn you, he'll find nowt up there but rocks, ice and snow.'

'Come with us,' Nompar told the squire. 'Throw not your life away chasing after his dreams. You know horses and you take good care of them, and I don't doubt your courage. I might recommend you to a dozen men who'd gladly give one such as you a good place in their retinue. Noblemen who'll reward you just as handsomely as Sir Alexander, and with better chances for advancement besides.'

'I'll not betray my master!' said Crawley.

'You were with Sir Alexander when he jousted at Guînes a few years ago,' said Nompar. 'So no doubt you know the truth of that scandal better than I: whether it truly was he who jousted in his blazon, or Sir Thomas Dotterell. But you must also know the story of how Lady Margaret Grosvenor was ravished, and blamed Sir Alexander, but he said she was prompted by a grudge she bore him, and it was one of his friends who had got her with child. Like Dotterell, the friend was disgraced, and has since become a lay brother in a monastery in a far country;

though the child Lady Margaret gave birth to nine months later bore a startling resemblance to Sir Alexander.

'And then there was the time he won a vast sum of money dicing with the Duke of Lancaster; though afterwards the dice Sir Alexander had been using were found to be weighted, so they would come up sixes more often than any other number. He put the blame on his squire, your predecessor. I know not what became of the lad, though I heard a rumour he was reduced to begging for alms in the streets of Lichfield.'

'Do you not see the pattern here?' Kemp gestured contemptuously at Bulchett. 'Those who give their loyalty to this caitiff are never rewarded with owt but treachery. He cares for none but himself and, if he feigns otherwise, it's only to bend folk to his will more easily. He'll stab you in the back as soon as he no longer has any use for you.'

'You don't know him as I do!' sobbed Crawley. 'He's a good man, a wise man, a brave man, a Godly man—'

'He's a turd. A worthless, selfish, stinking turd, shit out of a poxed pig's arse. And if you cannot see that for yourself, then you're beyond any help I can give you.'

'Martin!' Nompar pointed to where a mob of armed men rounded the spur behind them: Nixon and his reivers.

'Time to go,' Kemp told Crawley. 'The choice is yours. You can climb Ragman's Law with this back-stabbing turd.' He gestured at Bulchett. 'Perhaps you'll find Soulis' lair before the reivers slay you, but I doubt it. Or you can make for the border with us. But Nompar and I will not risk our lives to tarry a moment longer. If you're too great a fool not to see through this knave, then you're not worth saving.'

Motioning the *bourc* to follow with a jerk of his head, Kemp turned and waded across the stream, heading for a glen leading south out of the valley. Nompar followed. Kemp helped him out on the south bank, and they both turned to see if Bulchett and Crawley were following. The knight was back on his feet and had already set off towards Ragman's Law. A little disappointingly – if not all that surprisingly – Crawley still trotted along at his heels.

Kemp sighed. 'Come on,' he told Nompar, and the two of them continued towards the glen leading south. It led to a saddle between two more hills a couple of miles to the south, but though black crags protruded through the snow on the slopes on either side, it did not look insurmountable. Before they reached the glen, however, they had to cross the spur of one of the hills flanking its mouth. The ground was covered with thick snowdrifts, waist-deep in places. It seemed to take forever, and when they finally reached the crest of the spur, they paused, panting from their exertions and glad of an excuse to catch their breath, no matter how briefly. Gazing back the way they had come to survey how high they had climbed, Kemp was pleasantly surprised to see how far below the Mitre Stone seemed to be. Bulchett and Crawley were already distant figures, black against the snow as they ascended the slopes of Ragman's Law.

Nompar trudged up to stand beside him. 'Are you sure it was wise to let Sir Alexander go?'

'He can do us no harm.'

'And if it turns out there *is* a Brazen Head, and it grants him unlimited power?' Nompar asked him with a smile.

'I'll wager my life there is not.'

'I think we already have.'

Kemp shook his head. 'A safe bet, I reckon. There is such a thing as natural justice. Oafs like Sir Alexander always come to a bad end. Sooner or later his lies will catch up with him.'

'Do you think so? In my experience, such men swagger through their charmed lives, behaving as swinishly as they please, never once taking responsibility for the consequences of their deeds.'

Bulchett studied the crag overhead. It was sheer, but there was a ledge off to his left. It climbed over a cliff, no more than forty feet high or so, but high enough to kill anyone who fell off it. But he knew he could not die until he had fulfilled his destiny.

He walked along the ledge until he had rounded the corner of the crag above, only to find the ledge petered out. There was no obvious way up from there, unless... perhaps if he clambered up, he could grasp that nub of rock there, put his foot on that ledge there... yes, that would do it. He started to climb up, and had almost pulled himself up over the crag when the stone under his right foot broke away from the cliff face. It bounced off the ledge where Crawley stood and shot out into space, falling for what seemed like forever before smashing against the rocks below and shattering into a thousand fragments that flew in all directions, with a crack that echoed off the surrounding hills.

Bulchett was left dangling by his left hand. The soles of his boots scrabbled in vain at the rockface while his right arm flailed for something to catch hold of. It was only a few feet to the ledge below, but he knew if he fell, he could not help but fall backwards and plunge to the bottom of the cliff after the dislodged stone. At times like this, the disloyal thought crept into his mind that perhaps he was not destined for greatness after all.

But then Crawley was there, coming to his aid once more. 'Put your foot on my hands, Sir Alexander! I'll push you up!'

Trying to put his foot down, Bulchett missed Crawley's hands altogether and put his heel in the squire's upturned face, but that served just as well. He boosted himself up until he was able to clamber over the lip of the crag above. Puffing and blowing, he dragged himself to safety, sprawling in the snow of the more level slope above. He lay there, gasping for breath, while Crawley clambered up after him, making heavy weather of it if his grunts and gasps were any indication. Bulchett watched dispassionately as first one hand crawled spider-like over the precipice, found a handhold, and then was followed by its companion, before Crawley's strained face hove over the precipice after them. An inch at a time, the squire dragged himself to safety before collapsing in the snow next to Bulchett.

Having now caught his breath, the knight pushed himself to his feet. 'Well, don't just lie there lollygagging! We're but a few hundred yards from the entrance to Soulis' lair, I can feel it. And for the love of Peter, smarten yourself up! Is that mud on your face? Honestly, Rowland, when you look so dishevelled, it reflects poorly on me! I won't have it!'

'No, Sir Alexander. Sorry, my lord.' Crawley spat on his fingers and rubbed at his face.

Ragman's Law was rounded like a dome, so the higher up its slopes one climbed, the less steep they became, until the very peak was almost as flat as a plateau. Bulchett paused to survey the view, the chill wind blowing across the hilltop making his eyes water. All he could see in any direction were more snow-covered hills and glens, though the one he stood on seemed taller than any of the others. A cairn of stones marked the highest point.

The two of them searched the hilltop. Immediately below the summit, a precipice overlooked the glen to the north, with rocky crags jutting out of the snow. Here Bulchett and Crawley found a fissure in the rock widening to about three feet, leading down into darkness.

'You were right, my lord!' Crawley shrugged off the coil of rope and tied one end of it to a nub of rock close to the fissure. 'Not that I ever doubted you. It's all coming true, just as you foretold. It was wise of you not to tell Kemp and the *bourc* the true reason for coming to Ragman's Law. Had they known it, I warrant they would not have let us go so easily, and they would still be with us to demand their share.'

'The true reason? I already told you the true reason.'

Laughing, Crawley dropped the other end of the rope into the fissure. 'That there is a demon trapped in a Brazen Head? Come now, my liege! Such fairy tales may suffice to beguile peasants like Kemp and those others, but I know you well enough to know you are not such a fool as to believe them. Besides, I know the story of the Treasure of the Templars. Fear not: I'm not an avaricious man. I've only ever sought to serve you, my lord. Whatever share you see fit to give me as my reward for aiding you, I will be content.'

Bulchett pasted a smile on his face. He did not believe a word of it. If he had been in Crawley's shoes, he would have been scheming some way to cheat his master and claim the whole treasure for himself alone, and he could not imagine his squire was thinking any differently. 'Let's not get ahead of ourselves. First we must climb down and find the treasure.'

'Of course, my lord. But we're so close! I know it!' Crawley peered down into the crevice again. 'Perhaps I should go first? Make sure there is no danger?'

'Let's not rush into anything,' said Bulchett. As uninviting at the crevice looked, he was damned if he would let Crawley climb down first. The knight nodded grimly to himself. He should have seen it before. All the grovelling and fawning Crawley had done to him... nothing but empty flattery, while all along he had been planning to swoop in and steal the treasure from under his nose at the last minute. If that was his plan, he could think again.

'I'll climb down first,' said Bulchett. 'You keep an eye out for... what's that?' He looked sharply towards the crag of rock behind Crawley.

The squire turned. 'What's what?'

Bulchett whipped his knife from the sheath on his belt and buried it up to the hilt between Crawley's shoulder blades. The squire staggered away a few paces, then turned back, a pathetic look of disbelief and astonishment on his face, as if this was the last thing he could possibly have expected. He opened his mouth to protest, but no words would come. He took a couple more steps, then sank to his knees, before pitching forward, face down in the snow.

'That'll teach you, you back-stabbing devil!' Bulchett muttered.

Gripping the rope with both hands, he began to climb down. He sat down on the edge, lowering his legs into the crevice. A nasty stink wafted from below: a rank, acrid smell, the stench of pure evil; like the fart of a lapdog that had gorged itself on meat roasted with a garlic sauce.

Glancing down, he saw a nub of rock on the side, and lowered his right foot to it. Left hand, right hand, left foot, right foot, it really was quite easy once you got the—

His foot slipped off its ledge and his heart leaped into his mouth as he fell. He cracked his skull; it was fortunate he was wearing his bascinet, and the quilted hood of his gambeson beneath the coif of his habergeon provided more than adequate cushioning. His gauntleted hands lost their purchase on the rope. His feet briefly scrabbled in vain at the walls of rock shooting past him on either side, and then he was falling free into the yawning darkness below.

He did not have far to fall. He slammed feet first into something hard and unyielding, and yet at the same time oddly slippery. His legs shot out from beneath him and he fell on his back, slithering down an uneven, rocky slope. The last thing he remembered before he blacked out entirely was the shock of his legs slamming hard against rock, something snapping and a tearing pain in his leg.

-

Nixon and his men reached the Mitre Stone. 'It seems our quarry has had a falling-out,' observed Archibald, gazing first after Bulchett and his squire, then turning to look in the opposite direction after the Bourc of Cazoulat and the archer. 'What say you, Nixon? Half of us pursue Sir Alexander while the other half pursue the *bourc*?'

Nixon shook his head. 'The *bourc* is the greater danger. Frae whit Ah hear, Bulchett is nae more than a blustering buffoon. Rory and me will deal with him and his squire while ye go after the *bourc* and...' Nixon broke off, shaking his head. 'There's summat familiar about yon English archer... Ah'm sure Ah ken him frae somewhere, though Ah cannae think where... Och, well, nae matter. Ye'll have nae difficulty bringing them to heel if Ah send Howk and the rest of my men wi' ye.'

'Don't trust him, Sir Archibald!' said Sneith. 'This reeks of trickery to me!'

Nixon shrugged. 'As ye will, Sir Archibald. Ye and Sneith can go after Bulchett and his squire while my men and me pursue the *bourc*.'

'Very well,' said Archibald.

'No!' protested Sneith. 'He agreed too readily. 'Tis a double bluff: he wants us to think he's trying to trick us into going after the *bourc* so we'll agree to going after Bulchett. I say we should go after the *bourc* and leave him to catch Bulchett.'

'Have you any notion what he's talking about?' Archibald asked Nixon.

The reiver shrugged. 'Ye tell me, Sir Archibald. He's your man. But if ye want to go after the *bourc*, then by all means be my guest.'

'That's a trap!' said Sneith. 'He agreed to that too readily.'

'So you think we should go after Bulchett and leave him to get the *bourc*?' asked Archibald.

'No! That's what he wants us to think! But he knows we know that he knows that agreeing to something too readily is a sign that's not what he wants us to do, so we should do the opposite.'

'Which is?' asked Archibald.

Sneith opened his mouth, then caught himself, and frowned. 'Er... go after the *bourc*?' he suggested hesitantly, watching Nixon's face closely as if the reiver chief's reaction to the suggestion might give something away.

'That's fine by me,' said Nixon. 'If that's what ye want to do?'

'That's what we want to do,' Sneith said more confidently, as if Nixon's ready acquiescence was proof it was the last thing he wanted.

Archibald sighed wearily. 'Let's go, then.' He clambered down the bank of the stream and began wading to the opposite side.

Sneith followed him, then stopped in midstream. 'Wait! What if it's a triple—?'

Archibald gave him a solid clout around the back of the bascinet. 'We're going after the *bourc*,' he said firmly. 'I'm sure Nixon and Reid can handle Bulchett.'

Nixon exchanged grins with Reid. 'Take the rest of the men and go with him,' the chief told Howk. 'We'll catch up with ye in a few hours.'

While the rest of the band followed Archibald and Sneith across the stream, Nixon and Reid began striding through the snow to where they knew an easy path led up the west side of Ragman's Law. 'Rab, did ye jist pull off the smartest triple-bluff it's ever been my privilege to witness? Or is Sneith simply the biggest sumph this side of the black stump.'

'Ah dinnae ken why it is Ah have a reputation as some kind of trickster,' grumbled Nixon. 'In truth it makes nae odds to me which of us goes after Bulchett and which of us goes after the *bourc*. Ah mean, it's no' as if there really is a great treasure to be found in the cave below Ragman's Law.'

'So ye dinnae ken the story Ah heard when Ah was a bairn, about how – when the King of France accused the

Templars of heresy – he sent word out in advance to all his royal officers so they could round up all the Templars in the realm on the same day, and none would escape.'

'Everyone kens that.'

'But does everyone ken how rumours of the king's wicked scheme reached the Grand Master in Paris beforehand? How he had the treasure in the vaults of the Old Temple smuggled out of the city and hidden at a commandery in Picardy?'

'Och, if that were true, why did he no' flee France when he had the chance? Why stay in Paris, to be tortured by a Holy Inquisition until he confessed to denying Christ, and was burned at the stake?'

'Who can say? Maybe the power he wielded as Grand Master of the Order of the Temple lulled him into a false sense of security.'

'Maybe,' agreed Nixon. 'So whit happened to the treasure? In the version of story ye heard, Ah mean.'

'A band of serjeants of the order had it smuggled across the border into Flanders and loaded aboard a ship bound for Scotland. Wi' Robert the Bruce under a papal interdict, they thought the treasure would be safe at the Templars' preceptory at Ballantrodach, a few miles south of Dalhousie. Whit they didnae ken was that Lothian was under the iron hand of King Edward's father in those days. They didnae realise their error until they arrived. Fearing the English king would send men to seize the treasure for himself, six knights of the order agreed to carry it to a preceptory at Darvel in Ayrshire, where those loyal to the Bruce held sway. Knowing the English were on their trail, they travelled by a circuitous path, through Yarrowdale, hoping to reach Darvel via Clydesdale. But their route had been betrayed to the English by a traitor in their ranks, and they were ambushed in the Tweedsmuir Hills. There was a bloody skirmish in which all the Inglishers sent to arrest them were slain, and all but three of the Templars. The survivors hid the chest containing the treasure in the cleft on Ragman's Law but, no' trusting one another, they fell to fighting amongst themselves and there were nae survivors.'

'That's a good story,' said Nixon. 'Ah've only one question…'

The same question had occurred to Reid long ago. 'Ah know, Ah know: if there were nae survivors, who told how they hid the treasure in the cave on Ragman's Law? That's why Ah never bothered to take a rope up there and sclim down to see if there was any treasure there for myself. As Ah say, it's jist a story.'

'Och, well, ye were reet not to sclim down into that cave,' said Nixon. 'But no' for the reason ye think!'

Nineteen

Kemp and Nompar paused at the head of the glen to gaze back the way they had come. The men pursuing them were less than a mile behind. 'How many, d'you think?' asked Kemp.

'About two dozen.'

'Aye.' Frowning, Kemp turned to look at the *bourc*. 'There were about two dozen when we stood at the Mitre Stone. Didn't *any* of them go after Bulchett and Crawley?'

Nompar shrugged. 'I warned you: men like Bulchett are never faced with the consequences of their deeds.'

'If we only had a dozen to deal with, we might've ambushed them. A dozen – that's only six each. I could have shot down my share before they even reached us.'

'And leave me to deal with the other six, I suppose?'

'Remind me to teach you how to use a bow some time.'

'Two dozen is too many,' said Nompar.

'Two dozen is *definitely* too many,' Kemp agreed.

The *bourc* glanced over his shoulder, in the direction they had been heading until they paused. 'How far to the English border, do you think?'

'About a dozen leagues, I reckon.'

'And how far do you think we must run before they forsake pursuing us?' Nompar indicated the reivers following them.

'If we can stay ahead of them until nightfall, I reckon they'll lose interest.'

'And if not?'

'We must hope summat turns up.'

'Such as?'

'We'll know it when we see it.'

'And this is your notion of a plan, is it?'

'If you have a better one, I'm all ears.' Kemp sighed. 'If we head south-west, I warrant we'll find ourselves in Annandale. We can follow it down as far as Hoddom, and from there follow the ancient highway to Longtown. From there it's but three leagues to Carlisle.'

The two of them crossed the saddle between the two hills at the head of the glen. The world to the south came into view, white-clad hills and valleys stretching away in all directions. Kemp had an impression of being on top of the world, so high the impossibly wide, grey sky seemed almost to catch on the hilltops.

A precipitous path led down past a tarn where water flowed out from under the ice to rush through the bottom of a meandering glen. As they followed it down, the ground on either side became steeper. Tussocks of rushes thrust up through the snow. Occasionally Kemp and Nompar caught glimpses of a larger valley up ahead, even deeper still than the glen they were following. The lie of the land prevented them from seeing just how deep the valley ahead was, but it was evident they still had a way to descend before they reached the lowlands.

The winding path descended parallel to the burn, occasionally rising where it crossed a spur of land from the hill to their left. The banks of the burn became steeper: here there was a scar of exposed earth where it had undercut the slope above, there it curled around a dark crag jutting out of the snow.

Glancing over his shoulder, Kemp caught sight of figures cresting the brow of one of the spurs back up the glen, less than a couple of furlongs behind them. God damn it, but these Scots moved fast over difficult terrain!

Kemp and Nompar pushed on, running as fast as they dared along the path, which had become a ledge cut in the steep slope on one side of the ravine. In a few dozen yards they had rounded another spur and were out of sight of their pursuers, but they dared not stop to catch their breath. The terrain offered plenty of hiding places: at any other time of year they might have concealed themselves, and the reivers might have run past and missed them entirely in their haste. But there was no point attempting such tricks now, when their footprints in the otherwise virgin snow would betray them.

A hissing roar alerted Kemp to a waterfall up ahead: he could see where the stream to their right rushed into a rocky defile, and just beyond that the whole ravine seemed to drop into dead ground. Cresting the brow of the next spur, he finally saw the bottom of the valley up ahead in the V between the hills on either side, a dizzyingly long way below.

The bottom of the ravine twisted so tightly between the interlocking spurs it almost seemed impossible the burn could squeeze between them. At the end, it rushed out over another precipice into a yawning chasm. But Kemp saw a ledge there on the opposite bank, perhaps a couple of hundred feet below them. If they could just get down to the burn they might leap across to it. A second ravine came down the hillside on their left. Where the path ahead crossed it, the ravine was little more than a furrow, but further down it became deeper and rockier. There was a broad spur between the two ravines: steep, but not so steep that a couple of aspen saplings could not cling to it. If Kemp and Nompar could climb down to those, they might find a place where they could leap across the burn; perhaps even step over it, if they were lucky.

Kemp stopped, unslinging his bow stave and stripping off its bag. 'See if you can find a way down to yon path,' he told Nompar, pointing.

The *bourc* nodded. 'Will you not come with me?'

'I'll be right behind you.' Kemp braced the lower end of his bow stave against the inside of a foot to string it. 'But if we're still on yon path when Nixon's men come over the spur behind us, we'll make easy targets. I mean to persuade them to hold back.'

Nompar took a couple of steps towards the spur Kemp had told him to descend, then halted and turned back to the Midlander. 'Down there?' he demanded incredulously, pointing.

On the verge of turning to head back up the path to the tarn, Kemp nodded, and tarried, waiting to see Nompar start down the spur.

The *bourc* did not move. 'We'll break our necks!'

'We'll not throw Nixon off our trail by following an easy path!'

'Have you seen how easily these Scots cross rugged ground? We needs must find a path a goat would blanch at if we're to find one to make Nixon's men baulk.' Shaking his head, Nompar turned and began to pick his way gingerly down the spur between the two ravines.

Kemp tucked his bow-bag under his belt and hurried back up the path until he came to where he could just see over a spur to the path beyond where it curved around the next spur, about a hundred yards away. When Nixon and his men hove into view, they would be outlined against the sky behind them, while Kemp had the hillside at his back, not that it provided much concealment with its expanse of snow for a background.

He took an arrow from under his belt, frozen fingers nocking it with difficulty. He needed a 'sighter' to warm his bow, but with two dozen men chasing them and only a dozen arrows left in his sheaf, he dared not squander any.

The reivers did not keep him waiting long, which was just as well: waiting meant thinking, and any thoughts he had at a time like this would not be encouraging ones. The first man rounded the spur behind, loping along the snowy trail with long, confident strides. Kemp drew his bow, but tarried before loosing: at that range, he knew he had a better chance of hitting a gaggle of men rather than a lone figure, and sure enough two more men rounded the spur, then a bunch of half a dozen. Aiming for the bunch, Kemp let fly. The string slipped awkwardly off his frozen fingertips and the shaft veered to the left of the intended line of flight; not by much, but at that range it was enough to miss the bunch of men entirely, though the traitor-arrow plunged into the snow close enough to alert them to the fact an archer was shooting at them.

Cursing his own clumsiness, Kemp blew hastily on his fingers, flexing them, trying to get the chill off them before fumbling for another arrow. He had chosen a place where the path was narrow, with a sheer drop into the ravine on one side and a hillside too steep to climb on the other. There was no getting off it to try to outflank him: the reivers could only come on, or retreat. They came on.

Kemp nocked the arrow, drawing it back to his ear, aiming for the bunch once more. He let fly, and this time the arrow flew true. One of the reivers fell with a shaft sticking out of his torso. Another man tried to support him as he fell; two more ran back, and another two ran on. The three men ahead of the bunch had more room on either side of the path. Two of them ran for the cover of a boulder, while the third unslung his own bow and began to string it. Kemp picked him off with his third arrow. The man toppled off the path and plunged out of sight into the bottom of the ravine. Kemp did not see the splash, but he heard it over the rushing of the water. He ducked below the level of the spur he hid behind, running bent double as he headed back to where the *bourc* was trying to find a way across the ravine. He could only hope Nixon and his men would not realise he had gone, and waste time advancing cautiously.

There was no sign of Nompar at the head of the chasm but his footprints descending the spur. Kemp followed them. A few dozen feet down, the footprints turned into a single broad furrow where the *bourc* had shuffled down on his backside. Not very dignified, but perhaps not the worst idea Nompar had ever had. The slope below just seemed to get steeper and steeper, and Kemp could not be sure that if he slipped, he would not shoot down and plunge into the chasm. The craggy ridge of the spur jutted up to his right; he could hear the hiss of the waterfall on the other side.

It was as well Vertue was not with him: Kemp did not care for heights, and consoled himself by muttering a succession of blasphemies to distract himself from his fear. There was still no sign of Nompar, and Kemp wondered if he had slipped off the spur entirely. He did not like to think the *bourc* was dead, much less that he might have sent him to his death.

Then he was descending over a slight brow in the spur, the ground below it even steeper, but at least he could see Nompar clinging to the slope below, trying to peer around the ridge of the spur. Just seeing his tenuous position made Kemp's insides knot up. As he shuffled down, a piece of snow he dislodged rolled down before him, growing larger as it went, until it was a good-sized snowball when it shot off the precipice below Nompar. That got the *bourc*'s attention without Kemp having to call to him. Looking up, he gestured to Kemp. The Midlander did not much like the idea of climbing down to him, but he was damned if an Englishman would be too craven to go where a Gascon dared.

Nompar gestured even more frantically. *Have patience!* thought Kemp, slithering down. *I'm coming as fast as I can!*

Suddenly the snow beneath his feet crumbled away and he felt himself slipping. He dug his heels in, trying to stop himself, but he was moving too fast. His throat sought to outdo the knot in his stomach when he realised he was going to shoot out over the precipice and plunge into the chasm below, quite possibly striking Nompar on the way down and sweeping him to his death also. But by only digging one heel into the snow, Kemp found he could change his direction a little, even if he could not stop himself. He steered towards the lower of the two aspen saplings clinging to the spur. His legs shot out on either side of its slender trunk and his crotch slammed into it painfully, but the agony that flamed through his loins was mitigated by the realisation that he was not about to fall to his death after all. He clung to the tree, struggling to catch his breath, grinning through the tears of agony that streamed down his cheeks.

Nompar clung to the slope only a few yards to his right. 'Are you hurt, *mon amec*?'

Kemp nodded. 'Very much so!' he squeaked.

'Why did you come down?'

'You beckoned me.'

'I did not!'

'Yes, you did! You did this!' Kemp made a beckoning gesture.

Nompar shook his head impatiently and made a 'keep back' gesture, but he did it with a slight circling motion that the Midlander understood at once why he had mistaken it for beckoning. 'That's not how you motion someone to stay back!' he snorted. 'Keep your hand level, like this.' He took one hand off the trunk of the sapling he clung to so he could demonstrate. 'Otherwise it looks like you're beckoning.'

'If I had been beckoning, I would have had my palm turned towards me, thus.'

'I couldn't see which way your palm was turned from all the way up there, could I?' Gripping on to wiry sprigs of heather sticking out of the snow, Kemp pulled himself up gingerly until he could brace his feet against the bole of the sapling. 'Is there a way across?'

'If there was a way across, I would have been beckoning you to climb down to me instead of motioning you to stay back,' the *bourc* replied a little tetchily.

'Let me see.' Kemp started to traverse the slope to where Nompar clung.

'You will not take my word for it?'

'Maybe I'll see summat you missed.' Kemp climbed over Nompar and clambered to where he could look around the ridge of the spur. With his right hand he could cling to the heather above him, but there were no

296

handholds for his left: he could only press his palm to the lichen-covered rock. A thin curtain of white water rushed over a lip a few feet above him, falling into a narrow plunge pool before flooding out over a ledge and spraying into the chasm. The main cataract flowed too fast to freeze, but icicles had formed where spray accumulated on the rocks on either side and dripped down. A man might be able to climb up a series of ledges on the far side, but there was no way to reach them without jumping to the ledge with water rushing over it, a jump that would almost certainly end with the jumper slipping out over the precipice.

'There's no way across that,' said Kemp.

'I told you as much,' said Nompar.

'Climb back up to the path.'

'Is there time to reach it?'

'The sooner you stop asking foolish questions and start climbing, the more time we'll have.'

Plunging a fist into the snow to clutch at the heather below, Nompar started to pull himself up when an arrow whipped past him, narrowly missing Kemp as well. The Midlander glanced up to see a couple of bowmen had taken up position on the path above them. The second loosed, his arrow coming even closer to Kemp than its predecessor had.

'Any suggestions?' asked Kemp.

Nompar craned his head, trying to peer over the precipice below them. 'We could jump.'

'Are you crazy?'

'There's usually a deep pool at the very foot of a waterfall—'

'Aye, and if we jump blindly from here, I'll lay odds against us landing in it.'

Nompar pursed his lips, then shrugged and nodded. 'You're right, that is a crazy idea.'

Kemp turned his attention to the slope above. Perhaps if they got higher, they could find a place where the bowmen could not see them to shoot at them; and if they could do that, there was a chance they could outflank the bowmen and shoot them before the rest of Nixon's men arrived.

Bracing a foot against a nub of stone sticking out of the earth immediately above the precipice, he grasped a fistful of heather and tried to pull himself up. As he did so, the stone under his foot broke loose from the soil surrounding it and shot out into space. He slipped down, both his legs dangling over the precipice, only his hand clutching the heather preventing him from falling any further, except that with all his weight now depending on the heather, it was torn from his grip and he felt himself slither over the edge.

–

Bulchett awoke to find himself lying in almost pitch-black darkness with a foul, rank stench in his nostrils. Almost… a little light came from somewhere. He craned his neck and saw it shining through the rocky crevice in the ceiling of what was evidently a cave. He was not lying directly beneath it, so he must have moved after falling through. It came flooding back to him: the slippery stuff coating the rock he was lying on. Some kind of cave slime? He reached out to touch the surface he lay on: yes, there was something there, making the rock greasy to the touch. He moved his hand to his nose and took a sniff. He recoiled with a gasp: the slime was evidently the source of the stench. He retched.

He tried to stand. Searing pain shot through his right leg when he moved it. He lay still, sobbing. When the agony had subsided, he tried again, moving his leg more gently now, but the pain was just as bad as before. Had he broken it? He needed to examine it, and for that he would need more light than fell through the crevice in the ceiling. Fortunately his scrip still hung from his belt. Groping inside it, he found his tinderbox. He struck the flint within against the steel until enough sparks fell on the parchment tinder to make it smoulder. He blew on the embers until he could get them to light a splinter of wood. The glow spread through the cave, dimly illuminating the walls. Except there were no walls, just two sloping surfaces, one above and one below, which perhaps met in the shadows beyond the glow of the burning splinter, with stalactites hanging from above and stalagmites rising to meet them from below. There were no doorways, no passages leading out, no sign that any human being other than him had set foot in here since the Creation.

Damn that John of Glasgow! he thought bitterly. Evidently the passage in his *Chronica* explaining how Ranulf de Soulis had a lair in this cave had been an invention. A feeling of contempt squeezed bile from Bulchett's liver: if there was one thing he could not abide, it was liars! But that did not prove the Knights Templar had not hidden their treasure in here somewhere.

He looked at his leg. Even in the light of the burning splinter, he could see something bulging against his chainmail legging about midway between his knee and his ankle. Frowning, he leaned forward to touch it. Agony erupted from beneath the bulge. He shrieked, and swore, and cursed God for allowing this to happen to a man of destiny. He realised the bulge was made by a fractured bone that had splintered, tearing through the skin to press against the inside of the mail legging.

He glanced back towards the hole in the ceiling. The rope still dangled down. It was a good twenty feet beyond his reach, but in the pool of light from above he could see the bottom of it rested on the floor of the cave. If he could at least reach it, perhaps he could use the strength of his arms to pull him up to the hole in the ceiling. He rolled onto his stomach, wincing at the fresh shoots of pain that erupted from his broken leg. Clawing with his hands, pushing himself up the slope with his good leg, he began to climb towards the rope.

He was only a few inches away when it suddenly snaked upwards. Bulchett looked up in time to see the last few inches disappear through the irregular oval of sky visible through the hole in the ceiling which silhouetted the head and shoulders of someone peering down at him.

'Rowland! Is that you?'

'Nae, it's no' Rowland,' a voice with a strong Scottish accent called down. 'Is that ye, Sir Alexander?'

'Who's that?'

'Rab Nixon. Who's this feller wi' a knife wound in his back? Is yon your squire, Sir Alexander? Is it Rowland?'

'No!'

'Did ye stab your own squire in the back? That was a wicked thing to do! Whit did ye do that for?'

'It wasn't I that stabbed him!'

'Och, was it no'?' Nixon chuckled. 'Who was it, then? Was it some naughty pixies? Did the naughty pixies come and stab your squire in the back?'

'Throw that rope down!'

'Whit, so ye can escape? Ah dinnae think so. Ye see, Ah've got ye jist where Ah want ye.'

Bulchett grinned in the darkness. He had one last cast of the dice before his turn was up, and he reckoned they were loaded in his favour. 'Aren't you forgetting something?'

'Whit would that be?'

'The Treasure of the Templars. A fortune beyond your wildest imaginings! Gold coins, gems, jewels...'

'Ye've found it, have ye?'

'I have!'

'How did ye find it?'

'I'd heard the old story about it going missing when some of the old king's men ambushed some Knights Templar in the Tweedsmuir Hills; about how, before the survivors fell out and killed one another, they hid it in a cave.'

'Aye, but how did ye ken it was *this* cave?'

'I remembered the legend about Ranulf de Soulis having a lair in a cave in this part of Scotland. Then I got to wondering how it was the knights who hid the treasure knew the cave was there... unless they'd read about Soulis' lair in the Chronicles of John of Glasgow, which give the location of the lair as Ragman's Law.'

'Very clever!'

'To the contrary, perfectly elementary!' Bulchett replied smugly. 'But if you want a share of the treasure, you'll have to come down here to get it.'

'Nae, Ah dinnae think so.'

Someone turning down a fortune was something Bulchett could not comprehend. He shook his head. 'What do you mean?'

'That story about the battle in the Tweedsmuir Hills, it's no' true, ye ken. The part about there being nae survivors, Ah mean. There was one survivor... aye, it's true he died of his wounds a week later, but no' before he'd confessed his sins to a certain priest at a church in Moffat. Och, and all that talk of it bein' gold coins and gems and jewels worth millions... that's a gross exaggeration. It was nearer three hundred and twenty-seven gold coins.'

'How would you know?'

'The priest was my father. He sclimmed down here a couple of days later to retrieve the treasure for himself. He was a careful man; if there'd been millions of gold coins down here, Ah dinnae think he'd've been so careless as to miss any. It's all gone now, of course. Frittered away on drink, dice and whores decades ago. My father didnae stay a priest long when he got his hands on three hundred and twenty-seven gold coins, Ah can tell ye! No' that he'd been a plaster saint before then. Ah mean, Ah was past my eleventh winter when all this happened, so that should give ye some idea of whit manner of priest my father was. Well, it's been pleasant chattin' wi' ye, Sir Alexander, but Rory an' me must be on our way. Ah've got some business to attend to wi' your friends the Bourc of Cazoulat and... who is that archer with him?'

'I don't know. Some fellow called Kemp.'

'Kemp, Kemp... no' *Martin* Kemp?'

'Do you know him?'

'We crossed swords a couple of times, a few years ago. Was he no' at Berwick when the Earl of Dunbar besieged it last year? Aye, Ah reckon Ah've got a score to settle wi' Kemp. Och, dinnae fash yourself! As soon as that's done, we'll come back for ye. Ye may not be worth three hundred and twenty-seven gold coins, but Ah reckon your father will still be willing to pay a fair ransom for ye. So

Ah'll bid ye farewell for now… we'll be back in a day or twa.' The silhouetted head disappeared.

'Nixon!' bellowed Bulchett. 'Let down that rope, damn your nose! Nixon! Nixon?'

There was no reply.

A day or two… Bulchett was confident he could survive that long. Perhaps even recover enough to give Nixon the thrashing he deserved.

Something rustled above him. He looked up again, thinking perhaps the reiver had returned, but no silhouette broke the outline of the opening overhead. Taking out his tinder box again, Bulchett lit another splinter. As its warm glow spread through the cave, he slowly raised his eyes to the ceiling. Between the stalactites hanging down, something stirred…

Bats.

Hundreds of them – perhaps even thousands – hanging upside down from the roof. Beady black eyes in fanged, snub-nosed faces, leathery wings wrapped around their furry little bodies… Bulchett's skin crawled with terror at the thought. The saliva drained from his mouth. In the silence of the cave he could hear his heart pounding in his ribcage, and despite the cold, beads of sweat began coursing down his face. The stinking, slippery stuff he lay in was their accumulated droppings.

The shock of this realisation made him drop the splinter in his hand, and the flame went out when it landed in the filth. And then he was plunged into darkness, bleeding in bat shit, alone but for ten thousand or so bats.

He screamed.

Twenty

Kemp was not dead.

No one was more surprised by that than he was. He had been braced for that long plunge into the chasm below him, but it had never come. There had been no drop when he slipped over the precipice, just more slope. Steeper than the slope above the precipice, but there was enough to cling on to: one foot jammed against a projecting nub of stone, one hand gripping a tuft of moonwort growing out of a crack in the lichen-covered rock, the other pressed against the cliff-face as firmly as if Kemp wished to fuse his hand to it. He opened his eyes and looked up to see the smooth rock of the precipice above him, and something that looked like... yes, it was definitely Nompar's heel.

'Nompar?' he called.

'Martin?' The *bourc*'s voice burst with astonishment. 'You're not dead?'

'Nay. There's more slope down here.'

'How much more?'

Slowly, with infinite care, Kemp turned his head to look down. Beyond the nub of stone his right foot was jammed against was nothing, just the yawning void of the chasm and the hiss of the waterfall cascading into a plunge pool far, far below. Maybe there was more slope below the second precipice, but if there was, it was even steeper than the slope he now clung to. And the slope he clung to now was as close to a sheer cliff as damn it.

An arrow clattered against the rocks nearby. That had been aimed at Kemp rather than Nompar. Glancing up and to his right, he could still see the bowmen on the path above. And, more to the point, they could still see him.

He began to inch his way to the left, towards the ridge of the spur, his left leg scrabbling for a foothold. He found one: not much of one, but as good as he could hope to find under the circumstances. He slowly transferred his weight from his right foot to the left, keeping his grip on the moonwort lest the stone his left foot now rested on crumbled away. It was as well he did, for that was precisely what the stone proceeded to do. His grip on the moonwort held, but his whole body jolted, his stomach spasming with fear as his weight was forced back onto his right foot. He clung there for a moment, listening for the dislodged stone clattering against the rocks below, not daring to move, with his left leg hanging in space. He had decided the noise of the stone hitting the bottom had been drowned by the roar of the cataract when the clatter echoed up from the bottom of the chasm. *Hell's teeth, that's a long way down...*

He hung there, too frozen with terror to move, until another arrow narrowly missed him. He wondered if the bowmen were lousy shots, or just toying with him, trying to get him to fall from where he clung without killing him outright, so they could enjoy his scream as he plunged to his death.

His hatred of them spurred him into action: he would not give them the satisfaction. He raised his dangling left foot and tentatively explored the rockface below him with his toecap, finally finding a horizontal surface he could rest his foot on. It was probably no more than a couple of inches across, but he was in no position to be picky. Again he gradually transferred his weight to his left foot, bracing himself for the shock of it giving way beneath him. It seemed to hold. Making sure both his hands had good holds on the rock above him, he moved his right foot away from where it rested. Now all his weight was on the left. He began to explore the rock below with his right toecap, seeking a foothold closer to the spine of the spur. Finding one at last, he moved his left hand over the rock, feeling for a handhold. His fingertips detected a crevice and curled into it. He transferred enough of his weight to it so he could move his right foot and search for something else to put it on, something strong enough to bear his weight, something closer to the spine of the spur.

Inch by inch, he traversed the slope towards the spine. The spur had a natural camber to it: the further he moved to his left, the harder it was for the bowmen to get a clear shot at him.

He saw enough handholds and footholds on that side to enable him to climb over the precipice above and join Nompar further up the slope. But then he remembered the ledge he had seen partway down the cascade on the other side of the spine. It had been too far down to risk jumping to it from above, but from where he was now? He clambered across to the spine and looked around it. The ledge was level with his feet: if he could somehow work his way around the spine, he might reach it. From there he could practically step past the cataract to a ledge on the opposite side, then climb up the rocks to a place where the walls of the ravine were not so steep. They could climb out there and descend the opposite side of the chasm to the path below.

We can do this, he thought, allowing himself to dare to hope for the first time since the bowmen had begun shooting.

'Nompar!' he called.

'Yes?'

'If you climb down here, there's a place we can get across the waterfall.'

'Are you sure?'

'Nay. But right now it's our best hope.' *Our only hope*, he might have added.

Nompar began to lower himself over the lip of rock above. Dislodged chunks of snow fell past Kemp. He could see the *bourc*'s foot feeling for a hold, not finding the one a few inches below it.

'Stretch yourself a little more,' Kemp called up. 'There's a good place to put your right foot just three inches below it… another inch… that's it!'

Once Nompar was level with him, Kemp turned his attention to the spine. A cleft in the rock above his head gave him a handhold. He swung his left leg around. He tried to swing it to the ledge, but it would not reach. He strained, but it was hopeless: he was about six inches short.

There was nothing for it: he would have to swing himself across.

No sense in delaying. He was in no hurry to die, but while he clung to this rock with a chasm yawning below and a couple of reivers taking potshots at him, he could hardly claim his quality of life was such that there was any benefit in dragging it out even a few more heartbeats. The longer he delayed, the more time he gave himself to think about the consequences if he lost his grip, or his foot slipped on that ledge he was aiming for. If it came to pass, there would be time enough to worry about that on the way down…

He moved his right hand up until he could slide his fingers into the same cleft as the one the fingers on his left already occupied. He took a couple of breaths, then transferred all his weight to his fingers, only for the couple of heartbeats it took him to swing both feet around the spine of the rock to the ledge by the cataract; heartbeats that boomed in his chest like beats on the Devil's own drum.

Both feet found the ledge, but it was slick with spray. His left foot slipped off again, and he was at an awkward angle, his fingers still caught in that cleft, leaning over too far backwards, with only one foot on the ledge. He managed to extract the fingers of one hand, bracing it against the rock behind him while he extracted the others, pushing himself upright again. He teetered for a few seconds with his heart thudding somewhere between his tonsils. From here he could see where the cataract cascaded down to the pool far below, and a sick, dizzy feeling swept over him. He grabbed for the rock above and found something to hold on to: not enough to give him a secure grip, but enough – just – to steady him. Standing upright, he drew another breath, and turned back to where Nompar was looking around the spine of the rock at him, his visor raised to reveal the anxiety etched on his face.

Kemp resisted the temptation to look down again. 'Feel the rock above you.' He had to shout to make himself heard above the roar of the cataract. 'There's a cleft in the rock about a foot above your head. If you can get your fingers in there, you can swing across to this ledge.' There was plenty of room for them both to stand on it, provided Nompar did not fidget about too much.

The *bourc* did as he was bidden. He had already taken off his gauntlets to make it easier to find handholds; they were tucked under his belt. Finding the cleft, the *bourc* managed to swing both feet on to the ledge, but like Kemp he had difficulty pulling his fingers from the cleft in time to use his own momentum to swing himself upright. He tottered, grabbing instinctively at Kemp's arm and almost pulling him off. Kemp managed to grab hold of a ledge above them both and caught hold of Nompar's elbow, pulling him to safety. The *bourc* puffed his cheeks out in relief. 'As easy as "good day",' he remarked sardonically.

On this side of the spine, they were out of sight of the bowmen on the path above, but Kemp could see where the path continued along the slope of the hill opposite, less than a furlong away. It would not take them long to realise they only had to move a hundred yards down the track to resume shooting at their quarry, albeit at a greater range.

Kemp turned his attention to the rocks on the opposite side of the cataract. There was the ledge he had spotted opposite, but the gap between that and the ledge he now stood on – the gap the cataract plunged through – did not seem nearly as narrow as it had before. And now he saw the ledge opposite sloped, and was wet with spray, probably slick with algae to boot. But there was no other way off the ledge he and Nompar stood on, other than to go back the way they had come, and that was out of the question. Kemp tried to step across, then recoiled: it was too wide for that. He would have to jump. There was no room for a run-up. He bent his knees, took a couple of deep breaths, and sprang across. His body slammed against the rocks above the opposite ledge and he clung to them like a lover embracing a long-lost sweetheart. As he had anticipated, the slippery, sloping ledge he now stood on offered little purchase for the soles of his boots, and there was no room for Nompar to jump across until he had climbed out of the way.

Ascending the rocks a short way, he turned to watch Nompar jump across in front of the cataract. When the *bourc* landed on the ledge below, his feet slipped, but Kemp reached down to catch hold of one of his flailing arms. Once Nompar had regained his balance, they both turned and scrambled up the rocks. Moments later the two of them were out of the ravine, traversing the snowy slope of the hillside beyond.

They were back within sight of the bowmen on the path opposite. The first two had been joined by half a dozen friends, and it was not long before a hail of arrows came their way. The best way to avoid it was to keep moving, so they scrambled down the slope to the path below. It was steep, but not so steep they could not slide down it on their rumps, which was far quicker than trying to pick their way down on their feet. Reaching the foot-path at the bottom of the chasm, they followed it around a huge boulder which then hid them from the bowmen above. Kemp and Nompar ran along the path parallel to the bank of the burn, following it to where it flowed out of the chasm into the valley beyond.

Nompar glanced over his shoulder before grinning at Kemp. 'A pity we cannot tarry to watch them try to follow us across that!'

'They don't have to. Belike there's at least one amongst them who knows this valley well enough to know all they need do is descend yon hillside and follow the far bank of the stream till they come to yon ford.' Kemp pointed to where the burn widened up ahead and the banks, high and undercut for most of their length, sloped down on both sides to allow the road running through the valley to cross.

They jogged on in silence, keen not to squander the head start they had won with such difficulty. Kemp felt too exhausted by the exertions of descending the chasm to feel much exultation at having survived.

The valley was broad and deep, running from northeast to south-west. Kemp was confident if they followed the river downstream, it would lead them to Annandale in a few miles. It was growing dark, however: there was no telling where the sun was behind the grey clouds that seemed to roof the valley over, but wherever it was, Kemp guessed it was sinking behind the horizon.

When they were too weary to continue jogging, Kemp and Nompar slowed to a walk, but a brisk one. Dusk closed in and the snow turned from white to a dingy blue. Kemp looked about for a place where they could spend the night. The valley offered not even as much as a sheiling, but the slopes on either side were carpeted with trees, and when dusk turned to twilight Kemp and Nompar veered off the road to take shelter amongst them. Here the woods were surrounded by a ditch and an embankment, which suggested they were no longer as far from civilisation as all that, and the embankment would help to hide the light of a campfire.

'Dare we risk a fire?' asked Nompar.

'On a night as cold as this, I don't think we dare do without. Unless we'd have Nixon's men find our frozen bodies in the snow tomorrow.'

They found sticks half-hidden in the snow, enough to build a fire, and Nompar produced his tinderbox. He clucked his tongue when he looked inside.

'What's amiss?' Kemp asked him.

'I have used up the last of my tinder.'

'Try this.' Reaching into a compartment of the purse hanging on his belt, Kemp drew out a piece of folded parchment.

Nompar squinted at it in the twilight before looking up at Kemp in astonishment. 'This is the contract I signed to pay you those twelve hundred *escudoes* I owe you!'

Kemp shrugged. 'I think we can call that debt repaid several times over.'

'But… such generosity! I know not how to repay you.'

Kemp smiled. 'Get the damn fire lit and we'll call it fair and square.'

Once Nompar had the fire going, the two of them warmed their hands at it. '*Moun Dieu!*' groaned the *bourc*. 'My belly's tight! What would I not give for a dish of *pitre de guit amb tricandilles à la Bordelaise* right now.'

'*Pitre de* what?'

'*De guit*. Duck breasts with pig's tripe cooked in a sauce made from lampreys' blood.'

'Lampreys' blood?' Kemp pulled a face. 'That's a crime against pig's tripe. Onion gravy is what you want. Chitterlings cooked in onion gravy.'

Nompar rolled his eyes. 'You English and your lamentable notions of cuisine! You must come to Cazoulat one day, *mon amec*. I will take you to an inn where they cook the finest *tricandilles* in Gascony, washed down with a flagon of wine made from grapes from my father's vineyards…'

In the flickering glow of the fire, Kemp saw a shadow pass over Nompar's face. It was not difficult to imagine why: evidently the *bourc* had reminded himself of the news of his father's recent death… a death that still needed to be avenged. But that was a matter that would have to wait for another day.

Kemp shuffled uncomfortably, hugging his mantle tighter about him against the cold. 'I warrant you'd be glad of a bowl of tripe with onion gravy right now.'

Nompar pasted a smile on his face. 'I am so hungry, I could eat tripe *without* onion gravy!'

The two of them stared moodily into the fire, tormenting themselves with thoughts of the banquets they might have enjoyed had they been in Cockaigne, the magical land of plenty, rather than shivering in some woods in the wilds of Scotland in the dead of winter. 'Do you think the reivers will continue to chase us tomorrow?' Nompar asked at last.

Kemp shrugged. 'Maybe.'

'I think they will give up,' said Nompar. 'I think they will forsake chasing us and head back to Ragman's Law to hunt down Bulchett and Crawley.'

'Take care not to overhope.'

'You do not agree?'

'What was it you said earlier today about people believing what they want to believe?'

Nompar chuckled ruefully. 'You are right, of course. But not you…?'

Kemp smiled. 'Let's just say life's taught me to hope for the best and brace myself for the worst. Get some sleep. I'll take first watch.'

Kemp was woken at first light by Nompar. Given how cold and hungry he had been the night before, he was pleasantly surprised to discover he had got to sleep at all, but that was the only thing about his waking that was pleasant. The fire had burned out during the night and the morning was bitterly cold. He had been dreaming about being in Gascony in summer, and it was a cruel disappointment to realise that was just a dream and he was still in Scotland. There was no morrow-meat to start the day, but like most folk Kemp did not bother with food first thing in the morning; he preferred to get half a day's work under his belt before sitting down to dinner an hour before midday.

'It can't be much further to Annandale,' he said, looking to raise his own spirits with the prospect as much as Nompar's, for in his own quiet way the *bourc* was his usual chipper self. 'I warrant we'll find summat for our dinner in Annandale, even if we must steal meat from the hands of a hungry child.'

'I am so hungry, I could eat dog meat,' said Nompar.

They went into separate thickets to ease nature, then set out without further ado. Most likely Nixon and his men would give up this morning and turn back to Ragman's Law, if they had not done so already; but there was no sense in tarrying to find out whether or not they had.

As they set off, Kemp bowed his head and pinched the bridge of his nose between thumb and forefinger. 'Your head still aches?' asked Nompar.

'Aye.'

'The best thing for an aching head is to find something to take your mind off it,' said the *bourc*.

'Such as getting out of Scotland?' suggested Kemp.

'That might work.'

The further downstream they travelled, the wider the valley became, the less steep the hills rising on either side. At a distance, it was difficult to tell a snow-covered heath from a snow-covered field, but where there had been heather growing right up to the verge of the road, now only tussocks of rushes showed, and the sheep nuzzling the snow in search of grazing suggested they had left the moors behind and were back in pasturelands.

'I think it is a little warmer today,' Nompar remarked after they had been striding down the road for an hour or so. 'Perhaps the thaw is coming.'

'Perhaps,' agreed Kemp. 'I'll still prefer it when we're warming our bones in front of a roaring fire in Carlisle.'

–

'Here they are,' Nixon remarked to Reid when they saw Ayton and the rest of the reivers waiting by the trees. 'Remember: if anyone asks, Bulchett and his squire are both deid. Ah dinnae mind sharing the ransom wi' Howk and the others, but Sir Archibald and Sneith are both rich enough already – and it's no' as if they've did aught to help us catch Bulchett.'

'And if they learn later that Bulchett still lives? D'ye no' think they'll work out ye cheated them?'

'Of course they will. But by then the ransom will be in our hands. They can squawk all they like then.'

Reaching Ayton and the others, Nixon and Reid greeted them with nods. 'God give ye a good morning, lads. Where are Sir Archibald and Sneith?'

'Wi' Howk, jist through yon trees.' Ayton pointed. 'Ah think we've found the place where the *bourc* and his friend spent the night.'

Nixon and Reid ducked under the trees and found Howk, Archibald and Sneith studying the ground. 'Have ye no' caught them yet?' Nixon asked scornfully.

'Traces of a fire here.' Sneith pointed out what the rest of them could plainly see with their own eyes. 'This is where they spent the night.'

'What of Sir Alexander and his squire?' asked Archibald.

'Deid,' said Nixon.

Sneith narrowed his eyes. 'You slew them both? I thought you wanted to claim the ransom?'

Nixon shrugged. 'They widnae be taken alive. Whit could we do?'

'Nae bluid, nae banes, nae fur, nae feathers, nae crumbs,' observed Howk, still studying the ground. 'Looks like they lay down hungry and set off this morning even hungrier.'

'Chances are when we do catch up wi' them, we'll find them deid of cold and hunger,' said Nixon. 'This is no' the weather for going about with an empty belly.' Turning to Reid, he indicated where the tracks continued down the valley. 'It's clear they're heided for Annandale. Run on ahead and wait for them at Spedlin's Tower.'

'Aye, Rab.' Reid headed towards the trees on the far side of the clearing, where the ground below them sloped up towards the ridge on the south-east side of the valley. It did not bother him that Nixon had sent him on ahead to tackle two men single-handed. If anything, it would have flattered him, had he not felt supremely confident of besting them both. He would have to pick his ground carefully, of course: find a spot where the road narrowed so he could find a place to conceal himself where he knew his quarry would have to pass within a foot or two. He could easily kill the first before either of them knew he was there. Then it would be one against one, and Reid did not fear to fight any man on such odds. With any luck, he could kill Kemp and render the *bourc* senseless with a stunning blow: if they took him alive, they could claim the ransom for him as well as Bulchett.

When he emerged from the trees onto a crag of rock near the top of the ridge, he had a good view of the valley below. He could see the figures of two men a couple of miles to his left: Kemp and the *bourc*, he guessed. Nixon and the others were about a mile behind them.

Hearing footsteps scrunch in the snow behind him, he whirled, tugging his maul from under his belt with his left hand and his reaping hook with his right, but it was only Sneith toting his crossbow.

'Whit do ye want?' Reid asked him surlily.

'Sir Archibald thought you could use my help.'

'Ah dinnae need anyone's help. Least of all yours, ye bawsie juffler!'

Turning away, Reid returned his weapons to his belt and started down the track towards the saddle beneath Fauldside Hill without waiting to see if Sneith followed. If the man-at-arms fell and twisted his ankle crossing the moors, he need not expect the reiver to stop and tarry for him. When he reached Capel Fell, Reid knew he would have to climb all the way down into Craigmichen Cleugh before climbing up the far side, but from there it would be easy enough to follow the ridge all the way down through Auchenroddan Forest, and he could reach Spedlin's Tower hours ahead of their quarry.

Twenty-One

'Stop!' Kemp's legs ached, and his lungs felt raw from breathing the chill winter air. 'No more running. We've run far enough.'

Hearing him, Nompar, who had pulled ahead, turned and walked back, bending over to lean with his hands on his knees. He was breathing just as hard at Kemp. 'If you need to rest...' he panted.

Kemp shook his head. 'From the moment I entered Scotland last Allhallowstide, it seems I've done nowt but run. I'll run no more. Time we stood and fought.'

'Against two dozen men?'

'If that's what it takes. If we choose our ground carefully, we can even the odds.' Kemp looked around. They were following the ancient road that ran through Annandale. A watermill of the English kind stood on the riverbank nearby, its roof thickly heaped with snow. Kemp thought of it as 'the English kind' because most watermills in Scotland were little more than stone bothies built over streams with a horizontal wheel suspended to catch the current. They were open for anyone passing to use, which sounded idyllic until you realised that having no resident miller meant they were very often in a poor state of repair. But occasionally one saw larger mills like those in England, with vertical wheels, often the property of a local lord or an abbey, which employed a resident miller who charged folk for the privilege of having their grain milled, and the mill on the River Annan clearly belonged to that category.

A few hundred yards upstream, a channel had been dug from the river to feed the millpond, which was iced over, though water still flowed from under the ice through a little sluice gate into the mill race, where the mill's wheel turned, close to where the water from the pond ran back into the Annan. That put the mill on a sliver of an island, with the river on one side and the channel feeding the pond, the pond itself and the mill race on the other. The mill stood about three hundred yards from the road, linked to it by a path, with little in the way of cover on either side, a good, clear prospect for an archer.

Kemp pointed the mill out to Nompar. 'In there.'

A narrow wooden bridge spanned the mill race immediately upstream from the wheel. It was an undershot wheel: even Kemp understood that an overshot wheel generated more power, but not every locality had a river with enough of a fall to make an overshot wheel practical.

Kemp and Nompar crossed the bridge to the mill and knocked on the door. A dank, earthy smell wafted out as a bald, sharp-featured old man answered the door and looked them both up and down disapprovingly. 'Whit d'ye want?'

'You're the miller?' Kemp asked in surprise. Millers spent their days hefting sacks of grain or flour, and consequently they were usually hefty men. This fellow did not look as though he could heft a pouch of feathers.

'Aye. Whit d'ye want?'

'We want to borrow your mill for a few hours.' Nompar tried to press a couple of silver coins into the miller's purse. 'I pray this will cover any inconvenience.'

The miller would not accept the coins. 'Borrow my mill? Ah never heard of such a thing! Be off wi' ye! Ah've work to do this morning.'

A brawny man joined the miller in the doorway. 'Is there a problem, father?'

'These foreigners want to borrow our mill!'

'We're no' interested,' said the miller's son.

Kemp looked him up and down. Now it was obvious who hefted the sacks at this mill. 'You may take my friend's silver, or refuse it,' he told him. 'But we're borrowing this mill, come what may.'

'The De'il ye are!' The miller's son gave Kemp a shove in the chest, making him stagger back. 'Ye dinnae tell my father whit to do in his own mill.'

'I seek no trouble,' said Kemp.

'Then ye've come to the wrong place!' The miller's son gave him another shove, sending him staggering back onto the footbridge over the mill race. 'Trouble's all ye'll find here!'

'I don't want to hurt you,' said Kemp. 'But if you stand in my way, I must handle you roughly.'

The miller's son grinned. 'Is that so? Ye've got me pishing in my braies!' He gave Kemp another shove, sending him staggering back to the far end of the bridge. 'God-damned Inglishers, full o' pish and wind about—'

Kemp punched him in the jaw. The miller's son was spun around, spitting out a gobbet of saliva laced with blood and a couple of teeth, before sinking to his knees and clutching at the bridge's railing to keep from falling into the mill race. Kemp shook his hand as if he could shake the pain out of his bruised and aching knuckles. Then he seized the miller's son by an earlobe, hauling him to his feet and dragging him off the bridge. 'On your way, sonny!' he snarled, delivering a sharp kick to the lad's rump.

The rest of the family came meekly after that: the miller and his elderly wife, the son's wife carrying a squalling babe. 'If you head up the road to Moffat, you will meet Rab Nixon and a score of his men coming the other way,' Nompar told them. 'If you tell him he can find the men he seeks here, he will thank you for it.'

'One way or another, we'll be out of here before nightfall,' said Kemp.

The miller and his family headed up the road, though whether they were going to meet Nixon or simply going to take shelter with a neighbour for a few hours remained to be seen. There were not so many travellers on the road from Moffat to Lockerbie at this time of year that Nixon and his men would have trouble following his quarries' footprints in the snow.

Kemp and Nompar surveyed the interior of the mill. On the ground floor was a living space with two bed places and a crib for the baby. Kemp added some kindling to the fire burning in the hearth. In the next room the stout wooden kingpin connected to the waterwheel outside turned a large wooden cogwheel in a frame. The cog's teeth meshed with the teeth of a second cog that rotated on a vertical axle, presumably turning a millstone in the grinding room above. The sluice below the millpond must have been open, for the miller had already begun work that morning and the machinery turned, filling the mill with rhythmic groans, creaks and thuds. Ground flour sifted down a chute from the millstones on the floor above, slowly filling a big tub. Empty sacks were stacked nearby. Next to the housing containing the cogs, a ladder led up to the grinding room.

Finding a pail, Kemp carried it out through the back door, to where a flagstone path beneath the wide eaves of the mill led out on to the snow-covered ground of the island. He walked across to the shore of the millpond and tested the ice with a foot. It creaked under the pressure: if Nixon and his men tried to cross the ice, they would likely meet a similar fate to Vertue's. But the channel that fed the pond from the river was narrow enough for a bold man to leap across, so it was possible to outflank the mill from that direction.

Kemp filled the pail at the riverbank and carried it back to the mill. He suspended a kettle from the tripod over the hearth and poured the water into it. He noticed an earthenware pitcher and picked it up. It contained milk. He carried it outside, tipped the milk into the river and smashed the pitcher on the flagstones. It broke satisfyingly into a couple of large pieces and a lot of shards. He picked up the larger pieces and threw them on to the path further up, hard, so they too shattered into shards. The whole length of the path was littered with shards that would either crunch underfoot or chink loudly if someone inadvertently kicked them. If they did, Kemp could only hope he would hear it above the plashing of the turning waterwheel and the noise of the mill's machinery.

He climbed the ladder up and into the grinding room. A wooden chute descending from the ceiling fed grain into the centre of the two millstones that sat one above the other immediately above the cogwheels on the floor below. A door led through to the bower, with a single large bed for the miller and his wife, a trunk for fresh linen at the foot of it. Kemp opened the shutters on the window and looked out across the river. No doubt in summer it was a pleasant enough view; some might find it pretty with everything that was not water thickly draped with several inches of snow, but Kemp had spent too much time out in the cold over the past few days to see any beauty in it now. He leaned out of the window, but could not see the top end of the millpond.

Another ladder led up to an attic. There were no walls here, the timbers of the roof sloping up from the furthest reaches of the floor to reach an apex immediately overhead. Here were the grain bins that fed the millstones. There was a large door in the gable-end, and Kemp opened it to reveal a sheer drop to a loading platform below, with a hoist overhead so sacks of grain could be swayed up and emptied directly into the bins.

He gazed out across the countryside on the opposite side of the mill from the river. He could see half the millpond, and the mill race coming down as far as where it disappeared around the side of the mill where the water-wheel turned. Beyond he could see the road, and twenty figures coming down it, less than half a mile away now.

He descended to the ground floor and found Nompar sitting by the hearth, carefully honing the blade of his sword with a whetstone. 'Nixon and his men are coming down the road.'

Nompar just nodded, his face impassive, and went on honing his blade.

By now the water in the kettle was starting to simmer. Wrapping rags around both hands, Kemp lifted the kettle off the hook by its handle and carried it across to the front door. The water gave off clouds of steam as it met the cold air outside. He tossed it on to the planks of the bridge, where it froze almost at once. A trick his father had taught him when he was a boy, something no one had ever been able to explain to him, though anyone who had ever had the opportunity to put it to the test accepted it was true: hot water froze faster than cold. It left the planks of the bridge slippery with ice.

Kemp carried the empty kettle back into the living area and put it down on the wooden floor in one corner. 'Be wary if you step out on that bridge,' he told Nompar. 'It's icy.'

'It was not icy when we arrived.'

Kemp smiled. 'A frost must ha' come down.'

He glanced out of the window. Nixon and his men had reached the far end of the path leading to the mill. They huddled there, evidently debating the best way to approach. Kemp counted a score of them. He frowned: two dozen of them had chased him and Nompar from below Ragman's Law; he had shot two in the ravine above the waterfall, so there should have been two and twenty left. Two men were missing. Had Nixon sent them back, with a message for Lord Douglas perhaps? Or were they even now sneaking around the back of the mill to outflank Kemp and Nompar? The Midlander crossed to the back door and glanced out. The north end of the island was clear; they did not have to worry about anyone coming from that direction just yet.

'How many arrows have you left?' asked Nompar.

'Thirteen.'

Kemp climbed up to the attic and peered through the door beneath the hoist to where the reivers now spread out on either side of the path leading from the road to the mill. They were keeping well spaced out as they advanced, to make themselves more difficult targets for an archer than a single huddle of men would have been. Kemp's mouth was dry as he strung his bow, and his palm sweated where it gripped the bow stave. His upper arm ached where he had received a slight wound in the autumn; it was strange how one was more aware of everything in the moments before a battle.

It would be an unexpected twist of fate if, having survived Crécy, Calais, Guînes, Mauron and Berwick, he were to die in a brawl with a score of reivers at a mill in Annandale. But everyone died eventually. After everything Kemp had been through in his short life, in many respects it was a miracle he had lived this long. Perhaps today would be the day his luck ran out. If it was, no one would sing any songs about him and Nompar as they did about the victors of Crécy. Perhaps they would not deserve to have any songs sung about them. But the battle ahead of them would be as desperate as any Kemp had fought in, for all that. Today he was not fighting for his king, or for God, or for gold, or to impress his lady-love, or for any of the other foolish reasons a man risked his hide in the tumult of a battlefield. He and Nompar would be fighting for their lives. But at the end of the day, when the clarions sounded the charge and the arrows began to fly, the lofty causes men espoused at the start of the campaign were soon forgotten. Survival, for oneself and one's comrades, was all any man fought for in the heat of battle, be he English, Scots, French, Welsh, or from any other land.

The reivers were less than fifty yards away: close enough for Kemp to pick off individual targets if he chose to. 'That's close enough!' he shouted.

Nixon halted and signalled for his men to do likewise, those of them who had not already instinctively obeyed the Englishman's command. The brawny figure next to the reiver chief stood a head taller than the other men around him: Howk. *Sweet Jesu*, thought Kemp, *he's a big whoreson.*

'Are ye gaunae come out an' yield?' called Nixon. 'Or must we come in there and get ye?'

'Suppose we do yield?' Nompar called from below. 'What terms will you offer us?'

'If you hand over the Englishman and surrender yourself, we'll only demand a ransom of two hundred and fifty pounds for you.' This time it was Sir Archibald Douglas who spoke.

'And my arms and armour?'

'You must give those up.'

'What of the Englishman? What ransom will you demand for him?'

'Nae ransom,' growled Nixon. 'He must die. The corpse of Michie Liddell must be avenged.'

'But the man who slew Michie Liddell is already dead.'

'Oh aye? Whit about all the other Scots folk slain by the English marauders who marched across the border into Scotland at the end of last month?'

'What about the English folk slain by reivers like you, Nixon?' Kemp called back. 'Whose death will atone for them?'

'Must an Englishman die every time a Scot is slain by one of King Edward's subjects?' asked Nompar. 'Or a Scot each time an Englishman is slain by a vassal of King David? Are England and Scotland to be at one another's throats for eternity, striving against one another until the mists of history descend to obscure the original reasons for their enmity?'

'Ah'll no' soon forget why the English are our foes!' said Nixon.

'If you'd avoid bloodshed, Sir Nompar, you only need to yield and turn your friend over to us,' said Archibald. 'You at least will live to fight another day.'

'That I cannot do.'

'Why not?'

'He is my friend. Would I disgrace the name of Savignac by having it said I betrayed a friend? If you wish to avoid bloodshed, Sir Archibald, the power lies with you: march back the way you came, and before sundown Kemp and I will march back to England, never to return to your country. You have my word on it.'

'I dinnae trust the word of any damned vassal of Edward of England!' spat Nixon. 'Much less a Frenchman.'

'I am a Gascon,' Nompar corrected him.

'Same difference. You're all god-damned foreigners.'

'I'll give you one last chance,' said Archibald. 'Surrender now. Once we start our attack, we'll offer no quarter.'

Sensing the conversation had run its course, Kemp took an arrow from under his belt and nocked it to his bow. 'We'll ask for none.'

'Then there is no use in further talking!' Archibald knocked down his visor and drew his sword. 'Attack!'

Kemp drew, aiming at Nixon. He sensed that if anyone was directing the Scots today, it would be the reiver chief. Kill him, and he had cut off the head of the snake.

He let fly an arrow and saw Nixon reel. For a moment he thought he had got him, but the reiver chief stayed on his feet and pulled the arrow out of his chest – it looked as though it had penetrated part of his armour without injuring him – before tossing it aside.

A volley of arrows whipped through the second-floor doorway where Kemp stood, but he had been expecting it and had plenty of time to step out of sight before any of the shafts whistled past. The arrows thudded into rafters, walls and floorboards. If Kemp ran out of arrows, he would have to remember he could find more up here.

While the bowmen shot at Kemp's doorway, the hobelars charged towards the bridge spanning the mill race. But the narrowness of the bridge prevented them from coming at Nompar more than one at a time, and if he stayed in the shadows behind the door at the end of the bridge, he would be relatively safe from arrows. As long as he only had to fight the reivers one at a time, Kemp reckoned the *bourc* could outmatch any of them with a sword. Until his sword-arm wearied, at least.

Kemp picked off a couple of the bowmen, sending the rest scurrying for cover. The hobelars reached the bridge. The first slipped on the icy planks, clutched at the handrail, then lost his footing and slid out under the railing. Water fountained up where he landed in the mill race.

Seeing what befell the first man, the hobelar behind him slowed down as he stepped gingerly on to the bridge. But the third was not ready for it, cannoned into the second man's back and sent him skidding forward across the icy planks. No sooner had the second man disappeared somewhere out of Kemp's line of sight than the Midlander heard a dying shriek. It might have been Nompar's shriek, or that of the hobelar; Kemp's money was on the man having skidded helplessly onto the *bourc*'s waiting sword tip. Following him, the third hobelar approached the doorway more tentatively, watching his step on the icy bridge. He too disappeared from Kemp's line of sight, and a heartbeat later the ring of steel against steel echoed up the hatchway from below.

Half a dozen more men crossed the bridge. It was so close below the doorway under the hoist – yet slightly off to one side – Kemp could shoot down at them without putting himself in the way of the arrows from the bowmen. Waiting for their chance to get at Nompar, the remaining hobelars crowded on the bridge. For Kemp it was like shooting at fish in a barrel: a barrel so crowded with fish there was no room for any water. Some of Kemp's arrows glanced off bascinets or breastplates; others penetrated chain mail or quilted aketons. By the time one of his arrows had sent a fourth man toppling into the mill race, the remainder realised they were on a hiding to nothing. They dashed away from the front of the mill, giving him a chance to pick off another victim, shooting him through an unarmoured thigh rather than risk having an arrow glanced off his backplate. The man fell with a scream, then began dragging himself through the snow, leaving a crimson trail in his wake.

'How d'you fare?' Kemp called down the hatch.

'Just warming up,' he heard Nompar call back.

'How many did you get?'

'Three. You?'

'Seven, slain or *hors de combat*.'

'Braggart! Do you count the one who slipped off the bridge without you loosing an arrow?'

'Why not? It was my ice he slipped on.'

Ten between them: nearly half the opposing force slain in a few moments. That was a good start. But Nixon's men had begun cockily, seeking to overwhelm the two fugitives in the mill by a frontal attack in full force. They would not make the same mistake a second time. And Kemp only had three of his own arrows left.

It was too much to hope that suffering such heavy losses in their opening attack would convince the reivers to give up entirely. More likely it would make them all the more determined to avenge the companions already slain, even if more lives had to be thrown away to win that vengeance.

'Let me know if they approach the bridge again,' Kemp called down to Nompar.

'Where are you going?'

'They were kind enough to send me some extra arrows to replace the ones I loosed. I'm just going to gather them up.' Kemp moved to the opposite wall and grasped the shaft of the first arrow he found, trying to pull it free from the beam it was embedded in. He grasped the ash wood shaft and teased it up and down, trying to loosen the steel arrowhead embedded deep in the grain of the wood. Just when he thought it was finally about to come loose, the shaft splintered behind the head. Another wasted arrow: he threw it down with a curse.

'Martin!' Nompar called warningly from below. 'Fire arrows!'

Kemp made his way back to the door below the hoist. A little over a furlong away, the surviving four bowmen amongst the reivers were indeed gathered around a man with a burning torch. 'I'm surprised they have any.'

'Surely all they need is some arrows, and some flax wrapped around the shaft to set alight?'

Kemp laughed. 'If only it were so simple! You need curiously wrought arrowheads, and longer shafts if you are not to scorch your knuckles when you draw. I never carry any myself...'

'Evidently one of Nixon's men does!'

The bowmen broke away from the man with the torch, running to within a furlong of the mill and loosing their arrows, before running back out of range again. Like shooting stars in the gloom of the day, the four arrows arced high, trailing traces of smoke. The first plunged into the snow heaped on the porch over the door below, where it was immediately extinguished. The second plopped harmlessly into the roof. The third buried itself in the wall below the eaves, where the flames melted the snow above, which dripped down, extinguishing them.

The final flaming arrow came straight at Kemp. He ducked aside and it whipped through the doorway to bury its head in the wall behind him. Letting it burn there, he nocked one of his own arrows to the bow and let fly. The hobelars were taking care to stay out of range. Kemp let fly at the bowman who was running back after loosing the last fire arrow, but shooting at a lone man at that range was a chancy business and the arrow went astray. When his second arrow chanced to wound a man in the thigh and he fell to the ground, it boosted Kemp's confidence enough for him to loose his final arrow, but that too landed harmlessly in the snow.

Kemp crossed to where the fire arrow still burned in the wall. The steel arrowhead was longer than on an ordinary arrow, so the burning matter would not set the wooden shaft alight. Behind the head, the steel divided into three strands which curled about to form a little cage, before rejoining the socket where the wooden shaft was inserted. Some kind of burning matter was enclosed in that cage: probably tow, Kemp guessed. The flames scorched and charred the beam the arrow was stuck in, but did not set it alight. He grasped the shaft, teased the arrow out of the wall, and carried it back to the hatch, where he contemptuously tossed it into the snow below.

'As I was saying, I never carry any,' he called down to Nompar. 'Unless you're shooting at a thatched roof after a dry spell, they never work.'

'That's good to know!'

Kemp peered out towards the road. Nixon and his men had all disappeared. That made him nervous. If he could not see them, it was difficult to anticipate what mischief they would get up to next. Taking a chance, he risked exposing himself to the bowmen by leaning out of the hatch, trying to see if they were crossing the channel from the mill pond to the mill race.

'You see them?' he called down to Nompar.

'No. You think perhaps they have given up?'

Kemp laughed. 'No.'

He descended to the grinding room and entered the bower, opening the shutters to lean out of the window there. He craned his neck, trying to catch a glimpse of the channel leading from the river to the mill pond.

A shard of pottery chinked on the path at the back of the mill. Cursing, Kemp forgot about retrieving any other arrows. Holding his bow vertically so he could fit it through the hatch with the rest of him, he hurriedly descended the ladder to see a bowman and two hobelars step through the back door, one after another. Seeing him on the ladder, the bowman drew, and loosed an arrow. The Midlander had to jump sideways to avoid being skewered as the arrow flew between two of the rungs, level with where his stomach had been, before burying its tip in the wall behind him.

Kemp crashed to the floor. The reiver bowman must also have run out of arrows, for he threw down his bow. As

Kemp rose to face him, the bowman drew a knife from his belt and stabbed at the Midlander's stomach. Kemp tried to grab him by the wrist to stay the blow, but he misjudged his grab and the knife lacerated his palm. The cut burned as though he had grasped a red-hot poker, but there was no time to think about it: in the same instant, one of the hobelars came at him from the side, smashing the head of his spear into his ribs. The thrust broke a couple of the steel plates under the leather covering of his brigandine. It was like being struck with a sledgehammer. He felt something break – maybe a couple of links in his habergeon – and something else tore; his gambeson, or perhaps even his skin. So breath-snatching was the pain, he could not even be sure which. He staggered sideways, which at least helped him avoid another knife-thrust from the bowman. The hobelar drove his spear at Kemp again, with less force this time, but sooner or later he would realise he would be better off jabbing his spear at the Midlander's unprotected face.

Behind the bowman, the second hobelar likewise levelled his spear. Kemp grabbed hold of the bowman's brigandine and swung him in the way of the thrust. Whether or not the spear penetrated the bowman's back, Kemp could not see, but the bowman stumbled forward under the impact, crashing into the Midlander. His bascinet collided with the brim of Kemp's helmet and the shock carried through to his forehead. Scintillating flashes of light sparkled inside his eyes, dazzling him. Another blow slammed against his chest, and something hooked against the back of one of his ankles, tripping him. With a surge of panic he found himself falling, knowing that once he was down the three reivers would have him at their mercy. Someone knocked his helmet off. The bowman moved in – evidently the spear blow to his back had not pierced his brigandine – and delivered an agonising kick to his ribs.

Above the grunts of the reivers and the scuffling of their feet, Kemp heard the ring of steel against steel from the next room. 'I'd be glad of some aid!' Nompar called.

'That makes two of us!' Kemp shouted back.

One of the hobelars thrust his spear down at where he lay. Kemp rolled out of the way, then rolled back as soon as heard the spearhead thud into a floorboard. He grabbed the shaft of the spear and tried to tear it out of the hobelar's grip. The other hobelar raised his spear above his head as if aiming to slam it down into Kemp's face. The Midlander brought a leg up and slammed the sole of one foot into a kneecap. He felt the bone snap and heard the man sob in agony. As the hobelar doubled up, Kemp slammed his heel into his cheek. The man crumpled and stayed down.

The remaining hobelar was not giving up his weapon so easily, so Kemp used it instead to pull himself up off the floor. While he and the hobelar had a tug of war for possession of the spear, something jabbed him in the shoulder, the blade of a knife slashing the leather covering of his brigandine to score the steel below. Keeping hold of the spear with his left hand, Kemp flailed a fist at the bowman and felt it connect with something. The bowman fell back, giving Kemp time to grasp the hilt of his sword. He dragged it from its scabbard and thrust it at the hobelar, not wasting time trying to penetrate his brigandine but aiming for his unprotected legs. Kemp slashed the blade against the inside of a thigh, knowing there was an artery there which, once severed, could not be stanched. Blood splashed on the floor, but the man fought on, not realising his fate was sealed. Swinging his sword above the spear between them, Kemp slammed the pommel into the man's forehead, cracking his skull.

As the hobelar dropped, Kemp whirled in time to face the bowman who came at him again, stabbing. Kemp swung wildly in his haste; more by luck than judgement, his blade almost severed the man's thumb entirely, so that it hung down connected only by a flap of skin and sinew, while the knife fell from his ruined hand. Bracing the palm of his left hand against the pommel of his sword, Kemp slammed the tip into the man's eye. The bowman folded up, the blade embedded in his skull, almost tearing the hilt from Kemp's hand. As the Midlander braced a foot against the man's head to jerk it free, he was aware of the room growing darker as another man crossed the threshold.

Howk.

Seen close to, he looked even bigger than he had from a distance.

Kemp pulled his blade from the dead man's skull and levelled it at the giant. Howk pulled a battle-axe from under his belt and the two of them circled.

Howk lunged first, swinging his axe at Kemp's head. The axe head buried itself in one of the ceiling beams. *He's not overwise*, thought Kemp. *Maybe this will be easier than I reckoned.*

While Howk was still trying to pull the axe free, Kemp thrust the tip of his sword at the giant's midriff. Howk dodged aside — for such a big man he was surprisingly nimble on his feet — and caught Kemp's wrist in an iron grip. He twisted the Midlander's arm up between his shoulder blades, until Kemp found himself crying out in pain: he was sure his arm-bone was about to pop out of its socket. He could not help dropping his sword, it was an instinctive reaction. Keeping his arm twisted up behind his back, Howk kicked the blade, sending it skittering across the floorboards to slam into the foot of the rear wall, close to the back door.

Without releasing Kemp's arm, Howk pushed him across the room and slammed him against the housing supporting the cogwheels. One of the timbers splintered under Kemp's weight. Howk smashed a massive fist into one of Kemp's kidneys a few times — pain exploded through the Midlander's back — then tried to push his face into the teeth of the cogs where they meshed. Kemp barely managed to brace his arms in time, resisting Howk's overwhelming strength with all his might. Kicking back, he managed to scrape a heel against Howk's instep. The giant's grip loosened enough for Kemp to twist back to face him, clawing at his face with his left hand and trying to lift his knee into Howk's crotch at the same time. Howk twisted, catching the knee on his thigh, and released Kemp's wrist to throw a left hook at his jaw. Feeling his teeth rattle in his skull, Kemp sprawled back against the housing of the cogwheels, so dazed the scintillating lights returned to the periphery of his vision as if threatening to blind him.

Twenty-Two

If he was to have a chance of defeating Howk, Kemp realised he had to do it swiftly. He grabbed hold of the larger half of the broken plank in the housing and wrenched it free, jabbing the splintered end at Howk's face. The reiver brushed it aside, then grasped it, yanking it from Kemp's grip. He smashed it over his own knee as if it were made of earthenware and tossed the two pieces aside. Grabbing Kemp by the throat with his left hand, he slammed him back against the housing again and drove a massive fist into his stomach. Kemp felt it even through the articulated plates of his brigandine and the chain mail below. The wind driven from him, he sank to his knees, gasping for air.

He realised he was sitting on the floor next to the bin where the flour from the millstones fell from the bottom of the chute. Grabbing a fistful, he tried to dash it into Howk's eyes. The reiver saw it coming and averted his head before he was blinded, but it meant taking his eyes off Kemp for a moment. That gave the Midlander time to pick himself up and throw himself at Howk. He caught him around the waist, seeking to slam him back against the wall behind him. He might as well have tried to tackle an oak tree. As he continued to push futilely against Howk, the soles of his boots finding no purchase, he felt something slam agonisingly into his spine. Letting go of

Howk, he sank to his knees, and the reiver kneed him in the face. The blow connected with Kemp's cheek and bright lights seemed to flash inside his skull. He was not sure whether to pass out or throw up. He threw up, his spew splashing on the floorboards.

Howk turned away with a sneer of contempt and walked across to where the haft of his axe hung down from the ceiling beam where the head was embedded. *Going to deliver the death stroke*, thought Kemp. *On your feet, Martin. He'll slay you if you don't get up now!*

He hooked a hand over one of the timbers of the housing and pulled himself up, standing shakily on legs that felt like water. He reckoned he had about one punch left in him: he had to make it a good one. Clenching his fist, he staggered across the floor to where Howk stood, still tugging on the axe-haft. Kemp tapped him on the shoulder and Howk turned. Channelling his fear into rage, and his rage into his fist, Kemp threw it with all his might at Howk's jaw.

The reiver jerked his head aside so the punch sailed harmlessly past him, with such force that Kemp staggered and almost lost his balance.

Howk laughed. 'Got your second wind, have you?' Grabbing Kemp by the neck, he threw him across the room. The Midlander slammed into a wall and clung to it. The room whirled around him, making him dizzy.

Howk grabbed him and flung him across the room a second time. The floor seemed to pitch like the deck of a storm-tossed ship, then pain erupted from all parts of his body as he slammed into a wall. He tried to cling to that too, but it offered his fumbling hands no holds and he sank to the floor. Flailing about on his knees, he felt another blow slam into his midriff, a kick he supposed, but the scintillating lights at the periphery of his gaze had turned into a black fog that seemed to narrow his field of vision to a circle on the floor a few inches across. Someone grabbed him by the throat and haled him up, before something slammed into his jaw. He was aware of his legs moving beneath him, trying to keep him upright, then once again he slammed into a wall. His legs crumpled and he slid to the floor again. All he could see was the sign of the cross and he wondered if this was God's judgement upon him.

'Had enough yet?' jeered Howk.

Kemp realised that the sign of the cross was the blade, hilt and quillons of his sword, lying on the floor a few inches from where he slumped.

'Yes,' he said, grabbing the hilt. 'I've had enough.'

Howk's eyes widened when he realised his mistake in throwing Kemp so close to where his sword had fallen. He ran back to where the haft of his axe hung down, trying to tug it free again.

Bracing his left hand against the wall behind him for support, Kemp managed to push himself to his feet. Drawing his sword back for a thrust, he stumbled towards Howk. Hearing the Midlander's footsteps on the floorboards, the reiver left off heaving at the haft of the axe and turned to face him.

'A sword against an unarmed man?' he growled. 'Is that your notion of a fair fight?'

'You're a head taller than me,' slurred Kemp. 'Is that *your* notion of a fair fight?'

He thrust the tip of his blade clumsily at Howk's midriff. Once again the reiver dodged it easily, but when he tried to seize Kemp's wrist, the Midlander revealed his thrust had been a feint, swinging the blade at Howk's wrist. Ordinarily the blow would have lopped the reiver's hand off, but Kemp was too sick and dizzy to put all his strength into it. Still, it was enough to hack down to the bone, and dark blood spurted from the wound. Shrieking in terror at the sight of so much of his blood, Howk clapped his other hand over the wound and turned and ran for the door leading to the front room. Kemp went after him, hacking at his head from behind. The stroke missed, but it landed on Howk's shoulder, biting deep. The giant's legs folded beneath him and he sank to his knees.

With his left hand, Kemp grabbed a fistful of Howk's straggling hair and wrenched his head back, hacking at the side of his neck with his sword. The first blow opened the reiver's carotid artery and blood sprayed against the wall. Two more blows severed his spine. With a sawing motion, Kemp sliced through the last remaining flap of skin, and then Howk's body pitched forward onto the floorboards, leaving the Midlander holding his severed head in his left hand.

'*Now* it's a fair fight,' he panted.

A footfall sounded behind him. He turned to see Nixon on the threshold of the back door, nocking an arrow to his bow. Realising he could not reach him before the reiver drew and loosed, Kemp flung Howk's head at him. Nixon had scarcely begun to draw his bow when the head smacked into his temple. His fingers slipped off the bowstring and he loosed, the arrow pinging across the room with so little force, Kemp was able to snatch it out of the air with his left hand. Dazed and blinking, Nixon dropped his bow and staggered back against the wall behind him. Tossing the arrow aside, Kemp advanced on him, Howk's blood still dripping from the blade of the sword in his right hand. He let the tip rest against Nixon's breast somewhere between the third and fourth ribs.

'Wait, wait!' sobbed Nixon. 'Slay me now, and ye'll never ken whit—'

Kemp drove the tip of his blade into the reiver chief's heart. 'Never know, never care.'

Nixon's eyes momentarily registered a look of surprise before the light of comprehension faded from them entirely. Kemp jerked the blade free, and the corpse crumpled to the floor.

The sounds of combat from the next room had fallen silent. In the quiet that ensued, footsteps scuffled on the floorboards. Kemp barely had enough strength left to stay on his feet, let alone raise his sword. An armoured figure stepped through, his jupon slashed and bloodied, but the Douglas blazon still recognisable for all that. Kemp levelled his sword, but it was a bluff, for he felt so weak, he knew all Archibald had to do was strike at him, and any attempt to parry would result in Kemp's sword being dashed from his grip.

Then he saw Archibald was unarmed. Nompar followed him through the door, prodding the Scot in the back with the tip of his sword.

Archibald's eyes flickered to Nixon's corpse. 'You slew Black Rab Nixon.'

Kemp nodded. He wiped blood from the blade of his sword and slotted it back into its scabbard. Stepping into the front room, he found three dead hobelars on the floor: Nompar had been busy. Kemp peered cautiously out of the door at the front of the mill. He could see no one else. 'Is that the last of them?'

'I saw three bowmen turn and flee,' said the *bourc*.

Kemp stepped out onto the bridge. His foot slipped beneath him, belatedly reminding him how he had made the boards slippery, and he had to grab for the railing to avoid falling. No one shot any arrows at him, so he signalled for Nompar to bring Archibald out after them. Marching the Scots knight before them, they followed the snow-covered riverbank, heading downstream towards Annan.

After half a mile, they came to where a small wooden boat was tied up at a jetty. 'That can carry us all the way down to Hoddom Ferry,' said Kemp. 'From there it's but five leagues to Longtown. We can be in Carlisle before sundown.'

'Yon boat is not large enough for three of us,' said Archibald.

Nompar nodded. 'I could demand a ransom of three hundred scudoes for you.'

'If you could get me to Carlisle, aye. Though I cannot guarantee Lord Douglas would pay it.'

'If I agree to leave you here and forgo your ransom, will you give us your word of honour that you will do nothing to stop us from reaching England?'

'If you give your word both of you will head straight for the border by the shortest route, troubling no Scottish folk on your way, and swear that once you reach England, you'll never return to Scotland so long as you both shall live?'

Kemp and Nompar exchanged glances. 'Gladly!' said the Midlander.

He climbed down into the boat and sat on the thwart. Nompar followed him down, unfastening the painter. Kemp used an oar to push them away from the jetty before fitting both in their rowlocks. Archibald watched from the jetty, one hand raised in farewell. Kemp heaved on the oars, rowing them into midstream where the stronger current would carry them more swiftly.

'How's your head?' asked Nompar.

'Better,' said Kemp. 'I reckon you were right.'

'Oh?'

'Having summat to do *did* take my mind off it.'

—

Three leagues south of the watermill, where Spedlin's Tower glowered over the snowbound banks of the River Annan, Reid saw a boat approaching with two men in it. It had not occurred to him his quarry would steal a boat. If he flung his maul, he might get one... Then he remembered Sneith had a crossbow, and ran across to where the man-at-arms huddled under a tree, dozing.

Reid punched him in the shoulder. 'Wake up, ye pauchtie widdiefow! There's a boat coming!'

'Speak English, you jabbering rascal!' growled Sneith.

'Ah *am* speaking English, ye hallocked glunder! There's a boat coming.'

'Is it the *bourc* and the Englishman?'

'Of course it is! Ah can see their helmets. Besides, who else would be coming down the Annan in a boat in the deid of winter?'

'Any number of people.' Rising to his feet, Sneith stretched stiff and aching limbs. Taking up his crossbow, he walked across to the riverbank. The boat was nearer now: a figure wearing a brigandine and a kettle helmet sat on the thwart, his back to the prow, hauling on a pair of oars. A man-at-arms was slumped in the stern.

Sneith caught the hook of his pivoted steel 'goat's-foot' under the crossbow's string, braced the curved tines against the nubs on either side of the stock, and hauled the string back until it caught on the ratchet. He unhooked the 'goat's-foot' and hung it from his belt.

'Come on, come on!' Reid urged him impatiently. 'They're getting away!'

'They're doing nothing of the kind!' Sneith snorted. The boat was movingly slowly. It was within range, but extreme range: the river was only forty feet wide here, and the current would soon bring it much closer.

He selected a bolt from the quiver on his belt and slotted it into the groove on the crossbow, then braced the butt to his shoulder.

'Come on, damn your nose!' hissed Reid. 'Why d'ye no' shoot?'

'I'm waiting for the boat to come within range.'

'It's *in* range.'

'Yes, but not close enough for me to be sure of my shot. If I miss with my first shot, I'll not have time to reload twice!'

'Let me do it!' Reid grabbed the crossbow and tried to tear it out of Sneith's hands. He almost succeeded, but then the man-at-arms tightened his grasp on it and pulled it back. The two of them yanked it to and fro between them in a tug of war, while the boat floated past them on the river.

'Let go of it!' snarled Reid. 'Can ye no' see they're getting away?'

'*You* let go of it!' Sneith adjusted his hold on the crossbow's stock to get a stronger grip, only to crush the tricker below into its housing. The ratchet was released, the string snapped from an angle to a straight line, and the bolt flew from the groove to pierce Reid's brigandine. He let Sneith take the crossbow then and glanced down at the shaft of the bolt sticking out of his belly. It felt as though a white-hot poker had been driven clean through his guts and he felt his own hot blood coursing down his belly into his crotch.

'Now look what you've done!' snapped Sneith, oblivious to Reid's injury, as he took the 'goat's-foot' to span the crossbow again.

'Look whit *Ah've* done? Ye glaikit gowk! Can ye no' see ye've slain me?' Filled with rage at the man-at-arms' stupidity, Reid drew his reaping hook from his belt, pushed Sneith's visor up with his left hand, and hacked the tip of the hook's curved blade into the man-at-arms' eye. Sneith stumbled back with blood coursing down his cheek, then fell and sprawled in the snow.

'That'll teach ye!' Reid chortled, before sinking to his knees beside Sneith's corpse. Another spasm of agony erupted through his belly. The death rattle sounded in his throat as he pitched forward to lie alongside Sneith.

On the river, the two men in the boat continued downstream towards Hoddom, oblivious to the life-and-death struggle that had taken place on the bank.

–

Dragging his broken leg behind him, Bulchett groped blindly at the walls in search of a way out. In the darkest part of the cave, what he had before taken to be a shadow turned out to be an opening. Possibly it was just a niche, but he was determined to search every nook and cranny before he gave up all hope. *A melancholic like Kemp would have given up already*, he thought to himself. *That's why those of us blessed with a sanguine temperament will always overcome the melancholics.*

He walked on, arms stretched out before him, expecting his fingers to touch rock at any moment. But where they did, it was only because there was a bend in the tunnel, and off to his left he saw a distant glimmer of light. He walked towards it, and it became brighter and brighter until it formed a doorway. He stepped through into a vast, high-vaulted chamber carved out of the living rock, where hundreds of gargoyles smirked down at him. All manner of strange sigils had been carved in the marble floor, forming spirals within spirals, all leading towards a stone plinth in the very centre of the chamber. Resting atop the plinth, level with his own head, was a head cast entirely out of brass, a head with a face that was an echo of a human face, a woman's face that was so beautiful there was something weirdly inhuman about it.

By my faith! The legends were true!

The eyes were closed, but as Bulchett approached the eyelids flicked up, revealing two sapphires, and a seductive voice issued from the brazen lips, though they did not move.

Welcome, Alexander Bulchett! Without the lips moving, it was as if he heard the words in his own head. *Long have I awaited your arrival!*

'You know me?' Bulchett cried in astonishment.

Of course! I know all. And I know only one man would be wise enough, and courageous enough, to find me.

'You are Meridiana?'

I am. And you are the one foretold by destiny to be my master. Whatever you wish, it shall be my honour to bring to pass. Release me from this brass prison, and I shall be bound to do your bidding for eternity.

'How do I do that?'

Only place a kiss upon my lips.

'Let it never be said that Sir Alexander Bulchett hesitated to kiss a fair maiden!'

Placing his hands on either side of the head, Bulchett closed his eyes and pressed his lips to the cold brass. As he did so, he felt them become soft and warm, and opened his eyes again to find the brass head and the plinth it had rested on had vanished. Instead he held a naked young woman in his arms, large blue eyes gazing adoringly at him out of a face framed by golden tresses, her nubile body pressed excitingly against his.

'Meridiana?'

The woman clasped him close to her, crushing her full breasts against his chest. 'For my powers to reach their full, we must become one,' she whispered breathily in his ear.

His rampant lust would not be denied. 'If you insist!' he panted, before kissing her again.

As he probed her mouth with his tongue, her teeth felt oddly sharp to him. She exhaled into his mouth, and suddenly all he could taste was bat droppings. Bile rose to his gorge and she laughed maniacally as he pushed her away from him. Now he saw her body, while maintaining its earlier voluptuousness, was coated with a pelt of bristly black hairs. He looked up at her and saw her sapphire eyes had been replaced with beady black ones, her snub nose turned into a pig-like snout, and her lips parted to reveal a mouthful of fangs. As he shrieked in terror, she embraced him with her leathery wings and began to chew his face off—

He awoke with a start. *Only a bad dream*, he thought. 'Lord Christ be thanked!' he sobbed out loud. He trembled all over, whether from the fright of his nightmare or the cold he could not say, but it was cold, as bitterly cold in the cave as it had been from the moment he fell into it... when? Hours ago? Days? He had lost track of time. All he knew was that his parched throat and the tightness in his belly were pushing him to the brink of madness. His broken leg still pained him, and he felt limp and lifeless for lack of victuals. He was starting to wonder if Nixon was going to return after all.

Overhead, the bats rustled in their roosts. Unlike in his nightmares, they had sense enough to have nothing to do with him, except to shower him with their droppings. But there was another sound now: the bleating of many sheep coming from the fissure in the ceiling of the cave. He glanced towards it, and saw daylight shining through... it had been dark the last time he had looked in that direction, so at least a night had passed. Unless he had dreamed the darkness... or perhaps he was dreaming now. He had drifted through a thousand delirious dreams since he had fallen into the cave and had lost all track of where reality ended and the nightmares began.

A shadow moved against the sunlight falling on the rocks on one side of the crevice. 'Hoo there!' a voice with a Scottish accent called down. 'Is there someone down there?'

A shepherd, Bulchett thought dimly, and then exultation filled his breast, giving him renewed hope. If Nixon had only pulled the rope up without removing it altogether, the shepherd could lower it to him and haul him out. He was saved!

'Hoo there!' Bulchett called back.

'D'ye need any help?' asked the shepherd.

The knight bridled. Help? *Help?* Who did the shepherd think he was? The kind of fool that would fall into a fissure in a mountain, break his leg and get himself trapped? 'Of course not!' he snorted indignantly.

'Are ye sure?'

'Well, of course I am! You do not think that if I needed help, I would be such a fool as to deny it, do you?'

What am I saying? wondered Bulchett. *This could be my last chance to get out of here, of course I should tell him I need help.*

'Be off with you, you filthy lout!' he shouted up. 'I have no need of help from the likes of you!'

He clapped a hand to his mouth. What was wrong with him? Why would his lips and tongue not obey him?

'As ye will,' the shepherd called down mildly, and then his shadow faded from the rocks above.

Bulchett lay and listened to the bleating of the sheep until that too faded. *Good riddance,* he told himself with a giggle. *I have no need of help from a Scots caitiff! I'm Alexander Bulchett, King of the Bats! At my command, the bats will fly to me, seize me in their talons and lift me to safety! And then with their help I shall conquer the world and rule over it, as is my due!* He cackled hysterically at the prospect.

Three days later, covered from head to toe in bat droppings and driven quite insane by his ordeal, Sir Alexander Bulchett died, in agony, of dehydration. Occasionally folk would tell stories of the foolish things he had done, and wonder what had become of him. But he was neither missed nor mourned, and no one, not even his own father, doubted he had come to a bad end.

–

A few hours after passing Spedlin's Tower, Kemp and Nompar tied up the boat at a wooden landing stage on the west bank of the River Annan and walked the half-league to where Lochmaben Castle stood on the south side of

Castle Loch. Less than four months had passed since they had last visited it, and yet so many adventures had befallen them in the meantime it seemed like a lifetime ago. The castle's constable, Sir Richard Thirwall, knew them both and gave them a good supper, comfortable beds for the night, and sold them a couple of horses and saddles, at not too extravagant a price, to bear them to Carlisle.

The following morning dawned bright and clear, markedly warmer than the past few days, and most of the snow had melted with the rising of the sun, leaving only a few patches of white where the ground remained in shadow. By midday, Kemp and Nompar had crossed back into England by the bridge over the River Esk at Longtown, and an hour later they crossed the River Eden and entered the walls of Carlisle.

A strong fortress dominated by a great square keep built of red sandstone ashlar, the castle stood in the north-west corner of the city. As Kemp and Nompar approached the gatehouse, a flock of crows rose from where they stalked the bank above the castle's outer ditch in search of worms, cawing raucously as they settled on the battlements above. Having identified themselves to the sentinels at the main gate, the two horsemen entered the outer bailey, where they found Ieuan practising at the butts with some of the men from Kemp's former company.

Ieuan left off talking with the others to run across to where Kemp and Nompar swung themselves down from their saddles. 'Martin! God be praised! I'd feared you slain by the Scots.'

Kemp smiled ruefully. 'They came close, Ieuan. They came damned close.'

'Sir Nompar!' Emerging from the gate leading to the inner bailey, King Edward hailed the *bourc*, marching across to greet him with Sir Walter Mauny at his side. 'We thought we had lost you.'

Nompar and Kemp both knelt before their king before rising again. 'Nay, my liege,' said the *bourc*. 'We fell in with Sir Alexander Bulchett and a handful of his archers. He claimed to know the way to safety, but it seemed he was more interested in seeking the Brazen Head of Pope Sylvester.'

'The Brazen Head?' The king looked bemused. 'A legend, surely?'

'Sir Alexander seemed to believe in it,' said Kemp. 'Or at least, so he said. I soon learned to put little faith in owt he told me.'

'Has my elevation of him in your place made you jealous of him, Kemp?'

'Perhaps. But I still say he's a damned liar.'

'I wonder if you would make such an accusation were he here to defend himself?'

'He would,' said Nompar. 'As would I. But I do not think we shall see Sir Alexander again; a circumstance to rejoice at. If he is dead, it is no more than he deserves for his calumny against Kemp.'

'What calumny?'

'Blaming me for putting Haddington Greyfriars to the torch, sire,' said Kemp. 'I've good cause to believe he was there that night, and I reckon he was the one who started the fire, though whether he did so by accident or design I can't say.'

The king looked pointedly at Kemp's unshackled wrists. 'I seem to recall I ordered you be brought to Carlisle Castle in chains.'

'I ordered his chains struck off, sire,' said Nompar. 'With the Scots chasing us, it seemed for the best. And if I may be so bold, it was as well I did, for I doubt he would have been able to slay Black Rab Nixon had I not.'

The king looked at Kemp in surprise. 'Nixon is dead?'

The Midlander nodded. 'He'll not trouble the folk of Northumberland again. Though I warrant there will be plenty of others keen to take his place.'

'Even so...' The king gestured expansively. 'I fear I was hasty in my judgement against you, Kemp. Aye, well... what's done is done. No use shutting the stable door after the steed is stolen. Tell your men to polish their gear and present themselves for my inspection at dawn tomorrow.'

'My men, sire?'

'Your archers.' The king gestured to the men practising at the butts.

'You'd restore me to my captaincy?'

'I will even have you paid for the days Sir Alexander was nominally in command. No sense in Master Wykeham's accompts being disordered unnecessarily.'

'You are kind, my liege. But I must decline.'

'Decline?'

'Your offer of a captaincy.'

'Then I must insist. As your king, I command it.'

'And I must refuse.'

The king stared at him. 'You refuse your king? Where is your loyalty?'

'Where was yours, sire, when Sir Alexander blamed me for the burning of Haddington Greyfriars? You must have heard the same stories of Bulchett's treachery as the *bourc* had, yet you chose to believe him over me. Men like him are the root of much sorrow in this life, but only because men who should know better allow them to.'

The king's face clouded over. 'You are my vassal, Kemp! You owe me loyalty! You presume much, to suggest it should be the other way around.' He clenched his fists for a moment and then, with a visible effort, relaxed them again. 'Come now! You think I am ignorant of the good service you have done me over the years? Calais, Guînes, Berwick? Be my man, and the world shall be your oyster.'

'You are generous, sire. But again I must decline.'

'As you will,' the king said pettishly. 'You are not the only man capable of commanding a company of archers. Indeed, Master Ieuan has deputised right well for you in his absence.'

Ieuan dropped to one knee. 'You are kind, my liege. But where Martin goes, I go.'

'You would rather give your loyalty to him than to me, your king?'

'Meaning no disrespect, sire, but you've not saved my life as often as he has.'

'How will the pair of you make a living, then, if not in my service? I cannot see you turning to the cloister. Nay, wait: let me guess... I heard you were captain of the Company of the Dragon for a while, Kemp. You mean to return to Brittany and become a freebooter once more? But was not your captaincy of that band of brigands usurped by one of your own men?'

Kemp smiled. 'Aye, well. I'm minded to do summat about that.'

Historical Notes

The final phase of the Second Scottish War of Independence began towards the end of January 1356 and was over by the end of the following month. It went down in history as the Burnt Candlemas. There can be no doubt Edward III's intention was to avenge the Scottish attack on Berwick which had taken place late the previous year, while Edward had been campaigning in northern France. But the Scots were only avenging an attack made by Lord Neville on the lands of the Earl of Dunbar early in 1355, an attack intended to discourage any Scottish raids while Edward was campaigning overseas, yet one which had exactly the opposite effect to that intended.

As Edward III marched north across the Scottish border, a fleet paralleled his march off the coast carrying victuals for his army, just as a fleet had done off the coast of Normandy when he marched to Crécy ten years earlier. The Scots, meanwhile, withdrew north of the Firth of Forth, leaving behind little to plunder and less to forage. God appears to have taken the Scottish side – provoked by the despoiling of a Scottish church on the coast by some English sailors, according to some accounts – and sent a storm to sink some of the ships of the fleet and disperse the rest.

When news of this disaster reached Edward, encamped with his army at Haddington, he realised he could tarry no longer in Scotland if he did not want his men to starve, but must at once march back to England. I have perhaps been unduly kind to Edward III in suggesting it was never his intention to burn the Greyfriars at Haddington: none of the sources I consulted while researching this book suggested the burning of the friary was anything but an act of deliberate vandalism by the English, condoned by Edward and probably at his orders. But it seemed too good a way to introduce the bumbling, feckless Sir Alexander Bulchett, and to disgrace Kemp unjustly in the eyes of his king.

Edward split his army into three columns as it retreated to England, burning towns and villages as they went. His own column was ambushed by the Scots 'somewhere near Melrose'; Edward himself evaded capture and arrived with the bulk of his men at Carlisle before the end of February. Scottish historians argue he was chased out of Scotland with his tail between his legs, never to return; English historians tend to take the view that as there were no more major raids across the Scottish Border until 1388, eleven years after Edward III's death, he had achieved what he had set out to do, namely, pacify the Scottish Marches for decades to come. I will leave readers to make up their own minds which version is true, only pointing out that the two interpretations are not mutually exclusive; though one wonders if there would have been any trouble at all on the borders in the years 1355–6 if Lord Neville had not launched his pre-emptive raid. Certainly Sir Eugène de Garencières arrived in Scotland soon afterwards to urge the Earl of Dunbar to attack the English, paying him 40,000 gold *agnels* to do so; but that alone might not have been enough to provoke Dunbar to action, had there not been a raid on his lands to avenge.

Sylvester II was Pope from 999 to 1003 CE. Born Gerbert of Aurillac in France, before he became pope he travelled to Spain and studied mathematics and astronomy, Catalonian monasteries being well supplied with books on those subjects from Moorish Cordoba. It was presumably this association with 'Saracen sorcery' that led the monk William of Malmesbury to ascribe all manner of legends to Sylvester which cast him less in the light of a traditional pope and more like something akin to a necromancer. Foremost amongst these legends is that of the Brazen Head in which the demoness Meridiana was imprisoned. In the version Malmesbury tells in his Chronicle *De Rebus Gestis Regum Anglorum*, Sylvester was planning a pilgrimage to Jerusalem when he asked the Brazen Head if he would die there. When the head replied in the affirmative, Sylvester cancelled his pilgrimage, deducing that he only had to stay away from Jerusalem and he would be sure of eternal life. Of course, the trick with demonic prophesies is to read the small print: a few weeks later he was taken ill while delivering a sermon in the Church of the Holy Cross of Jerusalem in Rome, and died soon thereafter.

Born in Scotland (if his name is anything to go by) in 1175, Michael Scot was another student of mathematics and astrology who was believed to be a sorcerer after his death. Like Gerbert of Aurillac before him, Scot learned Arabic and travelled to Spain to study. Scottish folklore links him to William de Soulis, a former Lord of Liddesdale who fought for the English until Bannockburn, then switched sides when he saw which way the wind was blowing. The legends tell of a Lord Soulis who practiced necromancy until the locals decided they had had enough of him, and boiled him alive at Ninestane Rig, a stone circle half a league east-north-east of Hermitage Castle, though more likely this legend arose from a confusion with one of William de Soulis' forebears, Ranulf de Soulis, who was murdered by his servants early in the Thirteenth Century.

The Poor Fellow-Soldiers of Christ and of the Temple of Solomon — to give the Knights Templar their full title — were disbanded by Pope Clement V in 1312 following Philip IV of France's attempt to steal their wealth for himself by cooking up false charges of heresy, blasphemy, sodomy and black magic. Philip's plans were largely foiled when Clement decreed the wealth of the Templars should be handed over to the Knights Hospitaller. Legends tell that the treasure of the Templars was shipped to Scotland and concealed in the crypt of Rosslyn Chapel (144 years before it was built, mark you), along with the original crown jewels of Scotland, the Holy Grail, the Holy Prepuce, the Lost Ark of the Covenant, the Maltese Falcon, the One Ring, the only remaining print of *London After Midnight*, and an assortment of odd socks that went missing from a laundromat in Wolverhampton on the afternoon of 31st April 1973. And if you believe that, you'll believe anything.